THE
LIST

THE
LIST

J. A.
KONRATH

PINNACLE BOOKS
Kensington Publishing Corp.
www.kensingtonbooks.com

PINNACLE BOOKS are published by

Kensington Publishing Corp.
119 West 40th Street
New York, NY 10018

All Kensington titles, imprints, and distributed lines are available at special quantity discounts for bulk purchases for sales promotions, premiums, fund-raising, educational, or institutional use. Special book excerpts or customized printings can also be created to fit specific needs. For details, write or phone the office of the Kensington sales manager: Kensington Publishing Corp., 119 West 40th Street, New York, NY 10018, attn: Sales Department; phone 1-800-221-2647.

This book is a work of fiction. Names, characters, businesses, organizations, places, events, and incidents either are the product of the author's imagination or are used fictitiously. Any resemblance to actual persons, living or dead, events, or locales is entirely coincidental.

ISBN-13: 978-0-7860-4274-6
ISBN-10: 0-7860-4274-5

First Pinnacle premium mass market printing: June 2018

10 9 8 7 6 5 4 3 2 1

Printed in the United States of America

The general spread of the light of science has already laid open to every view the palpable truth, that the mass of mankind has not been born with saddles on their backs, nor a favored few, booted and spurred, ready to ride them legitimately, by the grace of God.

—THOMAS JEFFERSON

CHAPTER 1

"I found the head."

Tom Mankowski, Chicago Homicide Detective Second Class, pushed the chair aside and squinted into the darkness under the desk. The two uniforms who were first on the scene flanked him.

"Light."

The patrolman to his left flicked on his Maglite, letting the beam play across the head's slack and pale features. Tom righted his lanky frame and turned his attention back to the lounger on the other side of the apartment. The body was bound to the chair with duct tape, torso leaning slightly forward, blood still trickling from the neck stump. All of the fingers on its left hand were severed.

Ugly way to die.

Tom's hazel eyes tracked the carpet in a line from the lounger to the desk. There was a blood trail, and an odd one at that. He had been expecting a pattern of drops indicating the head had been carried. Instead there was a repeating arc pattern.

"I want a door-to-door on this entire floor and the one below it," Tom told the uniforms. "Then sweep the alley and check all the dumpsters. Wear gloves."

"Uh, we're off duty in twenty minutes."

"Not anymore. Check all Dumpsters in a two block radius. There's no way the perp left this apartment without getting blood on him. Maybe he ditched clothes or a weapon. Call the district and get four more guys to help, on my authority. You can put in an overtime request tomorrow morning when you give me the reports."

They headed for the door, grumbling.

"Hold on. Other than the front door, did you touch anything when you arrived?"

"Naw. The superintendent opened the door, we saw the vic and called it in. Then we stood around until you showed up to send us on Dumpster duty."

"You didn't turn off the TV? Or a stereo?"

The first guy adjusted his cap. "Oh yeah. I did. The CD player was cranked up all the way. Some classical crap."

"Make sure it's in the report."

Tom dismissed them and turned his attention back to the body. Forcing detachment, he examined the wound to the neck. There were no tears or ragged edges in the skin, just a continuous smooth cut. Tom had never seen anything like it before.

"Morning, Tommy. Coffee?"

Detective Roy Lewis entered the apartment and handed his partner a Styrofoam cup with a gas station logo on it. At six foot two, Roy was the same height as Tom, but that was their only shared trait. Roy was black, bald, with broad shoulders and a round face sporting a thick mustache. Tom was white to the point of pale, thin and angular, with sandy hair that was a touch too short for a ponytail.

Roy's jacket was dotted with droplets, some of them still snowflakes. It was the first week of April, but winter didn't seem to know that.

"Why is it when I buy coffee, it's *Starbucks*, and when you do it's *Phillips Petroleum*?"

"Because I'm a cheap bastard. What do we got here?"

"Vic is a male Caucasian, name of Thomas Jessup. Woman in the apartment below called 911 because blood was dripping from her ceiling."

Roy grimaced at the body, then took a sip from his cup. "Where's the head?"

"It rolled under the desk. I think the perp used some kind of sword. One cut. Clean."

"Not that clean."

Tom's stomach did a slow roll. Though he'd been in Homicide for six years, he still wasn't comfortable around bodies, especially the messy ones. Bad coffee made the nausea even worse. Tom stuck out his tongue and fingered off a line of coffee grounds. Not wanting to contaminate the scene, he wiped the dregs in his shirt pocket.

"This is like drinking sand."

"Yeah. It looked awful. That's why I got me a Coke. So what's up with the fingers?"

"Tortured. Perp took them off one at a time, then used twist ties to stop the bleeding. Music was up loud so no one heard the screams."

"Who was this poor guy, make someone want to cut off his fingers and lop off his head?"

"Let's find out."

Tom choked down the rest of his coffee and put the cup in his jacket pocket. Then he snapped on a pair of latex gloves. His partner did the same.

While they tossed the place, several techies showed up and began to take pictures and collect samples. The ME arrived shortly thereafter, formality making him take the corpse's pulse.

"Should we start CPR?" Roy asked.

The Medical Examiner ignored him.

Tom took the bedroom, and after a few minutes of poking through drawers found out that Thomas Jessup worked at the main branch of the Chicago Public Library. Check stubs put his standard of living at slightly more than average. A bank statement revealed only a few hundred in savings, but bills were paid in full and on time. The heat kicked on automatically, blowing around the strong smell of violent death. Tom checked out the bathroom, and after a thorough search he bent over the sink and splashed some water onto his face. The coffee felt like acid in his gut.

Afterward he joined Roy in the kitchen. "Anything?"

"This guy was a boy scout. No booze, no smokes, no drugs, no fatty foods in the fridge. A ton of books, not one of them with dirty pictures. What'd he do?"

"Librarian."

"Figures. You find any girl stuff?"

"Nope. If he had a girlfriend, they weren't intimate. At least not here. No women's clothing, no extra toothbrush."

"Found his wallet. On the computer. Sixty bucks inside. Poor guy just turned thirty. Hey, ain't your big three-oh coming up this week?"

Tom frowned. "Thanks for the reminder."

He looked in the cabinet under the sink and found half a box of garbage bags. They were the more expensive brand with the built-in handle—no twist tie needed. The perp must have brought his own to the scene. An earlier check of the front door didn't show any signs of a break-in. Someone Jessup knew and let inside?

Tom went back into the living room. The asses-and-elbows atmosphere of a murder investigation was in full swing, with almost a dozen professionals stepping over each other to do their jobs. A guy with a portable vacuum picked up hairs and fibers. A woman dusted for prints. A team armed with a spray bottle and an alternative light source illuminated blood droplets on the ceiling. All while a crime scene photographer snapped away and another techie videotaped everything.

In the center of the action, the Medical Examiner—a pale, thin, cadaverous looking man named Phil Blasky—was orchestrating the removal of the body. The duct tape was carefully unwound, cut into one foot strips, and bagged. It would be examined back at the lab. A stretcher, complete with body bag, was wheeled in. Once the body was freed from the chair, two cops donning plastic ponchos lifted it onto the cart.

"Now this is interesting."

The ME was bent over the legs, examining a bare foot. Tom got a closer look.

"I thought it was something he stepped on, but apparently it's a tattoo. It looks old."

"A tattoo? Where?" Tom's voice came out higher-pitched than he would have preferred.

"It's on the pad of the left heel. A blue number, about an inch long. The number 7."

Tom looked at the foot and paled. A lump in his throat made him unable to speak.

"I wonder what that means."

Me too, Tom thought.

He'd seen a similar tattoo. Also blue, about an inch long. The number 5.

He'd been seeing it on a daily basis for almost thirty years.

It was on the bottom of his own left foot.

CHAPTER 2

Springfield

Phillip Stang stared at the ceiling. His frail body desperately needed sleep, but he refused to give in. He was waiting for news.

The widescreen plasma TV played an old black and white war movie. Stang had muted it some time ago. The only sound in the room was the faint beeping and whirring of the machines that kept him alive. He lifted a pale hand to scratch his nose, then shifted on the bed from his one bad side to his other bad side. The pain moved in unison.

"Senator?"

The voice startled him, even though the volume on the intercom was set to low.

"Yes, Jerome?"

"Your son is on the phone."

Stang picked up the receiver. It was cold and heavy. When he spoke, his voice didn't betray the weakness or exhaustion he felt.

"It's two in the morning. You couldn't call sooner?"

"Sorry, Dad. There have been some, ah, complications. Jessup is dead."

"Did he know about the others?"

"He knew a few, but was only in contact with one of them. We put Jack on it."

"How about the girl?"

"Haven't heard anything yet. But with Jessup— there may be a little snag. The detective in charge of the case is Tom Mankowski."

If Stang had a sense of humor, he might have laughed at the irony.

"It doesn't matter. He'll be dead before he learns anything. It won't interfere with Project Sunrise. Call when you hear about Joan."

Stang hung up, not bothering to listen to his son's response. He shifted his attention back to the ceiling.

Waiting.

He was good at waiting. For more than three decades, he'd been biding his time. But a lifetime of patience would be rewarded within the next few days.

It was somewhat unfortunate that millions of people had to die to make it so.

CHAPTER 3

Los Angeles

Joan DeVilliers looked at her beeper and noted the number. Marty. She called him on the cell phone.

"Joan! You're impossible to get a hold of."

"Left my cell in the car."

She turned down Santa Monica Boulevard and pulled alongside of a limo. The windows were tinted and impossible to see into, but Joan waved and blew a kiss. Never knew who it might be.

"Did you check your email?"

"Not yet. I've been on location all day. Ridley and Tom were having an argument."

"Anything serious?"

"Everything is serious on a hundred mil picture. The gaffer has a hemorrhoid and it's serious. What was the email?"

"It was from me, telling you to check your voice mail."

Joan sighed. "Have you read the latest, Marty? About

how cellular phones are linked to brain cancer? I can actually feel the tumor growing in my head right now."

"I'll buy you a lead hat, hon. Check your voice mail and call me back."

Marty hung up. Joan punched the gas on the Jag to blow through a yellow light, then hit the speed dial for her voice mail. She rested the phone in the caddy to play it on the speaker.

"You have six calls."

BEEP.

"Joan, Bill at Paramount. I talked to Peter. Expect a call."

BEEP.

"This is Marty. Has Peter from Paramount called yet?"

BEEP.

"Joan, this is Peter at Paramount Studios. I'm green lighting the project. The contracts are being sent over. I look forward to working with you."

BEEP.

"Joan? Max. The reservation is at nine. Call if you need directions to Carmichael's. Looking forward."

BEEP.

"It's Marty again. Where are you? Have you been kidnapped? If you have been, let's negotiate for the option. Did Peter call?"

BEEP.

"Joan DeVilliers?"

Joan squinted at the phone. She didn't recognize the voice.

"I've scheduled your tattoo removal for tonight at your place."

Tattoo removal? Who was this?

"Expect it to be very painful. See you later."

"You have no more messages."

A horn blared and Joan swerved out of incoming traffic. She pulled over to the curb, her heart racing. Joan only had one tattoo, and she was certain no one in LA knew about it. Even on the rare occasion that she'd brought a man home, none had found any reason to examine the bottom of her left heel.

The phone rang and Joan jumped in her seat, banging her head on the roof of the Jag. She hesitated, then hit the speaker.

"Joan? Marty. Isn't it fabulous? Paramount bought it!"

"Fabulous, Marty."

"You're going to be producing two blockbusters at the same time! Aren't you excited? Joan, why aren't you excited?"

"Marty, did you know I had a tattoo?"

"No, I didn't. How modern primitive."

"When was the last time I changed my cell number? Last month, right?"

"I don't remember. Sounds right."

"How many people do you think have it?"

"I don't know. This is Hollywood, dearest. You *want* people to pass around your number. What's wrong? Peter did make the offer, right?"

Joan rubbed her eyes. Perhaps she was overreacting. It was probably a prank call, or a wrong number. Or, this being Hollywood, some kind of clandestine, high-concept movie pitch.

"I'm just being paranoid, Marty. Yes, I'm excited. I'll call you tomorrow."

"Night, hon."

Joan pulled down the sun visor and checked her eye

shadow. It hadn't smudged. She finger-combed her short blond hair and debated changing into evening-wear for her date, but the idea of going home alone made her nervous.

I'm being ridiculous, she thought. Some nut in the City of Mixed Nuts calls with a vague threat, and she was acting like a scream queen. Her security system at the house was top notch, her dog Schnapps would die to protect her, she carried pepper spray, and most important of all Joan was a second dan black belt in karate.

Any freak who tried to mess with her would have his hands full.

She wove back into traffic and was at her home twenty minutes later.

Joan's house was of moderate size—tiny by Beverly Hills standards, but more than enough space for her. It was nestled away in a small enclave of trees, the last lot on a tiny wooded hill. Private, quiet, a complete about-face from her high powered job. The occasional visitor was surprised to find the interior warm and rustic. Rather than harsh lighting, leather couches, Picasso lithos, and a bowl of cocaine on the bar, Joan had decorated like *Banana Republic.* The only thing chic about the place was her Jacuzzi, and even that was trimmed in cedar.

She hit the access code on her remote and the garage door opened. In her mind she went through her gowns. Max had already seen the Versace. Maybe the Christian Dior? The same dress had been worn by Jodie Foster to some awards ceremony. She and Jodie were the same size, though Joan would have bought the dress no matter how big or small it was. It was black, classic, and simply stunning.

Joan parked and closed the garage door behind her. She entered the house using the keypad entrance, and then quickly reset the alarm. Preoccupied with what she was going to wear, it took Joan a moment to realize something was wrong.

Schnapps.

A month ago, she'd bought the German Shepherd from the best handler in California. A trained guard dog, but a lovable one as well. He normally greeted her at the door. Joan's mind raced. Is he sleeping? Eating? Sick? Hurt?

Dead?

The phone call. Tattoo removal.

Joan reached into her purse and palmed the pepper spray in her right hand. In her left she gripped her car keys, making sure their jagged edges poked out through her fingers.

Then, without hesitation, she opened the door without punching in the code. This would set off the alarm and alert the police.

But nothing happened. No piercing siren. No lights going on. No immediate call back from the security company to see if this was a false alarm.

Joan bounded out the door and into the garage, almost bumping into the man leaning against her Jaguar.

He was average height, medium build, dressed in a black turtleneck and pants. On his hands were leather driving gloves, skin tight. He had deep green eyes, and a meticulous black goatee came to a point on his chin.

Joan forced back the shock and assumed a defensive

position. The man didn't appear to be armed. He smiled at her.

"Hello, Joan."

She attacked. In two steps she was on him, lashing out at the invader's face with her keys. He ducked away and sidestepped her, using her momentum to throw her against the car.

Joan absorbed the impact with her shoulder and spun, spraying mace in an arc as she turned.

He got inside of her arc and grabbed her around the waist.

"Aren't we feisty?"

His breath was garlic and peppers. She jerked back her head and smashed it against his face, and then threw a roundhouse left that buried her ignition key in his biceps.

He stumbled backwards, bleeding from two places, and Joan twisted out of his grip and ran into the house, locking the door behind her.

The phone was dead. Her cell was in the car.

"Eight thousand dollars worth of goddamn security!"

Quick choice—fight or run? He was stronger. Outweighed her. Smart enough to disable her dog and her security system.

Run.

Joan kicked off her heels and headed for the kitchen. She grabbed a paring knife from the butcher block on her counter. Resting on a mat by the patio door were her jogging shoes. Ears cocked, she slipped them on without bothering to tie the laces. Then she eased open the patio door and moved cautiously into her backyard.

The moon was out and it was a clear night. Joan

side-stepped her garden and headed to the back of the house. She decided to cut through the woods and head for the neighbor's.

She found her dog when she rounded the corner.

In the shadows, she first thought Schnapps had been hung. Moving closer, Joan realized he'd been speared on a big stick which had been driven into the ground. Her mouth opened, but she couldn't draw a breath to scream.

To her left was an even bigger stick, with a ladder set up next to it.

"That one is for you." A voice, from behind her. "Let's see if it fits."

Joan ducked a shoulder and rolled towards the intruder, coming up in a kick to his chest. He caught her foot and twisted. To avoid a broken ankle, Joan flipped with the twist and wound up on her back, her head swimming.

"Don't you want to know who I am? The last one had so many questions. I answered all of them, in the sixteen hours it took for him to die."

He removed a cloth and a small bottle from his pocket. In the moonlight, the blood trickling from his nose looked like motor oil.

"I'll give you a choice. Where do you want the stake, the ass or the crotch?"

Joan rolled onto her stomach and got up in a crouch. When she felt his touch she shot out both of her feet, mule-kicking him in the chest. Then she ran.

She had several advantages. She was in shape. She knew the area. And most of all, she was running for her life. It took her a few seconds to find the trail in the dark, but once she did she ran like hell. Branches whipped at her face, and twice she almost tripped on some unseen obstacle, but she continued full tilt until she'd reached the backyard of her closest neighbor.

Not bothering with the doorbell, Joan picked up a terra-cotta flower pot and smashed it through a window.

The siren wailed. The security lights came on.

Joan stood with her back to the house—the paring knife clutched in her hands and her eyes scanning the woods—and waited for the police to arrive.

CHAPTER 4

Chicago

Tom returned to his office at the 26th District, in the heart of downtown. He dragged along a large suitcase—Jessup's—that he and Roy had filled with papers and personal effects from the deceased's apartment. Roy had gone to the Harold Washington Library, where Jessup worked, to search his office and talk to his co-workers, leaving Tom to sort through the suitcase solo. Tom was fine with that—he was almost feverish with questions, and the suitcase might contain answers.

There was half a pot of old coffee set up on a table near the lockers, which Tom took back to his desk.

They'd worked the crime scene all morning, the discovery of Jessup's number tattoo fueling Tom's urgency. Tom hadn't found any obvious clues pertaining to it, or the man's murder. But the resemblance to his own tattoo was undeniable.

He'd asked his parents about the mark at an early age. They had no answers—when they'd adopted him at a few weeks old, he'd already had the tattoo. Some years ago, after becoming a cop, Tom had searched for his birth parents, but could find no evidence that he was even adopted. According to the county, he was naturally born to Joe and Laura Mankowski.

That was impossible, of course. His parents were both of Polish descent; short, dark, stocky. Tom was at least a foot taller, and several shades lighter.

He dug into the suitcase, pulling out some documents. Tom discovered he and Jessup were born at the same hospital. A labeled picture of Jessup with his parents showed that he also had little resemblance to them. Adopted as well? A long-lost brother?

"Not unless it was a really long labor," Tom mused. He and Jessup were born six days apart. He located a death certificate for Jessup's father, along with several US patents in his father's name. One of his patents was for a waterproof hairdryer, which in Tom's mind sort of defeated the purpose.

A recent birthday card from Jessup's mother wished him thirty more years of happiness, with love and kisses. Postmark from Des Moines. A piece of notebook paper with several book titles on it was found in Jessup's desk. Handwriting appeared to be his. Among the titles were several biographies of Thomas Edison, a bio of Lincoln, a book about the Declaration of Independence, a book about the Theory of Relativity, and an old Ira Levin thriller. Tom checked the inventory sheet. None of these books were found in the apartment.

Tom plugged a pen drive into his USB port—he'd copied Jessup's *My Documents* folder—and waded through spreadsheets, games, tax figures, and letters concerning library business. It took almost an hour and the remainder of the coffee before he found something interesting. A word processing file, BERT.DOC. It had no address heading, and was dated nine days ago.

Bert—

Looking forward to meeting you, to see if you live up to your many pictures. I realize it must be a shock, and even with the proof in the articles and in our birth certificates, you must still harbor some doubt. Besides the question of how, there are also many whys. Perhaps we can figure these out together, as well as find the others.

I'm enclosing a copy of a photo of you I recently found. Call me when you've made travel arrangements.

All best,
T. Jessup

Tom read it again, trying to find the hidden meaning. Was Bert a pen pal? Someone famous? Or had Jessup managed to find another person with a tattoo on their heel?

He printed the letter and logged onto the Internet. First stop, the Yellow Pages. It only took a few minutes to locate a Mrs. Emilia Jessup in Des Moines. He jotted down her number and called. Busy. Tom then accessed the CPD database and found out Jessup had no criminal record or outstanding warrants. Nor was there mention of him in the Chicago Tribune archives. He searched USENET, but Jessup's name and signature weren't on any of the big message boards. Google yielded nada. He tried to access Jessup's email account, but didn't have the password to get in from this terminal.

Switching tactics, Tom went to ViCAP—the Violent Criminal Apprehension Program run by the Feebies. Because the crime scene report wasn't finished yet, he couldn't fill out the long questionnaire to add Jessup's murder to the database. But he did go surfing.

Under a search for DECAPITATION, he found no less than seven hundred entries spanning the last fifty years. That was a lot of people losing their heads. TATTOOS OF NUMBERS gave him more than eight thousand hits. He combined the two for his next search, and added CAUCASIAN MALE UNDER 35.

Fifteen hits. They detailed some pretty horrible crimes, but none of them seemed related to Jessup. He refined his tattoo search to SINGLE DIGIT NUMBER TATTOO LEFT FOOT, and got a hit.

The crime took place last year in Tennessee. A twenty-nine-year-old Caucasian male by the name of Robert Mitchell had been found in the woods outside of Nashville. He'd been stripped naked and impaled upon a ten foot wooden pole. It had pierced his rectum and eventually exited through his mouth. The coroner theorized it took Mitchell a while to die.

He'd slid down the length of the stake an inch at a time. By the time it ruptured something vital, Mitchell may have been hanging there for over ten hours.

The pictures made Tom wince.

There were no witnesses, no suspects, and very little evidence. The investigation had been extensive and taken hundreds of man hours, but not a single lead panned out. Tom read on, and felt the coffee roil in his gut. Besides being well liked in the community, Mitchell had been a cop. He also had a one inch blue number on his left heel. There was a jpg attachment of the ink, and Tom clicked on it to enlarge.

A number 2. Done in the same style as his and Jessup's. Tom checked Mitchell's birth date and discovered Robert was only eight days younger than he was. Tom's mouth became very dry. He reached to pour more coffee, but the pot was empty.

Tom tried Emilia Jessup in Des Moines again. Still busy. He went back into the suitcase. Jessup's credit card statements showed no unusual purchases. The last few months of cancelled checks were all for food or utilities. There was an address book, but no one inside named Bert.

Jessup's phone company was local, one Tom had dealt with many times, but they still required a warrant to release phone records. Tom filled out the paperwork to set the wheels in motion, but it would take a few hours to get a list of all of Jessup's calls.

Unfortunately, Jessup didn't have a caller ID at his apartment. Strangely, he didn't have an answering machine either. Tom didn't know one single person who didn't own an answering machine, unless . . .

"Unless they have voice mail."

He searched the suitcase for previous phone bills and found one from last month. There was a charge for voice mail, but it didn't give Jessup's PIN. That was probably listed on Jessup's very first phone bill, when he was assigned the line. Tom had only brought along the bills from the last few months—he hadn't thought there would be a need to bring every single statement.

So it was back to Jessup's apartment. He wanted to

check the vic's email anyway, and if he hurried he could make it back before noon and grab a bite. He called Roy.

"Anything?" he asked his partner.

"Office in order. No known enemies. You?"

"I gotta run back to the scene, check his voice mail. We can compare notes over lunch."

"Meet you back at the district. I'm almost done here."

The day hadn't gotten any warmer, and the freezing drizzle had formed slush on his windshield. Tom climbed into his Mustang and stepped on a CD case that had fallen next to the gas pedal. Sting's latest album, unopened. His ex-girlfriend had given it to him, months ago, at around the same time his car stereo stopped working. He tossed it in the back seat.

Tom took Addison to Lake Shore Drive, south towards downtown. To his left, Tom could make out large ice patches on Lake Michigan. Ahead in the distance, the twin antennas of the giant John Hancock Building blinked in unison. Rush hour was in full force. Tom hit the siren, forging a winding path through traffic. One of the perks of being a cop. He exited on North Avenue and parked in front of a fire hydrant—another perk. The neighborhood consisted of upper middle class apartments, most of them recent college grads, all within crawling distance to the city's major hub of bars and clubs on Rush and Division. Tom walked to Jessup's residence and let himself into the lobby door with the key supplied by the superintendent.

The building was newly remodeled, brightly lit, secure. Jessup's door was taped off with yellow crime scene ribbon. Tom ducked under it and entered, turning on the lights.

The lounger that the body was taped to had been removed, taken to the lab to search for trace evidence. No one had been in yet to clean up, and the large brown blood stains on the carpet had grown funky. Tom went to the stereo, which was speckled white with fingerprint dust, and turned it on. A CD loaded automatically. Even someone as classically inept as Tom recognized Beethoven's Fifth. He lowered the volume and let it play.

Jessup's collection of old phone bills was in a file cabinet, and Tom searched until he found one with the voice mail personal identification number on it. Then he picked up the phone and pressed the keys to access the messages. There was only one.

"Hi, Thomas, it's Bert. The convention is running all week, and I have to man the table every day until eight. But I'm free all day Saturday, then I have to go back to Milwaukee. Can we get together then? You've got my number at the hotel. Call me later."

A robotic voice indicated the call had taken place yesterday afternoon at two-fifteen. Tom played it again, listening closely. It was a man, Midwest accent, a somewhat nasally voice. He didn't sound threatening or imposing. His manner was friendly, albeit harried. There was noise in the background. Tom repeated the message once more, trying to make out the sounds behind Bert's voice. It was the murmur of a large group of people. No street sounds, so they had to be inside. Bert had probably called from the convention he mentioned.

Tom closed his eyes, trying to pick up any key word in the background that would indicate what kind of convention it was. No luck. He pressed the star button on the phone to save the message, then sat back down on the kitchen chair. At any given time, there were more than two dozen conventions in the Chicagoland area. And hundreds of hotels. Bert mentioned that Jessup had his number. Would he have written it down somewhere?

There was no scratch pad by the phone. Tom hit the redial button on the receiver and got a local pizza shop. He went back to the second phone in the bedroom, but it didn't have a redial button. Punching *69 didn't work either. He would have to wait for the phone records to find out where Bert was staying.

Moving on, Tom booted up the computer and was able to access Jessup's email. Most of it was spam, with a few letters concerning the library. Tom was reading about the budget for a remodeling job when he heard movement behind him.

As a rookie, though he'd never admit it to anyone, Tom used to practice quick draws in front of a mirror. He got to be pretty fast. After being promoted to Detective, his hip holster disappeared and was replaced by the shoulder rig he now wore. Again, in the privacy of his apartment, he practiced drawing his gun from the new holster until he was just as fast.

So without even thinking, Tom's hand reached into his jacket and tugged at his 9mm Model 17 Glock pistol, eighteen rounds with the first already chambered. He was quick.

The intruder was quicker. A muscular arm snaked across Tom's chest and yanked him backward. Tom was violently flipped over the intruder's hip, chair and all, and he landed hard on his shoulders. His grip still solid, Tom cleared leather on his holster and aimed the weapon upward. A boot dug into his armpit and two strong hands locked on the gun, twisting it out of his fist. It was tossed aside.

Tom's vision stopped spinning and he focused on the man standing over him. Short, extremely so, but built like a tank on steroids. He had a crew cut and a blond Fu Manchu mustache. A chest-sized tattoo of a samurai was visible through his tight white T-shirt.

"Hi, Tom." The man's foot shifted from Tom's armpit to his neck. He stepped down hard enough to cut off oxygen. Tom twisted and yanked at the leg, but couldn't get free. It was like wrestling with a tree trunk. His lungs began to burn, and he could feel his face become bright red.

"So you wound up being a pig. A shitty one. Jessup put up a better fight than you."

The man smiled, his mouth a dungeon of gray teeth. Three were missing, and one protruding incisor was capped in gold. It caught the light and twinkled at him.

Tom was big but limber. Grunting with effort, he brought up his long leg, aiming for the gold. The man turned in time, but still received a nasty kick to the side of the face. He stumbled back, and Tom scrambled to his hands and knees, sucking in air. He did a quick scan of the floor for his gun, and not seeing it, launched himself at the smaller man.

Tom's charge was met with a solid right to the jaw. It was the hardest punch Tom had ever taken, and his knees melted as if made of butter. As Tom fell, his attacker completed a tight reverse-kick that connected with his chest. Tom landed on his side, unable to draw a breath. It felt like someone had parked a car on his ribcage.

His attacker wiped some blood from his mouth and snarled. He reached inside his long coat at hip level. With a simple, swift motion he withdrew an honest-to-God samurai sword. Tom tried to get up but he still couldn't breathe. He'd landed hard, and along with the pain in his chest and jaw, his nervous system sent him notice that he'd somehow hurt his ass. He felt for it, found he was sitting on something hard. His Glock.

The surprise must have shown on his face, because the man was out the door before he could bring the gun around.

Tom sat there for ten full minutes, his breath slowly returning, the Glock held in a shaky hand. When he finally felt strong enough to stand up, the world was still wobbly and his stomach churned as if he'd eaten a nest of weasels. He managed to get to the bathroom before he was sick.

Then he drank some water out of the faucet and called it in.

CHAPTER 5

Chicago

Roy came into the hospital room just as the doctor was putting the final stitch inside Tom's cheek.

"Ouch. Probably don't want this coffee, huh?"

Tom gave Roy a slight shake of his head. It was a gourmet brand too. His partner set it down on a tray, next to a pile of bloody cotton balls.

"While some guy was doing a Jackie Chan on your face, I gave Jessup's mom a call. You ready for this to get weirder?"

Tom made an affirmative sound around the doctor's fingers.

"The vic was adopted. Mrs. Jessup had some female problem, couldn't have kids. She and her husband were on waiting lists at adoption agencies. But here's the deal—some strange man just showed up out of the blue and dropped a baby off at their house, complete with birth certificates and fifty grand in cash."

Tom raised an eyebrow. Roy continued.

"She doesn't know who he was, or why he did it.

Never heard from the guy again. But she doesn't think it ended there. She thinks her son was being watched, all while he was growing up."

The doctor finished the knot and cut the thread. Tom thanked him and touched the side of his face, still numb.

"What do you mean, watched?"

"She said once, when Jessup was about four, he was playing in the backyard and she ran inside to get the phone. When she came out, he was lying on the ground, some guy leaning over him. She yelled at the guy, he took off. Her kid was soaking wet, coughing up water. Jessup had wandered into the woods and fell in a pond. The guy had given him CPR, saved his life. But here's the thing—there wasn't another house around for almost a mile. So that guy shouldn't have been there."

"Maybe he was hiking. Or a hunter."

"Dressed in a suit, in the middle of the woods? She said there were other times too. She'd see some person watching Jessup play in the park, then a few weeks later see the same person."

Tom mulled it over, wondering how much Jessup's story mirrored his own. Had this same mystery stranger also given his parents fifty K?

"Roy, there's something you should know."

He told his partner about his tattoo, and his adoption, and also about the cop in Tennessee who'd been impaled.

"And I just remembered something else. My parents used to joke that I had a guardian angel watching over me. I got into a bike accident when I was a kid—broke my leg in an empty warehouse. Bad break, I passed out. No one knew I was there, but somehow I woke up in the hospital. The doctors said some man took me there, gave my phone number, and left."

"This is some seriously weird shit."

"Did you get anything else from Jessup's mother?"

"I got a name. When the mystery guy dropped off Jessup, he also left birth certificates, already filled out. Not only the state one, but the one the hospital issued. Doctor in charge was a guy named Harold Harper, out of Rush-Presbyterian. Paper trail ends in New Mexico. I've got some guys working on it. What's up with your foot?"

Tom's shoe was off. It was setting on the cot in a plastic baggie.

"The guy who attacked me admitted to killing Jessup. I kicked him in the face. We get a DNA match off the blood on the shoe, case is closed."

"So you gonna walk around with one shoe?"

Tom tossed Roy his car keys.

"My gym bag is in the trunk. I'm parked in Emergency. Be a dear, would you?"

His sneakers retrieved, Tom signed his release and tailgated Roy back to the district. He wished he'd asked his parents more questions about his adoption when they were still alive, but it hadn't mattered at the time. Why question a perfect family? Tom's mother had been a saint, always loving and supportive. His dad, a Chicago Alderman, had been one of the best men Tom had ever known. Tom couldn't have picked better parents.

After dropping off the shoe at the lab, Tom and Roy hit the computer. It took Tom fifteen minutes to feed in details about his attacker, and the computer took .04 seconds to spit out an answer.

Arthur Kilpatrick. He had a rap sheet that read like Felony's Greatest Hits; assault, arson, burglary, rape, attempted murder. Two stretches in prison, and a current warrant out for his arrest. He'd seriously injured eleven people in a bar fight. Tom read the number again. *Eleven.* This was one major bad ass.

"Click under distinguishing marks."

Tom did, and discovered that among Kilpatrick's many tattoos was a blue number 9 . . . on the bottom of his left heel. He was eleven days older than Tom.

"Shit keeps getting weirder and weirder."

Tom agreed. If Rod Serling had chosen that moment to walk out of the closet, he wouldn't have been surprised.

"So why did this guy return to the crime scene, Tommy? You think he left something there?"

"We searched every inch of that place. What could he have been looking for?"

"Maybe he wasn't looking for anything. Maybe he was there because you were there."

Tom blinked. "He came there to kill me?"

"We got two bodies, Jessup and that southern cop, both with number tatts. Kilpatrick has a tatt, and you have a tatt."

"But how did he know I was there?"

"Could have followed you."

"It was rush hour. I used my siren to weave through traffic. No one could have followed me."

"Staked the place out?"

"Two entrances, front and back. Can't watch both at once."

Tom rubbed his chin, some of the feeling returning.

Was there any way he could have alerted Kilpatrick to his arrival at the apartment? A sensor, a phone tap, a silent alarm . . .

"When I first got there, I turned on the stereo."

Roy raised his eyebrows. "And he heard it? You think the place was bugged?"

"Only one way to find out."

Tom searched through his desk until he found the Foxhound, a souvenir from his days in Vice. It was a small silver box the size of a pager. The device scanned radio waves between fifty megahertz and three gigahertz, almost every available frequency.

"Check the batteries. It's been a while."

While Roy fussed with the battery compartment, Tom returned to the drawer for a gravity knife. He placed it in his pants pocket. Tom wasn't going to be caught without a back-up weapon again.

"I thought those knives were illegal."

"So? Call a cop."

Tom drove, sparing the siren now that traffic had died down. He parked in the alley next to Jessup's building.

"We going stealth mode or noisy, give him another shot at you?"

"Stealth. If we find anything, we can set a trap for him later."

Regardless, Tom pulled out his Glock and made sure a round was chambered.

"You look whiter than usual. You okay?"

"I'm fine."

"You can wait in the car, if you want. I'll find you a lollipop."

Tom gave him a glare. They walked in through the back entrance and up to Jessup's apartment. Tom opened the door as quietly as possible, one hand on the butt of his pistol. He flipped on the lights, and after a quick tour revealed the place was empty he relaxed a bit.

Roy took out the Foxhound and played with the dials. He started at the bookcases, waving the antenna in a serpentine pattern from top to bottom. Nothing happened, so he moved on to the near wall. When the antenna pointed at the electrical outlet, the red light began to blink and the Foxhound vibrated. He nodded at Tom and pointed.

Tom knelt next to the outlet and stared. It seemed completely normal. A lamp was plugged into the left socket. He switched it on and the lamp worked fine.

Tom went into the kitchen, where he recalled seeing some screwdrivers in a junk drawer. He found one and brought it back to the outlet. Then he unplugged the lamp and carefully unscrewed the cover.

It was definitely a bug. He removed two more screws and took out the entire assembly, careful not to jostle or disconnect it. The device was high-tech and professional. A flat platform mike was taped to the inside of the wall, with a long antenna running alongside. It drew power off of the apartment's electricity, and the current was live and allowed the sockets to function. Tom looked for any labels or markings, and wasn't surprised when he didn't find any.

He put the device back and joined up with Roy in the bedroom. His partner was kneeling next to another socket, the Foxhound blinking. Tom took the detector into the kitchen. Within two minutes, he'd found a third bug in an outlet next to the phone.

Neither one of them said a word until they were back in the car. Roy spoke first.

"Damn. That guy had more bugs than a housing project."

"Not homemade spy gear, either. That was some major league equipment."

"Even in Vice, we didn't have stuff that slick."

"So who does have stuff like that?"

"The government."

They exchanged a look. Tom started the car and pulled out of the alley, eyes on the rearview. "What next? Try a sting, draw Kilpatrick into a trap?"

"What else can we do?"

"Call the district, have Wally check the fax. I'm waiting on Jessup's phone records."

Roy got on the cell and Tom considered this new development. Whoever bugged Jessup's apartment was big league. Kilpatrick was the killer, but someone had to be behind him. Perhaps the mysterious Bert.

"Fax came." Roy dialed another number. "Jessup called the O'Hare Hyatt three times in the last few days."

"See if they have a convention going."

"Way ahead of you, partner."

Tom hung a ralph and headed for the expressway.

"Got it." Roy pocketed his cell phone. "The Hyatt is hosting a huge convention all this week, hotel is booked solid."

"What kind of convention?"

"It's an NFLCA expo."

"Enlighten me."

"The National Fishing Lures Collector's Association."

"That was this week? Damn it, I forgot to mark my calendar."

"Hurry. They said the Creek Chub auction starts in twenty minutes."

Tom patted his pocket, reassured that the knife was still there, and then merged onto I-90.

CHAPTER 6

"We can still make our reservation. You can throw something on."

Joan stared at Max, stunned. "You're kidding, right?"

"Not at all. Reservations at Carmichael's are very hard to get. *Everyone* eats there. The waiting list is months long."

"I can't believe you. Some maniac broke in my house, killed my dog, and tried to shish-kabob me—"

"Joan, you're being dramatic. Everyone gets robbed. This is LA."

"Stop the car."

"Don't be ridiculous."

"Stop the damn car."

Max pulled the Lexus to the curb in front of a McDonalds.

"Joan, let's not overreact."

"Overreact? You're a callous, arrogant, insensitive jerk."

"Insensitive? Who just picked you up at the police station?"

"Well, a million thanks for driving me home. Why don't you whip it out, and I'll pull up my skirt and hop on."

Max rubbed his eyes. His tortured look. She'd only seen him a half dozen times, and the look was becoming increasingly frequent—every time she offered an opinion, or her cell phone rang, or she talked about her day. Why was she with this guy anyway?

Joan found the door handle and used it. He rolled the window down.

"Joan, let me at least take you home."

She ignored him and walked into the restaurant. Maybe she was being a bit dramatic, but hell, the past few hours *were* dramatic. Joan tried to imagine how Max would react if he had some psycho chasing him. Big corporate hotshot would probably be sucking his thumb, begging for his mama.

But that wasn't really fair. No one really knew what they'd do in a crisis situation, until it happened. Maybe Max wasn't being insensitive—maybe this was his way of trying to be strong for her. Was his suggestion so outrageous? Perhaps the best thing for her would be to go out and have a good time. It sure beat going home and pulling Schnapps off of that stake.

Joan turned around, hoping Max was still there, or perhaps even coming through the parking lot after her.

Max was pulling out into traffic.

Asshole. Fine. She didn't care for him much anyway. He was too good-looking, and he knew it. Joan's Second Rule of Dating; never date a man prettier than you are. She'd broken that rule because she thought Max had some class. He was young, successful, and not in the life. That was Joan's First Rule. Never date a guy in the movie business. She had other criteria—no guys with back hair, no guys who wore Speedos or thongs, no guys who lived with their mom, but the first two were the most important.

Unfortunately, all that her rules got her was an empty social calendar and the feeling that she was somehow unworthy, even with her many accomplishments.

She went straight to the pay phone and punched in her pin number, calling the person she should have called when this first happened. Marty. Her assistant. Her friend. In her eyes, he was the perfect man. He'd make some guy really happy someday.

And apparently, that's what he was up to at that moment. When the call went through, another man answered. Tipsy, buoyant, enthusiastic.

Joan hung up. Lately, Marty had been about as lucky as she had with men. Good for him for scoring. She didn't want to intrude on that.

So, what now? Joan sat down in a plastic swivel chair, noting how stupid her sockless running shoes looked with her skirt. After the police arrived, she'd demanded to fill out the report immediately, hoping that the sooner they had a description, the sooner they could get the creep off the streets. The police complied, whisking her away to the station before she had a chance to change or even grab her purse.

And now, three hours later, after sitting with an artist and reviewing mug shots and telling her story a dozen times, she was stuck at a McDonalds without a ride, wearing these dumb shoes, afraid to go home.

Get tough, Joanie, she thought. *If you don't face it now, you'll never want to go back.*

Screwing up her courage, Joan removed herself from the chair and marched out to the street. It took her three shouts before a cab stopped.

Her sense of dread increased with every tick of the meter. When the cabbie finally pulled in front of her house and asked if this was the place, Joan didn't know if she could move.

"Lady? You okay?"

"Hold on. I have to go in, get some money. No purse."

"Meter's running."

"Be right back."

She controlled her breathing, pushing it deep into her stomach, and got out of the taxi.

No burglar alarm. Dark house. Dead guard dog. She didn't even have her keys. But the rear patio window was probably still open. That was in back, past Schnapps . . .

Joan followed the bushes around her home, moving quick and confident, refusing to look at her poor dog or the stake that was meant for her. The police, after checking out her house, had closed the patio door. An officer on her case had volunteered to hang around her house until she came home, and Joan kicked herself for refusing the offer. She figured she had Max, and the cop had been too good looking. Now, apprehension mounting, she wondered how she was going to get inside. Break her own window?

No need. The patio door was unlocked. Joan went into the kitchen, turning on lights as she went, and found her purse on the floor where she'd dropped it. After digging out her wallet, she walked out the front door and paid the taxi driver. The cab turned around in her circular driveway, and Joan watched the tail lights disappear down the hill. She felt very alone.

Back to the house. The front doorknob was covered with white powder. The police had determined this was the entry point, and had gone ahead and checked for prints even though she made it clear that the man wore gloves. Joan didn't know if she should admire them for the effort, or be irritated that they didn't believe her.

Once inside, Joan turned on her large screen television and changed the channel to CNN, grateful for the nonstop voices. She flipped on more lights, checked to make sure the doors and windows were all locked, and threw away her toothbrush, toothpaste, deodorant, soap, and shampoo. Anything he might have touched. Then she emptied her underwear drawer into the washing machine, her silverware drawer into the dishwasher, and started each of them on the highest heat setting.

She had an urge to vacuum, to scrub the bathtub and drain the Jacuzzi, but exhaustion was getting the upper hand. Her last effort to cleanse the house was changing her sheets, and then she kicked off her gym shoes and collapsed onto the bed.

Joan was able to relax for almost a full minute before paranoia reared its head. She picked up the phone and found it still disconnected. Her cell was in her car. Sleep would be impossible unless there was a phone next to her. Joan got out of bed.

She was padding through the living room when she saw the front door open. The scream was out of her mouth before he got into the room.

"Hello, Joan. Miss me?"

Same goatee. Same black outfit. Same gloves. He had some kind of metal device in his right hand. Lock picks. Joan willed herself to move, to run, to attack—anything but remain planted there like a deer in headlights. She took off toward the kitchen and went straight for the knife rack. With a steak knife in each hand, she turned around to face her tormentor.

He was standing in the kitchen, regarding her calmly.

"I knew you'd be a fighter. Perhaps I should burn you at the stake rather than impale you on one."

"Get away from me."

"Sorry. Can't do that, Joan."

"What the hell did I ever do to you?" Joan's voice came out steeped in desperation. She was close to cracking.

"To me? Nothing. The English may feel differently."

The guy was off his nut. That was good. She dealt with crazy people all the time in the business. She could handle crazy.

Joan moved her left foot, widening her stance. She assumed a defensive position, each hand holding its knife in a death grip. If he took another step forward, she'd try an attack. Keep him talking, don't telegraph it.

"You're crazy."

"I know about the tattoo. I know about the adoption. I know who your parents really are. Don't you wonder how I know all of that?"

With an easy, deliberate move, he took a bottle and a rag out of his left pocket. Something to knock her out while he dropped her on that sharp piece of wood.

Not in this lifetime.

Joan lunged. The man was nimble, trained. He dropped to one knee and trapped her wrist in his armpit, then lifted up his forearm to block the other knife.

But Joan didn't attack with the other knife. She went straight for the crotch, bringing her leg up and connecting hard. Her knee hit an athletic supporter. He closed his legs on her foot, trapping it. Joan dropped the knife in her pinned hand and grabbed his shirt. Then she let herself fall onto her back and flipped him over her head, her free leg planted on his chest.

The intruder released her wrist. Joan rolled onto all fours, still in attack mode. Before he could get up, she struck with the knife, aiming for the neck.

He saw the blow coming and moved to block it. The swing was deflected, but she still managed to bury the blade two inches into his shoulder. She released the knife and scampered for the front door.

"Joan? I really think you're overreacting."

Max, coming into the house.

"Max!" She ran right into him, yanking at his arm. "Come on!"

Max grabbed her, tried to hold her back. "You need to calm down."

This was the wrong time for talk. They needed to get out of here.

"There's a—"

That's all she got out. The intruder had pulled the steak knife from his shoulder and flung himself at Max, plunging it into his back. Max dropped to his knees. Joan shoved the intruder, but he backhanded her across the forehead, sending her sprawling onto the driveway just a few feet away from Max's Lexus. The car was running, the headlights on.

Phone, she thought. *Call for help.* She tugged the door open and slammed it closed, hitting the lock button. She looked around for Max's cell. It wasn't there.

"Dammit!" Joan looked out the window. The intruder was hunched over Max, working on him with the steak knife. She couldn't tell if Max was dead or alive, but then she saw it; a feeble twitching in his hands.

Joan leaned on the horn. The intruder stopped his attack and stared. Joan opened the window. "Leave him alone!"

"Is this your boyfriend, Joan?" The intruder grinned. "Handsome devil. But I can fix that."

He began to cut away at Max's face.

Joan thought about hitting the gas, running into him, but it would kill Max too. She clenched her teeth. *Fight or flight, Joanie? Fight or flight?*

Joan DeVilliers got out of the car.

The intruder stared up at her, his eyes widening. He let go of Max's hair and stepped over him.

"My, you are a brave one, aren't you?"

Joan pushed aside the fear and slowed her breathing. She didn't get to be a black belt taking a correspondence course. Joan could fight, and she could win. This guy was above her weight class, but she'd beaten men before. Joan planted her bare feet on the driveway and centered herself.

The man moved well, liquid and flowing. *Like a snake,* Joan thought. He was smiling and confident, but that could work to Joan's advantage. So far, she'd been reacting out of fear. He was underestimating her. If she stayed focused, she'd have a chance.

Time slowed down, as it often did when she was fighting. Sound seemed to disappear, and her opponent became sharper, clearer. Instead of treating him as a threat, she mentally divided him into different strike points. Joan could break boards with her hands and feet. Bones weren't much thicker.

He came in on her left, feinting with a hook and then round-housing with his right. Joan slipped the punch, spun, and landed a solid reverse kick in his face, dead center. She straightened her leg on impact, hitting him with all of her hundred and fifteen pounds.

It sent the intruder sprawling onto his back, his head bouncing on the asphalt, his nose a mashed tomato. Like many tournament fights, it was over in a heartbeat. Joan had knocked him out, cold.

For a moment, she didn't know what to do. Her brain told her to finish it, go for the death blow that she'd practiced so often but always pulled short in matches. But could she? Could she actually kill an unconscious man?

Joan approached cautiously. His eyes were closed, and he looked more pathetic than threatening. She knelt on his chest, raising her fist, aiming for the neck . . .

And couldn't do it.

A moan, from the doorway. Max. She got off her assailant and hurried to him. He was curled up in a fetal position, bleeding from several holes in his chest. His face looked like a lasagna. She turned his head to the side so the blood wouldn't run down his throat, and then felt in his jacket pocket for his phone. Joan dialed 911 and considered what she should do with the intruder. Tie him up somehow?

It didn't matter. When she looked down the driveway, the man was no longer there.

"Beverly Hills 911 Emergency, this is Mrs. Schmidtt."

"My name is Joan DeVilliers. I need an ambulance and the police here as soon as possible. I'm at 1445 Hillcrest."

"Can you explain what happened?"

"I was attacked." Joan's voice broke. "Again."

CHAPTER 7

Chicago

The O'Hare Hyatt Regency was one of the larger hotels in the area, with over a thousand rooms. The eight-story building had been constructed in a U-shape, with parking all around it. Tom circled slowly, trying to find a space. Even the handicapped spots were full. He put the Mustang in the Courtesy Bus slot.

The lobby was buzzing. The majority of people milling about were white males over fifty, many sporting novelty T-Shirts with slogans like GET HOOKED ON LURES and KISS MY BASS. The duo made their way to Check-In and waited for the smiling concierge to notice them.

"Are you gentleman here for the convention?"

"No, ma'am. I'm Detective Mankowski, this is Detective Lewis."

They held out their badges. The girl's smile held. She was young, blond, attractive. Upon noticing this, Roy sidled closer, becoming Alpha cop.

"What can we do for you, Detectives?"

"We need your help in a homicide investigation. We're looking for a suspect believed to be registered here. He's manning a table at the convention."

"I can check to see if he's registered. His name?"

"All we have is the first name. Bert."

"That may be tough. We have over fifteen hundred guests currently registered, and they're organized by last name."

"Can you look them up by address? We believe he's from Milwaukee."

"I can try." She pushed a few buttons on her computer. "Okay, here. We currently have a hundred and sixteen guests with a listed Milwaukee address."

"Anyone named Bert?" Tom tried to crane his neck over the top of the computer to see the screen. "It might also be variations—Robert, Herbert, Albert, Norbert, Cuthbert, Dilbert . . ."

"Q*Bert." Roy grinned. She batted her eyelashes at him. Tom had never seen a woman actually bat her eyelashes outside of television.

"It'll take a moment, I'll have to go through them name by name. Okay, here's a Robert. Signed in as Bob, not Bert. Not a seller. Whoever bought table space in the convention center gets a special room rate. Let's see. Michael. Jeffrey. George. Chris. John. Here's one. Albert Blumberg. He has a booth and he did sign in as Bert."

"Can we have his room number and table number?"

"He's in room 714, booth number 18-A. I'll give you a convention map."

"Any others?"

She spent a minute going through the rest of the names. A fat guy in a shirt that read MASTER BAITER walked through the lobby, proclaiming the auction was about to begin. It thinned the crowd considerably.

"No others. He was the only one."

They received a convention map and left the front desk, heading down a hallway to the Normandy Room, a huge warehouse-sized open space packed with people and display booths. Every direction they looked had tackle or men discussing tackle. A voice boomed over the loudspeaker.

"Next up, mint in box with papers, a Creek Chub Sucker #3900 in frog scale. Bidding starts at two hundred dollars."

"Two Benjamins?" Roy sneered. "That's why it's called a Sucker."

Tom consulted the map and led them through the ranks and files of booths, zigzagging to 18-A. The table was actually a glass display rack, showcasing several dozen brightly colored lures in neat rows. The man behind the display was thin, tall, in his fifties.

"Albert Blumberg?"

"No. He had to step away for a moment. I'm minding the store. You interested in one of his baits?"

Tom took a quick look in the case, noting all the prices were triple digits or higher. He doubted there was a layaway plan.

"Is he back in his room? We really should talk to him personally."

"I think so. He was bringing down more lures to display."

"He's tall, right? Long hair? About my age?"

"Wrong guy. Bert is short, short hair, big nose. Could be around your age."

Tom nudged Roy over. "You stay here, I'll check the room. Call if he shows."

"You do the same."

Tom took out his cell phone, making sure it was on and set to vibrate. A ringing phone was not a wise thing for a cop to have on him in precarious situations. The loudspeaker thundered. "Sold, for seven hundred and fifty dollars!"

There was scattered applause. Roy shook his head.

"Seven-fifty. What kind of damn fish can you catch worth seven-fifty? I cast that out, better reel me in a Mercedes."

Tom wove his way though the crowd and located an elevator, entering alongside two elderly men who were discussing worm burns. Tom exited on his floor and followed the hall to 714. He opened his jacket and stood to the left of the door before knocking.

"Hold on a second."

The voice seemed to match the one on the phone. Tom tensed a notch. The door opened.

The man was average height, with wavy brown hair and a closely clipped mustache. He was a couple pounds overweight, which showed in his hound dog jowls. Familiar looking, but Tom couldn't place him.

"Are you here about the Luny Frog? I can't go any lower than fifteen hundred. Not a single penny." He blinked. "Okay, fourteen hundred."

"Bert Blumberg?"

"Yes, that's me. The bait is in excellent-plus condition, and it's the first production model, complete with egg sinker. That fourteen hundred is firm. Solid. In stone. I won't go lower." Bert smiled, unsure. "Fine, I'll take thirteen."

"I'm not here about the Luny Frog."

"Are you sure? You look so familiar. Wait a sec . . . Thomas?"

Tom was surprised that the man knew his name. "Detective Tom Mankowski. How did . . . ?"

"The resemblance is uncanny. You're number five, right?"

The cop's eyes narrowed, accusing. "How can you know all of this?"

Bert squinted at him. "You don't know? Don't you have a tattoo on your foot?"

"What does it mean?"

"Tom Jessup figured it all out. I'm number six. Have you met Jessup yet?"

"He's dead."

Bert swallowed, his Adam's apple bobbing. "Dead? I just saw him a few days ago. How?"

"Murdered. I need you to answer some questions."

"Sure. Of course."

The room was small, tidy. A suitcase was open on the table, filled with lures individually encased in bubble wrap. Bert closed the door and paced to the table, then to the bed, then to the table again, staring at the floor.

"This is . . . this is bad. Very bad. He knew there was something wrong. I talked to him on Thursday. He said he was being followed. Am I next?" Bert looked at Tom, his eyes wide. "Could I be in danger? I buy and sell fishing lures, for the love of Mike. I never hurt anyone—I mean, sure, sometimes people get a hook in the finger—"

"Sit down, Mr. Blumberg."

"How was he murdered?"

"Please sit down."

Bert sat at the table and began to drum his fingers. Tom pulled up a chair, almost touching. He leaned close.

"Tell me about the tattoo, and how you know my name."

"You won't believe it."

"Try me."

"I didn't believe it either. Thought Jessup was a crackpot. But when I saw all the research, and the DNA . . ."

"From the beginning. Tell me."

"Tell you? No. No that's no good. You won't believe me. How about I show you?"

Bert went to the nightstand and opened the drawer. He took out some courtesy Hyatt stationary and a ballpoint pen and set them before Tom.

"Write a few sentences in cursive."

"What the hell are you talking about?"

"Do it. This is what Jessup did with me. Write some song lyrics, or what you did today, or whatever. Just do it in script."

Crackpot, Tom thought. But he'd play along if it got the guy to open up. He wrote the first few verses of the Doors' hit "L.A. Woman."

"Fine. Now what?"

"Just a second. I have to find it."

Bert located a briefcase at the foot of the bed and reached inside. Tom had his gun out and pointed before Bert could remove his hand.

"Hold it!"

"Jeez! Don't shoot me!"

"Take your hand out slowly, no quick moves."

"It's papers. Just papers. Jeez, I think I browned my shorts."

Bert, hand shaking, pulled a black leather binder out of his briefcase.

"It's Jessup's research binder. He wanted me to hold onto it for him."

"Bring it here."

"Stop yelling at me. I'm gonna have a heart attack, and you'll have to use CPR, and you won't do it because I had egg salad with onions for lunch."

Bert opened the binder and took out a piece of paper. He placed it in front of Tom. It was a print out of a handwritten rough draft, filled with crossed out words, brackets, and arrows. Very old looking. Tom began to read it, some lawyerspeak about quartering large bodies of armed troops, when something struck him.

The handwriting was his.

He looked at his song lyrics, and then back to the photocopy. All the letters matched. The *Ts* were crossed the same way, the *Ys* had the exact same curly bottom. Tom copied the phrase, *he has erected a multitude of new offices*, on his own paper, and found it impossible to tell the difference between the two.

"What the hell?"

"Does it match?"

"Exactly."

"Eerie, isn't it?"

"Who wrote this?"

"You don't recognize the words? Here's the first page."

Bert handed Tom another photocopy, this one with a

large scrawl on the top. He read, *"A Declaration by the Representatives of the United States of America, in General Congress assembled. What is this?"*

Bert smiled a goofy little smile. "It's a copy of the first draft of the Declaration of Independence."

Tom stared at him, incredulous. "So this means—what? I'm a reincarnation of Thomas Jefferson?"

"Close." Bert sat on the bed next to Tom. "You're his clone."

The words hung there like a crooked picture. Tom opened his mouth to say something, but nothing came out.

"Jessup knew about you," Bert said. "He was planning on contacting you soon. He just needed a final piece of verification. You were adopted, right?"

Tom nodded.

"Jessup didn't know how or why, but he did have some idea of who. He found me, and you, and two of the others."

"So . . . I'm Thomas Jefferson."

"Not convinced? Here."

Bert went back into the briefcase and took out a library book—Jessup's book on the Declaration of Independence. Tom stared at the face on the cover of the book. A painting of the Third President of the United States. Older, white hair, wrinkles. But it bore a striking resemblance to Tom's face. The broad chin. The deep-set hazel eyes. The tight mouth.

"This is insane."

"Insane?" Bert laughed. "Are you saying you don't hold this truth to be self-evident?"

"Funny. And who are you supposed to be, then? Groucho Marx?"

"I'm Albert Einstein."

"I bet."

"I'm serious. Look at this."

Bert took an Einstein biography out of the briefcase and handed it to Tom, the page opened to a black and white picture of the scientist as a young man. It was Bert, down to the big nose and droopy jowls. Tom pushed the book away.

"Impossible. Humans can't be cloned. Not thirty years ago. They didn't have the technology."

Bert spread his hands. "And yet here we are. Einstein and Jefferson, having a conversation."

"Who was Jessup?"

"Thomas Edison."

"And the others?"

"There's a guy in Nebraska who we think is Abe Lincoln, and a guy in Tennessee who is probably Robert E. Lee."

Tom's cell phone vibrated. He put it to his ear.

"Nothing happening down here, Tommy. 'Cept some guy just bought a lure worth more than my damn car. How're things up there?"

"Surreal. I'm with Bert in his room. Come up."

Tom hung up and stared at the Jefferson book, his mind a tangle. This had to be some kind of put-on. He flipped it open and found a description of the man. Six feet two inches tall. Thin and wiry. Sandy hair.

"There has to be more proof than this. I can see that I look like Jefferson, and write like Jefferson, but I could be a relative, a great-great-grandson or cousin or something."

Bert nodded, his jowls jiggling. "I figured the same thing. I mean, I flunked biology in high school. I get headaches when I do long division. But it all fits. I can explain it to you."

Someone knocked at the door.

"Ah. The guy who wants the Luny Frog. Fifteen hundred. Don't let me go less than fifteen hundred." Bert went to the door, pulling it open and pointing dramatically. "The Heddon Luny Frog, right? I've got it right here. Excellent plus condition. I couldn't go less than fourteen hundred for it. Maybe thirteen. You can touch it, you don't need to wear those gloves."

Tom shifted to see the person in the doorway. Male, white, medium build, with dark blue eyes and thick, almost feminine lips. His face appeared to be stretched too tight. He was wearing latex gloves and a poncho, even though it wasn't raining.

"*You can touch it, you don't need to wear those gloves.* I'm Jack. You're Albert. We've both made history before, Albert. Let's do it again."

Jack reached inside his poncho pocket but Tom was already on his feet with the pistol in his hand.

"Freeze! Police!"

Jack grabbed Albert by the sweater and tugged him forward, his arm around the smaller man's neck, using him as a shield. A knife came out, wickedly sharp with a long curved blade, the kind of crazy design that freaks bought from classified ads in *Soldier of Fortune* magazine. Fast as a snake he brought the point under Bert's chin.

"I could cut out his eyes before you pull the trigger."

Bert lost all color. "I like my eyes. They're my second favorite body part."

"Drop the weapon!"

"*Drop the weapon.* I know you. You're Jefferson.

I'm number ten. Saucy Jack. A hundred year old mystery revealed."

Tom's finger flexed lightly on the trigger, aiming for the perp's shoulder.

"Drop the weapon, now!"

"*Drop the weapon, now.* I don't think so. Maybe you drop the gun, hmm?"

The knife slid half an inch into Bert's chin, bringing forth a torrent of blood. Bert began to cry.

Tom let out a breath, ready to fire. Jack must have sensed his intention, because he pulled Bert backwards into the hall. Tom moved to follow, but then he heard Bert yell, "There's two!"

A trap. Coming in low, under his line of fire, was Arthur Kilpatrick. He'd been waiting outside the door. Tom couldn't bring the gun down in time and was caught in a flying tackle. Kilpatrick landed on top of him, his breath smelling of rotten meat.

"Hello, Mr. President."

Tom's gun was pinned next to his body, useless. But his left hand was only inches away from his pocket. The gravity knife. He yanked it out and flipped the switch. The blade sprung from the handle and locked into position. Tom jammed it into Kilpatrick's hip.

The small man howled, rolling off of Tom and hobbling for the door, the knife jutting out of his leg. Tom rolled to all fours and stumbled into the hall after him.

Kilpatrick had gone left, heading for the stairwell. Tom brought up his gun, hesitant to take a shot. The hotel was fully booked. If he missed, the bullet could easily go through someone's door.

Tom spun in the other direction, searching for Albert and Jack. Jack had vanished. Bert was on the floor, his

chest soaked with blood. Roy was kneeling next to
him, gun in hand.

"Where's the perp?" Tom yelled.

"Ran down the stairs. Go!"

Roy pulled out his cell phone to call an ambulance,
or back-up, or both. Tom took off down the hallway.
He reached the door to the stairs and turned the knob.
It didn't budge. Tom looked down and saw the wicked
knife blade jammed underneath it like a doorstop. Ex-
ercising bad judgment, Tom kicked at the blade, neatly
severing a large flap of rubber from the bottom of his
shoe.

He jogged back down the hall. Roy had taken off his
tie and was holding it tight under Bert's chin.

"Door's jammed. They got away."

"Kilpatrick again?"

"Yeah. Plus a friend."

Bert gasped. "Tourniquet. Tie a tourniquet."

"He okay?"

"Nasty cut to the chin, nothing fatal."

"I'm bleeding to death. Tie a tourniquet."

"Buddy, if I tie a tourniquet around your neck, it'll
strangle you." He turned to Tom. "What in the hell is
going on here, Tommy?"

"It's a long story. But I think I know the guy who
cut Bert."

"Did you see that knife? I come out of the elevator
and he was waving it around through the air like Jack
the freaking Ripper."

"Got it in one, Roy."

"Got what?"

Tom pursed his lips, eyes intent. "I think that was
Jack the Ripper."

CHAPTER 8

Chicago

"I have to get my lures."

Bert sat in the back seat of the Mustang, petulant. Five stitches in the chin did little to calm his resolve.

"I spoke to the hotel. They're keeping your things for you."

"You don't understand. There's, well, a lot of money invested in those. I want them by my side."

Roy turned around and faced him. "They set a trap for you. They knew you were there. If I didn't come out of that elevator when I did, you'd be on the slab waiting for an autopsy."

Bert folded his arms. "I need my lures. I won't say another word to you until I have my lures."

"Bert . . ."

"I want my lawyer."

"You don't need a lawyer. You're not under arrest."

"Then let me out right here."

"Dammit, Bert."

Bert leaned forward, his hands on their headrests. "Get me my lures, and I'll tell you how Jessup figured it all out."

"Figured what out? Tom, you know what he's talking about?"

Bert tapped Tom's shoulder. "You haven't told him you're Thomas Jefferson?"

Roy made a face. "Thomas—what?"

"This may take a while." Tom turned up the heat and gave Roy the quick version, telling him about the handwriting and the Jefferson book and the cloning. Roy was less than impressed.

"Maybe, just maybe, I could see you as Jefferson. But this guy is *definitely* not Einstein."

"I'll tell you the rest of it, but we have to get my lures."

Tom blew out a long breath and made a U-turn at the intersection, heading back towards the Hyatt.

"Okay." Bert let out a long breath and visibly relaxed. "Jessup first contacted me by email. Said he knew about the tattoo on my foot and what it meant."

"You knew you were adopted?" Tom asked.

Bert nodded. "I found out when I was a teenager."

"Let me guess. Mysterious man dropped you off, along with fifty grand?"

"How did you know?"

Tom ignored the question. "How did you meet Jessup?"

"Emailed me. Said that he knew about the tattoo, he had some amazing stuff to tell me, and he wanted to meet. I thought he was nuts, of course. But he sent me a picture of a thirty-year-old Einstein. Black and white. Looked just like me, except it was old and the clothes were out of date. So I agreed to meet with him in Chicago. The convention was coming up, so I figured I'd be here anyway."

Tom honked at some bozo ahead of him doing the speed limit. The guy merged into the right lane and Tom passed.

"So then he did the handwriting thing?"

"Yeah. And more pictures. Plus he showed me the article. A year before I was born, Einstein's brain was stolen from Dr. Thomas Harvey at Princeton. He had it in two jars. Jessup let me see a newspaper clipping on it. The brain was mysteriously returned the next month—it was thought to be some kind of college prank."

"Back up. How did he find you?"

"Oh. Our Birth Certificates. Every person has a birth number. He got in touch with the Cook County Clerk and looked up the person whose birth number came right before his. That was me."

"He already knew he was Edison?"

"Edison?" Roy snorted. "Am I the only one here thinks this is all crazy?"

Bert ignored him. "Last year he picked up a book on Edison and was surprised at the likeness. He wondered if he might be a relative. So he began to study him, gather information. He discovered his handwriting was identical to Edison's. Then he found a newspaper article about Edison's grave being vandalized, a year before he was born."

Tom reasoned it out. "Someone robbed the grave for a DNA sample."

"That's what he figured. So he paid to have a lab test his DNA, and then went to Edison's grave and . . ."

Roy turned around again. "He dug up Thomas Edison?"

"It was the only way to be sure. Jessup figured since he had a 7 on his foot, there must be six others. He knew if he was a clone, then he really wasn't born at Rush-Presbyterian Hospital, so those birth records were fake."

Tom filled in the rest. "So he assumed they were all sent to the local registrar as a batch, and the birth numbers would be consecutive."

"Right. The registrar assigns birth numbers in the order they're received. So Jessup began to search through newspapers from a year before he was born, looking for famous people whose graves had been disturbed. That's how he found the Einstein article, and took a guess that since my name was Albert, I might be Einstein."

Tom nodded. It fit perfectly. "The man who dropped the babies off—he insisted they keep their first names."

"My parents told me that too. Lucky, I guess. They wanted to name me Shlomo."

"So Jessup found out Jefferson's grave was disturbed."

"Yes. Along with Abraham Lincoln's and Robert E. Lee's. And coincidentally, number 1 and number 2 are named Abe and Robert."

"And he was planning on telling me?"

"After the tests came back. A few years ago, there was a sample of DNA taken from Jefferson, to prove if he ever fathered illegitimate children. Jessup tracked down the sample and was having the results sent to him. Then he was going to approach you."

"What were the other names? On the birth certificates?"

"I can't remember them all. I think there was a Jane, and maybe a Will."

Tom stopped at a red light and rubbed his eyes. Were they even his eyes? Or were they the eyes of a man who died two centuries ago?

"If—*if*—I buy into this cloning thing, and I'm Jefferson and you're Einstein, we still have a big problem. Jessup is dead, that cop who is supposedly Robert E. Lee was killed last year, and both of us are next on the list. So who the hell is doing this?"

Bert frowned. "Tom, that guy who tried to kill me. You said he was Jack the Ripper?"

Tom nodded. "He called himself Saucy Jack. The Ripper called himself that in a letter to the police. He also mentioned he was a hundred year old mystery revealed. But the clincher was the echolalia."

Bert raised an eyebrow. "Meaning?"

"It's a speech impediment, when you repeat back what was just said to you. A famous Ripper suspect by the name of Joseph Barnett had this disorder. He was a fish porter who dated the last woman the Ripper killed. Most enthusiasts think Dr. Francis Tumblety was the Whitechapel killer, but I think there are too many holes in that theory."

Roy shook his head. "It was Tumblety. The guy kept jars of female uteri in his closet."

"Tumblety was fifty-five years old. How many serial killers over fifty have you heard of?"

"I don't mean to interrupt here, but you two know so much about the Ripper because . . . ?"

"Police Academy. Mandatory course on suspect elimination. We had to study the Ripper case files and write reports about who we think did it."

"And you think that guy was Jack the Ripper?"

"If all this cloning stuff is for real, it's a possibility."

"Could be." Roy shrugged. "But if it was, it was Tumblety, not that fish porter cat."

"So who was that other guy with all the tattoos?"

"His name is Arthur Kilpatrick. He has a number 9 on his heel."

Bert leaned back and folded his arms. "Arthur . . . Arthur . . . what famous historical figured were named Arthur?"

They all thought about it for a moment.

"King Arthur," Roy said. "He had a sword too."

"Arthur Conan Doyle. The creator of Sherlock Holmes."

"Arthur Treacher. The fish and chip mogul."

Roy pulled a face. "Good one, Einstein. They clone Jefferson, Lincoln, and Arthur Treacher."

"It's better than King Arthur. He wasn't even real."

"Sure he was. Didn't you see *Camelot*?"

Bert rolled his eyes. "Oh, that's some good proof right there. That explains why he broke into song and dance."

"Maybe I'll dance a number on your face. Do an E equals MC ass whupping."

"You know, you've got some major issues, Roy."

"*I've* got issues?"

"You've got a whole subscription."

Tom made the decision right there to never have children.

"Here's the Hyatt, thank God. We'll pull up to the lobby. Bert and I will wait in the car. Roy, you run in and get his stuff."

"I should have two suitcases full of lures. Make sure

they cleared out my booth. I want receipts. Don't touch or break anything."

Roy gave him a look that would wilt flowers. Tom parked in front of the main entrance and turned off the engine.

"Call if there's trouble."

"The hotel should have an inventory list." Bert said. "Don't forget it."

Roy frowned. "Hundred fifty years of freedom, and the black man is running to get the white man's bags."

He got out of the car and took a good look around before heading into the lobby. Tom put his arm over the back of the seat and faced Bert.

"Can you please stop antagonizing my partner?"

"It's not me. It's him. I think he hates me because I'm Jewish."

"That's completely untrue. Race is not an issue with Roy. He hates everybody equally."

Tom turned back around just as his side window splintered. A sharp cracking sound filled his ears, the wind ruffling the hair on the back of his head.

"Get down!"

Tom lunged onto the passenger side, digging out his Glock. He chanced a look at the driver's side window and saw a spiderweb pattern with a one inch hole in the center.

Sniper rifle. High caliber—it punched through the glass, clean. Something slower would have shattered it. He looked in front of him and saw a divot in the upper portion of the passenger door. Based on the angle, whoever was shooting at him was higher up. The hotel was shaped like a big U, so he was probably in one of the rooms on the opposite side.

Tom considered starting the car and driving out of there, but he'd have to turn around, which would give the shooter a full front windshield to shoot through. And Tom was a big target.

"Stay down, we're going out the right door."

"Was that a bullet?"

Another hole materialized in the glass. The driver's headrest jerked back violently.

"Move!"

Tom tugged at the handle and pulled himself through the passenger side. He helped yank out Bert with his left hand and then closed the door, staying low. There was a loud *bang*. Tom hadn't heard any previous shots, assuming a supressor was being used. When the front end of the Mustang began to sink forward he realized a tire had been shot out. Tom called Roy's cell phone.

"Yo."

"We're pinned down. Sniper fire. He's in one of the rooms on the second or third floor, east side of the building."

"I'm on it."

Another *bang*. The rear tire. Tom opened the door and climbed back into the car, keeping under the line of fire. He took a deep breath, focused his concentration, and then he snatched the rearview mirror, yanking it off its base. He slunk back out of the car, mirror in hand.

"Stay behind the rim," he told Bert.

Tom crawled over to the front of the car, staying below engine level. He angled the mirror over the hood, looking for the sniper. He checked the windows on the second floor, one by one, hoping to spot movement or the glint of a telescopic sight. Nothing. He went room by room across the third floor and didn't find anything either. Strange.

"I haven't made peace with my family," Bert said, his head covered in his arms. "I can't die without making peace! There are things that need to be said!"

Tom ignored Bert's apparent breakdown, and tried to concentrate on the windows. Why couldn't he find the shooter? Tom started again on the second floor, trying to think like a sniper. A professional wouldn't be leaning out the window. A pro would be several feet away from the window, in a dark room. Tom located him near the end of the building. A window open just a few inches. No one else would have a window open in this weather. He dialed Roy.

"Second floor, third room from the last."

"Almost there. I'll leave you on. Stay quiet."

Tom put his finger in front of his lips, warning Bert to keep silent. He turned up the volume on the cell phone, keeping both eyes on the window.

"Police! Open the door!"

In the room Tom saw a muzzle flash.

"You want some of this?" Roy's voice, angry.

The gunshots could be heard without the cell phone, six in quick succession. Tom watched as the window flew open and a black clad figure crawled out with a rifle.

"He's out the window!" Tom yelled into the phone. And then he was up and sprinting across the parking lot. The sniper dropped, landing in some bushes. He noticed Tom advancing and raised the rifle. Tom veered to the left and dove into the bed of a pickup truck. A bullet pierced the sidewall and missed his leg by inches.

More gunshots. Roy from the window, firing down. Tom chanced a look and saw the figure running alongside the building and cutting around the corner.

"Tommy! You okay?"

"Yeah." Tom hopped out of the truck and held the phone to his ear. "He went around. I think it was our friend Jack."

"Be right there."

Roy went out the window feet first and dropped to the ground, landing on his ass.

Tom ran over to his partner, helping him up.

"You okay?"

"No. Sweet merciful Jesus! Something's stuck!"

Roy turned around, a large branch sticking into his right butt cheek. "Oh shit. Pull it out."

Tom winced. "We should wait for the doctor."

"Goddamit, Tom! Pull this goddamn stick out of my ass!"

Tom gripped the stick and tugged hard. It had been buried two inches in Roy's backside. The blood came freely, soon soaking Roy's pants.

"Should have left it in. I'm calling an ambulance."

"I'll do it. Go after him."

Tom nodded and ran to the corner of the building. He peered around cautiously. No sign of him, but there were plenty of cars for cover. Tom suddenly felt naked and out gunned.

"Do it," he told himself.

He ran around the corner, going in low. Low saved his life. The bullet grazed his scalp, taking off several layers of skin. Tom hit the ground and rolled behind a Nissan, bringing a hand up to the wound. It came away bloody, but there was no pain or disorientation. He crawled past the car and jogged in a crouch around the perimeter, trying to get behind the shooter. Tom ran by five cars before he saw him, crouched next to a red Buick. It was Jack, all right. And the son of a bitch was actually smiling.

Tom fired a quick group of four shots. It was a fair distance, and there was a light wind, but at least one of the bullets found its mark. Jack howled and rolled backwards out of sight, leaving his gun behind. Tom sprinted to the spot and scanned all directions. Too many cars, too many places to hide. Tom wiped some blood out of his right eye with his sleeve and picked up Jack's rifle by the barrel. Then he began walking through the parking lot, searching behind and under cars.

His cell phone vibrated. Tom answered.

"You okay?"

"I hit him, but he's gone. Got his gun."

"Bert's missing."

"Hell. Be right there."

Tom jogged back around to the front of the building. Roy was by the Mustang, holding his ass.

"Tommy, you're hit."

"A graze. Did you see Bert?"

"Got here, he was gone. Paramedics on the way."

Two black and whites, sirens wailing, pulled into the parking lot. Tom let Roy deal with them. He holstered his gun and ran into the lobby. A crowd of gawkers had gathered, parting as the frantic, bleeding man rushed in. He weaved through them, looking for any sign of Bert. Had Kilpatrick been there as well? Had he grabbed Bert while Tom and Roy were being distracted by Jack? Tom felt sick. Bert was annoying, true, but he'd been his responsibility. If anything happened to him . . .

Tom found Bert next to the front desk, kneeling by a suitcase and going through the contents.

"I got my lures," Bert said.

Tom wiped more blood out his eye and imagined the satisfaction he'd get if he pulled out his Glock and emptied a magazine into Bert's lures. He restrained himself.

"Come on."

Bert grabbed his cases and they made their way through the crowd, back into the parking lot. The number of squad cars had tripled, and Roy had organized a quick search party for Jack, uniforms fanning out through the rows of cars.

Tom felt the top of his head, which was now starting to throb. An inch lower and they would have been scooping up his last thoughts with evidence spoons.

He approached his Mustang, frown deepening. It would need two new tires, a new window, and a new headrest. Perhaps they could stick the rearview back on.

"What happened to your head?"

"I got shot, Einstein."

"I don't like it when you and your partner call me *Einstein*. It comes out sarcastic. Where's the guy with the gun?"

"He got away. Who knew you were staying here, at this hotel?"

"No one. Just Jessup."

"How did they know you'd come back for your lures?"

"I dunno. Lucky guess?"

"Did you tell anyone?"

"How could I tell anyone? I've been with you the entire time. We went from the hotel to the hospital, and from the hospital back here."

Tom thought it over. It wouldn't take long to set up a sniper in a vacant room, but how could Jack have known they were coming back for the lures? Was he just waiting around, hoping for the off chance? Unless Bert told someone, or . . .

Tom patted his pocket. The Foxhound bug detector hadn't been lost in the chase. He flipped it on and pointed the antenna at his car. It blinked and buzzed like a slot machine. Tom popped the hood and waved the antenna around, trying to get a fix. He found the bug taped to the side of the battery. The microphone snaked through the heat duct and led to the dashboard, and a line ran through his own car antenna. No wonder his radio didn't work.

He slammed the hood closed. They'd violated his car. His personal space. And by using his own car battery and antenna, the thing probably had a range of miles.

Tom went over to Roy, who was being led into an ambulance by some paramedics. One of them, a large white guy with a beard, began to undo Roy's belt.

"What the hell are you doin'?"

"I have to take off your pants."

"Damn. Aren't there any cute girl paramedics on duty?"

"No."

"Don't need to be so anxious. You're too anxious."

The medic looked at Tom. "Sir, you'd better come as well. We should take a look at that head."

Tom sat down next to his partner as a second medic attended to his head wound. He kept his voice low, no longer sure if everything he said or did was being monitored, and said to Roy, "The Mustang was bugged."

"When did they have time to do that? Case started only two days ago."

"That's the thing. It was hooked up to my car antenna. That's why my radio doesn't work."

"So?"

"So, my radio hasn't worked for about three months."

Roy blinked. "Dammit, Tommy. What the hell have you gotten into?"

Chapter 9

Chicago

"Help a brother blow up his donut?"

Roy held out the inflatable seat cushion, shaped like a small inner tube. The hospital said he'd need to sit on that to avoid ripping his stitches.

"No problem. Thanks for letting us stay here. I didn't want to go back to my place."

Tom figured his apartment was bugged, and probably being watched as well. Roy's place was clean; they'd swept it with the Foxhound earlier.

"Mi casa is your casa. Just don't let him touch anything." Roy stared at Bert and pointed. "Don't touch a damn thing. One thing out of place, and I break your face."

Bert folded his arms. "Why are you mad at me? I wasn't the one who told you to jump out the window, ass first."

"Both you and your damn fishing plugs are going out my window in about ten seconds."

"Maybe I should stay in a hotel."

"Bert, please. It would be safer if we stuck together."

"I know when I'm not wanted."

"You're wanted. Roy, tell him."

"Don't want him using my john, neither."

Tom walked his partner into the bedroom. Roy flopped onto the bed, face first. Tom debated helping him take off his pants, but decided to let them be. Leave the guy some dignity.

"Roy, I'm putting your pills here next to the bed."

"Thanks, Tom."

"You need anything, I'll be in the other room."

"Towels."

"You need towels?"

"I don't want him using my towels, neither."

Tom turned off the light and quietly closed the door. Bert was in the kitchen, rummaging through the fridge.

"At least he has good taste in beer. Russian Imperial Stout. Need one?"

"Yeah."

Bert grabbed two and sat next to Tom at the breakfast bar. There was a carved wooden bottle opener in the shape of a naked African goddess on the table. Bert opened both beers and handed one to Tom. The cop sipped it—sweet and malty, with a higher alcohol content than its English counterpart.

Bert took a swig from the bottle and looked around the apartment. There was a definite tribal theme here: voodoo masks on the walls, a tiger print rug, a black leather couch with a leopard throw on the back. The large rack of LPs, though practically antiques themselves, seemed too contemporary.

"Look, cut Roy a little slack. He's a good guy. He doesn't make friends too easily."

"That's surprising. He's such a warm and cuddly fellow. What's his story?"

"Roy grew up in Cabrini Green. One of the worst housing projects in Chicago, back then. Single mother, two younger brothers. Roy was the man of the family almost as soon as he could walk. But it was tough. He lost one brother to gangs, the other one to drugs. Took it real hard."

"I get it. He keeps people at a distance." Bert drank from his bottle. "I had an older brother, passed away when I was five. He wasn't adopted. I think my father wishes it was me instead of him that died. How about you? Brothers or sisters?"

"Just me."

"Lonely growing up?"

"Not really."

"That's because you never knew what you were missing. Never having something is different than having something and losing it."

Tom took another sip of stout and considered Bert's words. They made sense. He'd dated Donna for three years, and had even considered asking her to marry him. When she left, Tom felt like she took a part of him with her, a part that still was vacant and hollow. He wondered if he'd ever be able to fill that emptiness again.

Bert belched, interrupting his reverie. Tom lightly touched his scalp where the bullet had grazed him. Six stitches. The doctor had wanted to shave off the hair around the wound so it could be bandaged, but Tom wouldn't allow it. It was bad enough looking like Quasimodo—shaving half his head was out of the question.

He glanced at the clock on the microwave. Almost ten o'clock. After their trip to the hospital, it took three hours to debrief the Rosemont Police Department. RPD kept things cordial, considering they'd had their jurisdiction trampled on and hadn't been informed.

Tom's own boss, Lieutenant Daniels, hadn't been as charitable. She chewed them out, promising a full investigation of the incident, and demanding that next time they follow correct protocol for operating out of their territory.

Tom took another sip of beer, and found the bottle empty. He grabbed two more from the fridge. Bert took his, nodding a thanks.

"You know, when we were back there getting shot at, I had one of those moments where my whole life flashed before my eyes."

"So I gathered."

"I've had a boring life. Not a bad one—just very mediocre. But since Jessup told me that I'm Einstein, it's given me a new reason to live. I mean, I'm actually somebody now. You know what I mean?"

"Not really."

"Don't you feel any different, knowing you're Thomas Jefferson?"

Tom picked at the label on his beer with a thumbnail.

"I don't know how to feel. Suppose I am Jefferson. What does that mean, exactly? I may have the same genes, but I'm not the same man. I didn't do all of those great things that he did. I'm still Tom Mankowski, no matter what my face looks like. Aren't I?"

"I've been struggling with this one, too. Here I've got Einstein's brain." Bert tapped his temple. "The brain of the most brilliant man to ever walk the earth. And what am I doing? I buy and sell fishing lures."

Tom opened their beers and took a long pull. "You're just a salesman, I'm just a cop. Not quite living up to our genetic potential, are we?"

"Is there such a thing? Does anyone truly live up to their potential? Here's a good question for you—is greatness in a person born or made?"

Tom didn't have an answer.

"I think it's a combination." Bert scratched at the bandage on his chin. "Some people are born with a fire inside them. The will to succeed. It isn't a learned behavior. It's just some unknown biological factor that makes them try harder."

Tom stared into Bert's eyes. Einstein's eyes.

"Do you think you have that fire in you?"

Bert took a moment before answering. "Sometimes . . . sometimes I really think I do."

They finished their second beers. Bert went for the thirds, throwing out the empty six-pack container.

"Your friend's going to be upset we drank all his beer."

"He'll be fine. He was drugged up and in pain, that's all."

"He hates me."

"He doesn't hate you."

"He won't let me use the toilet."

"You can use the toilet, Bert. It'll be fine."

Bert opened the beers and set one before Tom.

"So what's the story with the lures?" Tom gestured at the suitcases. "Let me guess—your dad is a fisherman."

"Wrong. Physics professor. The lures are an investment. Look at it this way—things like stock, or gold, or real estate—they fluctuate with the market, but they more or less go up steadily. But with collectibles like dolls or toys or fishing lures, the potential for profit . . ."

"Hold on a sec," Tom interrupted.

This couldn't be a coincidence. Bert's dad was a physics teacher. Tom's dad was a politician. Jessup's dad was an inventor.

"That Tennessee cop, the clone of Robert E. Lee. You think his father was in the military?

"So?" Bert didn't see the connection. "My dad was in the army. Jessup mentioned his was too. Was yours?"

Tom's father had done a tour in Vietnam. He wondered if Bert had stumbled onto something. Was that how all of the clones' parents were chosen? Dad had the same profession as the clone, and had a link to the military?

Tom stood up, thoughts racing. He needed to get online. Roy was the last of the technophobes—he didn't even own a calculator, let alone a computer. Tom went to the kitchen and checked drawers until he found a phone book.

"Are you okay? What are you doing?"

Ignoring Bert, Tom looked up the name of a popular all-night copying center and located the one nearest to Roy. As he'd hoped, there was one only a few blocks away.

"I have to go out."

"Where?"

"I have to track down a lead. Stay here, get some rest."

"What if Roy gets up? If you're gone, he's gonna throw me out the window."

"It's only the third floor. Try to go limp right before you hit the ground."

Tom grabbed his jacket, gun, and Roy's keys, and was out the door.

The night had gotten cooler, freezing weather right around the corner. Tom stuck his hands in his pockets and hunched his shoulders, an act that caused pain flares in each of his injuries. He walked down an alley that let him out on Addison and hung a left, heading east.

Roy's neighborhood was a nice one. It was easy to spot Chicago's good sections—no graffiti and the sidewalks weren't broken. Even at this hour and temperature there were people out. Some high school kids, clowning around with a tennis ball against a brick wall. Four young women in short skirts on their way to one of the many clubs along the strip. Two guys, walking the opposite way, openly admiring the girls. An older couple, huddling close because of love or warmth or both.

Tom moved at a good clip, going left on Clark, easily spotting the copy shop between a submarine sandwich place and a liquor store.

It was busy, as expected; someone somewhere was always having a school or business emergency. Tom looked along the far wall and saw the computers available to rent by the hour. All were in use. He approached the counter and took out his badge.

"I need to use a computer."

The kid didn't even bother looking up at him. He was a twenty-something slacker type with a pink streak in his black hair and a Sex Pistols pin on his blue uniform shirt.

"Sorry. All booked up for the night."

Tom squinted at his name tag. Carl.

"This is a police emergency, Carl."

Carl glanced up, giving Tom the once over.

"You're a cop?"

Tom offered his badge as proof.

"Man, someone sure kicked your ass."

"You should see the other guy. They have to feed him through a tube."

"I bet. Hold on, lemme see what's going on."

He walked out from behind the counter and approached the computers. After a brief chat with a girl sitting in the third booth, he motioned Tom over. The girl who was booted gave Tom a dirty look as she left. He took her seat.

"My sister. She was here for free anyway. Knock yourself out."

Tom got on the net and went to the CPD database, accessing Arthur Kilpatrick's rap sheet. His parents were dead. Fire Marshall's report suspected arson. A few clicks revealed that Kilpatrick's father had also been in the army. The same went for that cop in Tennessee.

It was doubtful the Army would let him into its private database, but he wasn't going that route. All groups, no matter the size, were made up of people. And people had the tendency to stay in touch.

Within a few keystrokes Tom found a dozen websites whose sole purpose was to help a person find their old Army buddies. He hunkered down over the keyboard and cracked his knuckles, preparing himself for the task ahead. This might all be a waste of time, but it seemed like the way to go. So far, all roads lead back to the Army. It stood to reason that Harold Harper, the doctor from Rush-Presbyterian Hospital who was responsible for faking Tom's birth certificate, might have also been in the Army. He began to search.

The surname Harper was common. Tom found several Harolds on different sites, eliminating anyone who was too young to have been a doctor thirty years ago. Of those who did match, he clicked on their bios to get a background, looking for either medical training or a previous address in Chicago or New Mexico. After an hour of monotonous effort he hit pay dirt. An Army surgeon, the right age, with a current address in Albuquerque.

Tom checked his watch. New Mexico was an hour behind, right? It was late, but a doctor would be used to being awoken in the middle of the night. He took out his cell phone and dialed the number.

After five rings there was an answer.

"Yes?" The voice was male, deep and groggy.

"Dr. Harold Harper?"

"Yes?"

"The same Harold Harper who worked at Rush-Presbyterian in Chicago?"

"Who is this?"

"My name is Detective Tom Mankowski, Chicago Police Department. I'm calling—"

"Wait a moment. Did you say Mankowski?"

Tom paused. This was the doctor who had forged the birth certificates. Who's to say he wasn't in on this entire murder plot?

"Detective Mankowski? Are you still there? I believe I know why you called. When did you find out?"

The doctor sounded eager, genuine. Good guy or

bad guy? Ultimately it didn't matter. There had been two attempts on Tom's life in two days. It wasn't as if talking to someone could make it any worse.

"I found out today."

"How did you trace me . . . the birth certificates?"

"Yes."

"Wonderful. This is wonderful. I haven't seen you since your graduation from the Academy."

That came out of left field. "You were there?"

"Of course. Since the funding dried up, I've tried to keep tabs on the Lucky Seven—not always successfully, I'm afraid. You were always my favorite. You're a detective now? Wonderful. So, when are you going to fulfill everyone's expectations and go into politics?"

"Dr. Harper . . ."

"Harold. Call me Harold."

"You're getting ahead of me here."

"Yes. You must have many questions. Do you know about the others?"

"I've met Bert. He's the one who told me."

"Albert? Splendid. Is he still a stock market wizard?"

"He buys and sells fishing lures."

"Hmm. There's one for the social scientists to ponder."

"Harold, you just mentioned the Lucky Seven. I thought there were ten."

There was a long pause.

"You know about—*them*?"

"By them do you mean Jack the Ripper and Arthur Kilpatrick?"

"Oh dear. They're still in jail, I hope?

"I wish. Both of them tried to kill me last night."

Dr. Harold clicked his tongue several times. "They know as well? Oh dear. This isn't good. I warned him about this."

"Is that really Jack the Ripper?"

"Unfortunately, yes."

"And that other guy? Kilpatrick?"

"Attila the Hun."

Tom let out a breath. He felt a little better. It was a real ego blow to get beaten up by a short guy. But since the short guy was once the barbarian who conquered the world, it was a little easier to take.

"Harold, there's a lot to discuss here. Let's start at the beginning."

"Over the phone? Why don't you come out to the ranch? We could talk all you like. It would be lovely to finally talk to one of you, after all of these years."

Tom thought it over. Could be a trap, of course. And so much had happened in the last few days that leaving town now wasn't the wisest idea. But interrogating someone in person was infinitely preferable to over the phone. With cell phone rates what they were, it might actually be cheaper to fly down there.

"We might be able to get there tomorrow, if we can find a flight."

"Excellent. I can meet you at the airport in Albuquerque. Just tell me the time."

"I'll call you."

"I've thought about this many times. One of you finally figuring it out. Once or twice I almost called you up and told you, but you would have thought I was crazy. Listen to me, an old man rambling on. I'll wait for your call tomorrow."

Tom couldn't resist. "It's true, isn't it? I'm really a clone of Thomas Jefferson?"

"Yes, my boy, you are. I should know. I'm the one who did it."

"See you soon, Doctor."

Tom ended the call. Several people around him were staring. Their expression left no doubt they'd heard the conversation. Carl was among the bemused.

"How much do I owe you?"

"No charge—President Jefferson."

His expression was so smarmy that Tom wanted to yank the pink streak out of his head. Instead of resorting to violence, he glanced at the pay rate for computer time and fished out his wallet. He plunked down a five.

"Is there anything else you need to purchase? Stationary? Pens?" He smirked. "Louisiana?"

Tom left the shop, not sticking around to hear Carl's laughter.

Questions were about to be answered. And no one had a bigger stake in it than Tom did.

CHAPTER 10

Los Angeles

"You poor dear. This is horrible. Simply horrible."

Marty hugged Joan for what seemed like the hundredth time. He was more devastated than she was, bless his heart. Short, bald, immaculately dressed Marty, smelling of expensive aftershave even though he had a chic three-day beard. He was a genuine friend.

"I didn't mean to interrupt your date."

"Hush. You should have called after it happened the first time. Justin wouldn't have minded at all. Right, Justin?"

Justin came over for a group hug. "Of course not. I'm happy to be here for the two of you. Twice in one night. How horrible."

Joan felt smothered from all the embracing going on. She gently freed herself from the care-fest.

"I can get a room someplace, if I'm intruding."

"Nonsense." Marty and Justin said it at the same time.

"I have to be going, anyway." Justin gave Joan a

peck on the cheek and another hug. "I wish we could have met under better circumstances. Marty talks about you so much, I'm jealous."

Joan offered a gracious smile and a thank you. Justin gave Marty a more personal good-bye, and promised to call tomorrow to see how everything was going. He left with a big wave.

"How long have you been keeping him a secret?" Joan gave Marty a playful punch in the shoulder.

"Two weeks. I've been dying to tell you, but I wanted the test results first." Marty wouldn't get serious with anyone who didn't have a current bill of good health, signed and dated. "Isn't he gorgeous? He's into interior design, and he's my size. I just doubled my wardrobe."

"Congrats."

"But this isn't about me. Can I get you some coffee? Something stronger?"

"I'm tired. I'd like to get some sleep. Busy day tomorrow. Got those contracts to sign."

"Dear, I know you're joking. You can't go back to work after a shock like this."

"Well I can't stay at your place forever, peeking through the blinds."

"So brave." Marty brushed the bangs off of her forehead. "Would you like me to call the hospital again, see how Max is doing?"

"I'm sure his condition hasn't changed since twenty minutes ago. You can't get more stable than stable."

"It's so heroic that he came back to your place."

Joan kept her thoughts to herself on that one. She felt bad for Max, but any affection she may have had for him disappeared when he deemed Carmichael's more important than she was.

"I'll get your room ready. Extra towels are in the bathroom closet if you want a shower."

"I think I'd like that drink, actually."

"Vodka okay? It's imported. Super-premium, supposedly filtered five times."

"Sounds great, Marty. Thanks."

"Be back in two shakes."

Joan found her way to the couch and plopped down, displacing an unhappy Siamese cat. It arched its back and hissed before stalking off.

"Right back atcha."

She noted the time on the entertainment stand—Marty was so meticulous he actually set his DVD clock. Coming up on one in the morning. It felt so much later. Joan kicked off her running shoes, the same pair she'd worn to the police station on the first trip. Curling her legs up under her, she found herself staring at the bottom of her left heel.

Number 3. Her parents had never given her a straight answer about the tattoo. When she was younger, they told her things like *You're the third angel that came out of heaven* or *I love you has three words, and we wanted you to always remember that.*

Joan knew she was adopted from the moment she could talk. Her parents began their family late in life; her father had been career Army and was always flitting from one part of the world to another. When he finally settled down, he and his wife were already in their late forties.

Losing them had been unbearable. Mom from heart disease, and Dad from a broken heart, missing Mom so much. Joan so much wanted to call them right now, have them tell her it would all be okay.

But would it be okay? The psycho who attacked her knew about the tattoo. It seemed somehow tied in with the reason he wanted to kill her. *Someone wants me dead,* Joan thought. She shivered. There was something going on here that was beyond her understanding, and she didn't know who to turn to for help. The police didn't even file a report for the second attack— Joan watched as the detective in charge tagged it onto the end of the first one. Rather than offer to escort her home, they suggested she spend the night elsewhere. So much for protecting and serving.

"What would you prefer, hon, cranberry or OJ?"

Marty approached with a cocktail tray, complete with a small silver ice bucket and tongs. He was so cute, Marty.

"Just ice. Thanks."

Marty plunked some cubes into a rocks glass and poured her a healthy shot of vodka. Joan gulped it down like water. The burn made her stomach clench, but she held it down.

"Hit you again, Miss?"

"Please."

After he filled her glass, she patted the cushion next to her and Marty sat down.

"Is that the tattoo you were talking about? What is it, the golden arches?"

"It's a 3."

"How mysterious. What does it mean?"

Joan took a small sip of vodka. "I have no idea. I've had it since I was a baby."

"You know, I worked with a man who had a tattoo just like that. Not a three, though. I think he was number four."

"You're kidding."

"No. Same size, same blue color. We had a company party at the beach and I noticed and asked him about it. He didn't know where it came from either."

"Who was he?"

"He wrote ad copy at that agency in Santa Monica that you lured me away from. Gosh, this was years ago. What was his name? Began with a B. Bob, Brian, Buster, Bill . . . Bill. Bill Masterton. God, I'm so happy I'm out of the advertising biz. It's so cutthroat."

She rolled her eyes. "And the movie business isn't cutthroat?"

"Of course it is, but at least we pretend to be nice to one another."

Joan took another sip of vodka. "Do you think he still works there?"

"Why? Do he think he might be your long lost brother or something? How's that for a movie of the week—four children, separated at birth, each with a number to identify them, and an intrepid mother's search to track them down. I bet *Lifetime* would lap it up."

"What was the agency?"

"Hmm? Oh, *Chalmers/Sloan*. Kind of an eclectic client list. They do a lot of print stuff, not too much TV work."

Joan finished the drink and mulled it over. Another person with a number tattoo. It could mean nothing, or it could mean a lot. She'd have to check the guy out.

A yawn escaped her mouth, and the alcohol was taking the edge off her paranoia.

"Dear, you're exhausted. Let's get you to bed."

Silently, Joan followed him down the hall and to the

guest bedroom. Marty had turned down the blankets and left a large white T-shirt on the pillow.

"There's a new toothbrush on the sink. I'm one room over if you need anything."

"Thanks, Marty." She gave him one more hug. "Good night."

"Sweet dreams, hon."

She closed the door and undressed. The T-shirt had a Harley Davidson logo on it and smelled like fabric softener. She put it on and slipped into the cool, inviting bed, too tired to take her make-up off.

Sleep came fast and hard.

Joan jolted herself awake sometime the next morning.

She'd had a nightmare, a reoccurring one that went back to her childhood. In it, she was being chased by someone or something. She could never see its face. The closer it got, the harder it became to run—her legs got heavy, and her feet stuck to the ground, and it seemed like she was moving in slow motion. Joan would try harder and harder to get away, but no matter how much she strained the thing would always get her. That was when she'd wake up, often gasping for air.

This time it was worse than usual. When the thing caught her, it began to drag her to a large, pointed stake buried in the ground.

"Ass or crotch?"

She bolted upright in bed, her heart banging away, and tried to remember where she was. The sun was peeking through the blinds, and a clock radio she'd never seen before told her it was a little past eight.

Marty's place. Joan relaxed, leaning back and wiping the crust out of her eyes. She got out of bed and padded over to the bathroom. The mirror confirmed her fears. She looked like hell. Her eyes were red and baggy, her face was drawn, her hair resembled a dead plant.

Joan showered, brushed her teeth twice, found and used some Visine, and went back to the bedroom to change. Marty had already made the bed and laid her clothes out for her. There was also a big, foamy cup of cappuccino on the nightstand.

She didn't want to put on the same outfit again—it reminded her of yesterday. But she didn't have a choice. When finished, she checked her reflection in a framed Nagel print. Still haggard, but once she put her make-up on she might be able to fake being attractive. Joan took her coffee and met Marty in the kitchen.

"Good morning, sunshine. You look great."

"You're an excellent liar, Marty. Thank you."

"Were you up for breakfast? Croissant? Biscotti? Energy Drink?"

"The cappuccino is enough."

"If you want to change, I can drop by your place and pick something up."

"If you could take me there, that would be great."

"Are you sure you want to go back so soon?"

"Got to go sometime. If we hurry, we can just make rush hour traffic."

"You're the boss."

Marty owned a Corvette, which was a total waste because he drove like an old lady; always under the speed limit, slowing down for stale green lights in case they turned yellow, taking forever to merge. It normally made Joan nuts, but almost being murdered gave a person more patience for the little things.

"Here we are." Marty pulled into her driveway and parked. "You ready?"

Joan answered by getting out of the car and heading towards the front door. There were dark brown stains in the doorway. Blood. Max's blood. She pushed past it. Marty followed her in, eyes darting this way and that, obviously uncomfortable.

"I'll need the cleaning service to come by, take care of this blood. I'd also like the bathroom cleaned and the Jacuzzi drained. The phone needs to be fixed—I think the line was cut. And get some quotes on alarm systems. While you're at it, call up Stevensen Burglary and tell them their product stinks and I demand a refund. Also tell them to kiss my ass."

Marty grinned. "There's the tiger I know and love." He took out a pocket tape recorder and repeated her instructions.

Joan went into the bedroom and shed her outfit. She tossed it in the garbage. A shame, but she would never wear it again, with the memories attached. She stared momentarily at her wardrobe and went with her favorite power suit—a Claiborne red blazer with wide shoulders and a matching skirt. A white silk blouse and some red pumps rounded out the ensemble. After checking herself in the bedroom mirror, she switched from heels to flats. The pumps looked better, but you can't move fast in heels.

Marty had drawn the blinds over the patio doors, his tan complexion somewhat pale. He must have seen her dog. Poor Schnapps. She'd been so consumed with her own safety, she hadn't had time to mourn the death of her furry pal. She felt the tears well up, but refused to let them fall.

"Call . . . call someone to have those stakes removed."

"Should I arrange for . . . services?"

"Have him cremated. Pick out a nice urn. I didn't have him long, but he was a good dog."

The tears fell anyway. Joan went to the bathroom and forced composure. It took a few minutes, but she managed to get her breathing under control. Then she did the two minute makeover; a little foundation, a touch of eyeliner and mascara, and some quick, subtle lipstick. Feeling much more like herself, she grabbed her extra set of keys and led Marty out of the house.

"I also want a new front door lock. Something pick proof, if such a thing exists. Tell the locksmith I'm putting the keys in the mailbox." She did just that. "Do you mind if I drive, Marty?"

"Go ahead. I'd like to make some calls, get started on this anyway."

She put the Vette through the paces, cornering fast, pushing 90 mph on straight-aways, weaving through traffic with a liberating sense of abandon.

When they arrived at work, Joan felt good. She loved her office. *Joan DeVilliers Productions* began its life sharing space with an insurance agent in East Compton. Now, eight years and many movies later, she had a plush sixth floor spread on the Strip with a view and all the chrome and mirrors money could buy.

Marsha, her secretary, greeted her with a stack of messages and the FedEx from Paramount. Joan spent the next hour poring over the contract, making little additions and deletions to various clauses, the horrors of the previous day lost in a stream of legalese.

That done, she had Marsha free up her schedule for

the afternoon and got to work on reviewing some script changes for the Cruise film. Rather than her usual lunch at *Brisbeee's*, Joan ordered pizza and surprised herself by eating four slices. She was on her fifth when the intercom buzzed.

"Joan? The LAPD in on line two. Says it's urgent."

"Thanks, Marsha."

Urgent. Had they caught the creep?

"This is Joan DeVilliers."

"You broke my nose, bitch. You think it's over? I'm going to shove a stake so far up your—"

Joan slammed down the receiver. When her hands stopped shaking, she called the police.

CHAPTER 11

Albuquerque

"These aren't eggs." Bert poked at the airline food with his undersized plastic fork. "I think they're some kind of polymer. I shouldn't have paid extra for the meal."

Tom didn't care. He devoured them anyway, along with the stale bun, the dry sausage, and two cups of bland coffee. He also polished off Roy's meal while his partner snored, zonked out from the painkillers.

"So we're meeting with the doctor who created us?"

Tom frowned at the terminology. He didn't like the idea of being created. But then, he wasn't exactly born either. Or was he? The answers were less than an hour away.

"He's picking us up at the airport."

"I don't see why *he* had to come." Bert pointed his chin at Roy. He hadn't shaved, and it was tough to spot his stitches.

"He's my partner. We watch each other's backs. You

didn't have to come either. You could have stayed in Chicago."

"I have a right. I have questions, too."

"You didn't have to bring your lures."

"They go where I go." Bert reached up and switched off the blowing nozzle. "Recirculated air. I call these things *germ cannons*. You might as well be French kissing everyone on the plane."

Tom wiped the pat of butter off the little white square of cardboard and onto his third bun. Bert stored his tray in the upright position and fished a magazine out of the pouch on the seat ahead of him.

"Oh boy. An issue of *Macramé Monthly* that I haven't read yet."

The flight attendant collected their plates, but not before Tom forked the last sausage into his mouth. The cut inside his cheek had healed some, but the salty meat still stung. If indeed it was meat—it tasted more like a member of the rubber family. He didn't feel the wound on his head at all, and since his hair covered the stitches it wasn't even noticeable. The thing that hurt like hell was his ribcage; sleeping on Roy's soft leather couch had been a mistake. Every breath was like a fork in the chest.

Tom glanced to his left, over the lightly snoring Roy, out the window. Clouds obscured his view. To his right, Bert was absorbed in the magazine. It was strange to look at him, a face so recognizable that it was practically an archetype.

"So, Bert—since you found out about the Einstein thing, has there been any indication that you really are him?"

Bert set the magazine down.

"You mean have I ever had any brilliant thoughts or ideas?"

"Yeah."

"Nope. Not one."

"Have you ever taken an IQ test?"

"Like those Mensa puzzles? Figure out which number comes next in the series?"

"Yeah. Those."

"No. Never could get through them. I got slightly above average on my SAT, though. After my third try."

Tom noticed several strands of gray in Bert's wavy hair. In ten or twenty years it would become the great white mop known the world over.

"How about you, Tom? Do you feel any different? Since finding out?"

Tom was about to answer no, but he realized that wasn't the case. Though he still felt like himself, he was experiencing something akin to performance anxiety. He'd been struggling with it since last night, after Harold had asked when he was going to go into politics.

There was a whole big world out there. Shouldn't he be doing something more than just police work? Tom had always thought he was a good cop, good at his job, but now it didn't seem like it was enough.

"I don't feel like a different person, but I think I do feel a little inadequate."

"That will pass. Soon you'll feel completely worthless."

Bert went back to his magazine. Tom opened the little nozzle over his head, bathing his face with the germ cannon's cool, stale air. He smoothed out the wrinkles in the tan pants Roy had lent him. They were a little big in the waist, but otherwise fit fine. The loaned shirt was another story. Tom was swimming in it, and since putting it on he felt the urge to hit the gym and work on his pecs.

Bert hummed as he read. Something vaguely familiar. When Tom realized it was Britney Spears he shook his head. As far as nature vs. nurture went, Bert was a damn fine argument for nurture.

"What's 55 x 26?" Tom asked.

"Hell if I know."

"I thought you were a stock market wizard."

Bert looked up at him.

"How did . . . that doctor told you, didn't he? You said he kept tabs on us." Bert shrugged. "I did some trading. Made some fortunes. Lost some fortunes. That's behind me now."

"But you were good at it? Without dealing with numbers?"

"I didn't deal in numbers. I dealt in shares and dollars."

"Same thing."

"Not for me."

"Okay—if I had 85,552 dollars and wanted to buy some shares of stock that sold at 2 ¼, how many shares could I buy?"

Bert didn't hesitate. "You could buy 38,023 shares and have 11 cents left over." When the realization of what he just said hit him, he broke into a wide grin. "Hey! Do another one."

Surprised, Tom continued. "A guy wants to buy 351 shares of a stock that's at 6 ⅞s."

"He needs 2413 dollars and 12 and a half cents." Bert beamed. "Wow! I'm pretty amazing!"

"What's 18 x 45?"

Bert's smile faltered. "I don't know."

"That doesn't make sense, Bert."

"I know it doesn't make sense. But I just don't know."

"Okay, what if I wanted to buy 45 shares of stock at 18 dollars a share?"

"Eight hundred and ten dollars. This is weird, Tom. How come I can do it if it's a stock question but not when it's just simple multiplication?"

Tom recalled an old story he'd heard about Albert Einstein.

"Do you care about multiplication?"

"Hell no."

"Did you care about the stock market?"

"I lived and breathed to trade."

"There's your answer. Maybe you're a genius at what you care about. Einstein failed math in school. He just had no interest in it."

"You think that's it?"

"Could be."

Bert scrunched up his face. Tom could see he was puzzling it out.

"So now all I need to do is force myself to care about quantum mechanics."

"That's possible."

"But I don't care about quantum mechanics. It bores

the crap out of me. Do you care about life, liberty, and the pursuit of happiness?"

"As much as the next guy. I don't dwell on it."

"How are your writing skills? Essays and reports and things?"

"Well, I won that Pulitzer a few years back."

"So, in other words, I probably have Einstein's intellect locked up in my head somewhere. But you got buttkiss from Jefferson."

Bert delved into the magazine again, leaving Tom to dwell on that. The feeling was akin to being ten feet tall, but still unable to dunk a basketball.

As the plane emptied, Tom was reluctant to leave his seat. His self-esteem was at an all time low, and being told he was conceived in a lab under a microscope couldn't possibly help.

"Are you guys coming?" Bert already had his carryon in hand and his sunglasses perched on the end of his long nose.

"We here?" Roy yawned and stretched. "Did I miss breakfast?"

"I wouldn't phrase it like that."

Roy attempted to stand up, forcing his partner to move out of his way. Tom gripped the armrests and pried himself out of his chair.

"Don't forget your donut." Bert pointed to the inflatable ring on Roy's chair. The cop turned and picked it up, his face sour.

They were the last ones out of the plane; Tom and Roy had been required to fly with their guns locked up in the cockpit per FTA rules. The moment Tom stepped onto the runway he had to squint against the glare. He'd never been to New Mexico before, but it was exactly like he'd anticipated. Hot, dry, sunny, with mountains in the distance. The authentic West. The trio walked to the terminal, which was minuscule by Chicago standards. A sign welcomed them to the ABQ Sunport, and the air conditioning embraced them like a close family when they entered.

Tom asked for directions to the front entrance, receiving them in a pronounced drawl from a steward. He didn't have a cowboy hat to tip, but thanked the man just the same. The airport was quiet, serene, no large crowds or rushing people. It was unnatural. Perhaps there was some kind of sedative in the water.

"Hello!"

Dr. Harold Harper was stooped with age, tanned the color of mahogany, sporting faded jeans and a plaid shirt. He had a fringe of white hair encircling a bald dome speckled with liver spots. Tom knew his age to be seventy-two, but the doctor rushed to greet them like someone half that.

"Wonderful to see you! Let me look." He grasped Tom's shoulders and gave him the once-over. "My, it's simply amazing. You could have just stepped off a two dollar bill. And Albert—" Bert got similar treatment. "The mustache and everything. Did you have the mustache before, or grow it once you found out? And who's this?"

"This is Detective Roy Lewis. My partner."

"Hello, Roy, nice to meet you." He shook Roy's hand. "Actually, I suppose this is our first official meeting as well." He shook Bert's hand, then Tom's. "Harold Harper. Welcome to New Mexico. Do you have suitcases?"

"I do." Bert raised his hand.

"The luggage return is this way."

The elderly man took off at a quick clip, pointing out which airlines occupied which terminals, and where the restrooms and restaurants were, as if he were giving a tour of the Louvre. Bert's bags were the first off the carousel, but he insisted on opening them and inspecting the contents before they could move ahead.

"How could anything get damaged in those things?" Roy was referring to Bert's Samsonite suitcases. "Bet they're heavy as hell."

"These are classics. I don't even know if they make them anymore with a hard shell like this. They're waterproof, shockproof, and smashproof. Remember the commercial with the gorilla jumping on them?"

Outdoors again, the heat was like a hair dryer. Harold had parked close to the building, in a handicapped spot. He had a wheelchair sticker hanging from his rearview, but Tom couldn't guess what his ailment might be. The man had more energy that a two-year-old on crack.

The good doctor drove an old Jeep Wrangler with no roof or doors, just a roll bar to protect them from the elements. It was what could charitably be called a four-seater, though the rear two seemed built for embryos. Tom attempted to climb in back but Harold stopped him.

"Please. Do me the honor of sitting up front with me, if you would."

Roy shot him a look that would fry burgers, but Tom sat up front anyway. Bert played around with a bungee cord for several minutes, strapping in his luggage to the rear rack, while Roy placed his carryon between his feet and carefully positioned his donut. Harold took off before either had a chance to fully settle in. The doctor drove with the same sense of urgency he displayed while on foot. Traffic signals didn't appear to be applicable to him, and twice he had to swerve to avoid collisions. Tom liked him immediately.

"The ranch is about ten miles out of Albuquerque. Used to be twenty miles out, but the town is growing pretty fast. It'll reach three quarters of a million within the next few years, at the current rate."

Tom noted that as America aged, it tended to homogenize. Albuquerque could have been a suburb of Chicago—complete with strip malls, supermarkets, chain stores, and apartment buildings. The only difference was that every other vehicle was a 4 x 4. Tom checked the rearview, paranoid about being tailed. Rather than black sedans, he saw Bert sock Roy in the shoulder.

Bert grinned. "Slug bug green, no hit backs."

"Why did you just hit me, fool?"

"Volkswagon bug, right there. Don't you play the slug bug game? Every time you see a VW Beetle, you hit the guy next to you and say the color."

"You do that again, we play the physics game. I toss you out of the speeding Jeep and see how many times you bounce."

Bert folded his arms, glaring. "What is your problem? Why can't you have fun?"

"I have lots of fun."

"You act like you have a saggy diaper that leaks."

"Maybe you need to take your Shut-The-Hell-Up pill."

"I dare you to stop being a grump ass." Bert challenged.

"Fine—punch Bronco black."

Roy slugged Bert in the shoulder. Bert's eyes got wide. "What the hell was that?"

"I saw a black Ford Bronco, so I punched you."

"That's not the game. It's Volkswagon bugs."

"Now who's the one that isn't fun?"

Bert hit him back. "There. You didn't call no hit-backs."

"Fine." Roy scanned for a car, then he smacked Bert in the back of the head.

"Head whack Cadillac yellow, no hit-backs."

Bert elbowed Roy in the ribs. "Rib jab Buick Allegra red, no hit backs."

"Soon as I see a Toyota, I'm gonna break your jaw."

Harold leaned over and spoke to Tom out of the side of his mouth. "Are they always like this?"

"Neither of them plays well with others."

Luckily for all involved, Harold pulled onto a dirt road and they didn't see another vehicle until they reached the ranch. And a ranch it was. Tom, being Midwestern, assumed the term was used to describe any single floor house. But Dr. Harper owned actual acres of fenced-in property, complete with grazing livestock.

"What in the hell is that thing?" Roy pointed.

"That's Emma. She's an Israeli Black Ostrich."

Bert whacked him. "Israeli black ostrich, no hit-backs."

Roy hit him back anyway.

"You raise ostriches?" Tom regretted the stupid question as it left his mouth. They passed a dozen more birds before coming to a stop at the house.

"Largest of the ratites. Their meat is red, 80 percent leaner than beef. One egg is the same volume as two dozen chicken eggs. Shells and feathers fetch top dollar, and the leather is softer than lamb. Plus, they're a hoot to have around."

One of the birds walked up to the truck and stared at Roy, its head only a foot away from his face. Roy recoiled.

"No need to be afraid," Harold said. "She just wants her head scratched."

The bird's head bobbed up and down, seemingly in agreement.

"I don't like it. Make it go away."

Bert reached over and patted the ostrich.

"See? Very docile animal. You can even ride some of the larger ones. Perhaps you'd like to try it later."

The bird cocked its head and chirped. Then pecked Roy in the nose.

"Docile my ass."

Roy took out his gun. The ostrich screamed, then turned its tail and ran off.

"Oh, they hate guns." Harold got out of the Jeep. "We had some poachers here, years ago, killed four of the birds. Whenever they see a gun or hear a bang, they head for the barn."

There were two structures on the property, the house and the stable. Both had a rough hewn, rustic quality to their design, with unfinished log trim and cedar shingles. Bert unstrapped his luggage and Harold led them into the larger of the buildings.

Tom frowned when he wasn't met with air conditioning. Two fans spun lazily in the high, vaulted ceiling, pushing around the heat. In keeping with the log cabin concept, various pine support beams made criss-cross patterns throughout the great room. There was a large chandelier, made from several dozen antlers, hanging between the two fans, and a bearskin rug, complete with head, on the floor.

"Welcome to the Harper Ranch. Anyone for coffee? Nothing beats the heat like a hot beverage."

There were no takers.

"I'll just be a moment. Old man, need the caffeine." Harold left for the kitchen and Tom gave his partner a nod. Roy removed the Foxhound from his pocket and turned it on.

"What is . . . ?"

Tom slapped a hand over Bert's mouth and put a finger to his lips. Roy worked the room, waving the Foxhound's antenna this way and that. He was quick but thorough.

"Clean." He put the bug detector away just as Harold came back.

The doctor was holding an oversized mug of steaming coffee. He took a sip and set it on the table. Tom caught the aroma and had to admit it smelled pretty damn good.

"Fine, then let's sit down, shall we? Plenty to discuss, that's for sure."

Harold ushered them onto two sofas. Tom sat and stared at the ceiling-high stone fireplace. Why the house needed it was beyond his reasoning. Harold took the floor before them.

"The easiest way to do this, I think, is to start from the beginning. Forty years ago. I was one of only a handful of scientists trying to attempt in vitro fertilization—fertilizing an egg outside of the womb. My team worked with gametes from mice, then cows, and then finally with human sperm and ova."

Harold paused to sip some coffee.

"The work was funded in secret, done privately. We did it in Mexico. Not that we were breaking any US laws, per se, but pure science is always easier without regulation, and we had a doozy of a problem to solve. My first success took place right before we landed on the moon—this was almost ten years before Louise Brown, the first official test tube baby, was born."

"Who was funding you?"

"We'll get to that in a moment. But imagine, if you will, how excited we were that we'd created a person in a lab. And yet we couldn't publish, we couldn't go public. It was all very hush-hush. I found out why later. Our benefactor, it seems, was looking for more than reproductive technology. After proving that sexual reproduction was possible in vitro, he next wanted us to prove that asexual reproduction was possible in humans."

"Cloning?"

"Sort of. Asexual reproduction is having offspring with only one parent. This usually results in an exact genetic copy. Many things reproduce in this way— protozoan, fungi, seaweed, coral, insects, fish, lizards, even some birds under artificial conditions. The word *clone* comes from the Greek word for twig. Cut off a twig, plant it, grow a new tree. In theory, anyway."

The doctor was pacing before them, gesturing with his hands. He was talking at a terrific clip, the words coming out so fast they ran together. Tom thought of a champagne bottle, finally uncorked after decades in a cellar.

"It was hard work. How can you create life without a sperm and egg? We knew about chromosomes. Humans have forty-six, getting half from the mother and half from the father. But what if there was no father? Could we fool an egg into thinking it was a zygote, that it had been fertilized, using only the chromosomes of one parent?"

Harold shook his head sadly.

"Setbacks. Years of setbacks. We were trying to implant a karyoplast into the cytoplasm of a zygote. Nuclear transfer. Forcing a morula or blastocyst without two haploids."

"I don't know what the hell you just said." Roy got off the sofa. He gave Tom a look of intent, patting the Foxhound in the pocket. Off to check the rest of the place out. "Anyone want some water?"

"Kitchen is through there. How about you two? Am I going too fast?"

Tom ventured a guess. "You were scraping out fertilized eggs and adding your own genes?"

"Exactly. But it didn't work. We couldn't get the enucleated egg and the donor cell to fuse. We tried the Sendai virus, electrofusion—nothing worked. Then, as a control, I tried it with a nonfertilized ova. It fused into a zygote like magic."

"So all you did was put a human cell in an empty egg and it grew?" Bert seemed surprised.

"Well, my boy, you make twenty years of research sound simple. Actually, it was much more difficult than that. You had to actually put the donor cells in the gap-zero phase by starving them. You see, cells go through phases—"

"Doctor." Tom held up his hand. "You might as well be speaking Martian. We believe you when you say it was hard work."

"Darn tootin'. And we finally did it—grew an embryo in agar and transplanted it into the uterus of a woman, who successfully gave birth to a healthy baby. We did it many times, in fact. You can imagine how excited we were. But again, it had to be kept quiet, and again, it wasn't enough. Our next miracle was to bring dead cells back to life. Which, of course, is impossible."

"It can't be impossible." Bert leaned back and crossed his legs. "Because here we are."

"Oh, but it is impossible. Once tissue is dead, it's dead. Frankenstein's monster will forever remain in the realm of fiction. My team did enough work on that to settle the debate forever."

"So how . . . ?"

"Are you sure no one would like some coffee? You can't imagine how wonderful it is to tell this, after so long. I don't even have access to my notes. There won't be any memoirs, any posthumous Nobel Prize. He took everything."

"Who did?"

"We'll get to that in a moment. Anyhoo, once we proved that regenerating dead tissue was impossible, we did the next best thing. We copied it."

Tom raised an eyebrow. "You cloned it?"

"No, you can't clone dead tissue. The cell has to be alive, in the dormant G-zero phase, before we can take out the DNA. In a dead cell, the DNA won't replicate. It's a shell, a corpse. But since all DNA is simply building blocks made up of protein, all we had to do is reconstruct a dead person's genetic code. Rebuild it out of raw material, so to speak, in the exact same way as the original."

Roy came back with a glass of water. He shook his head at Tom and sat down carefully on his donut.

Tom puzzled over Harold's latest words but couldn't get them to ring true. Even with today's technology, it was impossible to build a strand of DNA from the ground up. There was just no way.

"Doctor, I'm afraid you've lost me."

Bert shrugged. "I got lost right after he mentioned the twigs."

Tom continued. "Maybe I can believe you doing all of these reproductive experiments years ahead of the scientific community, and I can even believe that you cloned a person from a live cell. But human DNA wasn't even completely mapped until a few years ago, and that took a decade, using the biggest super computers. I read the article in *Time*. Even then, it was only mapped—that's just the general picture. To get an exact replica, it needs to be sequenced, and that's still a long way off."

"You're right. We didn't have the technology back then to sequence the entire human genome. Let alone the genomes of the ten people that we cloned. There are over 50,000 genes in a human being, made up of billions of base pairs. We never could have sorted them all out and put them in the right order."

Tom leaned forward, arms on his knees. "So how did you do it?"

Harold's face lit up. "We took a picture. A very special picture. And from the picture we made a living cell."

"Please explain."

"In 1953, Watson and Crick used X-ray crystallography to discover the structure of a DNA molecule. They bounced radiation off of DNA and formed an image on photographic film, coming up with the double helix configuration. How much do you know about DNA?"

Tom thought back to high school biology, over twelve years ago.

"It's made up of four bases. They match up with each other in special orders. When the DNA replicates, it unzips, and then free floating proteins match up with the each side of the zipper and make a carbon copy."

"Excellent. The four nucleotide bases are adenine, thymine, cytosine, and guanine. When they stack up in specific combinations they make genes—sections of DNA that code for protein. Genes make up chromosomes, and chromosomes make up that double spiral staircase we call DNA."

"I remember this." Roy nodded. "The bases are A, T, C, and G. G always teams with C, and A always teams with T."

"Exactly! That was what made it work. We fooled the DNA into copying itself."

"You lost me again."

"Never even had me." Bert frowned. "I've been counting the antlers in that lamp."

"It was actually very simple." Harold sat on the coffee table and faced them. "We built a special camera. Its lens was an electron microscope—still not powerful enough for us to actually see every base nucleotide, but we didn't need to. Only the film did. Then we harvested some dead cells from each donor and took pictures of the nucleus—that's the center part of the cell where all the DNA is bundled up."

"So far, so good."

"Now, you all know how film works? It makes a negative, an opposite of the picture that is going to be developed. We used a film stock that was seeded with base nucleotides."

Tom smiled. "I think I get it."

"Hello!" Bert raised his hand. "Can you explain, for the benefit of the stupid people?"

"We took a picture of the DNA using film that had A, C, G, and T in it. Now, there are four forces in the universe; gravity, electromagnetic, strong, and weak. Many scientists believe they are all simply different applications of one universal force. Is the force that keeps the earth revolving around the sun the same force that holds atoms together? Or makes adenine always want to pair with guanine?"

"I'm going to go back to counting antlers."

"Stick with me, Bert. After taking a picture of the nuclear DNA with seeded film, we ran an electromagnetic current through the negative. It worked. When a free floating adenine saw the negative picture of a thymine, it tried to attach itself. It couldn't, of course, because that wasn't a real thymine molecule—it was only a picture. But it did line up correctly, along with all of the other molecules. We made half of the zipper. Then we scraped the negative, added more bases, and the other half of the zipper formed. The DNA rebuilt itself in the correct order."

Bert nodded. "I get it. It's like you took a picture of a skunk, and another skunk thought it was real and tried to mate."

This comparison temporarily stymied the doctor.

"Well, I guess, sort of. The base pairs lined up to the negative as if it were real. When we finished, we had a batch of fresh DNA. We inserted this into an enucleated liver cell, cultured them, put them in gap-zero, then removed the nucleus again and transferred it to an egg. From the egg it went to the mother, and nine months later, tada! Clones!"

"And the twig?"

"Get off the twig, Bert." Tom turned to Harold. "So I'm not an actual clone of Jefferson. I'm more like a copy?"

"Genetically, you're identical. You have an exact DNA match. But your body was never part of his, no. In fact, there are quite a few subtle differences. For example, the enucleated liver cells that we cultured your DNA in—they were mine. They were just empty shells, but still my genetic material. The same with the donor eggs from the mother—again they were scraped out, but the cell membrane was still from another human being."

"So I'm part Einstein, part you, and part Mexican woman?"

Harold shook his head. "No, Bert. You're all Einstein."

This brought a snort from Roy.

"But I wasn't grown from Einstein?"

"Exactly."

"Who else was cloned?"

"I did ten of you, all born within a few days of each other. The first was Abraham Lincoln. Then Robert E.

Lee, Joan of Arc, William Shakespeare, Thomas Jefferson, Albert Einstein, and Thomas Edison. Those are the Lucky Seven."

"Why these seven?"

"Phillip thought they represented the greatest figures in history. He believed they would have the greatest potential to benefit mankind. Or, more specifically, the US Government."

"Phillip?"

"We'll get to him shortly."

"Wasn't Joan of Arc burned at the stake?"

"The one place in the body that DNA never seems to dissipate, even after thousands of years, is in the teeth. From what I understand, Phillip had located her scorched jawbone, secreted away from the pyre by a zealot and locked up in some French monastery for years."

"You said there were ten."

"Ah yes. The others. Keep in mind, this was more than just a scientific breakthrough. It was a behavioral experiment as well. Just because we made a copy of Lincoln didn't mean he'd actually grow up to be Lincoln, with all of the traits we imbue Lincoln with. What makes a person who they are is much more complicated than their genetics. There are many factors—parents, environment, chance, socioeconomic conditions, illness, accidents—influences that we could only imagine. But we didn't know that, back then. And every good experiment needs some control subjects . . ."

"So you chose Jack the Ripper and Attila the Hun?"

"Jack was my fault. I'd always been a Ripperphile, and was convinced the killer was that fish porter,

Joseph Barnett. So we got a DNA sample and cloned him. I believe I was proven right. At age eleven he stabbed his adoptive parents to death."

Roy returned Tom's *told you so* look with a blank stare.

Harold went on. "Phillip chose the other two. Ancient leaders, known for their cruelty. Attila and Vlad."

"Vlad?"

"Vlad Tepes Dracula. Vlad the Impaler. Ruled Wallachia in the fifteenth century, tortured over a hundred thousand people to death. He'd spear them on long stakes—horrible man. His clone seemed to inherit the same sadistic streak. Set the family dog on fire when he was only six."

"Explain to us again why you'd clone the biggest psychos in world history and think it was a good idea?"

"The logic was sound at the time. If personality was inherited, then the Lucky Seven would grow up and be brilliant, and the Unholy Three would grow up as monsters. Of course, we only got it half right."

"The monster half." Tom frowned.

"Not to say that you didn't turn out fine," Harold quickly added. "We've watched you for years. That none of you rose to the greatness of your parental genotypes doesn't mean our experiment failed. But ultimately, our major success was with them. Perhaps the will to destroy is more easily transferable than the will to create. Monsters, all three of them."

"So this was just one big social experiment?" Bert sounded disappointed. "We weren't created to control the world or anything?"

"Phillip had planned to reveal you to the world, at

some point. But after watching you progress, there didn't seem to be any reason. Robert didn't become a great General. Neither Abe nor Tom have attempted to hold office. Bert, neither you nor the clone of Edison have made any grand discoveries or inventions. It was decided to never tell you. But yet, you figured it out."

"How could you have been at Rush-Presbyterian in Chicago if we were all born in Mexico?"

"I was a member of the staff, but have never actually been to the place. Phillip set it up, through his connections. It allowed us to fake all the birth certificates, make you US citizens. Phillip found suitable parents through his Army connections—the idea was to match the newborns up with fathers who were comparable to the clone."

"You keep bringing up this Phillip as the guy who set this whole thing up." Tom stared hard at the doctor. "Are you ready to tell us who he is?"

"He was, still is, one of the most powerful men in the world. Phillip Stang."

"Phillip Stang? *The* Phillip Stang?"

"Who's Phillip Stang?" Bert asked.

"A Democratic congressman from Illinois. His picture was all over the media last year, when he became Speaker of the House."

"I remember now!" Bert's face twisted in fear. "When I met with Jessup a few days ago, he thought he was being followed. He told me it started the month before, right after talking to some politician."

"It was Phillip Stang?"

"I didn't get the name. But what if it was Stang? He's one of the richest, most powerful men in the world. What if he's the one that wants us dead?"

Tom winced. This wasn't a pleasant development.

"I think this is a case of overreacting." Harold had finished his coffee but brought the empty cup to his lips just the same. "I've known Phillip Stang for years. Besides, you've got the wrong one. The Phillip that started the project with me is retired. His son, same name, is Speaker. Fine lad, too. Now there's someone with political aspirations."

It wasn't an intentional barb, but it stung just the same. Tom rose above it.

"We'll need some addresses. Anything you have on any of the clones. They have to be warned."

"Of course. But you have to be careful. You both seem to have adjusted well to the truth about your births, but it could be potentially traumatic to the psyche to suddenly find out you're someone else."

No kidding, Tom thought.

"We'd also like to talk with the elder Phillip Stang. Can you set that up?"

"Yes. Haven't spoken to him in a while. Last I heard, his health was failing again. Chronic kidney problems. He's got a home in Illinois, by Springfield."

"How about the others?"

"Not a problem. I know Abe is in Nebraska. He sells used cars, I believe. Joan went to Hollywood and is a hot shot producer. I saw one of her movies a few years ago, something loud with aliens in it. William is a writer. This thrilled us at first. He got great grades in college. Unfortunately, he wound up in advertising. I have their last names written down someplace, a few addresses."

"How about the other three?"

"Oh dear. No idea. They managed to disappear. Jack

was involved in the CIA for a while. His specialty was wet work, I believe they called it. He killed people for Uncle Sam. Vlad—we named him Victor—he escaped from police custody after murdering some young women in a particularly horrible way. Fled to South America. I've heard rumors that he worked as a freelance interrogator for various governments. And Arthur, Attila— in and out of prisons his whole life. Probably killed his parents. No idea where he might be."

"Do you know how they found out about everything?"

"The only thing I can think of is they must have been told. All three are above average intelligence, but I wouldn't say they had the savvy to dig up their pasts. Of course, that doesn't leave many people left. Even though I had a research team, none of my assistants knew exactly what we were doing. You were watched by various government employees while growing up, but they were never given details why. The only two people who knew everything about the experiments are myself and Phil, and even I didn't know everything."

"Did you tell them?"

"Tell them? My boy, if I saw any of them I'd run away as fast as my little old legs could carry me. I'm going for more coffee. Anyone care to join me?"

They declined. Harold plodded off into the kitchen.

"It's got to be Stang." Bert nodded smartly. "There's no one else left."

"All the high-tech listening devices point to a government operation." Tom agreed. "But what would the motive be? Why would he devote his entire life to this project, and then want to wipe it out?"

"Could Jack and Attila be working on their own?"

"I hope so. Because if Phillip Stang is involved, I won't be needing my donut anymore."

"Why?"

Roy frowned. "Because if we're being hunted by that cat, we can all kiss our asses good-bye."

CHAPTER 12

Albuquerque

"It tastes like beef."

Roy wiped some ketchup off of his mustache and took another bite of the ostrich burger.

"Softer." Bert smacked his lips. "Richer, too."

Tom reached for another sandwich, his third. He piled on the condiments.

"Harold, I have to say, this is the tastiest burger I've ever had. And I've tried them all—turkey, buffalo, lamb, alligator . . ."

"I tried raising alligators, years ago. It was a big mistake. I was also breeding beagles at the same time. Inquisitive dogs, beagles. Well, hindsight is always 20/20, isn't it?"

Roy pushed away his plate and poured himself another glass of lemonade, emptying the glass pitcher. Several ostriches had gathered around the picnic table, jockeying for scraps. A spectacular New Mexican sunset was dominating the western horizon, and the birds were darkening into silhouettes.

Bert tossed a piece of bun on the ground and the nearest ostrich pecked it up.

"There's something I still don't quite get." He threw more bun, and another bird muscled its way over and snatched it, long neck striking like a snake. "Why clone us at all? It must have cost a fortune. What did Phillip Stang actually get out of this?"

"Could be that Phillip was a bit of a philanthropist. Why did we go to the moon? Did it serve any real purpose? We did it to see if it could be done."

"Then why not go public with the results?" This had been bugging Tom as well. "Why not reap the fame and rewards of the greatest scientific development since, well, ever?"

"I have no clue. I was just paid to do it. It's the dream of every scientist; unlimited funds and no boundaries. I made some money, yes, but it isn't about the money, or the fame. It's about gaining knowledge, doing something no one else has done."

"And Stang felt the same way?"

"He never told me. When his son got into politics about a decade ago, Phil retired. You'll have to ask him yourself, after I set up a meeting."

The calm night was pierced by a scream—shrill, abrupt.

"Was that an ostrich?"

Two more followed, louder and closer.

"Coyote?" Tom asked.

"The ranch is fenced off. The only time they scream like that is when . . ."

Tom finished the sentence for him. ". . . when they see a gun." He stood up, taking out his Glock. "Let's get inside. Now."

They hurried into the house. Harold locked the doors while Tom and Roy killed all the lights. Ostriches were now stampeding in from the pasture, seeking the safety of the stable, climbing over each other to gain entrance. Their yelps had an eerie, surreal quality.

"Bert, Harold, in the kitchen. Call the police, then stay down below window level. Don't move unless I tell you to. Got the back, Roy?"

"Got my end covered. How are you on ammo?"

"I brought two magazines. You?"

"Same."

Tom opened the porch window and squatted on his haunches. He stared out onto the plains, letting his eyes adjust to the dimming light. The temperature had dropped, and a night breeze wafted in, cooling the sweat on Tom's forehead. He moved his eyes back and forth over the grounds, watching for light or movement, listening for people-sounds.

"Police will be here in ten minutes." Harold had crawled over.

"Shh. Go back into the kitchen. Do you own a gun?"

"No. I think guns are just a symbolic substitute for male genitalia, and I'm okay in that respect."

"Fine. If they get in the house, you can whack them with your genitals. Kitchen, now."

Harold scampered away. The cries of the ratites increased in volume. Something was spooking them badly. Tom looked hard at the barn, trying to spot anything man-shaped in the darkness.

A gunshot. Roy. Tom spun and ran for the rear entrance, keeping his head down.

"You see something?"

"How much you think these big birds cost?"

"Why?"

"I owe Harold for one."

"You shot an ostrich?"

"I wasn't sure what it was. Figured better safe than sorry."

"And now the bad guys know we're expecting them."

"Maybe I scared them off."

The gunfire seemed to erupt everywhere at once. Windows shattered and splinters flew and a sound like an exploding string of firecrackers echoed through the house. Automatic weapon fire.

Tom and Roy fell to their sides and curled up, protecting their heads. The destruction went on and on, lamps exploding and sparks flying and bullets chipping away at the stone fireplace and the couches hissing at them as the fabric shredded. Tom's gut was a clenched fist and his ribs screamed at the uncomfortable position but he refused to move.

After a lifetime, the shooting finally stopped. Tom didn't know if the ringing in his ears was a gun echo or his hammering heart.

"I'm going for the front." He couldn't hear his own voice and didn't think Roy could either. But his partner nodded and stuck his gun out the window, firing in the direction the bullets had come from. Tom sprinted in a crouch to the front door, both hands glued to his pistol, and he braced his back against the wall and peered through the broken glass. He caught sight of someone running behind the barn.

"Fire!"

Bert and Harold rushed out of the kitchen. Tom

could see the flickering orange they were fleeing from, with its accompanying smoke.

Roy met them by the sofas. "On my side too. They're torching the place."

"We have to get out of here!" Bert had his luggage in his hands and was heading for the front door. Tom grabbed his wrist.

"They want us to run outside so they can pick us off."

"So we're supposed to stay in here and roast?"

"Does this place have a basement? A cellar?"

Harold shook his head. "No."

"Okay, they're probably waiting for us on this side. So we have to go out the back way, through the fire."

Tom led them back into the kitchen, amazed at how quickly it had gotten unbearable. The rear entrance was a growing wall of flame, licking its way across the ceiling. Black smoke hovered at eye level, slowly inching its way to the floor. It had to be a hundred and thirty in there. Tom tried to make out the knob through the fire, but couldn't even see the door. He got to within three feet and the heat became so intense it was impossible to get any closer. The only window in the kitchen was the small one over the sink, and it too was surrounded by flames.

Tom went to the dining room, but that was a scene from hell, every single bit of furniture was a large, crackling bonfire.

"I think I'd rather get shot." Roy yelled into his ear. As the fire grew it became louder, a roar that was drowning out Tom's thoughts.

They went back into the kitchen, Bert and Harold hunched down under the falling veil of smoke. Tom looked around the room, hoping to see a magic escape route. His eyes rested on the refrigerator. It was a compact model, older, about five feet tall. He grabbed the sides and tried pulling it back. It was on rollers.

"Roy! Come on!"

They pulled the fridge out of its nook and yanked the power cord. The floor was tile and it moved easily. Tom positioned it ten feet in front of the burning back door.

"Ready?"

Roy nodded. They got behind the refrigerator and pushed it, gaining speed and momentum, hitting the back door at a full sprint.

Their aim was true. The appliance burst through the blazing entrance, flipping onto its side in the doorway. The flames rushed out of the kitchen in a big whoosh, starving for the new oxygen. They now had an opening.

Roy took out his gun and climbed over the fridge. Tom went back for Bert and the doctor. He was helping them through the door when the gunfire began.

Roy yanked Bert off the refrigerator and to the ground outside, the suitcases flying. Harold fell backward onto Tom, pinning him to the floor of the burning kitchen. Tom struggled out from under the doctor. Harold's plaid shirt was soaked in blood. His breath was faint.

"We can get you out of here. Try to hold onto my neck."

Harold shook his head. "You go."

Tom put his arm around the man's shoulders and began to lift him up. The doctor coughed violently, blood bubbling from his lips.

"Live . . ."

"Hold on, Doc. Just hold on."

Harold looked up at him, eyes dreamy and far away. A pleasant smile crossed his lips.

"Live . . . up to . . . expectations . . ."

His body went slack in Tom's arms. Flame began to close off the hole they'd made. Struggling with his balance, Tom gripped Harold tight and stepped up to the doorway.

The machine gun thundered again, and Tom leapt off the refrigerator. He landed hard, the ground erupting in little dust pockets as slugs ripped into the dirt around him. He got to his knees and continued to drag Harold away from the house.

Shots to his left. Roy, returning fire. He and Bert were on their bellies, behind Bert's suitcases. Tom took out his Glock and lay next to Roy.

"Where?"

"On the ridge, three o'clock, about a hundred yards."

"How many?"

"I spot one."

"I saw a guy in front earlier. So there's at least two."

Running in a crouch, Tom began a wide arc through the plains. The burning house was throwing off a lot of flickering light and shadows, but that worked to his advantage; a moving target would be hard to pinpoint.

More gunshots. Roy, firing far off to his right. Tom hunkered down and waited for the return barrage, trying to spot the enemy's position. When the machine gun let loose, it caught Tom by surprise. He was less than thirty feet away. The muzzle flash illuminated a short man with a crew cut, holding an Army issue M-16.

Arthur Kilpatrick. Or Attila, as Tom had begun to think of him.

Tom's response was automatic—he dropped to one knee, aimed for the head, and fired as fast as his finger could pull the trigger.

Attila pitched forward, rolling down the mound of raised dirt he'd been perched on. He didn't let go of the rifle.

Tom ran forward, firing wildly. If Attila got that M-16 around . . .

Movement on the ground, the rifle barrel raising. Tom jumped off the mound and belly flopped onto the smaller man, pinning the machine gun to his chest. He brought his Glock up to Attila's head and jammed it under his jaw. Anger and fear had released a potent adrenaline cocktail in his body, and Tom fought to keep his hands from shaking. Attila's body went completely limp.

"I'm not resisting arrest."

Tom's finger tightened on the trigger. He had one bad moment when he didn't think he could stop himself, but common sense prevailed. With his free hand he found the rifle and tossed it to the side.

"Roll onto your stomach, hands behind your head."

Attila complied, and Tom pressed his knee into the back of the man's neck.

"Aren't you gonna read me my rights, Tommy?"

"Who else is out there?"

"I'm all alone."

Tom put more pressure on his knee, pushing the smaller man's face into the dirt.

"You broke your neck in the fall. I don't think society will shed any tears."

Attila's voice was strained. "Jack's here too."

Tom fished out some disposable handcuffs—an unbreakable plastic line that tightened around a suspect's wrists and could only be taken off with tin snips. He looped one around Attila's hands and snugged it tight.

"How'd you find us?"

"GPS and a laptop. We put a tracker in Albert's luggage. We can trace it on the Internet."

Tom uncoiled another length of plastic line and wrapped it around Attila's ankles.

"How are you in touch with Jack?"

"Cell phone."

"Call him."

"Kiss my ass."

"Don't be stupid, Attila."

"So, you finally found out who I am." He rolled onto his side, facing Tom. "You think you know it all now? You don't know the half of it. I'll get another shot at you, soon enough. There isn't a place on earth you can hide from us."

Tom considered standing on his neck again, or giving him a swift kick to the stab wound, but decided against it. The police would be here any minute, and when they showed up Jack would run. They would have to get him another day. Tom took out his phone and dialed Roy.

"Got Attila. Jack's still out there. Stay alert."

"I called an ambulance. Won't help, though."

"Harold?"

"Took at least three hits. Long gone."

Tom hit the *END* button. He shoved Attila with his foot.

"So who's behind this? Stang?"

"I want my lawyer."

"Harold's dead. We got you for murder, clean and tight. And we'll hang Jessup's murder on you too. I don't know about New Mexico, but Illinois has the death penalty. Talk to me."

Attila grinned at him, his gold tooth sparkling in the glare of the burning house.

"How's your ribs?"

"How's your leg? I want my knife back, by the way."

"You have no idea how big this is. How deep it goes. You're in way over your head, Jefferson."

Tom didn't like being called Jefferson. And he really didn't like Attila's conceit. They had this guy, dead to rights, and he was acting like it was a parking ticket.

"You know what I don't get? You've got the same genes as the greatest warrior of all time. A guy who conquered the world. And you're just a petty thug who burned down his mommy's house."

Attila lost his smile.

"I'll be coming for you, soon. You and the rest of our siblings. The last cop that messed with us took sixteen hours to die. With you, it'll be twice as long."

Attila began to rant on about all of the horrible things he was going to do, but Tom tuned him out. He sat on the mound of dirt, exhausted, and waited quietly for the police to arrive.

CHAPTER 13

Albuquerque

"You've got to be kidding me."

Tom was gripping the phone so tightly his knuckles had lost their color.

"It's over my head, Mankowski. This is from the Police Superintendent herself. As of now, you and Lewis are on a mandatory leave of absence."

"I don't believe this, Lieutenant. Why would we get suspended—"

"It isn't a suspension. You're keeping your pay. But this goes high up, Tom. I don't have a say in it. Until this matter is all sorted out, consider yourself on vacation. One more thing—you have to turn in your guns and badges to the Albuquerque PD."

Tom was grinding his jaw so hard he could crush marbles.

"Lieutenant Daniels—"

"Just do it and get your asses back to Chicago. I'll do everything I can to find out what the hell is going on. You guys must have pissed off someone pretty important. The Super wanted your jobs. Put Lewis on."

He handed the phone to Roy and took a deep breath. Gerry Watterson, the Albuquerque Chief of Police, gave Tom a sympathetic frown from behind his office desk. The Chief was heavyset, tan, balding. A few hours ago he was their good buddy, organizing the fruitless search for Jack and extending over-the-top professional courtesy. Several phone calls later, the man put on his Pontius Pilate face.

"I'm sorry, Detective Mankowski. It looks like a clean bust to me. But my boss told me the same thing. I'll need to take your shield and weapon."

"What?" Roy yelled into the phone. "We catch the bad guy and you suspend us? Oh—paid vacation my ass!"

Tom put his hands on the desk, looking hard at Watterson. The Chief seemed like a good enough person, but then Lieutenant Daniels was a good person too. How could it have gone this way?

"Chief, you're making a big mistake."

"I don't have a choice in the matter. My hands are tied."

"My gun and badge?" Roy was screaming now. "You got to have a thousand mile dick, be fucking me all the way from Illinois!" Roy slammed down the phone and stared at Tom. "I cannot believe this. Can you believe this?"

"At least let us question the suspect." Tom tried to push his anger aside and appear rational. "The lives of several people are at stake here."

Watterson held out his hands, palms up. "I'd like to

help, but that's impossible. The suspect was taken into Federal custody an hour ago."

Motes swam in Tom's vision.

"Where the hell did they take him?"

"I have no idea."

"You don't understand—"

"No." Watterson was raising his voice now. "*You* don't understand. I know you guys are getting the shit end of the stick, but I can't do a damn thing about it, and neither can you. So give me your shields and your guns, and then go straighten it out on your end. I'm sorry, but there's no other choice here."

"Little back-ass redneck town." Roy spat. "You got a pointy white hood in that desk, Chief?"

A vein bulged out on the side of Watterson's head. "Arnolds! Johnson!"

Two Albuquerque uniforms came into the office. They had been on the crime scene earlier, helping Roy and Tom search for the second gunman. Now they also seemed to have undergone an attitude adjustment.

"These gentlemen have been ordered to relinquish their weapons, and are resisting the order."

Both cops drew their sidearms.

"Please put your hands behind your heads and lace your fingers together."

Tom and Roy exchanged a look. Tom sighed, then obeyed the command. Roy followed suit, mumbling obscenities under his breath. One cop covered them, while the other removed their pistols.

"Badges too."

"Sorry, guys." The cop did a quick frisk and took their badge cases and ID. He put them all on Watterson's desk.

"Thank you, Officers. Dismissed."

The two uniforms holstered their weapons and left the room. Tom decided to cross New Mexico off his list of future vacation spots.

"I'll take care of these for you." Watterson's eyes told them it was the truth. "Now get out of here."

"The guys that did this." Tom spoke with all of the urgency he could muster. "They're going to be waiting for us."

Tom could see that Watterson was considering this. After almost a minute, the man picked up Tom's Glock and chuckled.

"I don't see how you big city guys are comfortable with automatics. They jam, they misfire, you never know how many shots you have left."

Watterson took a key out of his pocket and opened up his lower desk drawer.

"In my book, nothing beats a Smith and Wesson 38 Special. Look at these beauties. Matching set, got them off a drug dealer."

He placed the revolvers before him on the desk.

"Probably stolen. Serial numbers have been filed off. We tried to do a search, couldn't find the owner."

Watterson swiveled around in his chair, facing the wall. Tom and Roy exchanged a glance, and then each took a gun. Tom spun the cylinder, noting it was loaded.

"Thank you, Chief."

"You mean for holding onto your guns and badges? No problem. Just do yourselves a favor and don't get caught in my county in possession of any type of firearm, or I'll have to bust your asses."

"Chief." Roy put the revolver into his holster. "About that pointy hood thing . . ."

"Apology accepted. Now get the hell out of here before I lynch you both." Watterson turned back around and gave them hard stares. "Good luck figuring this thing out."

They left the office and found Bert sitting in the hallway, going through his suitcase. He stared up at them, his face anguished.

"Did you hear? This is horrible."

"How did you find out?" Tom asked. "We were just told."

"Perhaps I can replace the rear treble, but the paint job is ruined. That's at least five hundred dollars off the price."

"What the hell are you talking about?"

"My Flying Helgramite. A three thousand dollar lure. Those maniacs shot it."

Roy was on him before Tom could intervene. The cop grabbed Bert by the shirt and pulled him close.

"It's your damn lures almost got us killed. There's a tracer in the suitcase."

Bert's reaction was totally unexpected. Rather than cower or cringe, he drove his heel into Roy's instep and rammed his head into the bigger man's chin. Roy staggered back, more shocked than hurt.

"I'm sick of you, and I'm sick of all of this!"

He squatted and began to close his suitcase.

"Bert." Tom put a hand on his shoulder. Bert shrugged it off.

"Don't touch me! I'm leaving."

"They'll kill you."

"Whoop-dee-doo. Like you care. Like anyone freaking cares."

Bert hefted both cases and began to walk down the hall. Tom followed.

"Look, Bert, this is stressful for all of us. But we have to stick together."

"I'll do fine by myself."

Tom grabbed his arm. Bert dropped the suitcases and spun around, holding out his fists.

"You want some of this? I won't put up with being bullied anymore."

"I'm not bullying—"

"Bull! If it isn't you, it's him, or Jack the Ripper, or my father—"

"Bert, please. We need you."

Bert blinked, some of the fire leaving his eyes. "You *need* me?"

"Roy and I were just suspended. Attila was taken by the FBI. For all we know he's back on the street already. If someone doesn't warn the other clones, they're going to be killed."

Bert's face went from angry, to thoughtful, to angry again. "I want him to apologize."

Tom beckoned his partner over. "Roy, come here and say you're sorry."

Roy folded his arms and pressed his lips together.

"Roy!"

Tom was bestowed with an evil glare, then Roy walked over to them, making it obvious he was in no hurry.

"I'm sorry, Bert."

"Say I can use your toilet."

"You can use my toilet."

"And your towels."

"And my damn towels."

"Now tell me one thing that you like about me."

"You've got to be yanking my—"

"Just kidding." Bert smiled. "Apology accepted. I'm sorry too. About the foot and the jaw thing. Self-defense course. It was just automatic. You okay?"

Roy's features softened a notch.

"I'm fine. But I swear, it gets out that Einstein busted my lip . . ."

Bert held out his hand. Roy gave it a halfhearted shake.

"Okay, team—what do we do first?"

Tom winced at Bert's enthusiasm, but the man was too excited to notice. "First, we locate that tracer in your suitcases and disable it. After that, I'm not sure. We have to find the others, and we have to talk with Phillip Stang."

"You think Stang was the one pulling the strings that got us suspended?" Roy asked.

Bert made a face. "Well, duh."

"Then I'd like to go pay the man a visit."

"He lives on a big estate in Springfield. Possibly guarded. He may not agree to see us, and we don't have our badges."

Bert frowned. "Stang can wait. If they're planning on killing the others, we have to stop it. Or at least warn them."

"How, Bert? Just call them up and say, 'By the way, you're a clone of William Shakespeare and you're being stalked by Jack the Ripper?'"

"So the others are just burgers at a fat farm?"

Tom had to think about that one.

"No, they're not. We don't even know who they are

or where they live, yet. That'll take some time. We can do it on the way to Stang's place."

"Harold's records all burned up. How we gonna find them? Just call Directory Assistance, say we're looking for Joan of Arc?"

Roy had a point. They didn't even have their last names.

"Their Birth Certificates!" Bert snapped his fingers. "That's how Jessup found me and you. We just get the birth numbers that came before us, and we'll have their names."

Tom nodded. "I'll need an Internet connection. Do you think this town has an all night department store?"

They hailed a cab. Tom made Bert sit in front to avoid any more slugging. Their first move was to have the taxi driver circle the block three times. When it was obvious they weren't being followed, they hit the nearest bank with a drive-thru ATM. The logic was sound— whoever had the power to get them suspended could just as easily have their bank accounts and credit cards frozen. Tom and Roy each took out a few grand. When it was Bert's turn, he waffled.

"Come on, man. You're part of this. You have to contribute."

"I'm okay."

"You gonna pay for your plane ticket with a Luny Frog?"

"I have some cash. It'll be fine."

They didn't push it.

The cab stopped at a 24-hour department store, and Tom went in and bought a portable laptop, extra batteries, and a Wifi card. He also got a fireproof lock box, and a replacement inflatable donut for Roy. As they drove to the airport, Tom used a credit card to activate a new wireless Internet account. A few moments later, he was surfing the Cook County database.

"Dammit. I don't have my birth certificate on me. I need the birth number."

"Got mine." Bert reached into his pocket and took out a blue piece of paper. Tom clicked on SEARCH and typed in 112-72-0040705. Bert's info came on-screen. Since Bert was number 6, and Jessup was 5, Tom typed in the same number minus two—112-72-0040703.

"William Masterton. I'm guessing this is Shakespeare."

"Who's next?"

Tom checked out number 3. "Joan DeVilliers. Joan of Arc."

The person right before her was Robert Mitchell—Robert E. Lee, the cop who was impaled last year in Nashville. A damn shame. They sure could have used him right now.

"Who's number 1?"

"Abraham Wilkens. Lincoln. Okay, those are the good guys. Let's see about the enemy."

Tom used the same trick, counting up instead of down, and found out Vlad the Impaler was number 8 and really named Victor Pignosky. Arthur Kilpatrick came next, and then Jack Smythe, the Ripper.

All of the players now had names. It was just a question of finding them.

Roy frowned. "I think my donut has a hole in it."

"Duh. Every donut has a hole in it."

"Ha ha, Einstein. I mean I'm leaking air."

"You probably don't have the nozzle in right. Let me see it."

Roy passed it to Bert, and Tom went back to the laptop. He started with Joan. Harold had mentioned she was a Hollywood producer. Tom tried the online Yellow Pages for LA and found over thirty listings for *DeVilliers*.

Switching tactics, he got on an engine that searched magazines, limiting his field to ENTERTAINMENT. He discovered an article in Variety that mentioned Joan DeVilliers and her company, JDP. Back to the Yellow Pages, and he had a phone number. Tom saved the page.

Next up was Abe. Harold had said he was a used car salesman in Nebraska. Tom tried a meta-search engine this time, using the words USED+CARS+ABE+NEBRASKA.

The first hit was *Honest Abe's Used Autos*. It was located in Lincoln, of all places. There was a large, captioned picture of Abe Wilkens, complete with beard and stovepipe hat, standing in the middle of a car lot. Did the guy know, or was he just playing up the obvious resemblance? Tom saved the info.

Shakespeare was problematic. Tom knew that he wrote ad copy, and that he got good grades in college, but that was it. Without a state or town, it would require some thinking to track him down.

"You have to push the nozzle all the way in, so it's flush."

Bert handed the donut back and Roy took a minute to adjust it to the proper position.

"Thanks."

"You're welcome."

How about that? Tom grinned. Actual civility.

"Next time push the nozzle in."

"I pushed the damn nozzle in."

"All the way."

"Maybe I should push your fat head into your neck, all the way."

"Don't get mad at me because you're too dumb to blow up a stupid tube. The instructions must have been killer: step one—blow it up, step two—push the nozzle in."

The cabbie was all too happy to spit them out at the ABQ Sunport. Tom tipped the driver exceptionally well. The group spent a good twenty minutes checking various terminals before finding a flight back to O'Hare. Before boarding, they commandeered a nice quiet table at a deserted café and tore into Bert's luggage.

"Easy! Please!"

Bert played the frantic mother hen, gingerly putting the bubble wrap around each lure as fast as Roy and Tom could open them up.

"Hey, Bert." Roy tossed him a feathered lure with the colorings of a mallard. "Duck!"

"Can we be mature about this, please? This all represents a rather large investment on my part."

"Okay, let's talk street value. How much is all this crap worth?"

"Current price guides put the collection at slightly over five hundred."

"Not how many—how much?"

"That is how much."

"Five hundred dollars?"

"Five hundred thousand dollars."

Roy and Tom looked at each other, then back at Bert.

"You got a half a million in these two suitcases?" Roy's voice was loud and squeaky.

Bert continued to wrap. "Yes. So please be gentle with them."

"Hold on. Time out." Roy made a T with his hands. "You got to tell us how you wound up with half a mil in old hooks."

Bert sighed, looking annoyed. "When I got out of college, my dad gave me a check for fifty grand. I made some investments. In a few years, I was worth somewhere in the area of eight million dollars."

Roy whistled. "That's a nice area."

"I had a big place, some cars. But all of my money was tied up in the market. It's not like I had eight million in a bank account someplace. Turns out, that's what I should have done. On October 27th, 1997, the market dropped 554.26 points. A 7.2% drop."

"That's not too bad. Seven percent."

"That's not quite how it works, Roy. It was the biggest crash in history. I lost everything."

"Everything? How?"

"Most traders diversify—they put money in a little bit of everything to hedge their bets. If gold drops, corn will protect them. But I didn't do that. I wasn't an investor. I was a niche trader. At that time, I had everything in technologies. They took the first hit, and dropped like crazy. I refused to sell, believing I could weather it. But there's a stampede effect. One person gets scared, the rest jump on the bandwagon. In a few hours, every one of my stocks became practically worthless. By the time they shut the market down, I had about fifty grand to my name. The next day I lost that, along with the house and the cars."

"Ouch."

"I had to borrow money from my father. I think it delighted him. Ever since I was a kid, he was trying to force me to be a scientist like him. When I decided to become a trader rather than a physics professor, it royally cheesed him off. It cheesed him off even more that I was so successful. I borrowed the money from him on the condition that I enroll in the graduate physics program at NYU. Instead, I took it and ran."

"And the lures?"

"I wound up in Wisconsin. After finding an apartment and getting a cheap car, I only had about twenty grand left. I didn't want to go back to the Market, so I did a little antique buying and selling to make ends meet. The biggest profits I made were on lures. You could find a Creek Chub Injured Minnow, new in the box, at an old bait shop for five bucks, then sell it for forty on the Internet. As I made money, I bought more expensive lures. And now here I am, in a New Mexican airport, winding bubble wrap around my net worth while you two make fun of me."

"And your dad?" Tom asked.

"I repaid the loan, but haven't talked to him in two years."

They finished sorting though the first bag and began on the second. Tom had no idea what a tracer looked like or how big it was. While Roy continued to unwrap lures, Tom went through Bert's toiletry bag. He found a toothbrush, a soap case, toothpaste, deodorant, another deodorant . . .

"Sweating problem?"

"Hmm? That one's not mine."

Tom popped the cap. A green stick stared up at him, smelling of pine. He tried to turn the dial on the bottom, but it didn't budge. Using his fingernails, Tom pulled out the sliver of green and peered underneath, finding an electronic gizmo.

"Unless antiperspirants have become very high-tech, I think we found our tracer."

He shook the contents onto his palm. It was a small bundle of wires attached to a circuit board.

"So that little thing can be tracked by satellite?"

"It's like a mini cell phone. Probably transmits its location every couple of minutes."

"Why didn't the Foxhound pick it up?"

"The Foxhound scans from fifty megahertz up. Cell phones transmit below fifty megahertz. I thought everyone knew that."

"Smart ass. So now what? Want to slip it in the pocket of some tourist going to Germany?"

Tom pulled the lead terminal from the lithium battery, effectively shutting the device off.

"I think I'll save it. You never know."

Tom and Roy helped Bert close up his suitcases. They took one more quick tour around the airport to make sure they hadn't been followed, and then went into the men's room. In the last stall, Tom wrapped his and Roy's revolvers in toilet paper and locked them in the fire box he'd bought at the department store. He wasn't sure if it was X-ray proof or not, anymore than he was sure if luggage was X-rayed at all. He figured he had a 50/50 chance of it getting on the plane. The only other choice was ditching the guns, and after the last few days Tom didn't want to be unarmed for any longer than necessary.

They went to the front desk and checked Bert's luggage and the box without incident. The steward announced their flight was boarding, and when Tom finally got in his seat he couldn't keep his eyes open.

"Hey, Tom."

He peeked at Bert with his left eye. "What?"

"What do you think will happen to all of those ostriches, now that Harold's gone?"

"I have no idea. The state will do something with them. A zoo. Sell them. Have a cookout. I don't know."

"Poor things."

Tom closed his eyes again. Funny that Bert should be worried about the birds. Especially when there were so many other things he ought to be worried about.

CHAPTER 14

Springfield

Tom cracked open a window, even though the weather was too cold for it. They'd cleaned up as best they could when they arrived at O'Hare, but they had no change of clothing and the last time any of them showered was Roy's place two days ago. Even with a liberal application of Bert's deodorant, Tom was feeling a bit rank.

They were on I-55, headed for Springfield and former Senator Phillip Stang. The trip was long and boring—there was nothing in the way of scenery but flat, featureless cornfields, and the radio was off limits because of an earlier Roy and Bert power struggle for control.

The only good thing that happened within the past 48 hours was avoiding arrest for smuggling the guns onto the plane. That little trick went off without a hitch, and Tom felt a lot safer with the Smith and Wesson in his shoulder holster.

"How much further?" Bert asked. He'd asked that no less than fifty times.

"How many times you gonna ask that?" That had been Roy's answer for each of the fifty.

"About as many times as you complain about your ass hurting."

"Springfield is coming up, next exit."

Three hours in the car and Tom's ribs were screaming at him, but that wasn't nearly as bad as the mental anguish he'd suffered, driving with Bert and Roy.

Stang didn't live in Springfield itself. His place was along Rte. 29, on the outskirts. They had to go through the town to reach it, and Tom was surprised to see how little it had changed in fifteen years.

Springfield was the resting place of Abe Lincoln, a status that led to its prosperity in the middle of nowhere and its being declared the state capitol. Like a mini Washington, DC, the town was packed with monuments and historic sites, and a field trip staple for just about every Junior High School in Illinois.

Tom remembered his trip fondly—not for the boring visits to Lincoln's tomb or the State Capitol, but because he'd gotten to second base with Shirley Valezquez when they strayed away from the tour group.

He ran into Shirley a few years ago. Married, kids, successful. Like so many of his peers. Tom could add a poor social life to his list of inadequacies. Perhaps after he went into politics he would find the right woman. He snickered, wondering which was the more realistic of the two.

Tom pulled the rental car into a fast food place. After filling their stomachs with grease, they climbed in the car again—Bert in front, having called shotgun—and headed for the Stang Estate, unannounced.

It looked like another Springfield monument, columns and carefully trimmed bushes and marble sculptures and fountains, visible from a mile away due to the flat terrain and lack of trees. As expected, there was a gate blocking the driveway. The small brick guardhouse wasn't occupied. Tom blew the horn.

A groundskeeper, complete with pruning shears, walked down the driveway and peered at them through the wrought iron.

"Yeah?"

"We're here to see Mr. Stang."

"He isn't seeing anyone."

"Tell him it's Mankowski and Blumberg."

"Mankoberg and . . . ?"

"Just say Jefferson and Einstein."

The man nodded and walked off. Minutes passed. Tom became increasingly uncomfortable. The mansion had two floors and a dozen windows facing the driveway. If Jack were waiting in one of those rooms with a rifle . . .

The gate made a clanging sound and began to roll backwards. Tom recovered from the brief shock and drove up to the house, parking in front of a six car garage.

"Is anyone else a little intimidated?" Bert asked.

They didn't answer. The front doors were cathedral style, double height, surrounded by ornate bay windows. They opened before Tom could knock.

"Good afternoon, gentlemen." A man, young and big-shouldered, wearing a trendy black suit. He had a broad, dark face, and a flat nose. American Indian, Tom guessed. "I'm Mr. Stang's assistant, Jerome. He's waiting for you in the drawing room. This way, please."

Jerome trotted through the gigantic foyer, past a wall-sized aquarium, and up the grand spiral staircase that seemed to be a standard in every mansion. They followed, feet sinking inch-deep into expensive carpet, large, dramatic paintings of battle scenes facing them on the stairway wall. Tom could take or leave art, but he found these repellant. They depicted ancient war atrocities—French revolution beheadings, Indian massacres, feudal disemboweling. One particularly offensive wood cutting reveled in a landscape of impaled bodies, some long dead and some still struggling on the stake.

"All originals." Jerome smiled mildly at Tom's distaste. "That particular piece dates back to the fifteenth century."

"It's adorable."

They strolled down a long hallway, coming to a halt at an intricately carved door. Jerome held it open for them.

Phillip Stang was in a king-sized bed, sitting up against a massive wooden headboard shaped like a setting sun. To his left were several large pieces of medical equipment, tubes extending to each of his arms. The machines chugged away with a faint locomotive sound.

"Is there anything else, sir?"

"Thank you, Jerome."

The door closed behind them.

"Welcome to the drawing room, gentlemen. I hope

none of you are put off by the pun. I'd prefer to see you under normal circumstances, but my poor, overworked kidney needs a weekly dialysis boost. Come closer."

Tom moved to the side of the bed, regarding the old man. He was like a white raisin—small, bald, wrinkled. Late seventies, Tom guessed. A gnarled hand picked up a remote control and turned off the big screen television playing across the room.

"Amazing." Stang had small, blue eyes, and they darted over Tom's whole body, taking everything in. "This is the first time I've seen you as an adult. You announced yourself as Jefferson, so you must know. What do you think? Pretty impressive work, I may say."

"We just visited Harold. He told us a lot."

"Harold? How is the old workhorse?"

Tom watched his face closely. "He's dead."

Stang smiled. "He lived a long life. These things happen."

"You're the one that killed him." Bert pushed Tom aside and got in Stang's face. So much for playing it subtle.

"Ah, Albert. I've followed your life with semi-interest. Shame about the stock market. What is it you're doing now, selling old worms and such? A disappointment. But let's try to be civil, shall we?"

"When did murder become civil?"

"You must be Detective Lewis. Oh, pardon me, you're not currently a detective, are you? I believe you've been suspended. Tell me, is your mother still working at that grocery store on Clark? She walks home, right? Even after the late shift? Dangerous, at night."

Tom had to hold Roy back. Stang's thin mouth twisted into a small smile.

"Let's come to an understanding here, gentlemen. You've apparently put two and two together, but I have no idea what you thought you'd accomplish visiting me. You two aren't even cops anymore."

Tom made sure Roy was calm before he approached Stang again. "We wanted to know why."

"Why, what? Why I did what I did, and am doing what I'm doing? Let's say that at one point in time you were necessary to me, and now you've become a liability."

Roy made a fist. "Right now I'm liable to knock you upside your bald head."

"I'd sue you for threatening me, but for some reason I don't think you will be around for the trial."

Bert's face became angry. "Are you threatening us?"

Stang smiled again, his dull eyes twinkling. "Mr. Einstein gets a gold star. I was worried I hadn't been obvious enough. Now is there anything else, gentlemen? I'm growing tired of you."

Tom tried to collect himself. He hadn't expected it to go like this. Stang had openly admitted he was going to kill them, and there wasn't a damn thing they could do about it.

"Whatever your little plan is, we're going to stop it."

It sounded lame as it came out of Tom's mouth.

"No, you won't."

"Sure we will." Bert said. "You're practically a

corpse now. I got half a tube of toothpaste that's gonna last longer than you."

"Au contraire. I'll be getting my eleventh kidney transplant tomorrow."

Tom knew people who have been waiting their whole lives for one, and this ugly bastard has had almost a dozen?

"I suppose being rich gets you to the top of all those donor lists."

"Something like that." Another twisted smile.

"Why'd you stop at Senator, Stang? An ego your size shouldn't have settled for less than President."

"Unfortunately, I was born in Germany. The Constitution—which you had a hand in writing, Tom—states that a President must be born in America. I tried three times, during my years as Senator, to add an amendment changing that. Each time I was unsuccessful."

"What a shame. I suppose there's always hope for Phil Jr. I wonder if he's involved in all of this? Maybe we should pay him a visit."

Stang's mood darkened. "Please do. I'll instruct the Secret Service to shoot you on sight. It will save me the trouble."

"Roy, do you get the feeling that daddy's little angel is involved in this too?"

"I think so. Maybe if we go to the media, make a big enough stink, something will shake loose."

Stang laughed, a short clipped sound like a dog bark.

"I'd like to see that. Go to the networks, tell them you're Jefferson and Einstein, and see what they do. There's no proof. No records."

"There's DNA testing."

"That takes weeks." Another wicked grin. "You don't have weeks. The remainder of your lives can be measured in hours. Jerome, would you mind escorting them out?"

Tom turned and saw Jerome in the doorway. He was holding a pistol casually at his side.

"Big deal." Roy opened up his jacket. "I got one too."

Tom patted Roy on the shoulder. This wasn't the time or the place for a shoot-out. "Come on. Let's go."

Jerome permitted them out the door, and followed them through the hall. Tom was angry. But even worse than that, he felt powerless.

"What the hell happened in there?" Roy shook his head.

Bert agreed. "I feel like a fly he just shooed away."

They went down the stairs, Jerome trailing closely behind.

"It's just round one, guys. We'll regroup, do it differently next time. At least we know what we're dealing with now."

"A rich, powerful, psychotic egomaniac?" Bert pulled a face. "I was happier not knowing."

Roy snorted. "Maybe we'll be lucky, he'll die during his operation."

"He's only part of the problem. We also have to deal with Vlad, Attila, and Jack. Plus this guy."

Tom pointed to a large portrait hanging at the bottom of the staircase. It was of an elderly Phillip Stang, sitting on a chair. Standing behind him, resting a hand on Phil's shoulder, was a young man who bore a striking resemblance.

"Phil junior. Mr. Speaker of the House. You think he's in this too?"

"Does the apple fall far from the tree?"

Jerome stood patiently in the foyer while they let themselves out.

"So what next? Do we go after Mr. Speaker?"

Tom shook his head. "How? Even if we could get to him, what do we do? Tape some wires to our chests and trick him into revealing his plot for world domination?"

"I say we go to the media."

"They'll laugh at us unless we have evidence. We need DNA tests. But even then, we'd need original samples."

"Well, we're in Springfield. Want to buy some shovels, dig up Lincoln?"

Tom actually considered it for a moment—proof that he needed some sleep.

"How about the FBI?" Bert asked. "Or the CIA?"

"We don't know how far Stang has influence. Between him and his son, I bet he could send the entire Army after us."

"Then can't we just kill them both? Pop some caps?"

"We're not assassins, Bert."

Bert climbed in back and passed Roy the donut. Tom sat in the driver's seat and drummed his fingers on the steering wheel, lost in thought.

"How about the Unholy Trio? Jack, Vlad, and Attila?"

"What about them?"

"Well, they're involved in this, and they're going to come after us, so we could set some kind of trap."

"I hate sitting around, waiting for things to happen. Plus, we caught one already, and they just let him go."

"And what about the other clones?" Bert asked. "They're on the list, too."

"Okay. Let me think."

Tom rubbed his temples. The situation seemed pretty hopeless. With the bad guy so high up in government, they couldn't expect any help through the official channels. They could try to go over his head, but Tom didn't have high hopes the President would take their calls.

"Stang said we're a liability."

"Yeah. What did he mean by that?"

"Obviously, us being alive is bad for him somehow. He wants us dead for a reason. And it can't be because we know too much, because he wants the other clones dead as well, and they don't know anything."

"I get it. There must be more at stake here than just killing us off. Maybe you were right about the world domination thing."

"Look, we're not cops now, right? So let's say we grabbed Attila or Jack. We wouldn't have to take him in. Maybe he'd tell us what's going on."

"He wouldn't want to talk."

Roy's face got very serious. "I can be persuasive."

Tom looked at Roy, then at Bert. "Do we all agree, then? We try to grab one of the bad guys?"

"What about saving the other clones?"

"We can do both."

"I'm in."

"Me too."

"Okay, then." Tom started the car and cranked up the heat. "We know Joan of Arc is in Hollywood, and Abe Lincoln is in Nebraska."

"Always wanted to see Hollywood," Bert mused.

"Me too."

"Sounds good." Tom cruised down the driveway and through the gate, leaving the Stang estate. "California here we come."

CHAPTER 15

Los Angeles

"Joan?" Marsha peeked in the door. "There are some men here to see you."

Joan checked her desk calendar and didn't see any scheduled meetings for that day.

"Are they anybody?" Anybody big in the business who wouldn't need an appointment.

"They said they're police officers."

"Thanks, Marsha. Send them in."

"Is everything . . . okay?"

"It's fine. I was assaulted last night. I'll tell you about it later."

Marsha's head disappeared, and a moment later three men came into her office. The first was black, big, cop written all over him. The second guy was smaller, a mustache, familiar in some way she couldn't place. Bringing up the rear was a tall, wiry man, with sandy hair. He's the one who spoke.

"Miss DeVilliers? I'm Detective Tom Mankowski.

This is my partner, Roy Lewis, and this is Bert Blumberg."

"Thanks for coming down, Officers. You're here
with good news, I hope. You caught the creep?"

"The creep?"

"The guy who attacked me."

For a moment they didn't seem to understand her.
Then the tall one, Tom, approached her desk.

"Was it one of these guys?"

He opened up a binder and handed her three color
computer printouts. The first picture was of a muscular
man covered with tattoos. She flipped to the second
page. Goatee. Green eyes. There was no doubt at all.

"This is him! Have you picked him up yet?"

"This man attacked you?"

"Twice. Tried to put me on a big stake. You've read
the reports. Right?"

None of them answered. Joan narrowed her eyes.

"Are you guys LAPD?"

"Miss DeVilliers—"

"I'd like to see some identification, please."

"Joan, listen, you're in danger."

"Do you have any ID or not?"

"Please, give us just a second. This is important."

Joan felt her face flush. Paparazzi. It was only a
matter of time before they caught wind of it. She hit
the intercom button in her desk. "Marsha . . ."

"We're not from LA. Roy and I are Chicago Homicide Detectives. We're following up on a murder investigation where the victim had a number 7 tattooed
on his heel. Just like your number 3."

Marsha's voice came through the speaker. *"Yes, Ms. DeVilliers?"*

The tattoo again. Joan stared at Tom. His suit was off the rack, wrinkled, and his face left no doubt he was exhausted. His partners shared the look. Joan tried to tune into any perceived threat, any bad vibe, any hint of them being media jackals. They were calm as calm could be.

"Hold my calls." Joan leaned back and crossed her legs. "You have my attention."

"The man who attacked you is named Victor Pignosky. He goes by the name of Vlad. He also has a tattoo on his heel, the number 10. I've got a number 5. Bert here has a number 6. There are ten of us, total. All the same age. All adopted by different parents. Vlad and two of the others are trying to kill the rest of us—me, you, Bert. They've already succeeded twice."

"Do you have any proof of this?"

Tom and Bert looked at each other, and then took off their shoes. Their tattoos matched the style of Joan's.

"Okay, so why does this Vlad guy want to kill me—us?"

"We're not sure."

"And what's the deal with the numbers? Are you guys my brothers?"

"Not exactly."

"Well, what exactly is going on?"

"We should tell her." The familiar guy, Bert, nudged Tom.

He shook his head. "How can we prove it? With her, we can't do the writing thing. There's no pictures, no

photos. Maybe we could look for old French paintings."

"You're going to have to tell her sooner or later."
The black man, Roy, shrugged. "She either buys it or
she don't."

"Try me. I'm a Hollywood producer. I've heard it
all."

"Fine." Tom took a deep breath. "This will sound
crazy. It sounded crazy to me, when I heard it. But all
ten of us, we weren't born, normally. We were—created. In a lab, in Mexico."

"Created, how? Are we talking mad scientists and
test tubes here? Some holy miracle thing?"

"We were cloned from famous historical figures."

Joan frowned. "You just lost me."

The little guy sighed. "He's telling the truth. I'm a
clone of Albert Einstein. He's Thomas Jefferson. The
guy who attacked you is Vlad the Impaler."

"And I'm . . . ?"

"Joan of Arc."

She hit the button. "Marsha, call Security."

Tom said, "Look. This thing is big. The police won't
be able to protect you. Victor—Vlad—isn't going to
stop. We're all on a hit list."

"Nice try."

"This is the truth."

Joan let out a slow breath, surprised she'd suspended her disbelief for so long.

"Well, it sounds like a movie pitch. The cloning
angle isn't bad, but it needs work. Maybe approach it
from a comedy perspective. You could call it *Send In
the Clones*."

"Security is on the way up, Ms. DeVilliers."

"We're staying over at the Chinatown Holiday Inn. Here's my cell phone number." Tom tossed a card onto her desk. "Call if you need us."

"Sure thing, President Jefferson. Now, I have some actual work to do. If you'll pardon me." Joan smiled. "Get it? Pardon me?"

Tom looked at her, hard. "Please, be careful."

Joan met his stare, and for a second almost believed him. She came very close to calling them back in, but the moment passed and rationality took over. She was no more Joan of Arc than those guys were Einstein and Jefferson. The little guy did look like Einstein, but it was all too far removed from reality. She wasn't buying.

But being stalked by some psycho—that was real. And they did have a picture of him, which implied some kind of connection. Joan didn't perceive them as a threat—there was something very benign about the trio—but the smartest move would be to call the police department and tell them what happened. Let the professionals take care of it. Joan would show up for the trial.

She located the number of the cop who took her report the night before. But before doing that, she called Marty into her office and had him set up some interviews for personal bodyguards.

Until this Vlad lunatic was behind bars, Joan wasn't going to take any chances. Even if she had to hire an entourage.

CHAPTER 16

"Well, what now? She didn't believe us."

Roy put on his sunglasses. "We knew she wouldn't. Be honest, I don't either. I figure this is all just some big white-person conspiracy."

They walked out of the building and stopped on the sidewalk. The California sun felt good. Tom inhaled deeply, trying to smell the ocean. He believed he caught a whiff of salt water behind the car fumes and the rotting garbage from the alley.

"At least we know Vlad is here. Roy, do we have any friends in the LAPD?"

"Not that I know of. We can always make some."

"It's a shot. I'd like to see those reports on Joan's attack. Maybe we can catch Vlad before he makes his next move."

"So, we're just supposed to sit here and wait?"

"That's the plan, Bert." Tom held up his hand to hail a cab.

"How about Lincoln? While we're here, Attila and Jack could be trying to kill him."

"What do you suggest?"

"I'll go after Abe."

Tom turned away from traffic and frowned at Bert. Maybe all the jet lag had caught up with the little guy.

"Bad idea. These are dangerous guys."

"If I want to go, you can't stop me."

"I could break your legs," Roy suggested. "Then you don't go nowhere."

"I'm not afraid of you."

"Don't matter. I can break your legs whether you're afraid or not."

Bert gave Roy his back and touched Tom's shoulder. "I'd be dead right now if you didn't show up when you did. Abe will be easier to convince. There's a handwriting sample in the leather binder, and the guy already knows he looks like Lincoln. We have to warn him, or he'll die."

"And if we leave LA, we miss our shot at Vlad and Joan will die."

"Why can't we save them both?"

"Let's vote."

"No voting. You guys will team up against me again. The choice is simple—you let me go to Nebraska, or I'll take off as soon as you both turn your backs."

A cab stopped by the curb.

"We'll discuss it back at the hotel."

"We'll discuss it now. There's a beat cop right across the street. All I have to do is start screaming that you two have guns."

Tom and Roy looked at each other. The cabbie leaned out the window. "You guys getting in or what?"

"I could keep an eye on him, make sure he's okay."

Tom couldn't believe that came out of Roy's mouth. "You're kidding."

Bert was just as amazed. "You want to come with me?"

"No, damn you both. I don't want to go with you. But if we don't have a choice, I'll go. We zip over there, warn the guy, make sure he's safe, zip back here. Could be back by tonight. I'm anxious to get back on a plane anyway. Been so long."

Tom considered it. Someone had to keep an eye on Joan, but it wasn't very likely Vlad would attack her again so soon. And, honestly, it would be nice to be alone for a little while. Tom had some personal issues to sort out, a difficult task when surrounded by constant bickering.

"Fine. Let's hit the hotel, we'll come up with a game plan."

The cabbie was fat, sweaty, and strongly smelled like a gym sock. The three of them climbed into the back seat. Roy was hesitant to sit down—Tom knew his donut was back at the hotel.

"You should have taken it with."

"And do what with it? Carry it around on my neck?"

"This is LA. I don't think anyone would notice. Slug bug red, no hit backs." Bert popped him in the shoulder. "And there's another one! Slug bug green, no hit backs." Bert hit him again, same spot.

The cabbie scowled at Roy. "Buddy, you need to sit down."

"I'm trying to sit down. This jackass keeps whacking me."

Tom questioned his decision to sit between them. The front seat seemed like the lesser evil.

"Chinatown Holiday Inn."

"Sweet Mary mother of Jesus wife of Joseph the carpenter!" Roy finally managed to sit down.

"So, you guys play the slug bug game?" The taxi driver grinned at them in his rearview. "I see that all the time. Lot of Beetles in Hollywood. Trendy."

"There's one." Roy reached over and pounded Bert in the leg. "Slug bug black, no hit backs."

"Where?"

"Right there."

"That's a BMW." Bert smacked Roy twice. "Wrong car, double hit backs."

"Can you guys quit this, please?" Tom looked ahead in the distance. "Oh God, no."

"Here it is." The cabbie pointed to his right. "Largest Volkswagen dealership in Los Angeles."

It was ugly. Real ugly.

When they got to the hotel, Bert and Roy were still laughing.

"I hurt my hand, smacking you so much."

"I got so many bruises, I'm going to be darker than you. How's your arm?"

"I need a Vicodin. You hit me sixty-five times in the exact same spot. But the one who really nailed me was Tommy. Man, you hit hard."

"No kidding." Bert patted Tom on the back. "You were jabbing so fast your hands were a blur. I didn't think you liked this game."

"Yeah, Tom. Next time, though, you have to call out the color of the car. You forgot to say anything."

"Did I?"

They entered the hotel lobby and got in the elevator. Their room was on the tenth floor. Tom opened the door with the keycard and made a beeline for the laptop. After logging onto Wifi, he went to the site he'd discovered last night after they got in. *Surveillance Technologies*.

"You're not taking your lures again, are you?"

"Everywhere I go."

"Can't you put them in the hotel safe?"

"I don't trust safes."

"But you trust the airlines? What if they lost your luggage?"

"Then they pay me the market value. I insure them every time I board."

Tom took the tracer he'd liberated from Bert's deodorant from his pocket and attached the lead terminal to the battery. Just below the battery, on the circuit board, there was a serial number followed the tiny word *BigTrack*. Rather than sleep last night, Tom had used these to trace the tracer back to its manufacturer.

Surveillance Technologies was an upscale spy store that sold bugging, tracking, and detecting equipment online. Their home page proudly advertised that the US government was one of their top customers. A disclaimer in somewhat smaller font stated that many of these products were illegal for civilian use.

The BigTrack series were tracers. By accessing the private area of the Surveillance Technology website, you could access the global positioning satellite to plot the tracer on an overlay as large as the western hemisphere, all the way down to a street map.

BigTracks were off limits for the public sector, and the tracking page required an ID and a password to access. Tom had spent almost two hours trying to get in. He used combinations of ATTILA, JACK, RIPPER, HUN, CLONE, GENES, STANG, BARNETT, and so on, hoping to luck into the right combination. He hit the jackpot with ID MARY and password KELLY. The Ripper's final victim.

He tried it now, and then punched in the serial number on the tracer. The screen loaded a map of the United States, with a small blip on the West Coast. He zoomed in to California, then to LA, then to Chinatown, and finally down to the street the hotel was on. Tom wondered if zooming in further would show a floor plan of their suite, but it was already maxed out.

"We call each other every four hours, starting when you arrive. I can trace you guys with this." Tom tossed the BigTrack to Bert. "Keep it on you."

"Yes, Mom."

Bert placed the transmitter into his thick wallet. Roy picked up Tom's carryon—Roy's had been lost in the fire in New Mexico. After the excruciating car trip back from Springfield, they'd stopped at their apartments to shower and change. Curiosity had prompted Tom to sweep his place with the Foxhound, and he found three bugs identical to Jessup's. Trying to sound natural, they openly telegraphed their trip to California, hoping one of the bad guys was listening. To make the trail even easier to follow, they purchased their plane tickets with credit cards.

Tom logged onto a travel site and searched for the next direct flight to Lincoln, Nebraska out of LAX.

"Got one. Southwest, leaves in two hours." He faced Roy. "Shall I also reserve a rental car for you, sir?"

"If you'd be so kind."

"I'll need a valid driver's license and a major credit card, please."

Roy tossed him his wallet. Tom followed the links and wound up at Hertz. He found an appropriate automobile and several keystrokes later, they had wheels.

"How did we survive before we had the Internet?" Tom wondered aloud.

"They were called telephones." Roy took his wallet back and placed his gun in the fire box. "Now don't be getting into any kind of trouble without me."

"You guys be careful. The bad guys will be watching. Good luck."

Bert offered Tom his hand, and they shook. "We'll be fine. We're gonna grab Lincoln, then maybe go see a play."

It was funny, but Tom didn't laugh. He felt uneasy all of a sudden.

"I don't know if splitting up is the smart thing."

"Why not?" Bert winked. "It always worked on Scooby-Doo."

"You just worry about your end, partner. Not that it'll be too hard guarding that body. She's a looker, that Joan."

"You think so?"

"Open your eyes, Tommy. If you're so preoccupied you can't see a beautiful woman right in front of you, it's time to reevaluate your life."

No kidding, Tom thought.

"Call when you get there, Roy."

They left the suite, leaving Tom alone.

Tom shut off the computer and closed his eyes, picturing Joan. Short blond hair. Blue eyes, small nose, full lips. Tom couldn't get a sense of her height, as she'd been sitting down, but she looked in shape and had filled out that blouse nicely.

Roy was right. She was attractive. Tom frowned. Now, in addition to keeping her alive, he also had to make sure he looked his best.

He checked his reflection in the bathroom mirror and winced. Stubble, baggy eyes, rumpled suit. A butter stain on his shirt from the breakfast bag on the flight in. The facial bruise from where Attila hit him was fading to an ugly yellow. Tom tried a smile on, and found some food stuck in his front teeth. How long had that been there?

"You're not living up to your potential," he told the mirror.

The mirror agreed. Tom decided to postpone his breakdown until later, and got back to work. He had formulated a quasi-plan to deal with Joan; follow her around and keep his eyes open. Since she would probably still be jumpy from the attack, the smart thing would be to inform her of his intention.

Tom fished out the business card he'd taken while visiting her office and dialed it.

"JDP, how may I help you?"

Tom tried to sound important. "Gimme Joan."

"May I ask who's calling."

"Mike Douglas."

"Just a moment, Mr. Douglas."

So far, so good.

"Mike? I haven't seen you since Cannes. How are you?"

"Actually, this is Tom Mankowski again. I figured you wouldn't take my call."

"You figured right."

"Please, just two seconds. I know you don't believe me. But you're still in danger."

"Thank you for your concern, Detective. But I've taken care of that."

"Call up the 29th Precinct in Chicago, talk to Lieutenant Daniels, or anyone else there. Ask them about me. I'm a good cop."

"I called Chicago. I was told you're on vacation. But yes, they did vouch for your character. I'm still not going for the Joan of Arc thing, though."

"That's fine. I don't blame you. I'm struggling with it myself. I just don't want you to freak out, because I'm going to be following you for a couple of days. Don't worry, I'll be discreet, stay out of your way. But Vlad is going to try again. Soon."

"That's hardly necessary. I just hired a personal bodyguard. He's one of the best in the business. Did security for the artist formerly known as Prince, who is known as Prince again."

"That's great. The more, the merrier. If you can just tell him I'll be hanging around, and ask him nicely not to shoot me. One more thing—your place is probably bugged. Maybe your office too. I don't know. Your security guy probably has a detector, have him check it out." Tom waited for a response. "Hello, are you there?"

"Bugged?"

He noted that she'd lost a bit of composure.

"That's what they did to my place, and to one of the guys they killed. It's been going on for a few months."

"A few months."

"Probably longer. We've been under surveillance for our entire lives. The guy who started this project is rich and powerful and has government backing. He's also a real nut job. Hey, for what it's worth, I didn't mean to come in and disrupt your life. Hopefully, it will all be over soon."

Joan hung up. Tom wondered if he could have told her about the bugs in a subtler way. It was a freaky thing to deal with. On a completely inappropriate note, Tom found that he enjoyed talking with Joan. Even if she thought he was crazy. Maybe if the circumstances were different . . .

If the circumstances were different, she wouldn't give him a second glance. She probably had a string of movie star boyfriends with perfect looks and tons of money.

Tom reverted back to acting like a professional. Hiring a bodyguard was an honest reaction on Joan's part, but he didn't believe it would do anything to deter the Unholy Trio. If someone really wants you dead, there are too many ways to get the job done. There wasn't much a rent-a-cop could do if Vlad flew a helicopter over Joan's house and dropped napalm on it, or sniped her from three hundred yards away, or put plastic explosives in her TV remote. The only way to be truly safe was to get the bad guys before they got you.

So that's how Tom decided to play it. First things first; he had to follow Joan around, get an idea of her schedule. He mentally began to check off all the things he'd need for a stakeout—food, water, a plastic jug, binoculars, sunscreen, a flashlight . . .

Tom went to the desk for a pad of paper and caught sight of himself in the dresser mirror. Maybe the very first thing he should do is shave. And do something about his wrinkled suit. He wrote down his list of items and added a new shirt. And some cologne.

Couldn't hurt.

CHAPTER 17

Los Angeles

This was worse than being attacked.

Joan watched as Rod removed another listening device, the third, from the electrical outlet in her bedroom.

"I think that's the last one." The bodyguard got up from one knee and eyed the bug in his palm.

"How long do you think they've been here?"

"Hard to tell. Could have been a while. To be honest, I've never seen a device this high-tech before. I've done a lot of corporate work, rival companies stealing secrets and such, but this is a different league."

Joan was sick. The thought that someone had been listening to her every word, her every private moment, was a violation unlike any she'd ever known.

"I know, it's a shock. These are some real bad people."

"I don't even want to live in this house anymore."

"A perfectly natural reaction. It will pass. Sometimes the truth is hard to take, but knowledge is power. We're on to them."

Joan didn't feel empowered. She felt helpless.

"Maybe I should call Tom. He's the one who told me to look."

"Bad idea. He showed up at the same time all the trouble started. He also knows the man who attacked you. It's likely he's involved."

"Then why would he tell me about the bugs?"

"To gain your trust. Believe me, I've seen it all in this line of work. Stay away from that one, he's bad news."

Joan glanced out the window, into her backyard. Earlier, she spotted Tom poking around through the woods behind her house. There was no sign of him now.

"So I can't trust anyone anymore? How am I supposed to run a business?"

"Someone is trying to kill you, Ms. DeVilliers. You can still go about your day to day life, with some slight modifications. As for trust, the only person you need to trust is me. That's the service you're paying for. I'm a professional."

No kidding. Joan had been with Rod for almost two hours now, and hadn't seen him smile once. She had no doubts he was formidable—the man was tall, muscular, proficient in six different martial arts, a weapons expert, a former Green Beret, extremely expensive, and serious as cancer. But his presence felt more like an invasion than a relief.

"Your intruder bypassed the alarm panel by manually disarming the system. He probably hid somewhere in the backyard and got the code by watching you through the window. That was a bad place to put the keypad. The new system will be much harder to beat."

Joan heard a beep. Her pager, in her purse on the kitchen counter. It was Marty—his home number, followed by 911. She picked up her phone and found it still wasn't working.

"Can I borrow your phone? Mine's in the car."

"Sorry, I have to keep it free for emergencies."

A glance at his face showed Joan he wasn't kidding. Irritated, she went into the garage and got her cell phone.

"Marty, it's Joan."

"Joan? Is that you?"

Marty was breathy, seemed out of it.

"You sound terrible."

"You remember, I had a checkup last week?"

"You did? What's wrong?"

"I got the results. Joan, it's bad." Marty started to cry.

"What is it, Marty? Cancer? HIV?"

"Can you come over?"

"I'll be right there."

Joan ended the call and wanted to scream at the universe. Marty was more than her longtime assistant—he was her best friend. She couldn't bear to have anything happen to him.

"Marty just called." Joan grabbed her purse. "I'm going over to his place."

"I'll come with."

"I'd rather go alone."

"Joan, I can't protect you if you fight me. If this is

going to work, you have to be able to follow orders. When I say duck, you duck without question. Whenever you go out in public, either I or one of my people have to be with you. That's just the way it is."

"Fine." Joan turned on her heels and went back into the garage. If Rod insisted on driving, she would fire him on the spot. But he slipped into the passenger seat without a word.

Joan drove too fast. Part of it was urgency, but it was also an effort to make Rod uncomfortable. It didn't work. Even when she blew a red light, he didn't so much as blink.

She wasn't sure exactly when it happened, but sometime in the past couple of minutes the bodyguard had become the enemy. Joan resented his lectures, his lack of emotion, and most of all his very presence. Now, with Marty in trouble, she felt as if he were mocking her with his stoicism. The big, strong man was here to save the poor, emotional little girl.

Joan parked in Marty's lot, slipping the Jaguar in between a Mercedes and a Beemer. Nice neighborhood, great apartment, famous friends, lots of money—both Joan and Marty were just as wrapped up in Hollywood culture as everyone else living here. But none of it ultimately mattered, did it? So many things were more important. She killed the engine.

"I'd like to be alone with my friend."

"I'll wait outside after I check the place out."

Joan kept her composure. "Can't you just stay here?"

"It's natural to resent me. I'm an intrusion in your life, and the very fact that I'm here reminds you that you're in trouble. If it's any consolation, you've taken it much better than most people. After what happened to you, I'm surprised you even had the courage to leave the house."

"Because I'm a woman?"

"Because you're a human being who was almost killed, twice. I've had years of training, and it's never easy having your life threatened. Remember, you didn't hire me because you're weak. You hired me because you're a fighter."

Joan's resentment toward the man eased a tad.

"Fine. If you could just give us some privacy, after you do your thing."

"Of course."

Marty's apartment building was new, but the architect had gone for that retro 50s look—lots of red brick and right angles. They walked to the security door and Joan pressed the button next to Marty's name on the intercom. He buzzed them in without a word.

The lobby was large, carpeted, home to several floor plants and framed prints of flowers. To the right was the rental office, closed at this hour. To the left were the door to the stairs and the hallway to the first floor apartments. Directly before them was the elevator.

Rod's eyes were scanning in so many directions that Joan was surprised he could walk a straight line. They took the elevator to the fifth floor, and Rod stepped out into the hall and checked both ways before letting her out.

"I'll go in first."

Joan wondered if he was also going to taste her food before she did, to check for poison. They walked to

Marty's door and she knocked. No answer. Another knock, more urgent.

"Marty? Are you okay?"

Rod checked the knob. It turned. He pushed Joan aside and reached into his jacket. A gun came out, black and ugly.

"You're going to give him a heart attack."

"Stay here."

"This is insane. He's probably in the bathroom."

Rod opened the door and went in quick, his pistol held alongside his leg. Joan watched from the doorway, her annoyance level rising, as he commandoed his way into the kitchen.

"I'm sure that . . ."

"It's a trap. He's dead." Rod looked from the floor to Joan. "Run."

The movement was so fast Joan couldn't be sure what she saw. At first, Rod was standing there checking behind the counter. Then there was a blur and he was toppling over, his head coming off his shoulders and rolling in the opposite direction.

Joan backpedaled, her mind unable to grasp what she just saw. A man stood over Rod's body and then glanced up at her. Short, muscular, and holding a long, thin sword. He grinned, exposing a single gold tooth.

Movement to her right. Another man, coming down the hallway. Dressed all in black, down to those leather gloves.

"Hello again, Joan." Vlad's voice was nasally. A large white bandage covered the bridge of his nose, and both of his eyes were bruised black. He had a gun leveled at her midsection. "No more fancy footwork this time."

Joan couldn't have imagined a worse scenario, even if she'd been paid to dream one up.

Both Vlad and the other man, the one from the picture that Tom had shown her, advanced. If they hadn't killed her yet, it could only mean they planned on taking her alive.

There was no way Joan would allow that.

She turned and ran down the hallway, to the elevator, and smacked the call button.

"I should shoot you," Vlad called after her, "but Attila and I have something else planned. A little ménage-à-trois."

Attila joined Vlad in the hall, slipping his sword into a sheath beneath his trench coat. They were a few yards away, and the elevator was still on the first floor.

It wasn't going to arrive in time.

Joan considered screaming for help, but any poor sap who opened their door would undoubtedly die for their bravery. Besides, it was her fight.

Joan dropped her purse. Then she unbuttoned her blazer and let it fall to the floor, ignoring the hooting and catcalls that followed. She was grateful for her decision to wear flats.

In an open space, she might have been able to put up a decent fight, even against two. But the hallway was narrow and left little room for maneuvering. Her only chance, and it was slight, was to make it to the staircase. That was behind them, on the other end of the hall.

She drew herself inward, sucking in a deep, calming breath, and focused on her strike points. Vlad was going to get another pop in the nose, and the man called

Attila was favoring his right leg, making the left her target.

Joan widened her stance and stood still while they approached. Her posture didn't seem to be what either of them was expecting, and Vlad lost his grin. They stopped within a few feet of her.

"If you make even the smallest move . . ."

Joan brought up her right foot, aiming for the bandage. Vlad flinched, but his howl told her she'd found her mark. The other, Attila, had whirled to the right and grabbed her hair. He yanked her so hard she almost lost her footing.

Joan fought to regain her balance and lashed out with the back of her left hand, going for his thigh. It was like striking a board, but his reaction was instantaneous. He grunted and released her head, both hands reaching for his leg.

Joan dodged past Vlad and sprinted down the hall with the duo two steps behind her. She wouldn't make it to the stairs. But Marty's door was still open. She flew into his apartment and got her weight behind the door. Someone's hand, Attila's, reached in as she was slamming it. Joan pinned his wrist, but she didn't have the strength or the leverage. They pushed their way in.

She turned and ran for the kitchen. Rod's body had fallen behind the breakfast bar, the gun still gripped in his hand. Joan dove for it and pried his fingers off.

A flash to her left. Attila, drawing his samurai sword. Joan brought the gun around.

The first shot went high, burying itself into the ceiling. The gun almost bucked out of her hands. Joan lowered her aim, tightened her grip.

Attila and Vlad were out the door.

She held her breath, trying to keep the gun steady. Had they gone, or were they still out in the hallway?

Wetness, seeping into her skirt. Rod's blood. She didn't dare to look. With her eyes and gun trained on the doorway, Joan got up from the floor and slowly walked into the kitchen, heading for the phone to call for help. Her foot touched something, and she briefly glanced down. Marty, his tortured eyes wide open and still teary, a large wooden stick shoved into his . . .

Joan looked away, a sob escaping her. The phone was no longer an option. She was going to end this, now. Both hands on the gun, walking carefully to avoid slipping in the blood, she moved towards the door.

Gunshots in the hallway. Joan ducked automatically, sliding on her knees behind the sofa. She heard yelling, and another shot. Joan peeked her head over the armrest, aiming at the doorway, seeing a man look into the apartment.

"Ms. DeVilliers?"

She fired, the bullet smacking into the doorjamb, throwing up a spray of splinters. The man shielded his face with his arm.

"It's me! Tom!"

The cop. Joan stood up from behind the sofa.

"Are you okay?" She walked over to him on shaky legs.

"Yeah. You?"

"Yes."

"You're bleeding."

"Not my blood." Joan's lip quivered. She fought to keep it together.

"Stay here. Call the police. I'm going after them."

Tom turned but Joan grabbed his arm. "I'm coming."

He stared at her, the same intense look he'd given in her office.

"Okay. Come on—they took the stairs."

Tom went off in a trot, his gun held at a downward angle away from his body. Joan held her gun likewise and followed.

"Have you fired a gun before?" He was talking over his shoulder, keeping the pace.

"No."

"Don't jerk the trigger. Squeeze it, like you're curling a barbell with your finger. Line up the back sight with the front sight and aim for the chest. Keep both eyes open, and lean into it slightly. It'll kick back."

"I noticed."

"Was it just the two?"

"That's all I saw."

Tom reached the door for the stairs and put his back against the wall alongside it.

"You open, I go in. On three. One . . . two . . . three."

Joan yanked open the door and Tom went in, low. He aimed left, right, and up in quick succession. Then he eased his arm over the railing and pointed his gun down the stairwell.

"They're about two floors below us," Tom whispered. "Stay quiet, move along the wall."

Tom kicked off his shoes and began to descend, moving fast. Joan did the same. The stairs were cool under her feet. Echoing up from the lower floors were footsteps. Attila and Vlad. They didn't seem to be hurrying.

"They're not expecting us to follow." Tom's voice was low, breathy. "Do they both have guns?"

"Just Vlad, I think."

The footsteps stopped, and Joan could hear a door open one flight down. Tom and Joan sprinted down the remaining stairs, stopping on the ground floor.

"Same as before, but quiet. One . . . two . . . three." Joan eased the door open and Tom went through fast.

Attila and Vlad had their backs to them, heading for the front door. But they weren't the only ones in the lobby. There were also a young woman with a baby stroller, and two kids waiting for the elevator. Tom spun back around, jamming his gun in his jacket.

"Shoot them," Joan said. "They're getting away."

"Too many civilians."

Joan tried to push past, bringing up her gun. Tom held her back.

"You start shooting, innocent people will die."

Joan clenched her jaw, but the tears came anyway. "They killed Marty."

"We'll have another chance."

"Can't we follow them outside?"

"You're covered in blood and we don't have shoes. How far do you think we'd get?"

She stared up at Tom, hate filling her entire being. "So we just let them go?"

"Sorry. Sometimes you have to."

Her body shook, and then the sobbing started. Joan felt deflated, as if someone had poked her with a pin and all of her strength had seeped out. She cried, and cried, and couldn't get herself to stop. She barely noticed when Tom took the gun out of her hand.

But she did notice when he put a hand on her shoulder, and then both arms around her. They swayed slowly back and forth, Tom patting her back, and she let all of the pain from the last two days come out in muffled sobs against his chest.

It didn't take long for Joan to regain control. She pushed out of Tom's arms, angry, embarrassed, refusing to look at him.

"The police are probably on their way. I have to go."

"I thought you were a cop."

"This gun is unlicensed. I get caught with it, I get fired or worse. If you wouldn't mind leaving me out of your deposition . . ."

She met his eyes, challenging. "The police—they can't help me, can they?"

"I caught Attila two days ago in New Mexico. They just let him go. The guy behind all of this has friends in high places."

"So what am I supposed to do? Just wait around until they come after me again?"

"I don't know. Leave the country, maybe? Take a long vacation, don't tell anyone where you're going. Pay cash, don't use credit cards. Keep a low profile . . ."

"I don't run away from confrontation."

"Look, Ms. DeVilliers, I don't have all the answers. I'm kind of floundering here myself."

"But you're going to get these guys."

"That's my intention. Yes."

Joan made her decision. It was more than a question of getting her life back. It was for Marty.

"I want to help."

Tom didn't hesitate. "The only way to flush them out is to set ourselves up as bait."

"It doesn't matter. I'm in."

"Okay. Then we need to get out of here without being seen." Tom put a gun in each of his pants pockets, then took off his jacket and draped it over Joan's shoulders. "That covers most of the blood. Let's just walk out, acting natural."

"Your holster."

Tom glanced at his shoulder rig, no longer hidden. He unstrapped it and tucked it under his arm.

"We'll take my car. I parked around back. I'm walking behind you to shield the blood on your skirt. Ready?"

Joan wiped away some stray tears and nodded. Tom opened the door and they walked out into the lobby, no one giving them a second look. They exited the building just as two squad cars pulled up, lights flashing.

"Don't act guilty," Tom said under his breath. "Act curious."

Joan was way ahead of him. "What's going on, Officer?"

"Please keep moving, ma'am."

They stood and watched for a moment as the police rushed into the apartment building, then Tom steered her around the corner and over to a green sedan parked in front of a fire hydrant.

"What happened to your two friends?"

"They went to Nebraska to warn one of the other clones. Lincoln."

Again with the clone thing. Joan got into the passenger seat and thought about it.

"So you really believe you're Thomas Jefferson?"

"Unfortunately, that's what it looks like."

"And those guys that just attacked me?"

"Vlad the Impaler and Attila the Hun."

Vlad had called the short man Attila.

"And that guy who looked like Einstein was really Einstein?"

Tom started the car. "As unbelievable as it all seems."

He let two more squad cars rocket past, and then pulled into traffic.

"So, have you found all the clones yet?"

"We're still looking for the last one."

"Is he number 4? Named William Masterton?"

Tom looked at her. "How did you know?"

"Marty knew him. He works in Santa Monica."

"Have you actually talked to him? Lately?"

"I called his company today, to see if he still works there. He does."

"How far away is Santa Monica?"

"Maybe twenty miles."

"Okay. You need to get changed first. And shoes would probably be a good idea."

"Do you remember how to get to my place?"

Tom made a U-turn, forcing a car on the other side of the street to slam on its brakes.

"So," Joan still wasn't buying this cloning angle, but she found herself willing to play along. "Who is this Masterton guy supposed to be, anyway?"

"William Shakespeare."

"This should be interesting."

"More like frustrating. We have to convince a total stranger that he's a clone of a famous historical figure, and you don't even believe it yourself."

"I'm trying to get used to the idea."

"Join the club."

She closed her eyes, picturing Jefferson's profile on a nickel. After getting a good mental image, she looked at Tom. There was a pretty good resemblance.

She also noted that he'd shaved since their earlier meeting in her office, and though he wore the same suit it wasn't nearly as wrinkled. Had the effort been for her? Joan wondered how she must look. She resisted the urge to check the vanity mirror. Nothing could be done about it anyway—she'd left her purse in the hallway. Marty's hallway.

Marty.

Before the grief could build, Joan pushed past it. While much of her wanted to wallow deep into the self-pity pool, it wouldn't help the task at hand. She could deal with all of that emotion at a later, more private time.

"Maybe if you filled me in on the whole story, I'd be more likely to believe it."

"It'll take a while."

"I'm a captive audience."

"I also have to warn you. If you do start to believe that it's true, that you're really Joan of Arc, it can really play hell with your psyche."

"My psyche could use a little shaking up."

"I'm serious, Ms. DeVilliers."

"Don't worry about me. I'm probably the most stable personality in LA. And call me Joan."

"Okay, Joan." Tom glanced at her and flashed a brief smile. "Here's how this whole mess started . . ."

CHAPTER 18

Washington, DC

"Your conference call is ready on your private line, Mr. Speaker."

"Thank you, Trixie. Hold my other calls."

Phillip Stang Jr. pushed aside the speech he'd been reading and reached across his expansive desk to tap the *speaker* button. His father had warned him that even with a secure line, using the speaker phone was a bad idea. But Dad was always overly cautious. A symptom of living through the Cold War.

"Dad? How are you feeling?"

"Tired, Junior. This doesn't get any easier as time goes on. At your age, I could transplant both kidneys at once and then go and play eighteen holes. These days, one is my endurance limit."

Phil could detect the drugs behind his father's voice, but the old man wasn't allowing them to muddle his thoughts. Good to know, for future reference.

"Is everyone else on the line?"

Attila said, "Yes."

Vlad said, "Yes."

Jack said, *"Is everyone else on the line? Yes."*

Stang sighed at Jack's response. Of all the infamous killers to ever walk the planet, they had to clone one with an annoying speech impediment.

"Updates, gentlemen. What have you got for me in the way of clearing obstacles?"

"Both Joan and Tom are in LA."

"Together?"

"Yes."

"There's one for the history books. Am I to assume that your third attempt failed as well?"

"We hadn't expected them to be together. He was armed."

"A cop with a gun. Go figure. Why is it, Vlad, that your genetic predecessor was able to kill upwards of one hundred thousand people, and you can't stick a knife in some bitch without fucking it up?"

Vlad paused before answering. Phil could imagine his teeth clenched in rage at the insult. Of the three, Vlad scared Phil the most. Jack was a psycho, Attila was a thug, but Vlad was evil distilled. That's why he only messed with him over the phone—you can't get burned if you play with fire long distance.

"It won't happen again."

"That's what I want to hear. Attila, hold his hand if you need to. We have a schedule here to keep, gentlemen. These loose ends should have been tied up days ago. How are things on your end, Jack?"

"How are things on your end, Jack? Fine. I should finish up later tonight. Albert is coming to Nebraska to visit Abe. I can get both at once."

"I like to hear this. Enough with the fooling around.

I know you guys love that torture shit, but save it for when we have more time. The keyword here *is fast.* I'll consider the topic closed, unless you want to add anything, Dad?"

"If it isn't done by tonight, it waits until after Sunrise. That's our main objective."

Phil nodded along with his father's words.

"Exactly. Are we all clear on that? Project Sunrise is the brass ring, here. I don't care if you've got one of the clones in your sights and are squeezing the trigger. You drop what you're doing and get on your planes by ten tonight. Have you all had a chance to practice with the equipment? You can handle the assembly? Yes?"

He'd tagged on the last word so Jack didn't have to repeat the entire previous sentence, the dumb bastard. All responded positively.

"Good. It's already been shipped to your destinations, along with your passes and make-up kits. I want your arrival confirmations tomorrow by eight AM. We're going to show the whole world that the best of the best are made, not born. This is history, gentlemen. I'm proud that you're all a part of it. Dad?"

"I do have something to add. We're doing more than altering history. We're creating a brave, new world. Immortality is within our grasp. We will not be denied!"

Phil grinned. While he shared so many of his father's traits, he lacked his way with words. The old man was eloquent, that's for sure.

"Get to it, gentlemen."

Phil hit the disconnect button and leaned back in his leather chair. He swiveled and checked out the view. It was raining, cloudy. The Washington Monument stood out, cutting through the weather like a giant exclamation point.

One day I'll have my own monument, Phil thought. And unlike all those other past suckers, this one would be built while I'm still alive. Maybe an image on a coin as well. Why revere the dead, when they can't reap the benefits?

"Mr. Speaker, your father on line one."

Oh, shit. He'd hung up on the old man.

"Dad? Sorry. Got disconnected. If I wasn't banging that useless secretary, her ass would be out."

"I suppose vulgarity is inexorably intertwined with your generation, but you need to show me some respect."

"Of course."

"I just watched your speech to the Oversight Subcommittee on National Affairs, International Affairs, and Criminal Justice. Taped it off of C-SPAN."

"And?"

"You looked fat. What have I told you about keeping that body fit?"

"My schedule has been killer, Dad. I haven't had time to hit the gym."

"Bullshit." The irritation in his father's voice was pronounced. "Spare me the busy crap. Cut out the four course lunches and get into shape. We're going to make the cover of *Time* magazine. You'd have us look like a bullfrog."

Phil took a deep breath before answering. "Government has changed since you've been in office, Dad. It's all about lunches."

"So eat a goddamn salad. This isn't a game, Junior.

This is my dream. Our dream. Almost forty years in the making."

"Why don't you give me a little credit, here? I've worked my ass off as much as you have. I'm the youngest Speaker ever elected to the House—"

"Don't forget how that happened, dear Phillip. Millions of dollars. My dollars. Sixty percent of Congress financed their campaigns on my money."

"It was more than that, Dad. As Chairman of the Steering Committee on Bipartisan Relations, I've been able to unite Republicans and Democrats on key issues like tax reforms, education—"

His father snorted. "Spare me. That simpering, middle of the road attitude is about to change. This country doesn't need a social lubricant in office. It needs a strong, determined leader. One who stands by his ideals, without bowing to special interests. Or to voters, for that matter. The President spends so much time trying to be popular, he forgot how to run the country. Other nations laugh at us, Junior."

"I know, Dad." He'd heard the speech, many times. Hopefully, he wouldn't get started on the Chinese.

"That's the whole point. To make being an American a source of pride once again. We're the protector of the free world. During the Cold War, we were feared. Now, every little camel jockey with an oil rig thinks they can flip us the bird without repercussion. Not to mention the biggest threat to humanity ever to exist, the Communist Chinese—"

"Dad, you're preaching to the converted, here."

"We can never lose sight of it, Junior. Even with an unlimited supply of kidneys, neither of us will live forever. But our legacy can."

"*I* said that. 'We cannot live forever, but our legacy as Americans—'"

"Kudos to your speech writer, Junior. Speaking of which, have you got the speech for Thursday?"

"I have it right in front of me." Phil picked up the packet and flipped back to the first page. "*It is in the times of greatest tragedy that we ourselves must also be great . . .*"

"I'd prefer to hear it live."

"It's a good speech. Nice mix of outrage and strength."

"For what we've paid, it should be."

"There's even a spot in it where I get a little choked up."

"What? Cut that."

"Why? It's a great line. 'I stand here humbled at our loss. But no matter the blows this country takes, we will not be reduced to a nation in mourning . . .'"

"You're not going to be humbled. Cut the line."

"But the people love—"

"This isn't about the people. The popularity contest is over. We're not out for approval ratings, Junior. Cut out any line that even hints at weakness. I also want you to lose the double chin in the next two days."

"That's impossible. Even if I starved myself . . ."

"Good idea."

Phil bit back his reply. He didn't kowtow to the old man, but he knew to pick his battles.

"Consider the double chin gone."

"Excellent. I'm tired now, but we'll talk soon."

"Get some rest, Dad."

Phil hung up and hit the intercom button.

"Trixie, who am I having dinner with tonight?"

"Those execs from Phillip Morris."

"Send them a rain check. Then see if the commissary is still open and find me a chef's salad. Chicken, no dressing."

"Yes, Mr. Speaker."

Phil picked up a pencil and began to go through the speech, trimming any signs of weakness.

America had been asleep too long, he thought. *It was about to get a serious wake-up call.*

CHAPTER 19

Los Angeles

"**A**nd then I followed you to your assistant's place, and you know the rest."

Joan couldn't get her mind completely around it. Tom had told the story in a truthful, straightforward manner. He obviously believed it, and it did sort of explain their current situation.

But Thomas Jefferson and Joan of Arc?

"This is a lot to swallow."

The evening had gotten cooler, so Joan rolled up her window. She cursed herself for not grabbing a jacket when they'd stopped at her house—she'd assumed jeans and a sweater were enough. Santa Monica was built on the coast, and the cool ocean breeze could get downright bitter.

"I'm not doubting your sincerity, but the story is so *out there*. I was cloned from the jawbone of a woman born six hundred years ago?"

"Well, technically, you're an exact genetic copy rather than a clone."

"Oh. That makes it a lot easier to buy."

Tom sighed and drummed his fingers on the steering wheel. Joan could sense his frustration, but there wasn't much she could do. Even after hearing the long explanation, she couldn't fully believe she was Joan of Arc. Tom was sincere as pie, but all delusional people were sincere.

"The writing thing did it for me—having my writing be identical to Jefferson's. I read somewhere that even if you try to disguise your handwriting, such as write with your opposite hand, the experts can still tell it's you. It's a mental thing. I wish there was some way to prove it to you."

"Well, sometimes I do hear the voice of St. Michael."

Tom gave her a sideways glance, and then smiled.

"That's a start. Do you like the French?"

"Doesn't everyone?"

"How do you like your steak? Burned?"

"Ouch. A *burned at the stake* pun. You just lost points."

Tom raised his eyebrows. "Really? I had points?"

It was creeping up on dusk, the road becoming harder to see. Tom flipped on the headlights, then passed the car ahead of him even though it was a no passing zone. He was even more aggressive behind the wheel than she was. Joan didn't know if this was a good thing or a bad thing.

"You know what's funny? That Joan of Arc movie came out a few years ago, and I turned down the script. I didn't like the character."

Tom laughed. "If it makes a difference, I like the character."

"The plucky Hollywood producer, drawn into a web of conspiracy that tops her own movies?"

"I think I'd call you spunky rather than plucky."

"Great. I'll pitch it to Reese Witherspoon. Go east on Wilshire. We're looking for 12th Street."

Tom hung a left, and they were confronted by a stop light. The streets were filled with people—walking, biking, blading, jogging, touristing. The affluence of the surrounding shops and buildings was reflected by the populace in their clothing, their attitude. Tom and Joan stared at a mime on the street corner, dressed in a hip tuxedo.

"Is that mime wearing Armani?"

Joan snorted. "Last year's."

The light changed and Tom hit the gas.

"I'm beginning to think California is one big resort."

"People come to LA for two reasons—to be a part of it or to get away from it."

"Why did you come?"

"To get away."

"From?"

"Hiko, Nevada. I had a real apple pie upbringing. Nice neighborhood, caring parents, perfect childhood."

"It sounds terrible."

Joan laughed. "It was nice. But without challenge. A little conflict can be a good thing. So I moved out of Mayberry and came to Hollywood."

"So you didn't arrive with dreams of making it big?"

"Hell no. I arrived with dreams of poverty, struggle, and heartache. I wanted to test myself, see if I could survive. I was twenty-one. Got a job waiting tables, had a roommate who sold pot, spent a year throwing up in trendy clubs."

"Living your dream."

"Exactly."

"When did you go from outsider to insider?"

"No one in this town does what they want. The businessmen want to write, the strippers want to act, writers and actors want to direct, the shop owners want to produce and the waiters want to be Kevin Smith. I worked with a few of those waiters. They needed money to make an independent film, I was pretty good with people, so I was able to get the money together. That's all a producer does, basically."

"The movie was a hit?"

"Hell no. Garbage. Didn't even get festival play. But it sold well on video, we made some money, brought in better talent. Next thing I knew, I was a hotshot producer, making big bank, hobnobbing with Tom Cruise."

"How is Tom Cruise in real life?"

"Short. He comes up to here." Joan put her hand next to her neck.

Tom laughed. He had a good laugh, deep and genuine. Without doing it intentionally, Joan went through her dating rules. Tom wasn't in the business, and though he was attractive in a rough sort of way, he certainly wasn't a pretty boy. Fair skinned meant no back hair, and she could tell he wasn't the Speedo type. Joan would bet her business he wore boxers, and the only tight fitting thing in his wardrobe were his socks.

"Here's 12th street. Which way?"

"North, I think."

"These are some nice houses. The copy writing business must be paying well."

No kidding. Joan had priced the area before buying in Beverly Hills. Some parts of the neighborhood were out of her range.

As they drove, the homes became less impressive, and soon enough they were in the half a million dollar area.

"It should be the next one on this side."

Tom pulled into a short driveway and parked next to a small, freestanding garage. A gas lamp illuminated the front lawn, and a porch light was on.

"Should I bring the gun?" Joan went to open the glove compartment.

"I've got mine. That should be enough."

They got out of the car and rang the bell.

The first thing that struck Joan about the man who answered the door was his hair. It had receded back to the crown of his head, a classic example of male pattern baldness. But sprouting out of his scalp, lined up like rows of black corn, were the worst hair plugs she'd ever seen. It looked like someone had punched yak hair into his forehead with a fork.

The second thing she noticed was that he bore an uncanny resemblance to Shakespeare—too much to have been coincidence. All he needed was one of those silly puffy collars.

"What?" The man had a squeaky voice, and his expression was a picture of extreme irritation.

"Bill Masterton?"

"It's my house. Who did you expect?"

"I'm Detective Tom Mankowski, this is Joan DeVilliers. We need to talk to you."

Bill's eyes got big. "The police?"

"May we come in?"

"I'm calling my lawyer."

Bill tried to slam the door but was unsuccessful. Tom's foot had gotten in the way. Joan looked down and saw that there was still a tag on the shoes. After stopping at her house they'd hit a K-Mart, as Tom didn't have a second pair with him.

"What the hell are you doing?" Bill shoved at the door.

Tom glanced both ways in a casual manner, then pushed his way in.

"We don't have time to screw around here, Bill. You're in some serious danger."

"I want you to go. Now."

"We will, after you've heard our story. Please. This is life or death."

Bill scrunched his eyebrows and chewed his lip. In the foyer light, Joan could tell that the plugs were slightly darker than the rest of his hair. Whoever did that to him should be sued, and sued hard.

"Okay, but make it fast. I have some stuff to do."

"Can we sit down somewhere?"

Bill led them to the living room, which was like stepping into a billboard. Everything had a corporate logo on it. Nike lamps and Coke clocks and Bud Light chairs and a Camel card table and a big white couch that had McDonalds on the seat cushions. Plastered over every wall were ads, posters, banners, mockups, and packaging from hundreds of different products. Joan felt as if she were at a flea market.

Bill shrugged. "I get a lot of free stuff."

Joan and Tom took the sofa. It seemed to be made of some kind of plastic.

"You're in advertising, right?"

"I'm a writer. Mostly catch-lines. You know, like *You deserve a break today, at McDonalds*."

"You wrote that?"

"No. But I'm working on something for the Trojan people right now. Booming industry, condoms. Lots of new markets opening up. I've got a great new tag." Bill held up his hands, as if the words were appearing in the air in front of him. "*The way to a man's heart . . . is through his fly. Trojans*. Good, huh?"

"Makes me want to run out and buy a pack."

"So, what's this life and death thing?" Bill asked.

Tom laid out the bare bones of the story in the same way he'd done in the car. Rather than be incredulous, or even interested, Bill spent most of the explanation fidgeting and looking at the clock.

"Here." Tom opened up his black binder and handed Bill a pad of paper and a pen. "Write a few sentences."

"Because it's supposed to match Shakespeare's writing?"

"It will. It sounds crazy, but you'll see."

"I think I'll get some coffee first. Either of you for coffee?"

"Uh, sure. I'll take a cup."

Bill got off the chair and left the living room. Tom turned to Joan.

"Was he following anything I said?"

"It didn't seem like it. To be honest, I don't like him much."

"That's because he's a creep. But he sure looks like Shakespeare."

"Exactly. Except for those hair plugs."

"Is that what they are? I thought he stapled a porcupine to his forehead."

Joan put her hand over her mouth while she laughed. "Isn't it bad? The color doesn't even match."

"Maybe he did it himself. Do they sell kits?"

Joan got an image of the unpleasant little man sitting in front of a mirror, stapling hair into his own head. She laughed so hard she snorted.

"I assume you have a gun, Tom. Take it out and put it on the floor."

Joan's laughter died in her throat. Bill had come back into the room. Instead of coffee, he was holding a nickel plated revolver. It was pointed in her face. She cast a frantic look at Tom, who seemed just as surprised as she did.

"I said take it out." Bill walked behind Joan and pressed the gun to her head. The experience was humbling. Her entire world became a small spot just above the nape of her neck, cold and hard. She could almost *feel* the direction the bullet would take, traveling up through her skull, exiting above her right ear.

Tom reached into his jacket and took out his gun, holding it by the butt. He placed it on the floor.

"You're in on it." Tom's voice was even.

"No shit. You sure you're not the Einstein clone? Now stand up, slowly. We're all going into the kitchen."

"What's the reason?" Tom asked. "Money?"

"You idiot. Of course it's not the money. The money is awesome, sure, but it's more than that. Now move."

Bill held Joan back while Tom walked a few steps ahead. His free hand was around her neck, cupped under her chin. The fact that every thought in her head might be her last made her knees knock. It was worse than being attacked, worse than finding the bugs in her house, it was even worse than getting shot at.

"Those people are horrible." Joan tried to keep the quaver out of her voice. "Why would you want to be on their side?"

"You have no idea what's happening here. What they're going to do. I'm going to be a very important, very powerful man."

Tom stopped walking forward and turned around slowly.

"How did you find out you were a clone?"

"Stang came to me. I was having some legal trouble. They said I took some money from my company. He helped me out, told me who I really was. He recognized my talent."

"Your talent?"

"My writing talent. I'm Shakespeare! And I'm stuck doing crap ad copy! That's like using a hurricane to blow out a match!"

The gun shook against Joan's head. She closed her eyes and willed it to stop.

"So he kept you out of jail, and now you're his little suck boy."

Bill took the gun off Joan and pointed it at Tom. The relief on Tom's face told her that had been his intention.

Brave bastard, that Tom. But was anyone in history braver than Joan of Arc? She found her voice, and when it came out it was strong and true.

"Don't blame him, Tom. Look at that hair. He couldn't have had a lot of love in his life. Not without paying for it, anyway."

Bill jammed the gun back in Joan's temple, hitting her so hard she saw stars.

"You want to say that again?"

"I'll say it. You pay for sex, Bill, because your head looks like a Chia Pet."

The revolver went back to Tom, and then Bill began to laugh.

"Good try, guys. Get me all upset. But I'm not the big loser in this room. You're Thomas Jefferson. She's Joan of Arc. You should be ruling this country. But instead you're a dumb cop and this one here makes stupid movies. I for one plan on fulfilling my destiny."

"By killing us."

"You make an omelet, gotta break some eggs. Now move it, open that door."

Tom didn't move. Joan could see he was getting ready to try something. She shifted slightly, so she could grab Bill's arm and toss him over her hip.

When the gun went off, she yelped in surprise.

Tom had crouched down, hands protecting his head. The shot had gone into the ceiling.

"Next one doesn't miss. Open the damn cellar door."

Tom righted himself and complied.

"Empty your pockets."

Tom removed his wallet, cell phone, and keys.

"Toss them on the table, then go down the stairs."

The staircase was wooden, dark. Tom took three steps down and turned. "Have you ever killed a man, Bill? Had another person's death on your hands?"

"I get the reference, and I won't have a problem washing the blood off."

He shoved Joan roughly through the doorway. She yelped, pitching head first down the stairs, but Tom caught her and held her steady.

"Besides," Bill said, "I'm not the hands-on type. I'll give Attila and Vlad a call. They have a lot more fun with this type of thing."

Joan stared up at him. "You should send them after the guy who gave you those hair plugs."

Bill sneered. "Sticks and stones." Then he slammed the door, engulfing them in darkness.

Tom's hand found her shoulder. "Are you okay?"

She was shaking, but she managed to answer. "I'm okay. Check the door."

Joan heard creaking, a grunt. "Locked. Solid, too. The door is heavy. Stand back." There was a loud thump. Then another. "I think I broke my heel."

"We have to get out of here. Do you have any matches? A lighter?"

"No."

Joan led the way down the stairs, proceeding cautiously in the pitch black. It was cool and damp, and she got the impression of a small space rather than a big one. Her hands brushed something stringy and dry. A spiderweb. She wiped it off on her blouse.

Reaching the floor, Joan inched forward, hands out in front of her, groping blindly for a wall. She hit one almost immediately. Her fingers felt wood, old and dusty, half moon cuts.

"It's a wine cellar."

"Try to find windows."

She continued to feel her way around the small room. In was not only devoid of windows, but wine as well. Joan felt behind the wooden racks and touched cold concrete.

"This is just the perfect way to end a perfect day."

"I'm sorry I brought you here."

"You're kidding. This was my fault. I'm the one who found Shakespeare."

"You believe he's really Shakespeare?"

"At this point, why not? And you want to know something? I always hated Shakespeare."

"Me too."

His words echoes in the small enclosure, and then faded. Joan shivered. Fear mounted with every passing second, as if the darkness were suffocating her.

Keep a clear head, she told herself. *Stay focused. Find your center. If you're going to go down, go down swinging.*

Joan broke the silence. "We should have rushed him."

"I saw the guy's eyes. He would have shot us."

"Isn't that a lot better than what's going to happen when Attila and Vlad show up?"

"You're right. I could have done something."

"I could have done something too. I could have flipped him. It was a simple move any yellow belt could have executed."

"You had a gun to your head."

"And it scared me. Next time I won't be scared."

"If this was one of your movies, how would we get out?"

"I would have written the scene so one of us has a weapon, or a hairpin to pick the lock, or we find a closet and there's a back hoe in it."

"Maybe we can pull down some of these old racks, make a weapon."

"It's a start. What's the chance of your friends somehow finding us?"

"Nil. I spoke to Roy when his plane got in, but

haven't checked with him since. He doesn't even know about Shakespeare. Maybe they can figure it out later and avenge our deaths."

"That would work cinematically. Doesn't help us much, though."

Tom got up. Joan listened to him shake the wine rack.

"Well built. But let's give it a shot."

Joan stood next to him and they both grabbed a corner support. On three they tugged, Joan putting her back into it, straining and groaning. The support creaked and abruptly gave way, the two of them falling onto their bottoms.

Joan weighed the little piece of wood in her hand. It was useless as a weapon. She sat with her back against the wall and hugged her knees, despair swallowing her up. *We're going to die,* she thought. The feeling multiplied within her, getting bigger and bigger, until she found herself gasping.

Tom bumped into her, touched her head, and then sat beside her. He put an arm around her shoulders, and then hugged her tighter when she began to tremble. The first really nice guy she met in California, and he wasn't even from California. Joan thought about home. Not her house in Beverly Hills, but the small town she grew up in. Joan had left to get away from the wholesomeness, but now she missed it so much she ached.

For some reason, Tom reminded her of home. She pressed against him, resting her head against his neck. After a minute or two, she was able to get her breathing under control.

"I just had a pessimistic thought," Tom said.

"Share it. Brighten my spirits even more."

"Well, neither of us expected Shakespeare to be one of the bad guys, right?"

"I was as shocked as the next girl."

"So, Roy and Bert are in Nebraska visiting Lincoln . . ."

"I follow. But I really can't picture Lincoln as a bad guy. He's America's poster boy for decency and honesty."

"He's a used car salesman."

Joan shivered. "God help us all."

CHAPTER 20

Lincoln

"Your vehicle is in the third space on the right. Thank you for using Hertz."

Bert picked up his bags and followed Roy out the door. When he saw their car he halted mid-step. Yellow. Round. Volkswagon.

They'd rented a Beetle.

"Slug bug yellow no hit backs!" Bert dropped his luggage in the parking lot and launched himself at Roy, his fist seeking out the sore spot on the larger man's shoulder.

Roy set his jaw and rubbed his arm. "Remind me to smack Tom upside the head for reserving this damn car."

"That's why this place is called Hertz."

Bert went back for his bags. He shoved them in the rear seat and got into the car. Roy unlocked the fire box and put the revolver in his shoulder holster. Then he fussed with his donut.

"Damn donut is leaking again."

"Is the nozzle pushed in?"

"Don't start with me. It's a hole."

"I may have something in one of my bags."

Bert scooted around and unzipped the panel on his larger bag. He found the metal box and set it in his lap.

"Camping emergency pack. Waterproof matches, candle, compass, flashlight, cable saw, tablets to purify water, fishing line, and a repair kit for patching tents. Gimme the donut."

Roy handed it over. Bert found the hole—a split in the seam—and dabbed on some rubber cement.

"It's gonna take some time to dry. Can you live without it for a while?"

"I guess I have to."

Roy got in the driver's seat, wincing as he sat down.

"Maybe you should turn the other cheek."

"Funny. Where the hell are we going?"

"Honest Abe's Used Car Emporium. He's on Route 2."

Roy turned the ignition and Bert consulted the complimentary map of Lincoln the rental company had provided. "When you get out of the lot you're going to get on 80. We can take 80 to 180, and that turns into 2."

"How's my donut?"

"Drying."

Bert set the camping kit by his feet, rather than bother putting it back in the suitcase. He reclined his seat a few more degrees and opened the window. The breeze felt nice. Not as warm as LA, but the air was fresh and clean. The sun was looming over the western horizon. It would set in about an hour or so.

Bert closed his eyes, thinking about the past week and the events leading up to it. He felt . . . alive. This went beyond finding out he was a clone of Einstein.

This was an actual adventure. He was a part of something, something big and scary and exciting. Bert had no
idea how this was all going to end up, but he wouldn't
have missed it for anything.

They drove in companionable silence. Roy managed to find Route 2, and a few minutes later they were
pulled up to a weather beaten billboard stamped with
"Abe's Pre-Driven Vehicles."

The Emporium wasn't anything more than a gravel
parking lot with a small brick building in the center.
Multi-colored plastic flags, cracked and faded, were
strung between two poles, and a sign proclaimed *"Huge
Sale This Week Only!"* in peeling paint.

Bert scratched his chin. "I think I expected more.
How many cars do you count?"

"Ten, if you include that rusty Buick up on blocks."

Before they could get out of the car, a tall man
rushed out of the little building to greet them.

"Welcome to Honest Abe's!" His voice was booming, grandiose, and he spread his arms out dramatically. One look at his face and there was no doubt at
all. This was Abraham Lincoln. The craggy features,
the square beard, the big ears. He even had the black,
stovepipe hat.

Bert opened the car door and Abe shook his hand en-
thusiastically. There was a cigarette burning in the corner of his mouth, which seemed strangely anachronistic.
The car dealer also wore jeans and a dirty T-shirt, neither of which matched that famous face.

"I see you're looking to trade up on this foreign hunk
of crap. I have just the car for you. A 1989 Chrysler
LeBaron. Made in the USA, built to last. Leather interior.

Air. I might be persuaded to trade it for this Eurotrash vehicle, because I like how you carry yourself."

"This is a rental."

"Of course it is. Perhaps I should be speaking to the driver." Abe looked at Roy, then back at Bert. "Does this Negro belong to you? Just kidding, of course. Welcome to Honest Abe's Car Emporium, where all men are free . . . to drive home in a great deal!"

He pumped Roy's hand. The look on Roy's face found him just as entranced by Abe's appearance as Bert was. He must have been; anyone else talked like that to Roy would have been nursing a broken nose. But when Abe said it, it was humorous and good-natured.

Bert likened it to meeting a celebrity. When he'd first met Tom, he knew his face from old portraits, but there was no spark of instant recognition. Lincoln was arguably one of the most recognizable individuals to ever walk the planet. This was real American history come to life. Being next to him made Bert's heart race. Even though it was irrational, he wanted to get the man's autograph and take some pictures.

"I have just the thing for you." Lincoln lead Roy into the lot. "A 1977 Cadillac Seville. Auto everything. Think of how the brothers in the hood will bug when they see you chillin' in this ride, homey."

Bert shook himself out of the momentary daze and went after them.

"Mr. Linc—er—Wilkens, we're not here about a car. We need to talk to you."

Abe stopped in his tracks, removing his arm from Roy.

"Mr. Wilkens? Oh, you must mean my boss. He's

out of town for the moment. I'd be happy to take a message."

"You aren't Abe Wilkens, owner of this lot?"

"Sorry, no. Good day, gentlemen."

Abe walked briskly back to the little building. Bert and Roy exchanged a look of amazement.

"Are you as weirded out as I am?"

"It's freaky. He is Wilkens, right?"

"Has to be. The resemblance was amazing."

"He tried to sell me a Caddy. Abraham Lincoln tried to sell me a Caddy." Roy was beaming. It pleased Bert that he wasn't the only one acting like a star struck idiot.

"Why'd he take off?"

"Let's find out."

They walked up to the building and Roy knocked on the door. "Mr. Wilkens?"

"What? Oh, he's not here, I told you. Just leave your name and whatever company you're from, and he'll get back to you."

"Company? I'm a cop."

There was a pause, and then the door opened and Abe's head poked out, sans top hat.

"You're not from any bank?"

"No."

"Credit card company? Loan officer?"

"Nope."

"Local organized crime?"

"Chicago Police Department."

"Well then, let's talk." Abe waltzed out of the office and put an arm around Roy again. "I'm a big fan of law enforcement, and would be honored to give you my special police officer discount."

Roy had a little smile on his face and Bert could sense his head wasn't in the game. He reached over and tugged Abe's arm.

"We're not here to buy anything. We're here about the tattoo."

Abe turned his attention to Bert. "You know about that?"

"A blue number 1 on your heel. You were adopted, right?"

Abe nodded, his pale eyes widening. "I was. Are you here to tell me it's true? I've been waiting years for this. You found my real parents, and I'm actually a relative of Abraham Lincoln. Right?" He grinned and clapped his hands. "I've had a feeling, since I was a kid. Always hoped it wasn't just a dumb coincidence. Is there an inheritance? Tell me there's an inheritance."

"It's actually, ah, more complicated than that. You aren't a relative of Lincoln."

"Are you kidding? Look at me! I'm the spitting image! I look just like the dead bastard!"

"Abe . . ."

"Why do you think I moved to Nebraska? I grew the beard, I got the dumb hat—"

"Abe, you aren't one of Lincoln's relatives. But you do have Lincoln's genes in you."

"What the hell are you trying to say?"

"You're actually Abraham Lincoln."

Watching Lincoln do a double take ranked among the greatest moments in Bert's life.

"Excuse me?"

"You're a clone of Abraham Lincoln."

"Are you trying to bullshit a bullshitter?"

"No."

"You can actually prove this?"

"Yes."

Abe began to laugh. He grabbed Bert and hugged him. "This is great! I'll be rich! Come on, you have to buy me lunch and tell me all about it. We'll take my car."

Roy and Bert followed Abe to his vehicle. It was, naturally, a Lincoln Continental. Older model, when they still made them big. Bert smiled. Lincoln, driving a Lincoln, in Lincoln. Rarely does reality offer up treats like that. He called shotgun and sat in front.

"Don't you need to lock up?"

"Hell no. The place is insured."

Roy had to move a large plastic garbage bag before he could get in the back.

"Don't you have garbage pick-up out here?"

"Those are aluminum cans. Top dollar at the recycling center."

"They're leaking."

"It's only water. I fill them all up a little bit before I take them in. Bumps their weight up."

Abe turned onto the street and hung another cigarette in his mouth. As he lit it, he gave Bert a once over.

"You know, you look sort of familiar. Harry's Pool Hall? Did we ever play poker together?"

"I'm a clone of Einstein."

Abe hooted and blew his horn. "I knew it! I knew it would finally happen for me. We'll go on tour. You play an instrument, right? I play bass. The Lincoln/Einstein World Tour! I'll sing 'The Politics of Dancing.' You can sing 'She Blinded Me With Science.' What do you play?"

"I played viola in high school."

"We'd have to work on that. Are there any more famous clones running around? Mozart? John Lennon?" Abe turned to Roy. "Tell me you're Jimi Hendrix."

"I'm Jimi Hendrix." Roy deadpanned. "Let me stand next to your fire."

Abe narrowed his eyes. "The voice is wrong. Plus you're too goddamn big. But, maybe . . . lose some weight, grow a beach ball afro. Do you play guitar? Here we are, Dinah's. Only place in five miles worth eating at."

Abe pulled into the lot. It had all the trappings of a roadside diner; the big sign that said Family Restaurant, the glass carousel of rotating pies and puddings, the permanent round stools at the counter. Bert wondered if the waitress was named Flo.

Abe parked himself on a stool and beckoned Roy and Bert to join him on either side. Bert could sense Roy's wariness about the seating choice, especially without his donut.

"Can't we sit in a booth?"

"I hate booths." Abe winked. "Especially John Wilkes."

There was laughter and much rib elbowing from the car dealer.

"Actually, my legs are too long. I get gum on my knees. Sit, stay a while."

Bert sat next to Abe and picked up a menu. There was a small stack next to a pyramid of mini cereal boxes.

"Everything is good, except the turkey. It's a loaf. Good evening, Meg."

The waitress was older, tired, and her pink lipstick matched her uniform. "Hi, Abe. Usual?"

"With extra bacon. And some coffee too, hon. This guy here is Einstein, and this large black man is Roy. Do you think he looks like Jimi Hendrix?"

"They're like twins." Meg hadn't lifted her eyes to look. "You guys know what you want?"

Roy didn't bother with a menu. "Burger and fries."

"How about you?"

Bert wasn't sure what he was in the mood for. They'd had chicken on the plane, or at least something purporting to be chicken. He decided to be adventurous. "Give me what Abe is having."

"Coffee too?"

Roy and Bert agreed to coffee. She brought over three stained cups and filled them. Lincoln added five packets of sugar, drained his cup without stirring, and then motioned for a refill.

"Now tell me. Everything. How can you prove I'm Lincoln?"

Bert gave him the abbreviated explanation, beginning with how he was contacted by Jessup. He glossed over the meeting with Harold, not really understanding the science behind it himself, and then talked about their disastrous confrontation with Stang. The grand finale was the writing test, comparing a sample of Abe's script with a Xerox of one of Lincoln's original letters.

"This is fantastic." Abe looked back and forth between the two papers. "I'm actually Abraham Lincoln."

"Didn't you hear the rest of it? Someone is trying to kill you."

"Every silver lining has a cloud."

"Has anyone threatened you lately? Attacked you?"

"No more than usual. Great, here's the grub."

Meg brought over three plates. Bert eyed his dinner dubiously. It looked quasi-pornographic.

"Francheesie," Abe explained. "They split open a quarter pound hot-dog, stuff it with cheese, then wrap it up in bacon and deep fry it."

Abe picked his up and took a large bite, grease dripping down his chin. Bert frowned. "I think I can hear your arteries harden."

"The secret is the lard. Some places use vegetable oil, and it just isn't the same."

Bert went to work on his fries.

"So what's the next step? Do we hit the newspapers, or go straight to Letterman and Leno?"

"We have to stop the people who want to end our lives."

"Yeah yeah, after that. Do you have any of this scientific evidence stuff?"

"Nope."

Roy's mouth was occupied by a burger that looked a lot better than Bert's choice. Maybe he'd trade.

"Hey Roy, half your burger for my francheezie?"

"Hell no. Looks like a fried donkey dick."

"What about that dead science guy? Didn't he take notes?"

"Stang has it all, and he's not going to hand it over."

Abe polished off his dog and licked his fingers. "Way I see it, we could do it three ways. Go through official channels and try to get the media behind us, then let them prove the truth. Or break into the Senator's place and get the proof ourselves. You gonna eat your donkey dick?"

"Help yourself. What's the third way?"

"We rob some graves. We can start with Lincoln and Jefferson. Where's your brain at?"

Roy grinned. "I ask him that all the time."

"Some guy has it at Princeton. Abe, you don't seem to understand how serious this is."

"You're right. We should probably get agents. Someone to negotiate all the offers when they start pouring in. I know a guy at William Morris. Bernie something. He's a big shot, represents Mr. T."

They had pie, and more coffee. Bert soon gave up trying to convince Abe that his life was in danger. The guy was on their side, and if they stuck together it would hopefully be enough.

"Where are you guys staying?"

"We haven't decided yet."

"There are a few hotels near the airport. Some pretty good bars, too. We're going out to celebrate, right?"

Bert didn't know if that was the smartest move.

"I'm up for a beer. You, Bert?"

"Well, Tom is—"

Roy nudged Bert with an elbow. "Tom is in LA with a hottie. We don't need to check in with him for another two hours. A drink or two can't hurt."

"Come on, Bert! Live a little!"

Peer pressure won, and they agreed to go to a bar named the Porter House, on Pine Lake Road.

"Only a few miles away, walking distance to the Ramada Inn. I'll point out the road when we pass it."

The sun had gone down, and the cold wind made Bert consider a jacket. They all piled back into the Lincoln, Abe verbally debating between rock stardom and a career in politics.

"I could be President, right? Wouldn't you vote for Lincoln?"

"Damn straight."

"Bert, you want to be VP? And how about you, Roy? Secretary of Defense? Then Jefferson can be Secretary of State."

"How about Joan of Arc?"

"She could cook for us. Keep the White House tidy. How could we lose with a ticket like that?" Abe pulled into his car lot and killed the engine. "I have to do some quick work here, roll up windows, move some cars. I'll meet you at the Porter House. Think you can find the place okay?"

"No problem."

"See you there, kids."

Abe waved and walked back into the little building.

"He's a pretty good guy." Roy shook his head, smiling. "It's like we hanging out with the Pope, or Michael Jackson."

"The guy has presence. But I wouldn't buy a car from him to save my life."

"Check to see if my donut is done. That stool gave me an awful ache."

They hopped into the Beetle and got on their way. Bert checked the patch. Dry. He blew up the donut and listened for leaks.

"Seems okay."

Roy adjusted the donut under him and sighed. "Thanks."

A sharp horn split the night just as they were passed by another vehicle. A tow truck, flatbed, going at least twenty miles an hour over the speed limit. Bert watched the truck speed into the distance until its tail lights disappeared.

"You think we should call Tom, let him know how the meeting with Abe went?"

Roy reached into his jacket pocket and took out his cell.

"You do it. He's on speed dial. Scroll down to his first name, it's alphabetical."

Bert found Tom's name and hit the *send* button. It rang. And rang.

"There's no answer."

"You got the number right?"

"I think so."

"Lemme try." Roy took the phone and hit some buttons. "He's not answering."

"Maybe the phone's not on him."

"Then he'd set it from vibrate to ring, and still pick it up."

Bert saw it before Roy did. The tow truck that had passed them moments earlier. It was in their lane, no headlights, coming right at them.

Roy barely had a chance to hit the brakes before the collision.

Bert didn't hear the crash. He felt it.

Impact. Spinning. Darkness.

When Bert opened his eyes, all he saw was white. He couldn't remember where he was. He could sense movement, a breeze. He looked to his right.

A shattered window. Lights, in the distance, moving by slowly.

He looked left. More white. He lifted a hand, pushed.

Behind the airbag. Roy. Blood all over.

A small stutter, then a stop. Someone opened his door.

A dwarf. Only a foot tall. Bert stared at the top of his head.

"Still alive? Good. We can have some fun."

The dwarf had a knife. He poked the airbag, deflating it, and reached over to unlock Bert's seat belt. Bert was yanked from his seat and he fell, fell, hit the street. His head was pounding. There was something, some kind of humming, in his ears. He looked up.

Not a dwarf at all. It was Jack. Up on the flatbed of the tow truck was a wrecked car. Roy, slumped over behind the wheel.

Slug bug yellow.

"Say good-bye to your friend."

Jack pulled a lever on the side control panel. The bed began to lift. The car began to tilt.

"Those old Volkswagons, they used to be able to float. Let's see how the new models do."

When the angle was steep enough, Jack pulled another lever. The Beetle rolled down the flatbed, over the railing of the bridge. Bert tried to move his head, to see. There was a splash.

"Need some help?"

Jack grabbed Bert's hair and dragged him over to the edge. Below, in the river. The bug. Bobbing. Then it began to sink.

"Roy . . ." Bert's throat was hoarse, painful.

"*Roy.* Well, now we know. The new bugs don't float after all."

Bert watched as the car went down below the surface of the water, leaving only bubbles in its wake.

"Roy . . ."

"*Roy.*" Jack dropped Bert's head. "Be happy for him. His pain is over. Yours is just beginning. In a few hours, you'll be begging to join your friend at the bottom of that river."

Bert felt a hand on his collar, and then everything went black.

CHAPTER 21

Lincoln

The cold shocked Roy awake. His feet felt like they were stuck in ice. It quickly moved up to his legs, and then to his waist. The reality of his predicament came to him in a rush.

He was in the car. Roy could remember the truck coming right at them. Trying to collide. Hitting the brakes too late.

He reached to his right, feeling in the dark for Bert. Not there.

Roy pushed aside the airbag, hands groping the dash. He found the switch for the interior dome light.

Flipping it on revealed that the situation was worse than he thought. The water was above the windshields, streaming in through a hundred different cracks. It was now up to his chest, freezing.

Roy attempted to open the door. Jammed. The button for the window didn't work. He tried to scoot over to the passenger side, but his seat belt held him in place.

Without warning the car lurched forward, like the first drop on a roller coaster. Roy's head fell into the airbag, and he was immediately surrounded by cold, rushing water. He tore at the bag, trying to get it out of his face. It pulled free, but the water was now over his head. Frantic, his hand sought the seat belt button.

The car jolted, hitting the bottom of the river nose first. For a moment it stayed like that, as if unable to make up its mind where to fall. Then, slowly, it lolled to the right, coming to a rest on its side.

Roy released the seat belt and strained his neck up to find oxygen. There was a small air pocket near the rear window. One of Bert's Samsonite suitcases floated by his head. He batted it away and managed to get one last breath before the water completely filled the interior. Then he turned towards the passenger door.

But that's what the car was resting on.

Don't panic, he thought, and then almost laughed. He was trapped in a flooded car at the bottom of a river. Why the hell shouldn't he panic?

The doors were blocked, but he could still get out through a window. Roy pushed at the front windshield with both hands, giving it all he had.

It refused to budge.

His gun. He could shoot through the glass. His hand went into his shoulder holster.

Empty.

The water that had filled the car was cloudy, dark. He tried to peer through the murk, searching for his revolver.

The dome light chose that moment to go out. Everything went pitch black.

Now it was panic time.

Roy groped the floor blindly, lungs burning, becoming frantic. His hands touched something metal. Not his gun. It was square.

Bert's emergency camping pack.

He unsnapped the case and felt around inside. Something long and round. *A flashlight.* He flicked it on.

The beam was thin but powerful, cutting through the haze. Spots appeared in Roy's vision, and he wasn't sure if they were floating debris or if he was about to black out. His brain screamed for oxygen. The light played across the floor, the back seat. No gun.

Roy aimed it up, looking for another air pocket. There were none. But floating over his head was the inflatable donut.

He grabbed it, seeking the nozzle, pulling it out. Roy exhaled, clamped his mouth around the opening, and squeezed it while he took a deep breath.

The air was stale, weak, not enough oxygen content. But it was enough to keep him in the game a little longer.

Giving up on the gun, Roy half crawled, half swam to the rear window. He gripped the handle of Bert's larger suitcase. Hard plastic shell. The one that the gorilla used to jump on in the old TV commercials. He brought it back and shoved with all his might at the windshield.

Once. Twice. Three times.

His vision became fuzzy again. He took another hit off the donut.

Four. Five. At six, the suitcase knocked the window out of its setting. Roy let go of the handle, watching it disappear through the new opening. He followed it out, straining and kicking, his wet clothes and shoes holding him back. No good. It was like trying to swim while tied up.

Don't blow it this close to the finish line, Roy.

He brought the donut to his face for the last time, lightheaded from all the carbon dioxide. He sucked out the remainder of the air and then struggled with his jacket, managing to free himself. Then he pulled off his shoes and kicked for what he hoped was the surface.

His mind began to drift, almost as if he were on the edge of sleep. His lungs were two burning paper bags. Roy's thrashing became gentler, feeble.

Almost . . . almost . . .

He broke the surface, and that first breath of fresh air was like being born again.

Roy flopped onto his back, trying to float, greedily filling his lungs. Something nudged him in the head. A suitcase. He clung to it, dizzy, shaking, happy as hell to be alive.

"Roy!"

He looked to his right, along the riverbank. It was Abe, waving at him. The tall man took off his shoes and his shirt. Then he waded into the water and swam up to Roy with even, powerful strokes. The two of them managed to beach the suitcase. Abe helped pull Roy onto the shore.

"I was just driving up when I saw that guy drop your car over the bridge."

"Was Bert with him?"

"I think so. He put someone in his truck."

"Which way did they go?"

"West. Into town."

Roy tried to stand up. His legs wouldn't support him. "We have to go after him."

"Shouldn't we call the police?"

"They won't help."

"You should probably see a doctor. You're bleeding."

Abe pointed to his head. Roy touched his hand to a sore spot, saw the blood glisten in the moonlight.

"Help me with this suitcase." Roy hefted it over to Abe. Twenty yards downstream, Bert's other indestructible piece of luggage was snagged on some sticks along the shoreline. "We have to get that one too."

"What's in them that's so important?"

"Half a million dollars."

"I'll get it."

Abe jumped into the river with more enthusiasm than he had when going after Roy.

The cop sat down on the riverbank and tried to gauge the extent of his injuries. His head was starting to pound, and his neck hurt like crazy. He felt his ass and wondered if he'd ripped the stitches. Roy coughed, and then spat. He was cold. He was in pain. But most of all, he was angry.

The bad guys had left him for dead. Big mistake. He was going to make sure they found out just how big.

"Got it!" Abe held the suitcase over his head like it was the Stanley Cup.

Roy began to shiver. He took off his shirt and wrung it out, but it was still too cold to put back on.

"We'll go back to my place." Abe heaved the suitcase next to its matching partner. "I have some clothes that will fit you."

"Do you have a cell phone?"

"I've got one in the car. How are we supposed to find Bert?"

"He's got a transmitter on him. If I can get in touch with Tom, I can track him."

Abe bent over and began to put on his shoes. "And what do we do when we find him?"

"Do you have a gun?"

"No."

"We'll figure something out. Let's get to that phone. Where's your car?"

Abe grabbed both pieces of luggage and made his way up the sloping bank. It wasn't steep, but in his wet socks Roy kept slipping. When he finally made it to street level he had half a dozen more cuts and bruises.

Abe's Lincoln was still running. Roy got in and turned up the heat. The cell phone was in the glove compartment. He dialed Tom's number. It rang and rang. Had they gotten to him too?

Roy hit the disconnect and dialed the number again, on the off chance he'd pressed a wrong digit.

No answer.

Roy punched the dashboard. "Dammit, Tommy! Where the hell are you?"

CHAPTER 22

Los Angeles

"That was a complete waste of time."

Tom and Joan had managed to tear down most of the wine racks. Their efforts didn't yield any usable weapons, or anything else that would get them out of the cellar.

"Not a complete waste," Tom disagreed. "At least we messed up his wine cellar."

"Good point. We sure showed him."

Tom sat down again, racking his brain for an answer. How many ways were there to open a door? Breaking it down was futile. The door and the jamb were solid oak, and the lock was heavy. They couldn't take off the hinges, because the hinges were on the other side. Picking the lock was out—even if they had a wire or a pin, Tom didn't have the slightest idea how to do that.

The final way, the one Tom saw a lot in his career as a cop, was called *loiding*. That meant sticking a thin piece of celluloid; a shim or a credit card, in between the door and the bolt, then easing it back. Unfortunately, Tom's wallet had been taken with the rest of his things.

"You wouldn't happen to have a credit card on you by chance?"

"Why? You want to go shopping?"

"I wanted to try to loid the door lock."

"Sorry. Left my purse at Marty's."

"Any jewelry? Rings, necklace, bracelet, watch?"

"No. Don't you have a watch?"

Tom did. But it was a leather band, useless. He needed something long and stiff. Maybe one of the pieces of wood they broke off, or . . .

"The nails in the boards. See if you can find any."

Tom searched along the floor, finding a corner section. He worked the pieces apart until he exposed a nail. It was thin, bent, about two inches long. Tom pounded it and the board against the concrete floor until it came out the other end.

He found his way up the staircase and examined the doorknob with his fingers. There was a metal plate along the jamb, which the bolt rested in. Tom stuck the nail in between them and tried to wiggle it back and forth. They were too close together, and the nail was too thick.

"Did it work?"

"No. Nail's too wide." Tom rubbed his eyes.

"I found a smaller one. Try this."

Joan climbed the stairs and handed Tom another nail. It was shorter, thinner. He wedged it in between the door and the jamb. With the tip, he could feel the bolt. But the nail was too short, and he didn't have any leverage to try to push the bolt back.

"It's not long enough."

"Do all the girls tell you that?"

Tom laughed despite himself. "You're not helping the situation. Try to stay focused."

"We could try kicking it again."

"It's a heavy door, with a heavy lock."

"Why don't you try kicking the other side, by the hinges?"

Why not? Couldn't hurt. Tom aimed at the bottom of the door. He kicked, hard.

Again. And again.

"I think it gave a little."

Two more kicks, and Tom was positive the door was moving.

"Let me try."

Tom let Joan have a go at it. After she put in six strong ones, Tom checked the integrity of the door. The lower portion was loose. He could push it forward almost an inch. Three more kicks and there was a small clinking sound. Screws falling out, hitting tile.

"Halfway there."

Tom couldn't kick as high as the top hinge, but now he could use the whole door for leverage. He rammed it with his shoulder and pushed hard.

"Lean on it."

Joan added her weight, both of them straining and groaning. Then, suddenly, the door was falling over and they tumbled out into the kitchen.

The lights were off, and the room was dark. There was a noise, a TV or a radio, blaring from another room. Tom crawled over to the counter, where his gun was setting. He grabbed it and held his breath, listening for movement in the house.

"Maybe he's gone." Joan was crouching down next to him.

"Could be asleep."

"Let's not hang around to find out."

Tom nodded in agreement. He reached for his wallet, keys, and phone. His phone was vibrating. Tom pressed the talk button and held it to his ear, silent.

"Tom? Jesus, where were you?"

Roy. Tom kept his voice low. "We have a little situation here."

"They've got Bert. But he's got the tracer. I need you to find him, now."

"Shit." The laptop was back at the hotel. "That may take some time."

"He doesn't have time!"

"Call you right back." He disconnected and turned to Joan. "We have to get on the Internet."

"Can it wait?"

"No." Tom held out his keys. "Take the car. Get out of here."

"You want to use Shakespeare's computer?"

"I don't have a choice. Go back to your place. You've got the gun in the car. I'll be by later."

"They could show up here any minute. Bill might even be in the house right now."

"Gotta risk it."

"You men and your macho bullshit." Joan grabbed the keys and hurried out of the kitchen. Tom felt a quick stab of sadness at seeing her go, then concentrated on what he needed to do.

"Okay, computer, where might you be?"

Tom didn't remember seeing it in the living room,

and it wasn't in the kitchen. But Bill was a writer, which meant he had to have a computer somewhere. Tom walked into the hallway. The TV sound got louder. He moved slowly past a closed door, probably the bedroom. That's where the noise was coming from, the volume cranked up high enough for Tom to hear every line of dialog.

He paused by the door, considering his options. He needed to interrogate Bill, but he didn't know if he was still armed. A shoot-out would be bad. Even if Tom did manage to capture him, how was he supposed to hold him while also messing around on the Internet? And what if Attila and Vlad showed up all of a sudden?

Bill could wait for two seconds. Tom made Bert the first priority.

There were more rooms down the hall. The first was a bathroom. The second was a home office. And on a desk was an IBM, complete with modem. Tom entered the dark room and switched the computer on. After it booted up, he adjusted the contrast so the screen was dim. The keyboard had one-touch Internet access, and it only took a minute before he was at the *Surveillance Technologies website*. Tom fished the BigTrack serial number out of his wallet.

His phone buzzed.

"Dammit, Tommy. Hurry up."

"Just a sec." Tom punched in the user name and password, and a few keystrokes later he was looking at a map of Lincoln, Nebraska. "It looks like he's on Talon Street. It's off of North Park Road, near the airport."

"Exact address?"

Tom squinted at the screen. "Doesn't say. But he's on the northwest corner of the intersection. Roy, be careful with Abe. Shakespeare was a real bad egg."

"Put down the weapon and hang up the phone."

Speak of the devil. Something pressed into the back of Tom's head. He didn't have to see it to know what it was.

"The phone and the gun, now."

Tom ended the call and placed the revolver on the desk top.

"Where's the girl?"

"She left to get the police. They'll be here any minute."

Bill gave him a hard tap on the head with the butt of the gun.

"Where is she?"

"She left."

"Where did she go?"

"I don't know."

The blow brought the stars out. Tom toppled off the chair and fell to his hands and knees.

"Let's get something straight, Jefferson. I'm the one with the gun. I ask the questions, you answer them."

He kicked Tom in the ribs. Tom groaned, a spike of agony running laps through his nervous system.

"What's the matter? Tender spot?"

Another kick, just as hard. Tom squinted up at him through the pain. There was something round and pink stuck to Bill's forehead.

"Do you have a roller in your hair plugs?"

Bill reflexively touched his head, then gave Tom the mother of all kicks.

"How does it feel, to get your ass kicked by William Shakespeare?"

Tom groaned. "It's better than reading your plays."

Bill reared back for another kick, but something to his left caught his attention and he stopped.

"Drop the gun."

Tom looked in the doorway. Joan. She had the semi-automatic in her hand, aiming at Bill's chest.

"Hello, Joan. Welcome to the party. I was giving one of our founding fathers a little lesson in humility."

"The gun. Drop it."

"This gun?" Bill smirked and pulled back the hammer. He pointed it at Tom's head. "What if I said no?"

"Then I'd shoot you."

"Playing hardball. I see. But do you know what the secret to playing hardball is? You have to know what you're capable of. How far will you go to win, Joan? Me, I'm willing to go all the way. Now I'm going to count to three."

"No, you're not."

Joan shot him in the chest. Bill took a step back, slack-jawed in surprise. He looked at the blood soaking his shirt, and then fell to his knees and slumped to the floor. Tom pried the gun out of his hand. The Bard's eyes were glassy, far off. A small gasp escaped his mouth, and then he didn't move any more.

"Is he dead?"

Joan appeared dazed. Tom got up off the floor, one arm protecting his ribs. "Yeah. He's dead."

"Should we call the police?"

"If you want to."

Joan walked over to Bill, slowly. She seemed someplace else. Tom recognized it as an early stage of shock. He went to her, taking the gun from her hand.

"If you didn't shoot him, we both would have died. You made the right choice."

Joan didn't answer. She just stared at the body. He stuck the gun in his waistband and gently touched her chin, turning her gaze away from Bill and on to him.

"Can you live with this?"

"I . . . I think so. What about the police?"

Tom thought it through. Even though it was a clear case of self-defense, he wasn't sure how far Stang's influence spread.

"I don't know if we can trust the police."

"So what should we do?" Her voice sounded strained. "Start wiping down all of our fingerprints?"

"We didn't commit any crime here, Joan. There's nothing to conceal. If we're ever questioned about this, we don't want to admit that we tried to cover it up. You saved my life. Both of our lives. Okay?"

She nodded. "Okay. What do I need to do?"

"We have to get ready for Attila and Vlad. They can show up at any time."

"What about . . ." Joan gave the body a sideways glance.

"Leave him. Go and wait in the living room. Keep an eye on the window, tell me if a car pulls up. Can you do that?"

Joan turned and walked out, somewhat robotically. Tom picked up his cell phone and dialed Roy. There was a recorded message, saying the customer had switched off his phone.

"Great. One more thing to worry about."

He left the den, deep in thought. Defense first. Tom locked the front and back doors, so the Terrible Two couldn't just waltz in. They'd probably call before they came. Tom didn't think he could convincingly speak like Bill, so he took the phone off the hook and put the hand set in a drawer so he wouldn't have to hear that annoying noise. Joan was sitting in the Budweiser chair, facing a crack in the blinds.

"How are you doing?"

"I think I'm okay. What's the plan?"

"We need to talk to one of them, to find out what's going on. If only one shows up, it's easy. I go around behind him while he's at the front door."

"And if they both show up?"

"Same thing. But if it goes bad, you'll be in here, aiming out this window. Vlad had the gun, so we go for him first. Can you do that?"

"Yes."

"I'm going to look over Bill's computer files, see if I can turn something up. Do you want anything? Some water? A sandwich?"

"I don't think I could eat."

"Right. Sorry. I'll relieve you in about an hour, okay?"

Joan nodded. Tom turned to leave.

"Tom?"

He stopped. "Yeah?"

"Have you ever . . . ?"

Tom knew where this was headed. He took a breath and let it out slowly.

"Killed someone? My second year. It was a 10-16. Domestic violence. We'd had calls about that address before. The husband drank, and he was a mean drunk. When my partner and I arrived, the guy took a swing at me. Big fellow. Strong. We jumped on top of him, trying to get the cuffs on. He fought pretty damn hard."

Tom hadn't talked about this in years, not since his mandatory visit to the police shrink.

"You shot him?"

"Um, no. We managed to get him subdued. But his wife . . . she came out of the bedroom with a gun. Shot my partner in the head. Defending her husband, I guess. Even though the bastard broke her nose."

"You killed her."

"I killed her."

"Self-defense."

"Yes."

"Just like me."

Tom nodded, slowly. "Yes."

Her shoulders shook, and then the tears. Tom went to her, arms open. She cried, and he patted her back and smoothed her hair, all while trying not to think about that October night, all those years ago, having to kill the woman he'd shown up to protect.

"You'll be fine, Joan. You're strong."

"I know."

"He was a bad man."

"I know."

Joan broke the hug, taking a step back. Tom could tell she'd found her strength again.

"Was that your friends on the phone, earlier?"

"Yeah. The bad guys grabbed Bert."

"Oh no. I'm sorry."

"Roy is going after him, but his cell phone is off. All we can do is wait."

"I hope they're okay."

"Me too."

"What was it you wanted to check out on Bill's computer?"

"I'm not sure. Just searching for clues, I guess. Something to make some sense of all this."

"Don't let me stop you. I'll be fine."

"You sure?"

"I've got window duty. You go be a cop."

"I won't be long." Tom gave her a little pat on the shoulder and then went back to the den, a bounce in his step.

He flipped on the light and tried not to look at the corpse. Sitting at the workstation, he logged off the Internet and opened up Bill's word processing file. Tom found fifteen documents. He clicked on the first one and began to read.

I address you today as the newly elected Speaker of this House of Representatives . . .

Ah-ha. Bill was writing speeches for Phil Jr., the third most powerful man in America. Tom decided to check the most recent speech, to see if it yielded anything interesting. He clicked on the last document and saw it was dated two days from now.

It is in the times of greatest tragedy that we ourselves must also be great . . .

As Tom read on, he was enveloped by a very real sense of dread. Halfway into the first paragraph, his fears were confirmed.

"Oh no."

He continued, and the speech got immeasurably worse. If this were true, if this were really going to happen in two days . . .

"We're in way over our heads."

Tom shook his head, his heart aching, because he knew there was no chance in hell any of them would be alive by the end of the week.

CHAPTER 23

Lincoln

The pain in his wrists woke him up. It didn't take long for Bert to figure out why.

He was hanging from them.

"Welcome back, Mr. Einstein."

Jack's thick lips were curved in a smile. He perched like a cat on the top step of a folding ladder, staring into Bert's eyes. The expression on his face was pure glee.

Bert took in the surroundings. It was an empty warehouse of some kind. Dark, dusty, abandoned. Looking up, he saw the rope that bound his hands extended up the ceiling and looped over a rafter. He followed it down to ground level, where it was tied to a massive metal shelving unit.

"Oh, God."

Looking down also revealed what he was hanging over.

"*Oh, God,*" Jack repeated. "There are a few tricks to a proper impaling. The stick has to be sharp, but not so sharp that it kills right away. It should be greased, in this case with some petroleum jelly, to help the body slide down. Too much and the game is over too quickly. Too little and it can take weeks. It's a little bit art, and a little bit science."

The stake was at least eight feet long, the pointy tip only a few inches away from Bert's crotch. The pain in his wrists suddenly became trivial.

"I know what you're thinking. Yes, it's going to hurt. It's going to hurt a lot. You'll scream for the first few hours, but no one will hear you. I'd prepared this for Lincoln, but lucky you, you get the trial run."

"Why don't you just shoot me?" Bert's voice was quivering badly.

"*Why don't you just shoot me?* What's the fun in that? Besides, I have some questions to ask, about where the others are, and this makes you much more receptive."

"I'll tell you whatever you want. I swear."

"*I swear.*" Jack patted Bert on the head. "Of course you will. Now perk up. We're going to spend some quality time, here. There are few relationships more in-timate than this one. You'll share everything with me, Albert. You'll open yourself up like you never have to anyone else. By the end, I hope we'll be good friends."

Bert fought back the tears. "You're insane."

"*You're insane.*" Jack laughed. "Of course I'm in-sane. I'm Jack the Ripper. The original serial killer. The most famous psychopath in history. But I'm not entirely bad. I'll prove it to you. I'll give you a phone call. You can call anyone you want."

"Why?"

"*Why?* To say good-bye, of course." Jack unclipped

the cell phone from his belt and held it out. "Give me a number. I'll dial for you."

Bert trembled with fear, anger, helplessness. He was going to die. The realization staggered him. It was too soon—there was so much he wanted to do, so much he hadn't yet done. This was supposed to happen when he was old. Not now, not this way, at the hands of a monster who fed on his pain. He wanted to spit in the man's face, but he held it back for the moment. There was a call he wanted to make.

Bert told Jack a number. Jack repeated it back, naturally.

"It's ringing." He put it to Bert's ear.

"Hello?"

When Bert heard the voice he wasn't sure if he could keep it together. "Mom? It's me."

"Albert! How are you? Where have you been hiding? I called the apartment three times, you haven't answered."

"Been busy lately."

"Too busy to call your mother?"

"Look, Mom, this is important."

"What is it, Albert?"

Bert's eyes teared up. "I want to say . . . I want to say thank you. Thank you for my life. For raising me." He swallowed, trying to keep his voice conversational. "You've been the best mother anyone could ask for. I love you, Mom."

"I love you too, son. Is everything okay?"

"It's fine. Is, uh, Dad there?"

"Albert . . . I don't know if he wants to talk to you."

"Please. Make him get on the phone. There's something I have to tell him."

Jack took the phone away and put his hand over the mouthpiece. "I just have to tell you, Albert. This is really touching. Really."

"Can you give me the phone back?"

Jack placed it next to Bert's ear.

"Yes?" His father's voice. Curt. Impatient.

"Hi, Dad. Look—I know we haven't seen eye to eye lately, but I wanted to say something."

"I'm not sending you any more money."

"Dammit, Dad, just listen to me. This isn't about money. It isn't about graduate school, or physics, or the stock market. This is about you and me. A long time ago, there was a man who told me I could do anything in life. The sky was the limit. He taught me to believe in myself."

Jack took the phone away again. "This is great stuff, Albert. Should I get some tissue?"

"Can I finish?"

"*Can I finish?* Sure." He held the phone out again.

Bert tried to gather his thoughts. "You were there for me, Dad. All throughout my life. You helped make me a man. I know I never lived up to your expectations as a son, but you lived up to all of mine as a father, and then some. I just wanted to thank you, for everything you've done. I love you."

There was a long pause.

"Did he say it back?" Jack asked.

Bert averted his eyes.

"You know, son, you haven't been by the house in a while. Your mother would love it if you came over, stayed for a few days. I've got these Nets tickets— they're having a great season so far. Heading for the playoffs for sure. Do you remember the first time I took you to see the Nets?"

"Like it was yesterday. They played the Bulls. Jordan scored 43 points."

"So you'll come out? They're playing on Thursday. I don't know what your schedule is like . . ."

Bert bit his lower lip. "I don't think I can make that game, Dad. But thanks."

"Well, another time then. Bert?"

"Dad?"

"I know . . ." He cleared his throat. "I know I haven't been the most affectionate father. That was always your mother's department. Hugs and kisses and birthday cards. But, I'm glad you called."

"I'm glad too."

"I love you, son."

"Thanks, Dad. Love you too. Bye-bye."

Jack took back the phone and pretended to wipe away tears. "I'm all choked up, here. Really. That was touching. The old man actually said he loved you?"

Bert refused to look at him.

"My dad loved me, too. It was a different kind of love, though. He had some—issues. Well, let's be honest. He got off on hurting me. But behind every attack, there was love. I've missed him every day since I killed him."

"You sick bastard."

"*You sick bastard.* That's all you can say? Well, maybe the insults will get more creative as the night drags on. I'll warn you, though. Try to get them all in early. Because later, instead of calling me names you'll be telling me you love me just to make the pain stop."

Bert took a deep breath, searched deep within himself, and found a little reserve of courage. He met Jack's stare head on.

"I'm a big, stupid, mama's boy."

Jack didn't even pause. "*I'm a big, stupid, mama's boy.*"

"And I play with dolls."

"*And I play with dolls.*" Jack's eyes narrowed. "I see what you're doing here."

"I have to repeat everything because I'm a moron."

"*I have to repeat everything because I'm a moron. Stop it. Now.*"

Bert racked his brain for more insults. He could remember a show he saw on cable about serial killers. Many of them killed animals, started fires, wet the bed . . .

"I wet the bed until I was twenty."

Jack's jaw clenched, and his head began to shake. "*I . . . wet the bed until I was twenty.*"

Bert raised his eyebrows. "Hey, I think we hit a nerve. I'm a bed-wetting little psycho and nobody loves me."

Jack slapped Bert across the face. The blow sent him swinging.

"*I'm . . . a . . . bed-wetting . . .*"

"Little psycho and nobody loves me."

"*Little psycho and nobody loves me.* You're going to wish you hadn't done this."

Jack hurried down the ladder. Bert watched him scamper to the shelving unit, where the rope was anchored. The thought of being dropped on that stake made Bert want to gag. His mind raced. Was there any possible way to get out of this alive? He didn't see any. Roy—poor Roy—was dead. Bert had only known him a few days, but he considered him a friend. Tom was in LA, and probably wouldn't find out about their deaths for a few days. No rescue, no escape. All the future held was a long, awful death.

Bert looked down, between his legs. He was still reeling from Jack's slap, and the stake swayed back and forth beneath him.

Maybe he couldn't stop death, but he could delay it for a little while. Bert kicked his legs out and began to swing.

"Stop that!"

Bert stretched out his leg, trying to reach the ladder. Maybe, just maybe, he could get onto it . . .

The rope went slack and Bert fell.

He stopped abruptly. At first, he thought he'd landed on the ladder and everything was okay. Then the pain hit. His left buttock. White hot, searing pain. Right to the bone.

"No!" Jack screamed. He grabbed the rope and held it tight. "Look what you did! It's supposed to go between your legs!"

Bert felt himself jerked upwards, being pulled off the stake. He looked down, saw the blood on the tip, felt his left leg go numb.

"If it hit an artery, you'll bleed to death!"

Good, Bert thought.

Jack tied the rope back to the shelves and climbed up the ladder. He spun Bert around and clucked to himself, inspecting the wound in a frantic, worried manner.

"I think it's okay. I think it's okay."

Bert blinked back the pain.

"I wear diapers."

"*I wear diapers!*" Jack grabbed Bert's shirt and pulled him close. "Do you want to play? We'll do it this way, then!"

Jack went to the top of the ladder and leaned on Bert's shoulder so he couldn't swing. Bert watched him take a long knife out of a sheath on his belt.

"This time, the stake won't miss."

Jack reached up to saw away at the rope. Bert closed his eyes and tried to brace himself. He couldn't swing. He couldn't get away. The stake was going to find its mark, and his terrible death would soon begin. Though not a practicing Jew, Bert's lips silently formed the only Hebrew words he knew. *Baruch atah Adonai.* Praise the Lord.

Then, suddenly, Jack cried out and there was no more pressure on his shoulder. Bert looked and saw the ladder tumbling over, Jack falling to the ground. And standing there, bare-chested . . .

"Roy!"

"Damn straight."

Jack hit the floor rolling. He came up in a crouch, still gripping the knife. His face registered surprise, and when he saw Roy it burned red with rage. He pointed the knife at him, shaking.

"You! I killed you!"

Roy had something big in his hands. It was a black garbage bag—one of the bags from Abe's car that had been filled with cans. Roy held it at his side.

"What's this I hear about diapers?"

"What's this . . . I hear . . . about diapers!"

Jack lunged, thrusting at Roy's stomach with the

knife. Roy danced away from the blade and swung the garbage bag like a baseball bat, smacking Jack in the face and chest with a hard, solid blow.

It wasn't filled with cans. When the bag burst open on impact, it covered Jack with a tangled mass of fishing lures. Hundreds of them.

Jack wailed and pitched to the floor. He rolled around, thrashing and kicking. Hooks were stuck in his clothes, his head, his neck. One hand was hooked to his chest, and the other was tugging at a bright orange object stuck in his eye.

The smart thing would have been to just stop moving and wait for help. But Jack became more and more hysterical. He somehow got to his feet, screaming like a little girl, and sprinted away from Roy, tearing off in the opposite direction.

Straight at Abe.

"Holy shit!" Abe took three steps back and raised something in his right hand. A tire iron.

"Get the hell away from me!"

Jack continued to race forward, gaining speed, blood spraying off him as he ran. Abe was backed up against the shelves and had no place to go.

Bert was transfixed, unable to turn away. Jack had so many lures stuck on him he looked like a decorated Christmas tree. He was four steps away from Abe . . . three . . . two . . .

Abe yelped and brought the weapon down, cracking it hard against the side of Jack's head. Jack flopped to the ground like a fish. He twitched twice, and then was still. Abe dropped the tire iron and staggered away.

"I think I'm having a heart attack."

Lincoln took three more steps and then fell to his

knees. His hand clutched his chest, and his face was scrunched up in pain.

"Abe!" Roy hurried to him, grabbed his arm.

"Chest pains. Bad. That guy . . . Jesus."

"Stay calm. I'll call an ambulance."

"Wait . . . wait . . . wait . . ."

Abe opened his mouth and let out an incredibly long belch.

"I'm okay. It was the francheesie."

Roy left him to his heartburn. He went to the fallen ladder and set it up under Bert.

"I got you, buddy."

"Hi, Roy. I thought you were dead."

"Naw. Just went for a brisk swim." Roy helped Bert get his feet onto the rungs. "Hey, Abe. Cut that rope."

Abe was smacking his lips. "That sure didn't taste too good the second time. Just a sec."

"My ass. It's killing me."

"Mine, too. We'll buy a couple of donuts. Try to stand up."

Bert stared into Roy's eyes. He saw deep concern. "You saved me."

"You're welcome."

"You're welcome? You hit him with my entire life savings. You couldn't find a brick, or a board or something?"

"Maybe I should leave you hanging there."

The rope was severed and Bert's arms came down. His legs were shaking, and Roy assisted him to the ground.

Abe came over with the knife and cut the rope tying Bert's hands. There were bloody ligature marks around his wrists, but that paled next to the pain of his circulation returning. It was as if Bert had stuck both hands in a barbecue grill. He moaned.

"Are you okay?"

"Half a million dollars." Bert looked around the warehouse, lures scattered all over.

Abe held up the knife. "We could, uh, get them back if you want."

Bert winced at the thought. His eyes fanned over to Jack's body. Moments ago, he didn't think there was any worse way to die than being impaled. Jack just proved him wrong. A horrible death, for a horrible man.

"Leave them. I just lost my stomach for the lure business."

"Well, your ass doesn't look too bad."

"Thanks, Roy. You've got a cute ass yourself."

"I meant, I don't think you're gonna bleed to death."

Bert laughed. "And just two minutes ago, I was hoping I'd bleed to death."

Roy eyed the stake. "I bet. Nasty."

"How'd you find me?"

"Tom. The transmitter. Shit, I should call him back. He doesn't have our number. Abe, gimme your phone."

Abe was squatting on the ground, picking up lures. "These things are really worth that much money?"

"The phone, Abe."

Abe pulled the cell out of his pocket and tossed it to Roy. Roy pressed a few buttons. "It doesn't work."

"Hit it."

Roy smacked it a few times. "Was that supposed to help?"

"Naw. Battery is dead. But don't you feel better?"

Bert made himself look at Jack again. He felt many

things—fear, revulsion, anger, even sympathy. He focused his eyes on the phone clipped to his belt.

"Jack's got a phone."

No one made any move to retrieve it.

"We should search him, anyway." Roy scratched his chin.

"Abe, you're closest. Grab his phone."

"No way. I saw this movie before. I go near him, he comes back to life and grabs me."

Bert made the decision. "I'll do it."

Roy shook his head. "No need, Bert. I got this one."

"It's okay. I don't want to spend the next thirty years in therapy, whining about my fear. I'd rather face it now."

Bert limped over to Jack, one hand pressed against the wound on his backside. With each step, he was less sure of himself. Deep in his psyche, Bert knew that confronting the horrific corpse of the man who almost killed him was somehow therapeutic. Shrinks talked a lot about closure. This was closure in spades. But it still scared the hell out of him.

He can't hurt me anymore. Bert said it over and over in his head. A mantra. He stopped next to the corpse, leaning down, focusing on the goal, reaching out a hand . . .

"Don't let him grab you!" Abe yelled.

Bert took the phone. Triumphant, he began to turn away, but something caught his eye. A piece of paper, sticking out of Jack's back pocket. Abe tugged it out. A plane ticket.

"While you're over there being brave, check his wallet." Roy said.

"No fair," Abe said. "I killed him, I get his wallet."

"We're looking for evidence, Abe, not robbing him."

Bert patted down Jack's pockets, careful to avoid getting hooked. He dug out a billfold, some keys, and a small plastic tube.

"You doing okay?" Roy had come up to him, put a hand on his shoulder.

"I'm fine." The case was black, about half the size of a pencil. It had a screw top. Bert shook the contents onto his palm.

"What is that? Drugs?"

"I don't think so."

The object was small, about two centimeters long. It looked like a miniature missile. Pointy on one end, tiny wings on the other.

"It's a dart of some kind." Roy carefully picked it up between his thumb and index finger and held it close. "Has some kind of mark. Squiggles, like Chinese writing."

"YOU!!!!"

The three of them whirled to see Jack. Somehow, impossibly, he'd gotten to his feet and launched himself at the trio, one arm stretched out for a pointy and lethal embrace.

Roy shoved Bert to the side and put out his hand to hold Jack back. As soon as Roy touched him, Jack's eyes rolled up in their sockets and he gasped, falling to the ground. His body jerked twice, and then he was still.

Abe nodded smartly.

"I told you that was gonna happen."

"Is he dead?" Bert asked. "What the hell did you hit him with?"

Roy shrugged. "I just poked him with the little dart thingy."

Bloody froth foamed out of Jack's mouth.

"It killed him that fast?"

"Apparently so. Let's try to avoid those things in the future. Gimme the phone."

Roy took the cell from Bert and pressed some buttons.

"Tom? Yeah, he's safe. Jack's dead. Okay, tell me."

Bert watched Roy's face. As Tom talked, it became grimmer and grimmer.

"Great. I was hoping this situation would become a lot more desperate. Jack had a ticket on him. Lemme see it." Bert handed it over. "Tomorrow night, to DC. Yeah, it makes sense. I'll break it to the guys, call you right back."

"What is it?" Bert braced himself for bad news.

Roy pocketed the phone. "Well, Shakespeare was a bad guy. He's dead. It looks like Stang's plot goes beyond just killing all the clones. Way beyond. The stakes have gone up."

"What do you mean?"

"Apparently, the day after tomorrow, Stang is planning on assassinating both the President and the Vice President at the same time." Roy let the words sink in. "And we all know who's next in line for the Presidency."

"The Secretary of State?" Abe looked up from the pile of lures he'd been gathering. "The Attorney General? The Prime Minister? Don't tell me, I know this. Oprah?"

"The Speaker of the House. Phil Jr."

Bert's stomach dropped. "If he becomes President, we're all dead."

"It's a lot worse than that. He's planning on blaming China for the assassinations."

Bert followed the line of thought. "Oh no."

"That's right." Roy's face creased with worry. "Get ready for World War III."

CHAPTER 24

Los Angeles

Tom clicked on the NEWS icon at www.whitehouse.
gov, to check the upcoming events for the President.
"He's in Canada for the next two days."

Joan asked, "Where?"

Tom checked where the Prez was supposed to be tomorrow at 4:15—that was the time mentioned in Bill's
speech. *At precisely a quarter after four, Eastern time,
our nation lost two of its finest leaders . . .*

"He'll be in Montreal. He's addressing the North
American Energy Commission, whatever that is."

"How about the Vice President?"

Tom couldn't find any mention of him. "I guess
he'll be presiding over the Senate. Roy mentioned that
Jack had a plane ticket to DC. They must be planning
on murdering him while Congress is in session."

"So we've got—what—twenty hours to try and stop
a double assassination?"

"We can place an anonymous call to the Secret Service, tell them the plot, and they'll take care of it."

"They'll want proof. Which we don't have."

"We'll be real convincing."

"You're kidding, right?"

Tom turned and looked at her. "What do you mean?"

"Do you honestly think that the President is going to cancel his speech because of an anonymous phone call? He probably gets threatened every day by nuts from all over the world. Suppose you got a call saying the mayor of Chicago was going to be killed at a speech. What would you do?"

Tom saw her point. "We'd beef up security."

"But we have to assume Stang can already beat security. Hell, the Secret Service may actually be in on it, with all of Stang's connections. Would the mayor cancel his speech?"

Tom shook his head slowly. "Probably not. He'd have faith in his security staff. Plus he'd want to prove that he's not easily scared. Terrorists can't push this administration around, that kind of thing."

"So an anonymous call is out. If we tried talking to the Secret Service in person, and told them the truth about everything that happened, how far would we get?"

Tom knew how that would go. "We'd get detained, and possibly arrested. We might be questioned for days, even weeks. Without due process, if Homeland Security got involved. And Stang would deny it all, of course."

Joan's face scrunched up in thought. "What if we went to the speech, and tried to warn him in person?"

"We wouldn't get within a hundred yards of him before the Secret Service swarmed all over us." Their options were dwindling. "How about the media? Could we tell them?"

"Same problem. We'd have to convince someone really high up before the President would listen, and we don't have any proof. Do you think Dan Rather is any easier to get a hold of than the President?"

"We have some proof. The speech."

"Shakespeare is dead. How can we prove he wrote it?"

Tom tapped his fingers on the desk, thinking. "What's left? Go after Stang?"

"Which one? Senior or Junior?"

"We probably couldn't get to Phil Jr.—he's protected by the Secret Service same as the President. But maybe we can pay Phil Sr. another visit, try to force him to call off his dogs."

"And then do what? Say he calls it off. Say we even take the next step, and murder him. Within a week, his son would have us hunted down and killed. Then he'd go ahead with the assassinations anyway."

This was ridiculous. The two most important people in America were going to die tomorrow, and there didn't seem to be any way to stop it. The same system that protected the President prevented Tom from helping him.

"So what can we do? Warning the President won't work. Showing up at the speech, if we can even get in, will just get us arrested."

"Jack had a ticket to Washington, so he was part of this. Attila and Vlad are probably part of it as well."

Joan let the implication of her sentence weigh on Tom.

"So, we wait for them to show up, and kill them?"

Joan folded her arms. "They're coming here to kill us."

"And you can handle this?"

"Yes. Maybe. I don't know. It's more than just the President. To be honest, I don't even like the guy. But if Stang becomes the leader of our country, he's going to start a war with China. You read the speech."

Tom nodded. To say the speech was inflammatory was putting it lightly. It blamed China for the deaths, and then made demands that the Chinese would never meet—the Communist government stepping down, a formal apology, restitution, the disbanding of the Chinese Army . . . This was more than just their lives and the lives of some politicians. There were millions, possibly billions, of lives at stake.

"What if this goes deeper than Attila and Vlad? We don't know how Stang plans to do it. He could fire a missile from miles away, for all we know. Besides, if they are the trigger men, they're already on their way to their destinations. A plane ride to Montreal is at least eight hours long."

"Then we somehow have to get the President and the Vice President away from those areas by 4:15."

They brainstormed for a few minutes, batting ideas back and forth. Some were bad, some were impossible, and a few were ridiculous. Joan chewed her lower lip.

"How about we fake an attempt? Like fire a few bullets into the air? Then they'd get the President out of there."

"We'd probably be killed before we could even fire

the first shot. Scratch that, we wouldn't even be able to get a gun anywhere near him. Where is this thing happening, anyway?"

Tom did a search for *North American Energy Commission* and found their website. He clicked on upcoming events.

"It's indoors. Invitation only, some kind of formal dinner. We couldn't get in if we wanted to."

Tom took out his cell and dialed Roy's new number. Maybe they had some ideas.

"How about we get one of those planes that do sky writing?" Roy suggested.

"The speech is inside. Last I checked, the Senate holds session inside as well."

"Maybe it'll be a nice day, they'll hold it on the White House lawn. Hold on, Abe has an idea."

Tom listened to some mumbling in the background. When Roy came back on, he laid it out. Tom was impressed.

"That's so simple it just might work," Tom said. "Do they have tours?"

"Bert says yes. He's been to Washington before."

"Will you be able to get what you need? It's a long time until the Fourth of July."

"Abe has got that covered. Think this can work for you, too?"

"I doubt it. We probably won't even be able to get in the building. Plus we don't have Abe. I'm not as recognizable in the public eye."

"Good luck. Call when you figure it out. We're going to stop by Abe's, then go to the airport. Good thing I took out the extra insurance on that rental car."

Roy hung up. Tom related their plan to Joan.

"Abe will probably get arrested. They'll put two and two together."

"He knows. But they won't be able to hold him for long."

"It wouldn't work for us."

"I know. But maybe we can use the same principle."

Tom sketched out an idea. Joan listened, and added to it. After bantering back and forth a few times, they had something that might actually fly.

"We'll need a sensor, or something that can pass for one. And uniforms."

"No problem. I'll call Stevie. He's been the prop master on my last two movies. He can get anything. Just find a logo."

Tom searched the Internet for Canadian companies. When he found a suitable picture he saved it to the hard drive. Then he enlarged it in Photoshop and printed out a high resolution copy.

"Perfect. Let me use your phone." Joan took it and left the room.

Tom searched through Bill's programs and found a business card creator. With it, he made some cards using the Canadian logo. He left the phone number blank, then printed up six on some card stock, three with the name Tom Johnson and three with the name Joan Smith. They came out looking professional, though it bothered him the printing wasn't embossed. Hopefully no one would notice. When he was finished, Joan approached the desk with a phone book.

"There's one magic shop nearby, but they close in twenty minutes. Are we convinced Attila and Vlad are a no show?"

"We don't have a choice. I don't know if we can get what we need in Canada. What about the other stuff?"

Joan handed him a piece of paper. "This is Stevie's email address. He wants you to send him a jpeg of the logo. If he gets it now, he can be ready in about two hours."

Tom looked at his watch. He still had to stop back at the hotel for his laptop and luggage, and then go to Joan's place. If they caught a late flight, they would get there late tomorrow morning, just enough time to get set up and work the kinks out of the plan. Tom emailed Stevie the logo.

"Do you have any other business you need to take care of before you go?"

Joan's eyes clouded. "I called Marsha after I talked to Stevie. She's going to close the business for a few days, make arrangements for Marty. The police found my purse, and they're looking for me."

"They want to question you, that's all."

Joan's eyes drifted to Bill's body, for the umpteenth time. Tom sensed her indecision.

"You don't have to go."

"Yes, I do."

"You can stay here, talk to the police, explain everything. I can manage in Canada without you."

He couldn't. Not by a long shot. But she was just a movie producer. She'd been through half a dozen traumas in just a few days. He had to give her an out.

"I've never run away from anything."

"I wouldn't call this a typical situation."

Joan met his eyes. "We have to hurry. The store is only a few blocks away."

Tom nodded, relieved. He gathered up what he needed and they headed for the car.

If they lived through this, he wanted to ask Joan if bravery came easily to her, or if she had to force it like everyone else. Tom had been forcing his since he arrived in LA. He wasn't sure how much more he had left.

CHAPTER 25

"Still no word from Jack?"

Phil Jr. took another sip of scotch. The tension was getting to him. He shouldn't have been drinking—not only because he needed a clear head, but because alcohol had a lot of calories. One more thing to worry about.

"No, Dad. He didn't check in when he was supposed to."

"Then why the hell don't you call him?"

Phil wanted to smash the speaker phone with his fist. The old man would never allow himself to be talked to like this, so why should he? They were cut from the same cloth. He bit his tongue and went over to the treadmill, putting his single malt in the beverage holder. Phil set the machine for a medium pace and began walking.

"We never call them outside of scheduled times, Dad. This is your rule, remember? So there's no connections."

"Use your brain, Junior. If Jack isn't in the game anymore, one of the others has to replace him. It's a long flight from LA to DC. What's that noise?"

"I'm on the treadmill. You told me to lose some weight."

"Call Jack."

"Fine." Phil drained his glass and switched the tread-mill off. He walked back to his desk and picked up his second line. As he punched in Jack's number, he held up a chrome letter opener and looked at a reflection of his chin. That wasn't fat. It was bad genetics.

"Yeah?"

Whoever answered didn't have Jack's voice. Dread crawled up Phil's back.

"Who is this?"

"Detective Roy Lewis, Chicago Police Department. Who is this?"

Phil covered the mouthpiece. "It's that cop, Tom's partner."

"God damn it!" Phil could picture his father's face turning red, that one squiggly vein in his head bulging out.

"What should I tell him?"

"Just hang up!"

Phil put the receiver on the hook and relaxed a tad. It amused him to hear his father frazzled. He poured himself another two fingers and turned the treadmill back on.

"Dad, you need to calm down."

"Call the others. Have Attila go to Washington. There's make-up in the kit, he'll have to cover up his tattoos. He trained on the equipment?"

"They all did. Have you seen it? Pretty cool set up. Those darts are wicked."

"They're called flechettes."

"Yeah, the flechettes. They don't even make a sound when they're fired."

"They use compressed air, a CO_2 cartridge. That's why I chose them. Silent, accurate, deadly. The perfect weapon of assassination."

The Secret Service wouldn't even know where the shot came from. The weapons were housed in fully functional digital cameras. Even if they were opened up, they looked perfectly normal. The flechettes were amazingly accurate, within a two inch radius from a hundred yards. Of course, they'd be fired at a much closer range. And even if the first shot missed for some reason, they each could fire four without reloading.

"They can actually take pictures, Dad. How would you like a snapshot of the President right when he gets a poison dart in the neck?"

Phil brought his hands up to his face, imagining he had the camera that killed the world's most powerful man. *Snap, you're dead.*

"Stay focused, Junior. Attila will need a press pass. You'll have to get a picture of him."

"Got one."

"Without the tattoos."

"The computer can take them off. Don't worry, Dad. It's under control. His press pass will be waiting for him at the hotel. He'll be right up front, have a nice, clear shot."

"And make sure their watches are synchronized to the second. Once one of them goes down, the Secret Service will rush to protect the other one. They have to die at the same time, or we won't get them both."

Like a broken record, his father.

"I'll make sure, Dad. Anything else?"

"Call me when they're in position."

His father hung up. Phil turned the speed up all the way and ran for a few minutes. When he lost his wind he hopped off and finished his scotch. After his breath returned, he called Vlad.

"This isn't one of the scheduled times."

Another Type A. Phil decided to surround himself with *yes* men when he took office.

"I'm aware of that, Vlad. Jack is out of commission. Arthur will have to go to Washington. I want you guys to leave, pronto."

"We're on our way to Bill's to take care of Tom and Joan."

"They can wait."

"Bill's line has been busy for a while. We should check."

"You should clean out your ears. I said they can wait. My father has a wild hair, and wants it done now. Besides, Bill always takes the phone off the hook when he's writing. Doesn't want to disturb the muse, or some such crap. Tell Arthur his ticket will be waiting for him at LAX. He'll be flying American Airlines. I want you both to call when you arrive."

"What happened to Jack?"

"No idea. I called him, that black cop answered. Could be in jail, dead, or on his way to DC himself. But we're not taking chances. Does Arthur know where to go when he gets in?"

"Yes." There was a wet sigh. "I'm really itching to get my hands on Joan."

"She'll be waiting for you when you get back. You

can have all the time you want with her, do whatever sick shit comes in your head. But right now, keep your eyes on the prize."

Phil hit the disconnect button, then dialed Bill's place. Busy. Odd that he'd take the phone off the hook when there was so much going on, but writers were a strange breed.

With Tom and Joan safely locked away in Bill's cellar, the only thing left to worry about was that black cop and the clones of Lincoln and Einstein. Phil mulled it over, but couldn't see how they could possibly be a threat. Even if they knew everything, there was no way they could stop it. Still, it was always smart to hedge your bets.

Phil flipped through his Rolodex and found Jerry's home number.

"Hello?" He sounded as if he'd been asleep.

"Jerry? Phil Stang. Look, I hate to bother you at this hour, but this is kind of an emergency."

"The Bureau is at your service, Mr. Speaker."

"I just had a phone call, two cops from Chicago. I think they're connected to the mob somehow. They wanted me to do something for them, I refused, so they threatened me."

"Are you okay?"

"I'm fine. But you can imagine. Calling my home number, saying they'd kill me. I've got my Secret Service guys on it, but I'd like it if you folks threw in as well."

"We'll make it a top priority. Do you know who they were?"

"Their names are Tom Mankowski and Roy Lewis. Go all out on this."

"When I'm done, even the Sheriff in Wasilla, Alaska will know their names. You mentioned organized crime. Do you know which family they're connected to?"

"No idea. But I'm sure you can find out. That's why you're Director of the FBI. They may have some accomplices as well. Let me give you some names. Albert Blumberg, Abraham Wilkens, and Joan DeVilliers."

"We'll take care of this for you, Mr. Speaker."

"Thanks, Jerry. I knew I could count on you."

Phil hung up. He would make more calls, to Justin at the Secret Service and Horace at the NSA. Then he had to get a ticket for Arthur and set up the press pass. But first; jogging or scotch?

He chose the scotch. During his last check-up, the doctor had cautioned him that he was in the early stages of cirrhosis. That didn't bother Phil in the least. Donor organs were easy to come by. He poured himself another drink and looked around his den. Even though the condo was among the best in DC, he wouldn't miss it at all.

His new accommodations were infinitely preferable.

CHAPTER 26

Washington, DC

When they finally settled in at the hotel, Bert had time to sort through his lures. He and Abe had gathered as many as they could, abandoning those stuck in Jack. The numbers were grim.

"What's the verdict?"

Bert shifted on his inflatable donut and made a face. "I'm out about two hundred grand."

Abe frowned. "You should have let me try to get the rest of them. We still can. The body probably won't be discovered for days. In fact, they'll be easier to remove when he's all bloaty and rotten."

Bert didn't care to dwell on that image. "In all honesty, I really don't care right now. The first time I lost my fortune, I was suicidal. Now, I just feel melancholy."

Abe sat on Bert's bed and began flipping through the cable guide.

"Near death experience. It'll do that to you. Your partner has been acting pretty laid back himself. He was stuck underwater for about five minutes. I thought he was dead for sure."

"Have you ever almost died?"

"Once, in high school. Some guys bet me that I couldn't stick my whole fist in my mouth. I did it, but couldn't get it out. Cut off my air. Some jock on the football team saved me. He had to step on my forehead and yank my arm."

"Did it change the way you looked at life?"

"Hell yeah. I haven't gone to a football game since. I still have the cleat scars."

"I meant in a more meaningful way."

Abe looked up from the magazine. "Like, did I analyze my life and decide to concentrate on things that were important like family and friends and stop wasting all my time sitting at home watching TV?"

"Did you?"

"For about a week. Now I think I watch even more TV than before. In fact, why am I here talking to you when I've got that big TV in my room?"

Roy came in through the side door. The three suites they'd rented were adjoining.

"The first four star hotel I ever stay in, and it's the Watergate. Remind me how I got talked into this."

Abe got up and clapped Roy on the shoulder. "We don't have time to play around. A hotel like this, everything is done for you. I need my suit cleaned, my hat blocked, the flyer copied, and a haircut. Plus, it's three in the morning, and they have 24-hour room service."

"These rooms cost more than our airfare. And we paid for yours."

"All in the name of patriotism. I'm ordering some prime rib. Anyone else want one?"

There were no takers. Abe nodded a goodbye and went back to his room, via Roy's.

Roy watched him leave. "That guy is a piece of work. You think he'll be able to pull it off tomorrow?"

"He doesn't have a choice. How about you?"

"We got the easy part. How's your ass?"

"The bleeding finally stopped. I could use another Vicodin."

"Way ahead of you." Roy handed him a pill bottle and turned to leave. Bert didn't want him to go just yet. He was overcome by a feeling that nothing should be left unsaid.

"Roy . . . Tom told me, the other day, about you losing your brothers."

Roy stopped and waited, silent.

"I had a brother too, died when I was a kid. I know what it feels like."

"You're getting weird on me."

"I'm not getting weird. Well, maybe I am. What I want to say, is, when I was hanging from that rope, you were there for me. Kind of like a big brother. I wanted to say thanks."

Roy pointed at him. "I will not hug you. Understand?"

"How about helping with this bandage?"

"Not even if you had gold bars coming out your ass. Now get some sleep. We can do this bonding shit over some beers, after we save the world. Night, Bert."

"Night, Roy."

Bert took two pills, then changed the dressing on his wound, being liberal with the topical antibiotic. It was deep and ugly, and probably could use a few stitches, but that would have to wait.

He killed the lights, brushed his teeth, and then crawled into bed. The Vicodin kicked in, and he slept without dreams.

"Wake up. Time to save the world."

Bert opened an eye and focused on Abraham Lincoln. Abe looked like he'd climbed out of a history book. His unruly hair had been professionally clipped, his beard was neatly trimmed, and he wore an antique black suit with creases in all the right places.

"How do I look?"

"Say something presidential."

Abe cleared his throat and put his hands on his lapels. "Four years ago, I scored seven times."

"I hope you have better material than that."

"Actually, I'm going to recite the Gettysburg Address. I memorized it back in school, for an assignment."

"Tell me you got an A."

"I got a D+. A few of the words slipped my mind. But I think I've got it down pat now. Why did Lincoln have four fathers?"

Bert couldn't tell if he was kidding or not. Rather than dwell on it, he rolled over and looked at the clock. It was going on one o'clock. He sat up in bed, a move that made him wince.

"Why'd you let me sleep so late?"

"We almost didn't go. The only way to get into the gallery while Senate is in session is with a pass. Roy spent all morning trying to get some. He finally had to call his boss in Chicago for help."

"But he got them?"

"I hope so. This haircut was thirty bucks."

Bert forced himself to his feet. The bandage was

stuck to him, and he had to take it off in the shower. Hurt like crazy, but no sign of infection. He slapped another one on and got dressed, jeans and a golf shirt. Room service sent up some aspirin—the Vicodin could wait until later.

When he was ready to go he knocked on Roy's door.

"Do you have the gallery passes?"

Roy was also in jeans, and the sleeves were rolled up on his gray button down shirt.

"Damn things were harder to get than Janet Jackson tickets. Luckily, my Loot knows some important cops in this town, or we'd be spending the whole day getting the run-around at the Senate Offices."

"I thought she suspended you."

"I'm on vacation, remember? I can visit the nation's Capitol like anyone else."

They pulled Abe away from the TV and the three of them took a cab to the Capitol Building. It was a cold, gray day. Bert hadn't been in DC for almost ten years, but he couldn't conjure up much enthusiasm for the several monuments they passed. He was nervous. There was a potential for disaster that they hadn't discussed. What if, despite their diversion, the VP got assassinated anyway? The Secret Service could mistakenly connect them with the crime. While Bert was all for saving millions of lives, he didn't want to spend the rest of his on death row.

The driver let them out at the east side of the building. It had begun drizzling, and in the haze the dome of the Capitol looked dirty and oppressive. They walked up the entrance ramp slowly, hemmed in by a big crowd also waiting in line. Apparently the average American's taste for tourism wasn't limited to theme parks. Though Bert could probably make an argument that Washington, DC, was the biggest amusement Mecca of them all.

"Did we remember the matches?"

"Got them. Relax." Roy patted his pants pocket.

"Everyone make sure their watches are synchronized. I checked mine this morning against CNN. Coming up on 2:38 right . . . now."

Abe set his watch. "When do I start?"

"At 4:12. We don't know how long you'll have before they try to remove you. Are you okay with this? You know you'll get arrested."

"No problem. When it gets out that I'm a national hero, think about the chick factor."

Bert didn't bother telling him that it might never get out.

"Okay, are we all clear on everything? I don't want any talking once we go in. Nothing to draw attention to ourselves."

"Draw attention?" Bert snorted. "We're two limping guys walking with Abraham Lincoln."

"Don't worry about it. Everyone will be looking at Abe. We'll be invisible, especially once the show starts. Right, Abe?"

"Hmm? I wasn't listening."

Roy gave him a tap in the back of the head. "The future of the world depends on what we do in the next ninety minutes."

"Gotcha. I'm all about helping the world. I freed your people, remember?"

The line moved at a steady pace, and after a tense moment walking through the metal detectors they were inside the Capitol Building. It was bigger than Bert remembered, all columns and arches and big works of art. There were three more long lines. Two had turnstiles and dividers, separating those who wanted to take a guided tour and those who preferred the self-guided option. All had to wait for tickets, which were free. The third line was for the gift shop.

Abe said, "What tour is complete without an official *I Love America* T-Shirt and the Strom Thurman in a snow globe?"

Roy ushered them over to the side, next to the Law Library doors.

"We're supposed to meet some Senator's aide at three. He's going to take us."

Bert noted, with some satisfaction, that Abe was drawing even more attention inside than he had outside. Maybe they could pull this off after all.

"Mr. Lewis and party?"

The kid was barely out of high school, pimple faced, red hair. He wore a tan blazer and brown slacks, and the knot in his tie was uneven.

"That's us. You're Senator Biltmore's aide?"

"Kevin Dermont. Nice to meet you all. Does everyone have their pass? Go ahead and clip them to your shirts. Have you seen the rest of your party?"

"The rest of our party?"

"I believe nine businessmen, visiting from Japan?"

"I think they're over there."

Roy pointed to a group of well-tailored Japanese men, standing near the entrance of the rotunda and chatting among themselves.

"Of course, please follow me."

They tailed Kevin to the group, where he failed to impress everyone with his halting Japanese greeting.

"We're grateful for this opportunity," one of the businessmen answered in flawless English. "Extend our thank you to the Senator."

"Does everyone have a pass?"

"We received them at the Senate Appointment Desk, thank you."

The kid led them through the lines and to the first of many guarded doors. Bert noted that the Capitol Police were abundant. All had uniforms, and all were armed. Maybe they wouldn't even make it to jail. Maybe they'd be shot and killed before given the chance.

They walked through a hall, decorated with large paintings of fat guys with white wigs. The air was cool, dry, and it smelled like a museum. The Japanese seemed more interested in Abe than in their surroundings. They were too polite to point, but their stares were obvious.

"Our first stop is the Old Supreme Court Chamber." Kevin bypassed another guard and ushered them into the room, where several dozen others milled about. "The impressive umbrella vault ceiling was designed by Benjamin Latrobe . . ."

He prattled on about some marble busts and the original desks and chairs, and before they could get a good look around they were on to their next stop. Bert picked up a tour pamphlet from a kiosk and looked through it.

This was not good. Apparently, there were only two more rooms to view before the Gallery. At this pace, they'd finish the tour before four o'clock, too early to save the VP.

The group went up the grand staircase and made their next stop the National Statutory Hall.

"This is actually the old House of Representatives Chamber. It was converted in 1964, and then later restored to its original appearance in the 1970s. Feel free to take a complimentary brochure."

The room was semi-circular, filled with marble columns and dozens of white, black, and gray statues of various dead guys. Kevin led them on a brisk walk-thru, pointing out the Car of History Clock, the Fireplace with the Declaration of Independence above the mantle, and the Liberty and the Eagle relief above the South entrance. Then he headed for the way out.

"Uh, Kevin? Can we take pictures?"

Kevin turned to Bert and frowned. "You don't have a camera."

"But several others in the tour do have them." Bert turned to the group. "Would you gentlemen like to take some pictures?"

There were several enthusiastic nods. Kevin put on a fake smile and said, "Of course. Take your time, enjoy the many works of art."

It bought them ten minutes, but that still wasn't enough. Bert's watch read 3:45. They had to somehow kill half an hour in the next room.

"This is the Old Senate Chamber. The Senate met here from 1810 until 1859. Then it became the Supreme Court Chamber until 1935. There, you can see the historic Franklin Stoves. Now, onto the gallery, where the Senate is currently in session."

Bert and Roy exchanged a glance of extreme panic. It was much too early. They had to stall the tour.

"What, uh, were some of the historic things that happened in this room?" Bert's voice came out more urgent than he would have liked.

"Quite a few. Did you have any particular event in mind?" Kevin's smile was in place, but it was obvious he had no desire to answer questions. He was probably still bristling from having to spend ten extra minutes in the Statutory Hall.

Bert racked his brain. High school history class was fourteen years ago, and he could barely recall any of it. But he was Einstein, dammit. He had one of the greatest minds to ever grace mankind. It should still be in there someplace.

He closed his eyes, willing himself back to that class. In his head, his old history textbook appeared. It was diffuse, out of focus, but he forced it to become clearer. The details came slowly. The brown paper shopping bag he'd cut up to use as a book cover. His name written inside, right under a person named Sam Gold. He saw the table of contents, surprised that he was able to read it. As if it were right in front of him, Bert opened the book to the 1800s . . .

"Didn't the Webster-Hayne Debate take place in this room?" Bert asked, meeting Kevin's stare.

"I don't recall. Perhaps you can enlighten us?"

"I believe it started as a plan to curtail western land sales in 1830. Senator Robert Hayne from South Carolina believed that an agricultural system built on slavery could only survive with an unlimited supply of cheap western lands, and argued that the states should have the right to set aside certain federal laws if they wished."

Bert glanced at Roy, who nodded, urging him on.

"Senator Daniel Webster of Massachusetts extrapolated the debate to one of State's rights versus national power. He argued for two days that the nation wasn't just an association of separate states, but a government by the people. As such, it was responsible to the people and could be modified only if the people, not the special interests of the government, chose it to be."

Several of the Japanese businessmen had gathered around Bert to listen.

"Thank you for that information. Now moving along—"

"This was also the room where the famous Missouri Compromise was reached, correct?"

"Yes, that's correct. Now if—"

Bert addressed the tour group. "Missouri had petitioned to enter the Union as a slave state, which would have tipped the balance of power because free and slave states were equally represented."

"Uh . . . did they allow it?" Roy asked.

"The compromise was that Missouri was admitted as a slave state only if Maine was admitted as a free state. And then slavery was barred from the rest of the land comprising the Louisiana Purchase. This kept the nation together for forty more years, until the slave states tried to secede over the issue, bringing about the Civil War. Almost as well known is the Compromise of 1850 . . ."

Bert went on to talk about the debate among Henry Clay, Daniel Webster, and John C. Calhoun. It culminated in a Mississippi Senator actually pulling a gun on a Missouri Senator. This led to another Clay story, about the censuring of President Andrew Jackson in 1834, and Bert followed that up with the famous tale of the attack on Senator Charles Sumner by South Carolina Representative Preston S. Brooks. Brooks had taken exception to an address Sumner had given, and beaten the Senator with his walking cane in this very room.

The more Bert talked, the better his delivery became. He began to move around the floor, using his hands to gesture and point. While he couldn't quite understand where the information was coming from, he didn't stop to question the phenomenon. He just went with it.

When Bert checked his watch again, it was just after four o'clock.

"I could go on, but I'm sure you're all anxious to see the new Senate Chamber, where many other acts of deceit and violence have occurred."

Kevin gave Bert a weak smile and led them out of the room.

"How the hell did you remember all of that?" Roy took him aside, whispering.

"I have no idea. It was like I was reading it in my head."

"You'll have to teach me that trick. I have trouble remembering my phone number."

They took the stairs to the third floor. There was another guard by the entrance, this one standing behind a desk. "Good afternoon, Gentlemen. We ask that you please leave all pagers, portable phones, and cameras here. The Senate is currently in session, so there is to be no talking. You're welcome to walk anywhere around the upper level."

He opened the door. Bert looked at Abe. His forehead was glossy from sweat, even though the building was cool. Then he turned to Roy, and the cop appeared positively sickly.

"Here we go," Abe said to himself. He took a deep breath and held it.

They went in.

CHAPTER 27

Montreal

Tom tried his best to sleep on the flight, but exhausted as he was, his mind wouldn't allow it. There was too much to think about.

Even if they did pull it off—if they could save both the President and the Vice President, it wouldn't be over. Stang would simply try again. The man had too much money and power. Out of morbid curiosity, Tom had accessed the FBI Most Wanted List on his laptop, and wasn't surprised to find himself on it. The others were as well. Unless they all desired to spend the rest of their lives hiding, surfacing only to stop assassination attempts, they had to end this.

Tom knew of two ways; killing Stang and son or gathering evidence. Since he was a cop and not a hit man, the choice was made for him. They would pay the former Senator another visit and try to find all of Harold's notes on the cloning experiment. Maybe then they'd have enough to convince the authorities.

Of course, that also meant going public, and Tom

wasn't sure he could handle that. He was still having some trouble dealing with the fact that he was Thomas Jefferson. Once the world found out, the media attention would be never-ending. He would no longer be an average guy with an average job—he would be outed to celebrity status and become public domain. Tom Mankowski would no longer exist. While that might work for Joan, who already had a career in the spotlight, it wasn't what Tom wanted out of life.

Of course, all of that was assuming they'd actually live through this.

He turned to Joan. She was sleeping, her head against the window. *Remarkable woman,* he thought. Strong, pretty, successful, smart, funny. Under different circumstances, she never would have given him the time of day. But fate, if you could call it that, threw them together and Tom sensed that she felt the same pull of attraction that he did.

Tom didn't put too much stock in that; crisis situations tended to heighten emotion. Joan was a woman who really did have everything. What could Tom possibly offer her? Kids and a little house in the suburbs? That's what she went to LA to get away from.

As if the situation was complicated enough, add some hormones to the mix.

Tom closed his eyes, thinking over their plan. It lacked the elegant simplicity of Abe's idea. There were too many things that could go wrong, cause them to fail. Hopefully, they'd prepared for them, but real life tended to pay scant attention to plans, no matter how well thought-out.

Disaster scenarios coursed through his head—failing to save the President, getting arrested, getting killed. He tried to block them out, but couldn't. If they failed, there could easily be a nuclear war in the immediate future.

Something touched Tom's shoulder. He opened his eyes. Joan had switched positions, her head now resting on his arm. She snored softly. He lifted up the armrest between them and put his arm around her. She nuzzled against him, and all the bad thoughts were wiped from his head. He was asleep a few minutes later.

They arrived at Mirabel-Montreal Airport at a little after eleven in the morning, Eastern Time. Tom had seen so many terminals in the last few days that they were all beginning to blur together. This one had the distinction of being bilingual. All of the signs and all of the announcements were in French as well as English.

Joan looked good, certainly not like someone who had just spent eight hours on a plane. Somehow she'd managed to climb over his seat and freshen up without waking him. Her hair and make-up were pristine, and her blouse was wrinkle free. In contrast, all Tom had done to start the day was splash some cold water on his face and brush his teeth with his finger.

Joan handed the Custom's Agent her passport, and Tom pulled out his driver's license.

"And how long do you plan to stay in Canada?"

"A week," Joan answered.

"Business or pleasure?"

"Pleasure."

"Do you have anything to declare?"

Joan nudged Tom with her elbow. "The gentleman does."

Tom raised an eyebrow. "What do I want to declare?"

Her smile was full wattage. "Independence."

Tom resisted the urge to groan. "How long have you been waiting to say that?"

"All flight. That was the high point of my entire week."

"Better than that movie deal you just landed?"

"Sometimes it's the little things."

He thought about her snuggling next to him on the plane. "Can't argue with that."

They located the rental car place and got wheels, and then took a room at the Montreal Ramada, using the name Mr. and Mrs. Johnson. If Tom had any illusions about sharing a room with her, they were thwarted when Joan suggested they get a double.

"We can each have a bed."

Even though she looked bright-eyed and bushy-tailed, Joan insisted on a shower. Tom went through the phone book and located six local fire departments. He jotted down their numbers. Then he found a nearby copy shop and noted the address.

There were still three hours before the shindig was to begin, but already the police were out in force. On a drive-by, Tom counted at least a dozen uniforms and plainclothes cops swarming around the entrance. Also standing vigil were several Secret Service agents, complete with Ray Bans and earpieces. A block away, three Mounties on horseback waited on the corner.

As Tom had expected, they'd never be able to get very far into the building, let alone the room where the President was speaking.

After Tom took a quick shower, they stopped at a nearby restaurant and located the pay phone by the restrooms. Tom made sure it worked, and then copied down the number.

Their next stop was a department store, where they got a digital camera. From there it was on to the copy place Tom had found in the phone book. Like its American counterpart, it offered a variety of services. Tom rented some computer time and got to work.

An hour later, they had business cards with the restaurant pay phone number printed on them. Using the camera, they also made and laminated some picture IDs, complete with the Canadian logo. *Enbridge*. Tom punched holes in them and attached some alligator clips. He also bought a clipboard, and spent a few minutes hunting through the various waste baskets in the store, stuffing it with official-looking papers.

Back at the hotel, Joan showed him how to work the meter. It was a technical-looking piece of equipment the size of a portable radio, complete with dials, switches, lights, and a red needle.

"It's from the movie *Galaxy Invaders*. The heroes used it to detect the heat given off by the alien."

"It detects heat?"

"It doesn't detect anything. It's phony. See this button? Press it and the needle jumps and the red light blinks. This button here makes it beep. The rest are decoration."

Tom hefted the prop by the handle, waving it to and fro, pressing the buttons on the sly to make the needle jump. While he practiced, Joan unpacked her suitcase.

"I hope this fits. I guessed you were a 42 long."

Joan tossed over a bright orange jumpsuit. Tom inspected it. Not only was his name embroidered on the vest below the *Enbridge* logo, the logo was also on the back.

"This is perfect."

"Got you this too."

She tossed Tom a white hard hat, also with the logo. They shrugged their jumpers on over clothing, as they were meant to be worn. Tom noticed that they even had some grease marks on them, appearing as if they'd been in use for a while. A nice touch.

"You ready?" Tom noted that even with the hard hat on, Joan looked cute.

"Ready. Are you sure you want to be the point man? I took some acting classes in school."

"I'm a cop. I'm used to dealing with uncooperative people."

Joan furrowed her eyebrows. "I just wish we had a back-up plan, in case this ones tanks."

Tom felt the same way. But they didn't have a choice. "We can do this."

She nodded. Tom checked his watch. It was 3:48. Less than half an hour to save the President's life.

They got on their way.

CHAPTER 28

Washington, DC, and Montreal

Bert went to the railing and looked down upon the Senate Chamber one floor below him. From this vantage point, he could see everything.

The room was big and round, brightly lit. Rows of mahogany desks were arranged in a semi circular pattern, and Bert was surprised to see half of them empty. Occupying the remainder were Senators, running the gamut of race, age, and sex. Their dress was as varied as they were, three piece suits to business casual. They drank coffee and bottled water and had little side conversations with each other and their aides while a voice thundered over the loud speakers in a monotone that sounded quite bored.

Elsewhere, activity. Interns and messengers coming and going, a group in a box off to the side that included some reporters and photographers, most of whom looked supremely disinterested. Several video cameras were in operation, recording everything for C-SPAN.

Not what Bert had been expecting. Perhaps he'd

harbored images of important men in robes making grand speeches that held the audience in rapt attention. This was more like a college seminar, except less formal.

Bert turned his attention to the central dais. Sitting above the Senate was the Vice President, holding what looked like a white rock in his hand. Bert figured it was a gavel. There were several people on the tier below him, and Bert could see someone standing diligently in the rear that was undoubtedly Secret Service.

Bert looked around the gallery where he stood. It was a large hallway that wrapped around the Chamber, kind of like a long, circular balcony. Several dozen onlookers milled about, many staring down at the proceedings, but just as many whispering to each other or walking around. Bert counted four Capitol Policemen among them, and assumed there were more he didn't see. Everything was relaxed, casual. Roy caught his eye and gestured for him to come over. He was standing next to a large bust of a familiar face. Thomas Jefferson.

"Almost time."

Bert checked his watch. Eleven minutes after four. They had less than three minutes. Bert searched for Abe in the crowd, but couldn't find him.

Fifteen minutes earlier, in Montreal, Tom had dropped Joan off at the restaurant and was attempting to drive through the large group of people that had gathered around the hotel storefront. Waiting for the President to make his exit, Tom guessed. They were being kept off the sidewalk and away from the entrance by velvet ropes. Tom honked, cutting a swathe through the crowd, eventually edging the car up to the hotel. He was instantly surrounded by cops and the Secret Service.

"What the heck is going on?" Tom made a show of looking around.

"Sir, you'll have to move your vehicle."

Tom pointed to the ID clipped to his chest.

"I'm from Enbridge Natural Gas. Just got a call there's a leak in the building."

An agent, eyes impenetrable behind his sunglasses, consulted a clipboard. Then he spoke quietly into his lapel mike.

"What's going on here?" Tom made a show of looking around him. "Some kind of party?"

"The US President is speaking."

"Hey, buddy, I don't care who's speaking. I need to get some readings."

"You'll have to wait in the car until you're cleared to enter the building."

"I don't need to enter the building. I need to check the foundation first."

The secret service guy was impassive.

"Look, if you don't let me check for a gas leak, you're endangering this entire block. Once the saturation reaches five percent, it's flammable. Anyone in there lights a cigarette, plugs in a toaster, rubs their socks on the carpet—BOOM!"

The agent made his decision and allowed Tom out of the car. Tom grabbed his prop meter and followed him to the front of the building. When he got there, two men frisked him.

"What the hell?"

They searched his pockets and came out with the

phony business cards. Tom watched as one of the agents called the phone number on his cell while another examined his gas detector.

"Careful! That's sensitive equipment."

The agent on the phone asked several questions. Tom had to assume Joan was following the script, answering as Enbridge Natural Gas and confirming both the leak and Tom. When he hung up he gave Tom a small nod.

"Go ahead, take your readings."

Tom frowned at them, looking annoyed, and then took off his hard hat and ran his fingers through his hair. While doing so, he palmed the three small vials that were taped inside the hat band.

Then he took the meter back and began to point it around the sidewalk. He eventually moved up to the front doors of the hotel and hit the button on the handle, making the needle jump.

"Uh-oh. It's a leak alright. Can you open the door?"

"We still don't have internal confirmation," one agent said to another.

Tom snapped a vial in his fingers, softly breaking it and releasing the liquid. A rotten egg smell drifted up from his hands.

"Can't you smell that?"

The smell was mercaptan. It was the primary ingredient in stink bombs, a novelty shop classic. It was also the chemical used by gas companies to add scent to otherwise odorless natural gas. Harmless, but nauseating. Tom glanced at the agents and could tell they noticed the smell. One even fanned the air with his hand.

"You better let me take a reading inside."

They had a brief talk among themselves, and then

allowed him in, accompanied by two escorts. The lobby was full; more cops and Secret Service, and several hotel employees. Tom broke another vial and hit the switch on the sensor to make it beep.

"The levels are high. You'd better get these people out of here."

"Which people?"

"The whole damn building. The whole damn block. Do you see these levels?" Tom pointed to his meter needle, which he held in the red. "You've got to clear this place out, shut off the main. I don't even want to be standing here."

The guy turned away, speaking into his microphone. Tom looked at his watch. It was already 4:11. They were badly behind schedule. Where was Joan?

At that same moment, hundreds of miles away in Washington, DC, Bert frantically searched the crowd for Abe. He finally spotted his stovepipe hat on the other side of the gallery. Bert wiped his palms on his jeans and swallowed hard. The moment of truth had come.

"Friends, Senators, citizens!" Abe's voice bellowed, matching the volume of the droning Senator who was on the house sound system. "I came here today because it is the historic anniversary of the Gettysburg Address."

The gallery focused on Abe. Bert stared down into the chambers and noted that many of them, too, were staring up. Some were chuckling. The Senator who had the floor had stopped speaking. Bert had no idea if it really was the anniversary or not—he guessed not.

But like everybody else he was momentarily spell-bound by Abe, his words, his presence.

Abe didn't hesitate. He launched right into it.

"Four score and seven years ago, our forefathers brought forth on this continent a new nation, conceived in liberty and dedicated to the proposition that all men are created equal. No matter how they were, uh, created . . ."

Bert stared as two of the Capitol Police had begun to move on Abe. He turned his attention to the Senate floor and saw that the Vice President appeared amused.

"There, in the box." Roy nudged him. "That guy with the camera. I think it's Attila."

"Now we are engaged in a great civil war, conceived and enduring, consecrating great brave men who greatly and bravely braved great things with, um, bravery."

Bert watched the man, whose camera was aimed at the VP while every other eye in the place was on Abe. Warning bells went off in Bert's head. That little poison dart they'd found on Jack . . .

"We need to do this. Now."

Roy reached into his jacket pocket and removed an unwrapped pack of Black Cat firecrackers. A string of fifty.

The police grabbed Abe, and he threw his hands up in the air dramatically, tossing out dozens of sale fliers for Honest Abe's Used Car Emporium. They cascaded down into the Senate chambers.

"We are met on the great battlefield of that war!" Abe continued, even as a third policeman jumped on him. "This is America! I have a right to free speech! You can't silence me! I won the war, dammit! I freed the slaves! I probably did a whole bunch of other important stuff!"

Bert screened Roy from view as he lit the match. He kept his eye on Attila and held his breath.

The firecrackers began to go off while still in the air. They fell onto Chambers with the rapport of machine gun fire, causing instant panic on the floor. Senators ducked under desks, covered their heads, screamed out loud. The Secret Service man dove on the VP, pulling him to the floor. Bert turned to look at Attila. He was making his way through the crowd, heading for the exit. But had he gotten his shot off?

Roy tried to pull Bert to the ground, to imitate what everyone else was doing. But Bert had to see, had to know if they'd completed their mission. Finally, after almost a minute of waiting, a swarm of agents and police had surrounded the Vice President and were taking him out of Chambers. The VP appeared shaken up but alive.

Bert let out a breath, unaware he'd been holding it.

"We did it. We saved him."

He turned to look for Abe. The cops were pulling him roughly out of the gallery, the cuffs already on. As he passed Bert he grinned and gave him a wink.

"I assure you gentlemen I had nothing to do with that outburst. I just wanted to sell some cars . . ."

They hauled him off. The room became a hubbub of commotion, everyone talking at once, everyone unsure as to what had just happened. Bert checked his watch. Seventeen minutes after four. They had done their job.

But how about Joan and Tom?

*   *   *

At 4:12 in Montreal, Tom had almost succumbed to panic. The authorities weren't evacuating the building, and there was no sign of Joan.

Then, like an angel sent from heaven, Joan stepped into the hotel lobby, more Secret Service agents around her. She had an official-looking clip board at her side and Tom's cell phone in her hand.

"Oh my God. Can you smell that? What are the levels, Tom?"

"Three percent." Tom broke the last vial, almost gagging at the stench.

"We've got to clear these people out of here now!" Joan dialed a number on the phone and pretended to talk to their home base. Sirens could be heard in the distance, getting closer. Before showing up, Joan had called all six of the local fire departments and told them about the gas leak. In a few minutes it would be pandemonium.

Tom checked his watch. It would be close. Were these lunkheads going to get the President out of there or what? Finally, six agents went running off down the hallway. Bravely rushing to save their leader, Tom hoped.

"There's a gas leak!" Tom shouted to everyone in the lobby. "Nobody panic!"

They panicked. Tom flowed out of the lobby with the rest of the people, just as several fire engines arrived. He met up with Joan and they melded into the crowd and watched. The Secret Service allowed the firemen in, and shortly began to assist in evacuating the building. When Tom saw people coming out wearing tuxedos, he guessed the Presidential dinner had been evacuated as well.

"Looks like we did it."

Tom nodded. "They probably ushered the President out a side door." He checked his watch and noted it was 4:17. If the assassination had happened, the Secret Service would be corralling people for questioning rather than letting them leave. The relief he felt was like a drug, purging everything bad from his body.

Joan made a face. "For just saving the world, that was kind of anticlimactic."

"You think so? I was fighting the whole time not to throw up. Let's get out of here, find out how the others did in DC."

Tom made his way through the crowd, having to push and shove because it was so densely packed. When he got to the car he took off his hat and turned around to talk to Joan.

She was gone.

CHAPTER 29

Montreal

The guy to Joan's left uttered a small gasp, and then dropped dead on the asphalt.

Before she could even react to what was happening, someone had grabbed her arm and pulled her away.

"Poison dart. Move, or you're next."

The man had a beard and mustache, and he was wearing glasses. He had a large, odd-looking nose, too big for his face. But the eyes—those deep green eyes—were instantly recognizable.

Vlad.

He was pressing a camera up against her. Joan guessed it was just a housing for his weapon—that's how he'd planned to kill the President.

"I said move, or you'll die where you stand."

She looked for Tom, but he'd vanished into the crowd. Then she turned to Vlad. His face was red, his lips pursed. He was seriously angry, and Joan had no illusions that he would kill her if she didn't move. But would it be better to die here, quick and easy, or go with the psycho someplace private, where he could take his time?

Her feet began to move of their own volition and he led her away. Joan could guess the horrors in store for her, but she didn't want to die. Even if she'd regret it later. They made their way to the other end of the street, Vlad with his arm locked around hers, the camera pressed to her side. He cut through an alley, taking her away from the commotion, the people, Tom. Every muscle in Joan's body was coiled. She kept waiting for something, anything, that would give her an opportunity to get away. The farther they walked, the less likely it seemed she would get one.

"How do you think Stang will react when he hears you failed?"

Vlad's rage was instantaneous. In one motion he released Joan's arm and backhanded her across the face. She hadn't been prepared for such a sudden blow, and found herself falling backward, landing on the tarmac. Her hard hat had flown off, bouncing against a Dumpster. Bright motes swam in her vision. She brought a hand up to her face. It came away red. Nosebleed.

"Hurts, doesn't it?" He reached up and pulled at his own nose, removing the fake latex one, exposing the swollen, discolored one underneath. "Put this on to hide the bruise."

The rubber nose bounced off of her chest. Joan blinked back tears of pain and tried to quell the ringing in her head. The camera was at his side, no longer pointed at her. Now was the time to escape.

She didn't have the chance. Quick and savage, Vlad kicked her in the right side. Joan managed to shift so he mostly hit her arm, but the blow sent her rolling.

She'd taken kicks before, by shoeless opponents of equal size. None hurt like this. Her entire arm began to go numb, and the motes she saw became blurry.

Vlad came again, grinning lasciviously. Joan tried to bat away his hand as he reached for her, but he managed a good grip on her hair. He yanked, forcing her head back.

"I'm not going to beat you to death in the alley. It won't be that easy. I have a place nearby. Someplace private. All my tools are there. We're going to have hours of fun."

Joan flailed out her leg, kicking at the camera. He kept it out of reach.

"What's going on?"

A man was standing at the mouth of the alley. Young, short hair, muscular build. He took a step towards them.

"Don't . . ." Joan started to say.

Too late. Vlad pointed the camera and a second later the guy was doubling over, blood foaming from his mouth.

"Now there's a Kodak moment."

Joan ground her teeth together and made her decision. If she was going to die, she would die trying to get away, not cowering in a corner. She scrambled to her feet and ran for the mouth of the alley. At any moment, she expected to feel a dart penetrate her skin. It looked painful, but quick. Better than being dragged back to his place.

But the dart didn't come. Instead, something hit her in the back of the head. Joan lost all motor function. Her world began to spin and she fell onto all fours.

Vlad kicked again, his foot burying itself in her stomach and sending her rolling into a brick wall.

"Get up."

Joan coughed, spit some blood. She sat up. "No."

Vlad began to shake, and then went from zero to psychotic is less than a second, kicking and punching and swearing at her. Joan tried to keep her head, blocking some blows, letting others land where they didn't do much harm, until he made the biggest mistake of his entire life.

He swung at her with the camera.

Joan met the swing with a flat palm, knocking the weapon from his hand, sending it spinning through the air and cracking against the ground. Now they were evenly matched.

Vlad, in a rage state, was oblivious to the loss of his weapon. He continued to punch and pummel, snarling like an animal, spittle spraying from his mouth. Joan saw the opening and lashed out her foot, hitting him solidly in the solar plexus. Vlad stumbled back, holding his gut.

Joan got to her feet. She hurt all over, but she pushed the pain aside. She'd beaten him once. She could beat him again.

She widened her stance. Vlad attacked. Joan spun into a reverse kick and connected solidly with Vlad's jaw. He left his feet and smacked hard against the asphalt, landing on his back, arms and legs splayed out. His head bounced on his neck.

Joan wiped blood off her face, using her sleeve. Then she took a running start and punted Vlad right between the legs, trying to kick his testicles up into his skull. He howled, curling up into a ball. Joan knew she needed to kill him. For what he did to her. To Marty. She had to end this, here and now.

But in her mind's eye she saw Bill, his dead eyes wide open after she'd shot him. It made her feel sick, empty. And that had been done to save Tom's life. She hated this man cowering before her, but he was defenseless. As much as he deserved to die, Joan couldn't find it in herself to do it. Not with her bare hands. Not like this.

As she hesitated, Vlad managed to get to his feet. He limped out of the alley, heading for the street. She thought of all the people Vlad must have murdered, and all the ones he would eventually murder if she let him get away. She thought about spending the rest of her life looking over her shoulder, wondering when he was going to try to get her again.

Joan made her decision. Maybe she couldn't kill him, but she could take him out of the game. Permanently.

She took three steps and launched herself into the air, aiming her flying kick at Vlad's back. He fell, face forward, onto the sidewalk. She ran to him, knowing what she had to do, wondering if she had the courage, the stomach, for it. Fate made it easier. Next to Vlad, in the gutter, was an empty beer bottle. She broke it against the pavement and grabbed Vlad's head by the hair, turning it to face her.

Two pokes, and Vlad's green eyes were gushing red. His screams were shrill, almost inhuman. Joan released him and he scrambled to his feet, bleeding and howling and permanently blind, his hands clamped to his eyes. He ran straight into traffic.

Joan watched it happen as if it were slow motion. Vlad staggering into the street. The sound of the horn. The screech of brakes.

The bus hit him head on. Vlad's arms reached out and grabbed the bumper as his legs went under the front tire. He wasn't dragged, exactly. It was more like he was erased. Pinned between the wheel and the street, Vlad's lower half was scraped away, leaving a wide streak of gore for almost thirty yards, like a big red skid mark.

Joan limped out of the alley, holding her side. She followed the trail up to the bus. The driver had gotten out, staring at Vlad in utter disbelief.

"He just jumped out. He just jumped out."

"It wasn't your fault." Joan placed a hand on his shoulder. "He was trying to kill me."

The driver looked at Joan, dazed. Vlad's upper body was still pinned under the tire. His lower body was . . . gone. Joan watched as his face contorted, his mouth opening and closing like landed fish. The pain must have been unimaginable.

Then, after a moment, the twitching stopped.

Joan turned on her heels and walked away. She hadn't gotten half a block when someone honked from the other side of the street. Tom. He parked and hurried to her, his face awash with concern.

"Are you okay?"

She nodded, unsure of her voice. At any moment, Joan felt as if her legs would give out.

"What happened?"

"Vlad."

Tom looked around, focusing on the traffic back-up. "Where is he?"

"He . . . caught a bus."

Tom reached out to her, took her hand. Joan hurt in a dozen places, and her emotions were fried. She made a sound that was halfway between a laugh and a sob, and then she hugged him. He wrapped his arms around her, holding her close, patting her back, rubbing her hair, rocking her gently to and fro.

"I talked to Roy. They saved the VP. You okay?"

"Remember what I said earlier, about it being anti-climactic?"

Tom nodded.

"I take it back."

Joan buried her face into his chest, letting go of the fear and pain. They stood like that, embracing each other, until the ambulance came and scraped up what was left of Vlad. The horrors of the last few days, and the emptiness Joan realized she had been feeling for years, all seemed to melt away in Tom's arms. For the very first time since she moved away from home, she felt safe.

And it was the best feeling in the world.

CHAPTER 30

"I want them dead."

Phil had never heard his father so upset. He stared at the speaker phone, trying to imagine the look on his face, but none came to mind. There was no precedent for it.

"Dad, calm down, we'll have another chance."

"Have them killed, Junior. Hire mercenaries. Pay the Mafia. I want them hunted down and gutted like deer."

It unnerved Phil more than he cared to say. Dad was always a pillar, a rock. But his voice was cracking and he seemed to be losing all control.

"We'll get them, Dad. We've got the airports covered. We froze their credit and their bank accounts. I've got people in LA tying Joan and Tom in with the murder of her assistant. And we also have Abe in custody."

"Is he giving anything up?"

"So far he's not saying anything. We can only hold him for 48 hours without pressing charges."

"Then charge him with something, dammit!"

"He really didn't do anything, other than disturbing the peace."

"Make something up! Use your brain!"

Dad went on a coughing jag, and Phil poured himself some Scotch. For the first time, the very first time, he was beginning to doubt his father. It scared Phil, because it was like doubting himself.

"Dad, I'm taking care of it. You need to rest. The operation—maybe it's left you a little unnerved."

There was a pause. Phil wondered if he had perhaps pushed too far. When his father finally answered, his voice was small, quiet.

"This is our dream, Junior."

"I know, Dad."

"Thirty-five years in the making. We've sacrificed so much. Even with a new kidney, I won't be around forever."

"You'll always be around. I'm your legacy."

"Cut the sentimental bullshit. I'm the one who started this. I want to be around to reap the rewards. If I can't be there to see you take the oath, it was a waste of my whole life."

"I spoke to the Secret Service. They don't even know that there were any assassination attempts. We can try again soon, same plan. There will be another chance later this month."

"First we have to get rid of those damn clones!"

Another coughing fit. Phil drained the scotch and reached for the bottle.

"Maybe I should come down to the house, visit for a few days."

His father was silent.

"I'll free up my schedule." Phil thought out loud. "I haven't seen you in a while, anyway. Maybe we can throw the ball around, like old times."

"We never threw the ball around."

"Yeah, well, it's never too late to start."

His father's voice became very cold. "I don't need you to worry about me. I need you to do your fucking job."

"I'll see you in a day or two. Bye, Dad."

He hung up the phone and called his travel agent to book the flight. Dad was wrong. Phil wasn't worried about his father in the least.

He was worried about himself.

CHAPTER 31

Springfield

  1 cordless drill
  1 portable step ladder
  1 funnel
  1 crowbar
  9 cans foam insulation
  1 20# bag powdered cement
  2 rolls duct tape
  1 caulking gun
  1 gravity knife
  2 M18 Taser guns
  1 can Guard Alaska bear repellent
  1 aluminum police baton
  4 Kevlar vests with trauma plates

Tom looked at the equipment spread out on the motel bed. Bert and Roy arrived the day before Joan and Tom, and had done the shopping.

"It's a good thing Springfield had an Army surplus store."

Joan seemed unimpressed. "This is all we'll need to break into Stang's place?"

Roy nodded. "Bert and I checked the place out. Security is tight, but can be beaten. The only rough spot will be Stang's assistant, Jerome Huntington. Did a background check. Would you believe that guy was a Navy SEAL?"

Tom could believe it. Not too many people in the health care industry carried pistols. Besides, there was something about Jerome, some sort of vibe he gave off, that frightened Tom.

"Shouldn't we get some guns or something?" Joan gave Tom a nervous glance. They'd left theirs in LA rather than risk taking them on an international flight, and Roy had lost his in the river. Illinois had a mandatory waiting period to buy firearms, so they couldn't get any by tonight.

"The taser is almost as good. It shoots two probes up to fifteen feet away, a hundred feet per second. Sends a pulse that completely overrides the skeletal muscles, causing uncontrollable contractions and massive disorientation for up to 15 minutes. Even works through a bulletproof vest."

"And I'm fine with this." Bert picked up a can the size of a small fire extinguisher and read from the label. "Shoots a thick fog of blinding pepper spray up to twenty feet away, guaranteed to stop a rampaging grizzly or your money back."

Tom wondered who would be alive to receive the refund if the product didn't work, but he kept that to himself.

"Bert and I got you a police baton, Joan." Roy handed her an aluminum billy club with a black rubber grip, roughly two feet long. "We figured, with your martial arts background."

Joan palmed the weapon and did something very fast with her fingers that made it twirl. Tom detected the tiniest trace of a smile on her lips.

"This will do," she said.

When 2 a.m. finally rolled around, they loaded up the gear and drove to Stang's place. Tom parked off road in a copse of trees about a mile away. The night was windy, and dark in the way it never got in the city.

They hoofed it the remainder of the way, ducking in the ditch alongside the road when the infrequent car drove past. It was slow going—the equipment was heavy and everyone was nursing injuries. Even though he was cold, Tom's hands were sweating in his latex gloves. There was no doubt that Stang would recognize them, but none of them were keen on leaving finger-prints.

The iron fence around the perimeter of the mansion was for show rather than security. Roy was able to pry a bar loose and they all slipped through, onto the grounds. The house and lawn were reasonably well lit. After a brief discussion, it was decided the northwest corner of the building would be the best approach. Not only was it harder to see things on an angle, but most of the windows on those two sides appeared to have their shades drawn.

Between the fence and the house was about an acre of carefully maintained grass. They took it in a sprint, moving as fast as they could. Midway there Tom tripped over a recessed sprinkler head, the step ladder clattering to the ground before him. Roy and Joan helped him up, kept him going. When all of them finally had their backs against the cool brick wall of the mansion, they took a few minutes to catch their collective breath. Tom listened to the wind, expecting at any moment to hear a police siren approaching. None did.

They began the break-in. Roy pointed out the first annunciator. It was a large metal box, the size of a medicine cabinet, painted white and attached to the wall about ten feet high off the ground. Inside was the horn, and a big one by the look of it.

Tom set the ladder underneath and climbed up to get started. There were slats cut into the box, like vents in a school locker. Using a penlight, Tom peered through a slit to see the cover lock. It was wired. Opening the box would set off the alarm.

Bert handed up a can of aerosol foam. Tom attached a tube to the nozzle and stuck it through the slats, filling up the annunciators horn. The foam was used in basements and attics to seal cracks and leaks and prevent heat loss. It dried quickly and had excellent insulating properties.

When the throat was full, Tom used two more cans to completely cover the outside of the horn. Then he sealed the vents with caulk, drilled a hole in the top of the box, and used the funnel to pour in dry concrete. That would fill in any remaining pockets of air inside the box.

The principle was simple. Sound traveled through the air in waves. By replacing a gas with a solid, the sound waves had no way to escape, and were effectively muffled. It would be like trying to scream with your head under water, except powdered concrete and foam insulation were quite a bit denser than H_2O.

After getting the knack of it, Tom was able to finish

the second and third annunciators quickly. When he was done, he found Roy and the others at a first floor window. They'd completely covered the glass in duct tape.

It was no longer a question of finesse. They were simply going to jimmy the window open. The alarms would go off, but hopefully they'd been dampened enough so that no one would hear them. The duct tape was to prevent the glass from shattering and making noise. Tom and Roy shoved their crowbars in the window jamb and jacked it up. There was some soft creaking when the pane splintered. Tom found the magnetic switch, recessed in the frame and fully open.

"Check the annunciator."

Bert walked under the nearest one and cocked up an ear.

"I hear a faint whining sound, really quiet."

They were in.

Tom eased himself through the window and onto the carpeted floor of a dark room. He briefly flicked on his penlight. Shelves. Books. A library. Tom made his way to the door and put his ear to it. No sound. He gripped the handle and turned slowly, easing it open. It let out into a hallway. To the right, around the corner, was a faint light. Tom motioned for the others to follow.

The hallway ended at the foyer. The wall sized aquarium glowed blue, peppering the grand staircase with streaks of muted light.

Tom went up quickly—the stairs were a bad place to get surprised. The taser felt comfortable in his hand. It was lighter than the revolver he'd been carrying, but his muscle-memory treated it like any normal gun; finger on the trigger, ready to point and shoot. In the darkness, the horrific pictures on the wall looked even worse. Shadows seemed to intensify the many expressions of pain. Tom ignored them, pressing onward.

Movement, at the top of the staircase. A pair of glowing eyes stared down at him. Functioning on instinct, Tom leaned to the side and fired. The two probes hissed through the air and made a faint crackling sound when they found their target. Tom climbed the last few stairs, taking a look.

On its back, four legs sticking straight up in the air, was a cat. It jerked every few seconds as the gun continued to pulse.

"You get him?" Joan whispered from behind.

Tom turned off the juice and pulled out the probes. He reloaded them into the gun barrel. The cat went limp, but it seemed to be breathing fine. He changed the gas cartridge and checked the battery. The feline rolled onto its feet and stared at them, one eye crossed. All of its fur seemed to be standing on end, so it kind of resembled a porcupine.

"Sorry, kitty."

The cat walked on wobbly legs to the second floor railing and squeezed through the bars. Then it fell twenty feet straight down, hitting the foyer floor with a thump.

"I thought cats always landed on their feet," Joan whispered.

Tom put his fingers to his lips and looked down the hallway. Dark and quiet. If Stang was still recovering from his operation, there was a good chance he might still be in the drawing room. That's where Tom decided to check first. He moved warily, as if he were in a haunted house and anything might jump out at any moment. When he reached the door there was a dim light coming through the bottom crack. He held his breath and listened. Faint snoring.

Tom went in fast. Stang was on the bed, his head propped up against the giant headboard with pillows. A thin line of saliva was escaping his open mouth. The dialysis machine next to him was silent, and a small night-light plugged into the wall bathed the room in a faint yellow glow. Tom was on him in two steps, gravity knife pressed to the old man's flabby neck.

"Wake up."

Stang peeked his eyes open. When he saw who was standing over him they widened to almost comic levels.

"Where's Jerome?" Tom asked.

"Two rooms over, same side."

"What kind of weapons are in this house?"

"He has a gun."

"How many?"

"Just one."

Tom took the knife and held it front of Stang's face, near his right eye. Fear made the Senator's thin lips tremble.

"How many?"

"A lot. A shotgun, an M-16, some bladed weapons." Stang's voice was soft, defeated. He was a far cry from the confident, cocky man who'd threatened their lives only a few days ago.

"Anyone else in the house?"

Stang looked away, saying nothing. Tom lowered the knife to the old man's waist.

"I'd be happy to reopen these stitches for you."

His frail body shook. "My son is here. Room across the hall."

Tom motioned for Joan to come over.

"This is the guy who sent Vlad after you. Keep an eye on him."

Joan twirled a baton and swung at the old man's head, stopping the club an inch before his eyes. Stang yelped, and she gave him a light tap on the nose.

"He won't give me any trouble."

Tom corralled Bert and Roy into the hall. "Bert, that's Mr. Speaker's room. If he comes out, give him the Gentle Ben treatment."

Bert nodded and crouched before the door like a defensive tackle. The bear spray was clutched in both hands, pointing forward.

"Jerome is heavily armed," Tom whispered to Roy. "Shotgun and an M-16."

They sidled up to his door, silent. No sound was coming from inside. Tom gripped the knob and counted quietly. On three he yanked the door open and Roy went in low and to the right. Tom flanked him, covering the left. The room was a moderate size. Tom scanned it quickly—desk, dresser, open closet, bed . . .

Empty. On the nightstand, next to a lamp, was a baby monitor.

"Enough talking."

Joan's voice came through the speaker. That meant the transmitter was in Stang's room, and Jerome had heard everything. He might already be on the phone with police. Tom hurried to the nightstand, reaching for the receiver.

The bullet hit him in the lower back, the force of the

shot knocking him forward. The pain was instant and terrible, like being whacked with a ten pound pick-ax.

Tom fell to the floor face first. He heard the boom of the second shot, felt the impact between the shoulders. It knocked the wind out of him, and hurt so bad Tom wondered if the bullets had somehow gone through the vest. Was Jerome using something high caliber, or an armor piercing slug that could penetrate a Kevlar weave?

Tom tried to roll over, to fire back, but his body wasn't responding correctly. The best he could manage was turning on his side. He saw Jerome, crouching under the desk. The pistol was aiming away from Tom, towards Roy.

But Roy was faster. Tom watched as the probes hit Jerome in the neck and chest, a tiny arc of blue electricity causing his upper body to snap backwards like a jack-knife. The desk toppled over and the gun went flying. Jerome began to jerk and twitch. Then he doubled over into a fetal position, his whole body shuddering as the taser sent pulse after pulse into him.

Roy set down the gun and hurried to Tom.

"Am I bleeding?"

His partner's fingers probed the vest.

"No. Vest stopped them both."

"Doesn't feel like it."

There was a scream, from the hallway. Roy yanked Tom to his feet and they hurried out of the room. Phil Jr., in pajamas, was rolling around on the floor, clawing at his eyes.

"It hurts! It hurts!"

Bert was standing over him. He looked at Tom and shrugged. "I only gave him a little squirt."

Tom took a deep breath and gritted his teeth. He hurt,

even worse than his ribs did after Attila had kicked him. The people who sold bulletproof vests hadn't bothered to mention this little fact. There might have been less pain if the bullets had gone all the way through.

Tom unclipped a roll of duct tape from his belt and walked over to Phil. He placed a knee on the small of his back and applied pressure.

"I'll give you fifty thousand dollars to wash off my face!"

Tom pried Phil's hands away from his eyes and taped the wrists together behind his back.

"Please wipe it off! Sweet mother of mercy!"

"Mr. Speaker, if you keep screaming, I'm going to let him spray you again."

The third most powerful man in America rubbed his face on the carpet and whimpered.

Roy dragged Jerome out into the hall. He was also trussed up with duct tape, but Roy had taken the added precaution of wrapping his legs as well. It seemed kind of redundant—the guy was down for the count.

"Here's why it hurt so bad." Roy walked over and handed Tom a large semi-automatic. "He shot you with a .45."

A .45 caliber handgun was military issue, a real cannon. But it was preferable to a shotgun or M-16. Tom felt incredibly lucky. Joan poked her head out of the drawing room and stared at the group.

"Everything okay out here?"

"I got shot." Tom held up two fingers. "Twice."

"You've got a vest on."

"But look how big the gun is." Tom showed her the .45.

Joan disappeared back into the room.

Roy patted Tom's shoulder. "Some ladies are hard to impress."

Bert managed to get the blinded Phil to his feet and lead him down the hall. Tom and Roy dragged Jerome after him.

They gathered around Stang's bed. The old man's face was pure malice. With his bald head and wrinkles, he looked like a snapping turtle.

"You need to hire better help." Roy pulled Jerome into a corner of the room. "I know nurses at County General who can shoot a lot better than this guy."

Tom sat on the bed and held the gun in front of Stang's face. "Where are all the research papers?"

"In the basement. There's a secret door on the first floor. Junior will show you."

"Dad! I can't see!"

Roy gave Jerome a light slap on the cheek. Jerome began to snore. "This one's in no shape to show us around neither."

"That leaves you to guide the tour, Senator."

"I'm recovering from a major operation."

"Bert, I think Phil Jr. needs more bear juice."

Bert aimed the canister at the younger man's face. The Speaker of the House cringed. "Take them, Dad! Take them!"

Stang snarled. "There's a wheelchair in the closet."

Tom opened it up and found the latest electric model. Stang gave instructions on how to work it, and Bert drove it next to the bed. Roy and Bert lifted the old man and set him in the padded seat.

Joan looked at Tom. "How can a wheelchair go down the stairs?"

"Pretty damn quick."

Stang glowered. "There's an elevator."

Tom instructed Roy and Bert to keep watch over the hostages, and held open the door. Joan went out first, followed by the whirring sound of Stang in the automatic wheelchair. So far everything had gone more or less according to plan. If their luck held, it would all be over very soon. *If* their luck held. Tom checked the clip in the .45. Six bullets left.

"The hard part is over, Tommy. From here on out, it's cake."

Bert nodded in agreement. "Let's finish this up, get out of here."

Tom gripped the gun tightly and walked out the door, hoping they were right.

CHAPTER 32

Springfield

"The lift is on the other side of the hallway."

Stang's voice was tired. He pushed the little joystick on the armrest all the way forward, but his chair didn't roll any faster than walking speed.

"There's something I wanted to ask." Tom rested the gun on Stang's shoulder. "Why the hell did you create us, anyway?"

"I'm asking myself that same question right now. It was all about power."

"Explain."

The old man cleared his throat. "I couldn't ever be President, being born in Germany. So, from birth, I've been grooming my son for the job. But winning an election has little to do with ability. Sometimes it comes down to different hot issues, or party support, or running mates, or looks, or a hundred other ridiculous reasons. I decided to stack the deck."

They reached the end of the hall. An old-fashioned

elevator, complete with metal folding gate, was waiting for them. Tom opened the door as Stang talked.

"So I cloned the greatest people in history, to align them with my son. It was a no lose situation. If greatness was genetic we'd have all the political savvy of Jefferson and Lincoln, all the brilliance of Einstein and Edison, Shakespeare to write the best speeches, the military strategy of Robert E. Lee."

The Senator had become more energetic, gesturing with his free hand and raising his voice.

"And even if you turned out to be idiots, you still had the famous faces, the famous names. Tom, I'd planned for you to become Vice President. Name someone in America who wouldn't vote for you? Democrat, Republican; it wouldn't matter. If my son had you as a running mate, and announced Lincoln as a future Secretary of State, Einstein as Secretary of Education, and so on, he'd be a sure thing. Robert E. Lee would capture the southern vote, Joan of Arc would get the women, we'd be unstoppable."

Tom shut the door to the elevator and Stang instructed him to pull the switch down. He did, and the lift began to descend.

"You think America would vote for clones?"

"Of course not. But I had papers made, all proving lineage to the people you'd been cloned from. Tom, you were Jefferson's great great great grandson. All of you had the genealogy. America would have eaten it up."

"Let me guess what happened. Edison figured out he was a clone."

Stang sighed. He appeared to partially deflate. "It started before that. I'd managed to recruit some of the others—Vlad, Attila, Jack, and Bill. But when I tried to recruit Robert E. Lee, he refused. Threatened to go public. That wouldn't do—the United States would vote for a descendant of Robert E. Lee, but mention the word clone and everyone starts crowing about religion and messing with the forces of nature."

"So you killed him."

"Of course. And then Jessup—Edison—figured it out by himself. I knew he did, because I've been keeping tabs on all of you since you were born. But when I offered him the chance to join he balked as well. By then Einstein knew, and you. Since none of you showed even a shred of political potential anyway . . ."

Tom followed the twisted train of thought. "You decided to cut your losses and get rid of us."

The elevator stopped on the first floor, but Tom didn't move to open the door.

"I created you. It's my right to destroy you. If you play God, you're allowed to play it to the hilt."

Tom felt like throttling the guy. Everything, all the death, all the fighting. Just because of some megalomaniac's ego.

"But I had no idea." Joan looked down at Stang. "Why try to murder me? I would have lived out the rest of my life not knowing."

Tom had one of those moments where everything suddenly became clear. He knew the reason, the real reason, why Stang had to kill them all.

"You were still a possible threat. Stang had to make sure no one ever knew that human cloning was possible. He said it himself, the United States would never elect a clone." Tom stared at Stang. "Especially a clone of a man who was born in Germany."

Joan looked at Tom, confused. Then her eyes got big. "The Speaker of the House?"

Tom nodded. "Phil Jr. A chip off the old block. Stang couldn't become President, so he cloned himself. If his clone became President, it was almost the same thing."

Stang looked like he'd bitten into a lemon. "I had a right to hold that office. One stupid, archaic law kept me out."

"So you created all of us to help your clone win the election, and when it turned out we would do more harm than good . . ."

Stang looked ready to spit venom. "I found another way to win the Oval Office. Without an election. Without a platform. Without a group of worthless freaks like you. I've watched you both, your whole lives. Pathetic. A woman who once saved France, reduced to a pimp who makes bad movies. And a man who once created a new nation, now just another dumb pig." His eyes were narrow, and flecks of spit dotted his lips and chin. "My son, he's my blood, my genes. He's me. You two are just some chemicals we cooked up in a lab. You aren't even human."

"I'm not sure you're the right person to judge humanity, Stang."

The old man slumped in his chair. Tom opened the folding gate and they went into the hallway.

"Where?"

"The next room. There's a hidden door."

It was a trophy room, deer heads and trout mounted on oak plaques and hanging on all four walls. A fireplace was in one corner, a matching sofa and chair arranged around it on the wooden floor. Tom checked the room out, top to bottom, and couldn't find any evidence of a hidden door.

"That's because it's hidden," Stang snapped. "Go to that bookcase and take out the volume of *Moby Dick*."

Tom found the book and pulled on it, half-expecting a secret passage to open. None did. He flipped through the book and it appeared normal.

"What's the deal?"

"Hold the book against the wall, just above the light switch. It's a magnetic lock. Then flip the switch up."

Tom did as instructed, and there was a clicking noise. Several wood panels in the center of the floor had risen up about an inch. Tom knelt down and realized it was a trap door, the seams hidden by the natural cut of the wood. He pulled open the hatch and flashed his penlight into the hole. A staircase.

"At the bottom there's a keypad. The code is 61694. Punch it in and the door will open. There's a short hallway, and at the end of the hall there's another door with another lock, same code. That's my safe. The papers are in there."

Tom sniffed the air. It was stale, and something else. Musky.

"Want me to go?"

Tom shook his head at Joan. "Stay here. If anything happens to me, tell my partner to snap Stang's neck."

He took the stairs slowly. When he reached the bottom he figured he was about twenty feet underground. A large aluminum door blocked his path. Tom found the keypad to his left and punched in the numbers. There was a clang and a hiss, and the door clicked open.

Tom was hit by a wave of cool, damp air. The musky

smell was stronger, more acrid. He pushed the door inward and aimed the penlight down the dark hall.

"There's a light switch," Stang called to him, "on the wall to the right."

Tom located the switch. He flipped it up, bathing the narrow hallway with pale yellow light. Looking ahead about fifteen feet, he saw another metal door. This one appeared larger, stronger. It also had a big metal slat in the center, with a slide bar. Tom had seen a similar contraption on a door in the solitary confinement wing at Joliet State Penitentiary. It had been the food slot. Violent inmates could receive their meals without the risk of opening the door.

"Hey Stang, what's this thing in the middle of the door?"

"I can put valuables into the safe without opening it up."

Tom didn't know if he bought that. His back hurt, his ribs hurt, and he now felt a sharp stab of paranoia. He approached cautiously, gun in hand. Being careful, he pulled back the slat on the door and tried to peer inside. It was dark, and his penlight didn't penetrate very far. An awful stench came through the slot—the smell of death. Tom thought it over. What if this wasn't a safe at all? What if it was some kind of private graveyard?

Actually, that would be a good thing. If Stang was burying dead bodies under his house, they wouldn't need all the cloning evidence to put him away. Local law enforcement would take care of him, and the media would take care of his son.

Tom punched in the code and the door unlocked. This one opened outward rather than inward. He peered inside the room, awash in the awful smell, trying to see in the darkness.

He called to Stang. "Is there a light?"

"On the far wall. It's only a few feet inside."

"What's that awful smell?"

"A, uh, an animal burrowed under the house and died. We haven't been able to find it."

That sounded like a big grandaddy lie. Tom took a step into the room, trying to steel himself against any possible shock.

He didn't see it, but he immediately sensed something directly in front of him. The hairs on his neck stood up, and he aimed his gun forward. By then there was movement on both sides of him as well.

Tom managed to fire twice before he got knocked off his feet. He landed on his back, hard. Something was on top of him, moaning and snarling. Tom felt rancid breath, hair, teeth. Mad dog?

No. Worse. Much worse.

He managed to push the attacker at arm's length and got a look. It was a man, with wild eyes, long hair, and a ragged beard. Black and jagged teeth. On his forehead, beneath the grime, Tom could make out a long scar. Deep, and old. And if the shock couldn't get any greater, Tom was stunned to recognize the face.

It was Stang.

The man tore at Tom with filthy fingernails. Another man stood over them both. He was also Stang, with a similar scar on his forehead. But this one was cleaner looking. Tom saw that he was holding something at his side. A white bandage, stained with some blood. Right in the spot where a kidney would be.

No wonder Stang was able to get so many organ transplants. He had his own personal supply, locked away down here. And always a perfect tissue match. Stang must have kept all of Harold's early cloning experiments, and then raised them to be spare parts. The thought horrified Tom. Have they been locked up here their whole lives?

The clone on top of him continued to growl and attack, and Tom noted that three more scrambled out of the darkness of their cell and ran down the hall.

"Jo—" Tom tried to call out but a grimy hand forced its way into his mouth, cutting off his voice. His gun arm was pinned. Tom grunted, and with all of his effort managed to roll his attacker over and get on top of him. He brought up his gun and aimed at the clone's chest, firing two shots.

Almost immediately he was hit from behind by another clone. His gun was knocked from his fist, skittering across the floor. The man on his back began to pound on him with both hands, each blow bringing stars to Tom's eyes. Then he was suddenly dead weight on Tom, mashing him onto the corpse below him. The weight doubled as another clone tried to climb over them, and another, and another.

Tom was being crushed by the pile of bodies, and very close to blacking out. He tried to fight it, tried to hold on, but he couldn't draw a breath and the pain and claustrophobia were so intense he felt he might go insane. Tom tried one last time to scream out Joan's name, to try to warn her.

All that came out was a weak moan.

CHAPTER 33

Springfield

"So you're a clone of your father?"

Phil Jr. nodded under the towel. Bert had finally tired of the complaining and was wiping his face.

"I'm going to be President and—"

They were interrupted by a sharp report, muffled but obvious. A gunshot.

Roy went to the door, taser in hand. "Stay here."

Bert shook his head. "If Tom's in trouble, we both go."

Roy nodded. He hadn't even taken one step out of the door when Bert saw the blade flash.

Roy fell into the hall, his taser clattering to the floor where he stood. And then the man came into the room. Bert mouthed his name.

"Attila."

His samurai sword was held in both hands. Bert noticed the blood dripping from the tip.

Roy's blood.

"Attila!" Phil's voice was cracking with emotion. "What took you so damn long?"

The small man grinned, exposing a single gold tooth in a field of rotten ones. "Needed eye gear."

On Attila's head were a set of swimming goggles, held on by an elastic band. He pointed his sword at Bert and slashed an X in the air.

Goggles or not, Bert let him have it with the pepper spray. He squirted Attila in the chest and face, a powerful eight second blast. When the fog lifted, the man was still standing there. His face was bright red, puffy, and the goggles appeared tighter on his eyes. His breath came in rasps, and his lips were swollen to double their size. But he could still apparently see, because he lunged straight at Bert with the sword.

Bert tripped backwards over Jerome and fell onto his ass, narrowly dodging the blow. But the pain from his gluteus maximus was like getting impaled all over again.

"Kill him!" Phil yelled.

Still gripping the can, Bert sent another stream of pepper at Attila, wondering what could possibly be keeping this man on his feet. It was bear repellent, for God's sake.

Attila continued to advance, slashing at the spray with his sword. He'd begun to howl, his face so swollen he looked like a Cabbage Patch doll. The sword came, closer, closer, and Bert felt that he was going to drop dead from fright before Attila even touched him.

Another lunge. Bert rolled away. The pepper fog in the room was now so bad that Bert was having trouble keeping his eyes open. It hurt like crazy. He blinked away the tears and tried not to breathe too deeply.

Attila planted both his feet and slashed, swinging at Bert's head like a baseball player. Bert ducked, and the sword neatly cut off a lock of his hair. He dove onto Stang's bed and tried to crawl across the mattress. A quick look over his shoulder found that Attila was standing directly behind him, puffy face grinning, ready to bring down the blade.

Someone yelled, "Hey!"

Attila paused, turning at the doorway, his swollen eyes squinting through the goggles.

Roy shot Attila with the taser. The probes hit him squarely in the chest, and Bert watched in awe as the first arc of blue electricity ignited the alcohol-based pepper spray soaking Attila's clothing.

It was like throwing a match on a gas grill.

Attila dropped the sword and screamed, trying to beat out the flames that had exploded all over his body. He just made it worse. Soon the bed canopy was also on fire, and the drapes, and some of the carpet.

Phil Jr. backed away from him, his face pure panic. "Help me!"

Bert watched in horrific fascination as Attila took two, three, four steps towards the Speaker of the House. Phil Jr. had run out of room and was cowering next to the railing, hands raised in supplication.

"Stay away!"

Attila collapsed on top of him, tangling his limbs in Phil's, setting his benefactor on fire.

Their screams mingled into a high-pitched cry that seemed to go on and on. Bert turned away from the horror, focusing on Roy. The cop shuffled into the room, holding his left shoulder. Blood dripped down from his fingertips. Across his chest was a twelve inch slash in the Kelvar vest.

"Time to go."

Bert hurried to him, took a quick look at the wound on his arm. It was deep and ugly, possibly an artery.

"We have to get out of here."

They made it into the hallway, just in time to see two people running at them. Tom and Joan?

When the figures came into view Bert almost yelped.

They looked like cave men, dirty and hairy and loping in a strange gait. Bert didn't stop to think about who they were or what they wanted. He still held the bear repellent and he fired straight at them. They rolled onto the floor, wailing and pawing at their faces.

Roy mumbled. "Jesus. They look like Stang."

Bert pulled Roy's arm over his shoulder and tried to bear his friend's weight. They half-walked, half-stumbled to the staircase. Another one of the crazy people was lumbering up the stairs, covered in blood. Bert brought up the spray and pressed the trigger. Empty.

He threw the can, bouncing it off the lunatic's head. The man kept coming, flailing his arms, eyes crazy. Bert tried to brace himself for the impact, but it was all he could do to hold up the sagging Roy. The man jumped on them, pulling and kicking. Bert reached for the railing, trying to keep his balance, and then all three of them were tumbling feet over head down the long grand staircase.

CHAPTER 34

Springfield

Joan heard the gunshot at the same moment she saw the man running up the stairs. He was followed by two more. Joan took two steps back and widened her stance. She kept the baton in front of her in a defensive position.

The first man emerged, hairy, bewildered. Joan did a double-take. It looked like a bearded, dirty Phil Jr. Another clone? She tightened her grip, ready to attack.

But instead of running at her, the man launched himself at Stang. The old man whimpered, bringing up both frail arms to protect himself. He was quickly yanked out of his wheelchair and thrown to the floor. The other two men came up the stairs and joined in the fray, scratching and slobbering and pulling him to pieces.

Joan didn't stick around to watch. She took the stairs two at a time, moving as fast as she could. Barely one step into the lower hallway a man reached for her, pulling at her hair. Joan brought the baton down onto his collarbone and he crumbled to the ground.

Ahead of her was a human pile of unwashed, hysterical Stang clones. Joan spotted a hand protruding from the giant mound of bodies. Tom's. She sprinted to his aid.

Her first impulse was to grab the gun, start shooting, but that would leave him buried in dead weight. Instead she pulled, and pushed, and smacked arms and legs and noses to get the clones to move. Gradually she uncovered Tom's head, bright red from pressure and oxygen deprivation. She grabbed him by the vest and yanked, her feet pushing against the body beneath him. Once his upper body came free he made a sound like a vacuum cleaner. Joan put an ear to his mouth, listening for breath. It was fast and steady.

The clones had given her a wide berth, nursing sore arms and heads. There were at least six of them in the hall, and God knew how many more in that dark room.

"Thanks."

Tom had opened his eyes, and was staring at her.

"What the hell is going on, Tom?"

Tom coughed. "Stang's personal organ bank. You can guess the Catch-22. If kidney disease is genetic, he keeps replacing his bad kidneys with other bad kidneys."

"What's wrong with them? Are they crazy?"

"Those scars on their heads are from lobotomies. To keep them from knowing what's going on."

Joan helped him to his feet. But instead of going back down the hall, Tom limped into the dark room where the clones had been kept.

"What are you doing?"

Tom coughed. "I think Stang was telling the truth. I think the papers are in here. Could you come up with a safer place to keep them?"

"Maybe there are no papers. Maybe they were destroyed."

"Stang's ego is too big. He'd never destroy evidence of his scientific triumph."

Tom picked up his penlight, groaning at the exertion of bending down. He flashed it into the room. Joan assumed a defensive posture, unsure of what horrors may await, and followed him in. The smell was overwhelming—stale body odor and rotten food. Tom played the small beam of light over three rows of stained cots, maybe twenty in all. In the corner was a toilet and sink, cracked and filthy. Along the near wall was a pile of tin dishes, seemingly out of place because they were neatly stacked.

Tom flashed the light on the far wall. There was another metal door, complete with keypad.

"What was that number?"

Joan approached the panel and tapped in 61694. The door clicked open and they peered inside. Two file cabinets, dusty and old. Tom opened the top drawer. Manila folders.

"We found them." He tried to tilt the file cabinet up onto its side. "Heavy. Maybe we can find some suitcases or—oh shit . . ."

Tom directed his flashlight beam behind them. Joan gasped. Twelve of the clones had returned, and they were coming closer.

"I only have five bullets left."

"Maybe they won't attack."

The clones attacked.

Joan lashed out with the baton, cracking the nearest clone in the head. He fell backwards, howling. Tom's gun boomed in her eardrums, and another clone went down.

"Get to the door!"

Tom tried to grab her wrist but she held him back. It was a bad move, defensively. Better to keep their backs to the wall, so they couldn't be surrounded.

She spun and hit another clone with a reverse kick. Someone grabbed her leg and she bounced a baton off his face. Another shot, and a moan. Joan rabbit punched the clone in front of her, driving the aluminum club into his stomach. A second clone tugged at her arm and brought it up to his mouth to bite. She tried to pull away, but another slipped behind her, getting her in a choke hold. Joan watched, horrified, as the biter grinned. His mouth was a sewer of black and rot, and saliva dripped down his chin as he prepared to take a hunk out of Joan's wrist.

Joan pivoted, flipping the choker over her hip, dislodging the biter before he had a chance to break the skin. She glanced to her right and watched Tom fire two more shots, then get tackled. Swinging her baton like a sword, she slashed her way past several clones and reached Tom, cracking the man on top of him across the temple. He crumpled, and Tom pushed him off. She helped him to his feet, and they faced the horde.

Tom fired his last shot. Another Stang dropped. There were still seven left.

Joan drew in a breath and tried to center herself. Fear would kill her if she didn't keep cool. She held up her weapon and let them come to her.

The first came at her, howling madly, arms outstretched. She jammed the baton into his solar plexus, and when he doubled over she smacked him in the back of the neck. Before he hit the floor she had spun around, connecting with the forehead of another clone, her weapon breaking the skin and blinding him with blood. Someone grabbed her waist. She crunched her heel down on his instep, then jerked her head backward, cracking it against his jaw. The impact made her dizzy, but he released her.

Next to her, she watched Tom swing a clone into the wall, then use the gun like a hammer and smash him across the face. Two more leapt at him, but before she could come to his aid she was lifted up in a horrible bear hug.

Joan's arms were pinned at her sides, and she couldn't throw a punch or swing a baton. Her legs dangled uselessly almost a foot above the ground. The smell—body odor and piss—choked her. She tried to twist, tried to pull away, but the clone's grip was too strong. Then she felt his mouth press against her neck.

Joan screamed, shaking her head from side to side, dropping her weapon and making her fingers into claws. She scratched at his side, her right hand finding a bandage, and stitches. This was Stang's recent kidney donor. She tore at the sutures, opening the wound, sticking her fingers in deep.

The clone howled, releasing her and dropping to his knees. Joan used the heel of her hand to break his nose, then looked for Tom. He was buried under three clones, while another advanced on him, wielding her baton. He raised it up to strike Tom's head, but Joan was on him in two steps, launching herself into the air and snapping his knee like a two-by-four.

Taking the baton away from him was child's play, and she made easy work of the three clones atop Tom, each getting a vicious crack in the head. She spun to face the final attacker, flipping the weapon in her hand like a six-shooter.

The clone blinked, then turned and ran out the door.

"Are you okay?" Joan helped Tom up. His nose was bleeding and he had a large scratch across his chin, but otherwise seemed intact.

"Yeah. Thanks. Let's grab the files and get the hell out of here."

They went back to the file cabinets and took what they could carry. It would take a few more trips to get them all, but Roy and Bert could help. Joan led the way through the hall, up the stairs. She tried not to look at Stang's body, but curiosity made her look anyway. He'd been torn to pieces—an arm missing, a leg missing—and in some places the flesh was ripped down to the bone. Joan also noted that several of his organs seemed to be missing. The clones had taken them back.

"Do you smell smoke?"

They hurried through the mansion, the hallway getting brighter with every step. When they reached the foyer, the blaze already descended half of the staircase. It was a huge wall of flame, roaring and out of control. Joan had never witnessed anything that provoked such a primal fear in her. She looked up and saw the fire was actually crawling across the ceiling, sparks and flaming bits of wood and plaster falling down like rain and igniting the carpeting.

"Roy!"

At the bottom of the staircase were two figures, lying on the ground. Tom and Joan ran to them, the heat increasing with every step. Through the thickening smoke, Joan could see Tom kneel down next to Roy. She looked at the other man. It was one of the clones, neck bent in a funny position.

The fire crept slowly down the stairs, engulfing paintings and wallpaper, kicking up the temperature with every step down. A cinder flew onto the files and they caught and began to burn. Joan dropped them all and kicked them away.

"Where's Bert?"

Joan heard a horn. She spun around and noticed one of the front doors was open. In the driveway was a black Cadillac. The window rolled down and Bert waved frantically from the driver's seat.

"Come on!"

Joan noticed that one of the manila folders she'd dropped had the word CLASSIFIED stamped on it. On impulse, she bent down and shoved it into her vest. Then she hurried to Tom and helped him drag Roy toward the front door, the fire close behind them.

A section of ceiling collapsed to their right, and when it hit the floor they were showered in sparks. Joan batted out flames in her hair, on her pants, and on Roy's chest. When she looked up, she almost wet herself.

Standing in front of the doorway was Jerome. In one hand he held a shotgun, and in the other, an ax. His muscular upper body was bare, and his chest and face were covered with streaks of something. It took Joan a moment to realize what it was—war paint. Fire flanked him on both sides, shadow and light flickering across his stone-like features, smoke rising behind him. He looked like a demon risen from hell.

Jerome leveled the gun at the trio and fired just as Tom yanked her to the side. She felt a tug in her leg, as if someone had slapped her, and then the pain came.

Tom pulled her and Roy behind a leather couch. The shotgun boomed again, and more flaming plaster fell from the ceiling, causing the sofa to catch fire. Joan took a quick look at her leg, and the blood appeared black in the orange glow. She tried to stand up, but it couldn't support her weight.

Tom grabbed an end table, which was partially engulfed in flame, and tossed it at Jerome. He dodged it, running to their left. Joan noticed he had a strap over his shoulder, and on his back was a machine gun.

Joan looked at Roy, semi-conscious on the floor, and then turned to Tom. He was tying his shirt around his bloody arm, and she realized that he'd also been shot. The doorway was less than twenty feet away, but it might as well have been twenty miles.

Joan knew, with startling clarity, that they were all going to die.

CHAPTER 35

Springfield

The sound rose above the cracking of the flames, and it made Tom's blood freeze. He recognized it from old Westerns—an Apache war cry. He chanced a look over the couch and watched Jerome pump the shotgun and aim. Tom ducked, realizing it was futile; the pellets would rip through the sofa easily. He wrapped his arms around Joan, hoping his body would shield her from the blast, and braced himself.

There was a gunshot, but not in their direction. Tom looked down the hall and saw a Stang clone do a bloody pirouette and collapse in a pile. Two more clones hopped over their fallen brother and bee-lined for Jerome.

Buoyed by the thought of living a few more seconds, Tom scanned around him for a weapon. There, in Roy's pocket. The taser. He grasped it, checking the battery and the CO_2 cartridge. It seemed functional.

Another shotgun blast. And then another. Tom peered over the couch and saw Jerome was now wrestling with a clone for the gun. He let go, shoving the clone away, and took the tomahawk from his holster, swinging it wildly and emitting another war cry.

Tom crawled around the sofa, his bleeding arm shaking badly because it was supporting most of his weight. His other hand gripped the taser, pointing it at Jerome. He got within twenty feet. Fifteen feet.

Jerome finished mauling the clone and stared impassively at Tom. He dropped the bloody ax and unslung the M-16 hanging on his back.

Tom wasn't sure if he was within the range of the taser, but he didn't have a choice. He aimed. Fired.

Missed.

Jerome brought the rifle around, his finger seeking the trigger. Tom knew there was nothing he could do, no place he could run. The M-16 would chew him into hamburger before he even had a chance to blink.

Then Bert came rushing through the front door, and swatted Jerome alongside the head with the step ladder. Jerome released the gun and fell to his knees. Bert raised the ladder to hit him again, but Jerome blocked the blow with his forearm. Tom dropped the taser and crawled like mad for the shotgun, lying next to the hacked-up clone. He pulled it away from the mangled body and racked a shell into the chamber.

"Bert! Duck!"

Bert ducked. Tom fired.

This time he didn't miss.

The blast knocked Jerome backward, leaving a mist of blood where he previously stood.

"Behind you!" Bert shrieked.

Tom rolled onto his back and aimed at another Stang clone, running straight at him. He pumped, and fired, and the clone went down. Tom squinted through the smoke and saw Joan, slowly dragging Roy toward the front door. Bert ran to her, helping out. Tom went to join them, then was forced to dive to the side when the grand staircase collapsed, causing a giant wave of fire to wash over the room.

Tom smelled burning hair, realized it was his, and dropped the gun to pat it out. He searched for Joan but visibility was near zero. Tom couldn't even see the front door.

"Joan!"

"Tom! Here!"

Tom crawled toward the voice, through the smoke, around pockets of burning floor. Soot stung his eyes, burned his throat. Was this even the right direction? The fire was roaring now, loud as a thunderstorm, and he wasn't even sure if . . .

Someone touched his hand through the haze. Joan?

No. Jerome.

The man's fingers locked around Tom's wrist like a bear trap. Tom tried to pull back but this was his wounded arm and the motion brought agony. He pried at Jerome's iron fingers, but they wouldn't budge. Tom's legs also became ridiculously hot, and he swiveled his head around and saw his pants had caught on fire. He twisted, trying to pat them out, but couldn't reach with Jerome's death grip on his wrist.

Tom panicked, frantically feeling the floor around him for some sort of weapon. His fingers brushed something wet. The ax. Tom cried out in pain and fury and brought the blade down on Jerome's wrist, severing their bond. Then he sat up and tried to beat out the flames on his legs. When that didn't work, he stretched out lengthwise and rolled for all he was worth. He kept rolling until he hit something hard—a wall or a piece of furniture—but he was still on fire, and it was getting bigger. The heat had begun to burn.

Tom felt behind him, hoping to find drapes, but instead his hand met cool glass. He noticed the faint blue light through the smoke and realized he'd bumped into the aquarium. The ax still in hand, Tom crashed it against the glass, showering himself in salt water and tropical fish. The tank was huge enough to forge a path through the fire, which Tom crawled through.

"Tom!"

Joan. And this time, Tom was sure the sound came from his left. He followed it, felt someone grab his leg, raised the ax . . .

It was Bert. He tugged Tom the rest of the way, through the front door, out into the cool night air. There were sirens in the distance, approaching fast.

"We have to go." Bert helped Tom into the back seat of the Cadillac, next to Joan. Then he hopped into the driver's seat, made sure Roy had his belt on, petted the cat in his lap, and punched the gas.

Tom turned around in the back seat, to look at the house one last time. He was surprised at how large the fire had gotten. The whole house had become an inferno. Flames had broken through the roofing, sharp fingers tearing at the night sky, blocking out the stars with black smoke.

He felt pressure on his bad arm. Joan's hand, trying to stop the bleeding.

"How's Roy?" Tom asked no one in particular.

"I think both legs are broken," Bert answered. "But he's breathing okay. How about you two?"

Joan gave Tom a squeeze. "We'll live. But a hospital might be a good idea."

Tom nodded. "But not in Springfield, Bert. Go east on 72 to Decatur. We don't want to be connected to this."

Bert glanced in the rearview, his eyes locked on Tom's.

"What happened to Stang Senior?"

"If you wanted to be technical, I guess you could say he killed himself."

Three big fire engines passed them on the road, racing towards the mansion. Tom closed his eyes and took a deep, cleansing breath. It was over. They had won.

"Hey." Joan shook him lightly. "One more thing."

"What?"

Joan moved closer. Her face was covered in soot, and one eyebrow was singed off, and she had some blood on her cheek. But her blue eyes were clear and wide and focused. Tom could feel her breath, and her hand on the back of his head. She was, no doubt, the most beautiful thing he'd ever seen in his life.

Tom didn't know if she kissed him, or if he kissed her. But he did know that, when their lips met, every ache and pain in his body disappeared.

CHAPTER 36

Decatur

Tom switched off the news on TV and turned to look at his partner in the hospital bed.

"They think it was some kind of slavery operation." Roy's words were dulled by the pain medication. Both of his legs were in casts, and his right arm was in a sling. This was the first time in almost a full day that he was well enough to talk.

"It's a good guess. Lots of burned bodies, but only four who had dental work. Plus a dungeon in the basement."

Roy smiled, sleepily. "Be interesting to see what happens if they run DNA tests."

"It sure will."

"We cool here?"

Tom nodded. "Told the doctors it was a hunting accident. Pretty dramatic one. Campfire out of control, falling trees, shooting at a bear. If you were awake, you would have enjoyed the story."

"Joan okay?"

"She came out of surgery after me. She's fine."

"Bert?"

Tom laughed. "Completely unscathed. He saved all of our lives, coming back for us."

"I'm starting to like that guy. Reminds me of my little brother."

Tom crossed his legs, wincing at the pain. The burns were only first degree, but stretched from his butt to the soles of his feet. His butt actually got the worst of it. The hospital had actually given Tom an inflatable donut. His arm wound wasn't serious—he'd caught a few pellets and would be sore for a while, same as Joan. Roy had taken the brunt of the damage. Tom didn't bother to tell him that his dislocated shoulder probably had nothing to do with the fall, but rather their attempt to drag him out of the burning house.

"How about the FBI?" Roy asked.

"I talked to the Special Agent in Charge in Chicago. He's driving here tomorrow. I figure we tell him the truth. There should be enough evidence still intact at Stang's house to back it up."

"Five bucks says the government keeps it hush-hush."

"I won't take that bet."

"Is this a private party, or can anyone attend?"

Roy and Tom smiled at Bert as he walked into the hospital room. Tom was especially pleased to see who Bert had brought with him. The face. The eyes. The beard. All perfect. He felt like he was in the presence of a celebrity. Tom extended his hand.

"Mr. Lincoln."

"Mr. Jefferson." Abe winked at Roy. "Mr. Hendrix."

Roy shook his head and grinned. "Hi, Abe. How was jail?"

"Good. I made some friends, caught up on my reading, got all that free publicity. Best thing I ever did."

Tom nodded. "I saw the morning paper. Something about Congress suppressing free speech in the Capitol Building. You've become a poster boy for the First Amendment."

Abe winked. "I just landed a talent agent. We're considering commercial work. Starting small. Coke. McDonalds. Chevrolet. I told Bernie to try and land me a porno, but he didn't think it was good for the image."

"What brings you out this way?" Roy asked.

"I had something to give to Bert."

Bert beamed. "Monthly Lincoln Police Department auction. They raise money by auctioning off things they've confiscated. You know; stolen cars, bikes, antique lures found at a murder scene . . ."

"I actually thought forty bucks was kind of high," Abe said, "but since I was there I felt obliged to buy something."

Roy laughed. "Why, Abe, how honest of you."

"Least I could do. If it wasn't for you guys, I'd still be selling cars instead of making the big Hollywood bucks."

"So you're back in business?" Tom asked Bert.

"Actually, no. I sold the rest of my lures and bought some property in New Mexico."

"You didn't . . ."

"It's going to take a few weeks to get my new ostrich farm up and running, but I expect all of you to visit when I do. Especially at Thanksgiving."

Roy smiled wide. "Good for you, buddy. I'm proud of you."

"Hey, I got you guys something. This is for you, Tom"

Bert handed him an envelope. Tom dumped the contents onto this palm. It was green, with hooks.

"A Luny Frog. Thanks, Bert."

"You probably need to clean it. There are still some small bits of . . . uh . . . Anyway, you should clean it. This one's for you, Roy."

Bert took a DVD out of his pocket. *The Love Bug.*

"Slug bug yellow no hit backs!" Bert whacked Roy in his good arm.

"No fair," Roy laughed. "Beating up on a cripple."

Bert's face became serious. "How are you doing, Roy?"

"Because I was on vacation when it happened, I only got partial disability. Gonna walk with a limp, probably for life. They say I could come back to work in a limited capacity. But pushing papers—I dunno. It ain't for me."

Bert stared at Roy, hard. "You know, I'm going to need a lot of help on the ranch."

"You're serious? Me and you, in the desert, chasing giant chickens around?"

Bert nodded. "Eating jumbo omelets."

"Might be something to consider."

Tom noticed that the small hospital room was becoming a bit cramped, but he felt his heart rate increase when one more person joined them.

"Oh my God, is that Abe Lincoln?"

Joan came into the room, and Abe gave her a big hug.

"Pleased to meet you, Ms. Arc."

Joan closed the door and faced them, looking serious. "I'm glad you're all here. We need to talk."

Tom noted the manila folder Joan was carrying, with CLASSIFIED written on the side.

"Is that from Stang's?"

"Yes. It's the only file I managed to save. You all need to look at this."

Bert opened the file and flipped through it. As he read, his face became progressively grimmer.

"Don't keep us in suspense," Roy said. "Spill."

Bert held up a paper. "This first page. It's a list of the ten clones Dr. Harold created. Me, you, Abe—the others with numbers on their heels."

He handed it to Tom. "Yeah. These are the ten. So?"

Bert handed him the next page. Tom stared at it. The first name that stood out was Jerome Huntington, the crazy Navy SEAL Stang had working for him. Printed next to his name was CLONE OF GERONIMO.

Tom scanned down the page, seeing many other famous names, some of them real doozies. And just like the first page, there were numbers next to them. Eleven through twenty.

"Let me see." Roy took the paper and read through it. "You mean to tell me there are ten more clones of famous people running around?"

"Nine more." Tom frowned. "Minus Geronimo."

"Nine more?" Abe reached for the page. "Tell me one of them is Marilyn Monroe."

"So what do we do about this, Tom?" Bert asked.

Roy nodded. "Yeah, Tom?"

Tom shook his head. "The FBI can take care of it.

I'm done. I did my part. This is no longer my business."

"There are some very bad people on this list, Tom." Joan put a hand on his shoulder. "Who knows what they could be doing in the world?"

Tom couldn't believe that came from Joan.

"Don't you want to go back to living a normal life? A safe life?"

"Can anyone in the world be safe with number 17 running around?"

"Number 18 is even worse," Bert said. "And 20 is pretty bad too."

Tom's shoulders slumped. "It's not our fight."

"You know," Abe grabbed his lapels and rocked back on his heels. "There were a lot of people who didn't want to stand up to King George in 1776. A lot of them said it wasn't their fight. But a few of them did. One of them was a guy named Thomas Jefferson."

Tom sighed. Corny as it sounded, Abe was right. Ultimately, it didn't matter why Tom was the way he was. It might have been genetics. It might have been the way he was raised. It might have been something totally unique to him. Tom had no choice but to follow his nature, wherever his nature came from.

"Okay," he said, standing up and taking Joan's hand. "Who should we try to find first?"

Turn the page for an exciting preview.

Bestselling author J.A. Konrath digs into the vaults and unearths this terrifying thriller from the depths of hell . . .

1906—Something is discovered by workers digging the Panama Canal. Something dormant. Sinister. Very much alive.

NOW—Project Samhain. A secret underground government installation begun 103 years ago in New Mexico. The best minds in the world have been recruited to study the most amazing discovery in the history of mankind. But the century of peaceful research is about to end. Because it just woke up.

When linguist Andrew Dennison is yanked from his bed by the Secret Service and taken to a top secret facility in the desert, he has no idea he's been brought there to translate the words of an ancient demon.

He joins pretty but cold veterinarian Sun Jones, eccentric molecular biologist Dr. Frank Belgium, and a hodge-podge of religious, military, and science personnel to try and figure out if the creature is, indeed, Satan.

But things quickly go bad, and very soon Andy isn't just fighting for his life, but the lives of everyone on earth . . .

ORIGIN
by J. A. Konrath

Coming in December 2018
Wherever Pinnacle Books are sold.

"Where is it?" Theodore Roosevelt asked John Stevens as the two men shook hands. Amador, Shonts, and the rest of the welcoming party had already been greeted and dismissed by the President, left to wonder what had become of Roosevelt's trademark grandiosity.

Fatigue from his journey, they later surmised.

They were wrong.

The twenty-sixth President of the United States was far from tired. Since Stevens's wire a month previous, Roosevelt had been electrified with worry.

The Canal Project had been a tricky one from the onset—the whole Nicaraguan episode, the Panamanian revolution, the constant bickering in Congress—but nothing in his political or personal past had prepared him for this development. After five days of travel aboard the battleship *Louisiana*, his wife Edith sick and miserable, Roosevelt's nerves had become so tightly stretched they could be plucked and played like a mandolin.

"You want to see it *now*?" Stevens asked, wiping the rain from a walrus mustache that rivaled the President's. "Surely you want to rest from your journey."

"Rest is for the weak, John. I have much to accomplish on this visit. But first things first, I must see the discovery."

Roosevelt bid quick apologies to the puzzled group, sending his wife and three secret service agents ahead to the greeting reception at Trivoli Crossing. Before anyone, including Edith, could protest, the President had taken Stevens by the shoulder and was leading him down the pier.

"You are storing it nearby," Roosevelt stated, confirming that his instructions had been explicitly followed.

"In a shack in Cristobal, about a mile from shore. I can arrange for horses."

"We shall walk. Tell me again how it was found."

Stevens chewed his lower lip and lengthened his stride to keep in step with the Commander-in-Chief. The engineer had been in Panama for over a year, at Roosevelt's request, heading the Canal Project.

He wasn't happy.

The heat and constant rain were intolerable. Roosevelt's lackey Shonts was pompous and annoying. Though yellow fever and dysentery were being eradicated through the efforts of Dr. Gorgas and the new sanitation methods, malaria still claimed dozens of lives every month, and labor disputes had become commonplace and increasingly complicated with every new influx of foreign workers.

Now, to top it all off, an excavation team had discovered something so horrible that it made the enormity of the Canal Project look trivial by comparison.

"It was found at the East Culebra Slide in the Cut," Stevens said, referring to the nine mile stretch of land that ran through the mountain range of the Continental Divide. "Spaniard excavation team hit it at about eighty feet down."

"Hard workers, Spaniards," Roosevelt said. He knew the nine thousand workers they had brought over from the Basque Provinces were widely regarded as superior to the Chinese and West Indians because of their tireless efforts. "You were on the site at the time?"

"I was called to it. I arrived the next day. The—*capsule*, I suppose you could call it, was taken to Pedro Miguel by train."

"Unopened?"

"Yes. After I broke the seal on it and saw the contents . . ."

"Again, all alone?"

"By myself, yes. After viewing the . . . well, immediately afterward I wired Secretary Taft . . ." Stevens trailed off, his breath laboring in effort to keep up with the frantic pace of Roosevelt.

"Dreadful humidity," the President said. He attempted to wipe the hot rain from his forehead with a damp handkerchief. "I had wished to view the working conditions in Panama at their most unfavorable, and I believe I certainly have."

They were quiet the remainder of the walk, Roosevelt taking in the jungle and the many houses and buildings that Stevens had erected during the last year.

Remarkable man, Roosevelt mused, but he'd expected nothing less. Once this matter was decided, he was looking forward to the tour of the canal effort. There was so much that interested him. He was anxious to see one of the famed hundred ton Bucyrus steam shovels that so outperformed the ancient French excavators. He longed to ride in one. Being the first President to ever leave the States, he certainly owed the voters some exciting details of his trip.

"Over there. To the right."

Stevens gestured to a small shack nestled in an outcropping of tropical brush. There was a sturdy padlock hooked to a hasp on the door, and a sign warning in several languages that explosives were contained therein.

"No one else has seen this," Roosevelt confirmed.

"The Spaniard team was deported right after the discovery."

Roosevelt used the sleeve of his elegant white shirt to clean his spectacles while Stevens removed the padlock. They entered the shed and Stevens shut the door behind them.

It was stifling in the small building. The President immediately felt claustrophobic in the dark, hot room, and had to force himself to stand still while Stevens sought the lantern.

Light soon bathed the capsule setting before them.

It was better than twelve feet long, pale gray, with carvings on the outside that resembled Egyptian hieroglyphics to Roosevelt. It rested on the ground, almost chest high, and appeared to be made of stone. But it felt like nothing the President had ever touched.

Running his hand across the top, Roosevelt was surprised by how smooth, almost slippery, the surface was. Like an oily silk, but it left no residue on the fingers.

"How does it open?" he asked.

Stevens handed his lamp to Roosevelt and picked up a pry bar hanging near the door. With a simple twist in a near invisible seam the entire top half of the capsule flipped open on hidden hinges like a coffin.

"My dear God in heaven," the President gasped.

The thing in the capsule was horrible beyond description.

"My sentiments exactly," Stevens whispered.

"And it is . . . alive?"

"From what I can judge, yes. Dormant, but alive."

Roosevelt's hand ventured to touch it, but the man who charged up San Juan Hill wasn't able to summon the nerve.

"Even being prepared for it, I still cannot believe what I am seeing."

The President fought his repulsion, the cloying heat adding to the surreality of the moment. Roosevelt detected a rank, animal smell, almost like a musk, coming out of the capsule.

The smell of the . . . *thing*.

He looked it over, head to foot, unable to turn away. The image seared itself into his mind, to become the source of frequent nightmares for the remainder of his life.

"What is the course of action, Mr. President? Destroy it?"

"How can we? Is it our right? Think what this means."

"But what if it awakens? Could we contain it?"

"Why not? This is the twentieth century. We are making technological advancements on a daily basis."

"Do you believe the public is ready for this?"

"No," Roosevelt said without hesitation. "I do not believe the United States, or the world, even in this enlightened age, would be able to handle a discovery of this magnitude."

Stevens frowned. He didn't believe any good could come of this, but as usual he had trouble going toe to toe with Roosevelt.

"Speak your mind, John. You have been living with this for a month."

"I believe we should burn it, Mr. President. Then sink its ashes in the sea."

"You are afraid."

"Even a man of your standing, sir, must admit to some fear gazing at this thing."

"Yes, I can admit to being afraid. But that is because we fear what we do not understand. Perhaps with understanding . . ."

Roosevelt made his decision. This would be taken back to the States. He'd lock it away someplace secret and recruit the top minds in the world to study it. He instructed Stevens to have a crate built and for it to be packed and boarded onto the *Louisiana*—no, better make it the *Tennessee*. If Mother found out what was aboard her ship she might die of fright.

"But if the world sees this . . ."

"The world will not. Pay the workers off, and have them work at night without witnesses. I expect the crate to be locked as this shed was, and the key given to me. Worry no more about this John, it is no longer your concern."

"Yes, Mr. President."

Roosevelt clenched his teeth and forced himself to stick out his hand to touch the thing; a brief touch that he would always recall as the most frightening experience of his life. He covered the fear with a bully Roosevelt *harrumph* and a false pout of bravado.

"Now let us lock this up and you can show me that canal you are building." Stevens closed the lid, but the smell remained.

The twenty-sixth President of the United States walked out of the shed and into the rain. His hands were shaking. He made two fists and shoved them into his pockets. The rain speckled his glasses, but he made no effort to clean them off. His whole effort was focused on a silent prayer to God that he'd made the right decision.

CHAPTER 1

"*You have reached Worldwide Translation Services. For English, press one.Por Español...*" BEEP. "*Welcome to WTS, the company for your every translation and interpretation need. Our skilled staff of linguists can converse in over two dozen languages, and we specialize in escort, telephone, consecutive, simultaneous, conference, sight, and written translations. For a list of languages we're able to interpret, press one. For Andrew Dennison, press two. For a...*" BEEP.

The business phone rang. Andy glanced at the clock next to the bed. Coming up on 3 a.m. Chicago time. But elsewhere in the world they were eating lunch.

If he didn't pick up, it would be forwarded to voice mail.

Unfortunately, voice mail didn't pay his bills.

"WTS, this is Andrew Dennison."

"Mr. Dennison, this is the President of the United States. Your country needs you."

Andy hung up. He remembered being a kid, sleeping over at a friend's house, making prank calls. It seemed so funny back then.

He closed his eyes and tried to return to the dream he'd been having. Something to do with Susan, his ex-girlfriend, begging for him to come back. She'd told him that would only happen in his dreams, and she'd proven herself right.

The phone rang again.

"Look, kid. I've got your number on the caller ID, so I know you're calling from . . ."

He squinted at the words WHITE HOUSE on the phone display.

"Mr. Dennison, In exactly five seconds two members of the Secret Service will knock on your door."

There was a knock at the door.

Andy jack-knifed to a sitting position.

"Those are agents Smith and Jones. They're to escort you to a limousine waiting downstairs."

Andy took the cordless over to his front door, squinted through the peephole.

Standing in the hallway were two men in black suits.

"Look, Mister—uh—President, if this is some kind of tax thing . . ."

"Your particular skills are required in a matter of national security, Mr. Dennison. I'll brief you in New Mexico."

"This is a translation job?"

"I can't speak any more about it at this time, but you must leave immediately. You'll be paid three times your normal rate, plus expenses. My agents can explain in further detail. We'll talk when you arrive."

The connection ended. Andy peered through his

peephole again. The men looked like secret service. They had the blank stare dead-to-rights.

"Do you guys have ID?" he asked through the door.

They held up their ID.

Andy swallowed, and swallowed again. He considered his options, and realized he really didn't have any.

He opened the door.

"As soon as you're dressed, Mr. Dennison, we can take you to the airport."

"How many days should I pack for?"

"No need to pack, sir. Your things will be forwarded to you."

"Do you know what language I'm going to be using? I've got books, computer programs . . ."

"Your things will be forwarded."

Andy had more questions, but he didn't think asking them would result in answers. He dressed in silence.

The limo, while plush, wasn't accessorized with luxuries. No wet bar. No television. No phone. And the buttons for the windows didn't work.

Andy wore his best suit, Brooks Brothers gray wool, his Harvard tie, and a pair of leather shoes from some Italian designer that cost three hundred dollars and pinched his toes.

"So where in New Mexico am I going?" Andy asked the agents, both of whom rode in the front seat.

They didn't reply.

"Are we going to O'Hare or Midway?" No answer.

"Can you guys turn on the radio?"

The radio came on. Oldies. Andy slouched back in his seat as Mick Jagger crooned.

Chicago whipped by him on both sides, the streets full of people even at this late hour. Summer in the city was around the clock. The car stopped at a light and three college age girls, drunk and giggling, knocked on his one way window and tried to peer inside. They were at least a decade too young for him.

Their destination turned out to be Midway, the smaller of Chicago's two airports. Rather than enter the terminal, they were cleared through the perimeter fence and pulled directly out onto the runway. They parked in front of a solitary hangar, far from the jumbo jets. Andy was freed from the limo and led silently to a Lear jet. He boarded without enthusiasm. He'd been on many jets, to many places more exotic than New Mexico.

Andy was bursting with curiosity for his current situation, but sleep was invading his head. It would probably turn out to be some silly little international embarrassment, like a Pakistani Ambassador who hit someone while drunk driving. What was the Hindko word for intoxication? He couldn't remember, and since they didn't let him take his books, he had no way to look it up.

At a little past four a.m. the pilot boarded and introduced himself with a strong handshake, but didn't offer his name. He had no answers for Andy either.

Andy slept poorly, on an off, for the next few hours.

He awoke during the landing, the jolt nudging him alert when the wheels hit the tarmac. After the plane came to a stop, the pilot announced they'd arrived at their destination, Las Cruces International Airport. Andy rubbed some grit from his eyes and stretched in his seat, waiting for the pilot to open the hatch.

The climate was hot and dry, appropriate for the

desert. The pilot informed Andy to remain on the runway and then walked off to the terminal.

Andy waited in the powerful sun, the only human being in sight, his rumpled suit soon clinging to him like a close family. A minute passed. Two. A golden eagle rode a thermal in the distance, circling slowly. Andy wondered when his ride would arrive. He wondered why this town was called The Crosses. He wondered what the hell was so important that the leader of the free world woke him up at 3 a.m. and flew him out here.

From the opposite end of the runway an Army Humvee approached. Andy noticed the tags, Fort Bliss. The driver offered him a thermos of coffee and then refused further conversation.

They drove west on Interstate 10 and turned onto highway 549, heading into the desert. Traffic went from infrequent to nonexistent, and after they passed the Waste Isolation Pilot Plant; a large complex fenced off with barbed wire, they turned off road and followed some dirt trail that Andy could barely make out.

The Florida Mountains loomed in the distance. Sagebrush and tumbleweeds dotted the landscape. Andy even saw the skull of a steer resting on some rocks. This was the authentic West, the West of Geronimo and Billy the Kid. He'd been to several deserts in his travels; the Gobi in China, the Rub al-Khalia in Saudi Arabia, the Kalahari in South Africa . . . but this was his first visit to the Chihuahuan Desert. It left him as the others had—detached. Travel meant work, and Andy never had a chance to enjoy any of the places he'd visited around the world.

The Humvee stopped abruptly and Andy lurched in his seat.

"We're here," the driver said.

Andy craned his neck and looked around. Three hundred and sixty degrees of desert, not a building nor a soul in sight.

"You're kidding."

"Please get out of the Humvee, sir. I'm supposed to leave you here."

"Leave me here? In the desert?"

"Those are my orders."

Andy squinted. There was nothing but sand and rock for miles and miles.

"This is ridiculous. I'll die out here."

"Sir, please get out of the Humvee."

"You can't leave me in the middle of the desert. It's insane." The driver drew his pistol.

"Jesus!"

"These are my orders, sir. If you don't get out of the Humvee, I've been instructed to shoot you in the leg and drag you out. One . . ."

"I don't believe this."

"Two . . ."

"This is murder. You're murdering me here."

"Three."

The driver cocked the gun and aimed it at Andy's leg. Andy threw up his hands. "Fine! I'm out!"

Andy stepped out of the Humvee. He could feel the heat of the sand through the soles of his shoes.

The driver holstered his weapon, hit the gas, and swung the Humvee around. It sped off in the direction it had come. Andy watched until it shrank down to nothing.

He turned in a complete circle, feeling the knot growing in his belly. The only thing around him was scrub brush and cacti.

"This is not happening."

Andy searched the sky for any helicopters that might be flying in to pick him up. The sky was empty, except for a fat desert sun that hurt his eyes. Andy couldn't be sure, but the air seemed to be getting hotter. By noon it would be scorching.

He looked at his watch and wondered how long he could go without water. The very idea of it made his tongue feel thick. A day, maybe two at most. It would take at least two days to walk back to the airport. He decided to follow the truck tracks.

"Andrew Dennison?"

Andy spun around, startled. Standing twenty yards away was a man. He wore loose fitting jeans and a blue polo shirt, and he approached Andy in an unhurried gait. As the figure came into sharper focus, Andy noticed several things at once. The man was old, maybe seventy, with age spots dotting his bald dome and deep wrinkles set in a square face. But he carried himself like a much younger man, and though his broad shoulders were stooped with age, he projected an apparent strength. *Military,* Andy guessed, and upper echelon as well.

Andy walked to meet the figure, trying not to appear surprised that he'd just materialized out of nowhere. The thoughts of vultures and thirst were replaced by several dozen questions.

"I'm General Regis Murdoch. Call me Race. Welcome to Project Samhain."

Race offered a thick and hairy hand, which Andy nervously shook. It felt like shaking a two-by-four.

"General Race, I appreciate the welcome, but I think I've been left out of the loop. I don't know . . ."

"All in good time. The President wants to fill you in, and you're to meet the group."

"Where?" Andy asked, looking around.

The General beamed. "Almost a hundred years old, and still the best hidden secret in the United States. Right this way."

Andy followed Race up to a pile of rocks next to a bush. Close inspection revealed that they'd been glued, or maybe soldered, to a large metal plate which spun on a hinge. The plate swivelled open, revealing a murky stairwell leading into the earth.

"Cutting edge stuff in 1906, now kind of dated." Race smiled. "But sometimes the old tricks are still the best."

Race prompted Andy down the sandy iron staircase and followed after closing the lid above them. The walls were concrete, old and crumbling. Light came from bare bulbs hanging overhead every fifteen steps.

Only a few hours ago I was asleep in my bed, Andy thought.

"Don't worry," Race said. "It gets better."

After almost two hundred steps down they came to a large metal door with a wheel in the center, like a submarine hatch. Race stopped in front of the door and cleared his throat. He leaned closer to Andy, locking eyes with him.

"Three hundred million Americans have lived during the last century, and you are only the forty-third to ever enter this compound. During your time here and for the rest of your life afterwards, you're going to be sworn to absolute secrecy. Failure to keep this secret will lead to your trial and inevitable execution for treason."

"Execution," Andy repeated.

"The Rosenbergs were numbers twenty-two and twenty-three. You didn't buy that crap about selling nuclear secrets, did you?"

Andy blinked. "I'm in an episode of the *X-files*."

"That old TV show? They wish they had what we do."

Race opened the door and bade Andy to enter. They'd stepped into a modern hospital. Or at least, that's what it looked like. Everything was white, from the tiled floors and painted walls to the fluorescent lights recessed into the ceiling. A disinfectant smell wafted through the air, cooled by air conditioning. They walked down a hallway, the clicking of Andy's expensive shoes amplified to an almost comic echo. It could have been a hundred other buildings Andy had been in before, except this one was several hundred feet underground and harbored some kind of government secret.

Andy asked, "This was built in 1906?"

"Well, it's been improved upon as the years have gone by. Didn't get fluorescent lights till 1938. In '49 we added the Orange Arm and the Purple Arm. We're always replacing, updating. Just got a Jacuzzi in '99, but it's on the fritz."

"How big is this place?"

"About 75,000 square feet. Took two years to dig it all out. God gets most of the credit, though. Most of this space is a series of natural caves. Not nearly the size of the Carlsbad Caverns two hundred miles to the east, but enough for our purpose."

"Speaking of purpose . . ."

"We're getting to that."

The hallway curved gradually to the right and Andy noted that the doors were all numbered in yellow paint with the word YELLOW stenciled above them. Andy guessed correctly that they were in the Yellow Arm of the complex, and was happy that at least one thing made sense.

"What's that smell?" Andy asked, noting that the pleasant scent of lemon and pine had been overtaken by a distinct farm-like odor.

"The sheep, over in Orange 12. They just came in last week, and they stink like, well, sheep. We think we can solve the problem with Hepa filters, but it will take some time."

"Sheep," Andy said. He wondered, idly, if he'd been brought here to interpret their bleating.

The hallway they were taking ended at a doorway, and Race ushered Andy through it and into a large round room that had six doors along its walls. Each door was a different color.

"Center of the complex. The head of the Octopus, so to speak. I believe you've got a call waiting for you."

In the middle of the room was a large round table, circled with leather executive-type office chairs. Computer monitors, electronic gizmos, and a mess of cords and papers haphazardly covered the tabletop as if they'd been dropped there from a great height.

Race sat Andy down in front of a screen and tapped a few commands on a keyboard. The President's head and shoulders appeared on the flat-screen monitor, and he nodded at Andy as if they were in the same room.

"Video phone, got it in '04." Race winked.

"Mr. Dennison, thank you for coming. You've done your country a great service."

The President looked and sounded like he always did, fit, commanding, and sincere. Obviously he'd had a chance to sleep.

"Where do I talk?" Andy asked Race.

"Right at the screen. There's a mike and a camera housed in the monitor." Andy leaned forward.

"Mr. President, I'd really like to know what's going on and what I'm supposed to be doing here."

"You were chosen, Andy, because you met all of the criteria on a very long list. We need a translator, one with experience in ancient languages. You've always had a gift for language. My sources say you were fluent in Spanish by age three, and by six years old you could also speak French, German, and some Russian. In grade school you were studying the eastern tongues, and you could speak Chinese by junior high."

Only Mandarin, Andy thought. He couldn't speak Cantonese until a few years later.

"You graduated high school in three years and were accepted to Harvard on scholarship. You spent four years at Harvard, and wrote and published your thesis on giving enunciation to cuneiform, at age nineteen.

"When you left school in 1986 you lived on money left to you by your parents, who died in a fire three years before. After the money ran out you got a job at the United Nations in New York. You were there less than a year before being fired. During a Middle East peace talk you insulted the Iraqi ambassador."

"He was a pervert who liked little girls."

"Iraq was our ally at the time."

"What does that have to do with—"

The President held up a hand, as he was so accustomed to doing with reporters.

"I'm not sitting in a seat of judgment, Andy. But you're entitled to know why you were chosen. After the UN fired you, you started your own freelance translation service, WTS. You've been making an average living, one that allows you to be your own boss. But business has been slow lately, I assume because of the Internet."

Andy frowned. In the beginning, the World Wide Web had opened up a wealth of information for a translator, giving him instant access to the greatest libraries in the world. But, of course, it gave everyone else access to those libraries too. Along with computer programs that could translate both the written and the spoken word.

"So you know I'm good at my job, and you know I could use the money."

"More than that, Andy. You're single, and you aren't currently seeing anyone. You don't have any relatives. Business is going poorly and you're behind on your Visa and your Discover Card payments, and you've just gotten your second warning from the electric company. Your unique mind, so active and curious years ago, hasn't had a challenge since college.

"You didn't talk to the media after the incident at the UN, even though reporters offered you money for the story. That's important, because it shows you can keep your mouth shut. In short, by bringing you in on this project, you don't have anything to lose, but everything to gain."

"Why aren't I comforted that the government knows so much about me?"

"Not the government, Andy. Me. No one else in Washington is aware of you, or of Project Samhain. Only the incumbent President knows what goes on there in New Mexico. It was passed on to me by my predecessor, and I'll pass it on to my successor when I leave office. This is the way it's been since President Theodore Roosevelt commissioned construction of this facility in 1906."

Andy didn't like this at all. His curiosity was being overtaken by a creepy feeling.

"This is all very interesting, but I don't think I'm your man."

"I also know about Myra Thackett and Chris Simmons."

Andy's mouth became a thin line. Thackett and Simmons were two fictitious employees that Andy pretended to have under salary at WTS. Having phantom people on the payroll reduced income tax, and was the only way he'd been able to keep his business afloat.

"So this is a tax thing after all."

"Again, only I know about it Andy. Not the IRS. Not the FBI. Just me. And I can promise you that Ms. Thackett and Mr. Simmons will never come back to haunt you if you help us here."

"What exactly," Andy chose his words carefully, "do you want from me?"

"First you must swear, as a citizen of the United States, to never divulge anything you see, hear, or learn at Project Samhain, under penalty of execution. Not to a friend. Not even to a wife. My own wife doesn't even know about this."

Not seeing an alternative, Andy held up his right hand, as if he were testifying in court.

"Fine. I swear."

"General Murdoch will provide the details, he knows them better than I. Suffice to say, this may be the single most important project this country, maybe even the world, has ever been involved with. I wish you luck, and God bless." The screen went blank.

"It's aliens, isn't it?" Andy turned to Race. "You've got aliens here."

"Well, no. But back in '47 we had a hermit who lived in the mountains, he found our secret entrance and got himself a good look inside. Before we could shut him up he was blabbing to everyone within earshot. So we faked a UFO landing two hundred miles away in Roswell to divert attention." Andy rubbed his temples.

"You want some aspirin?" Race asked. "Or breakfast, maybe?"

"What I want, after swearing under the penalty of execution, is to know what the hell I'm doing here."

"They say an image is worth a thousand words. Follow me."

Race headed to the Red Door and Andy loped behind. The Red Arm hallway looked exactly like the Yellow Arm; white and sterile with numbered doors, this time with the word RED stenciled on them. But after a few dozen yards Andy noted a big difference. Race had to stop at a barrier that blocked the hallway. It resembled a prison door, with thick vertical steel bars set in a heavy frame.

"Titanium," Race said as he pressed some numbers on a keypad embedded in the wall. "They could stop a charging rhino."

There was a beep and a metallic sound as the door unlocked. The door swung inward, and Race held it open for Andy, then closed it behind him with a loud clang. It made Andy feel trapped. They came up on another set of bars fifty yards farther up.

"Why two sets?" Andy asked. "You have a rhino problem here?"

"Well, it's got horns, that's for sure."

Race opened the second gate and the Red Arm came to an abrupt end at doors Red 13 and Red 14.

"He was found in Panama in 1906, by a team digging the canal," Race said. "For the past hundred years he's been in some kind of deep sleep, like a coma. Up until last week. Last week he woke up."

"He?"

"We call him Bub. He's trying to communicate, but we don't know what he's saying."

Andy's apprehension increased with every breath. He had an irrational urge to turn around and run. Or maybe it wasn't so irrational.

"Is Bub human?" Andy asked.

"Nope," Race grinned. The General was clearly enjoying himself. *Didn't have visitors too often,* Andy guessed.

"So what is he?"

"See for yourself."

Race opened door Red 14, and Andy almost gagged on the animal stench. This wasn't a farm smell. This was a musky, sickly, sweet and sour, big carnivore smell.

Forcing himself to move, Andy took two steps into the room. It was large, the size of a gymnasium, the front half filled with medical equipment. The back half had been partitioned off with a massive translucent barrier, glass or plastic. Behind the glass was . . . "Jesus Christ," Andy said.

Andy's mind couldn't process what he was seeing. The teeth. The eyes. The claws.

This thing wasn't supposed to exist in real life.

"Biix a beel," Bub said.

Andy flew past Race, heading for the hallway.

"I promise not to tell anyone."

"Mr. Dennison . . ."

Andy met up with the titanium bars and used some of his favorite curses from several different languages. His palms were soaked with sweat, and he'd begun to hyperventilate.

Race caught up, placing a hand on his shoulder.

"I apologize for not preparing you, but I'm an old man with so little pleasure in my life, and it's such a hoot watching people see Bub for the first time." Andy braced the older man.

"Bub. Beelzebub. You've got Satan in there."

"Possibly. Father Thrist thinks it's a lower level demon like Moloch or Rahab, but Rabbi Shotzen concedes it may be Mastema."

"I'd like to leave," Andy said, attempting to sound calm. "Right now."

"Don't worry. He's not violent. I've even been in the dwelling with him. He's just scary looking, is all. And that Plexiglas barrier is rated to eight tons. It's as safe as visiting the monkey house at the zoo."

Andy tried to find the words. "You're a lunatic," he decided.

"Look, Andy, I've been watching after Bub for over forty years. We've had the best of the best in the world here—doctors, scientists, holy men, you name it. We've found out so much, but the rest is just theory. Bub's awake now, and trying to communicate. You're the key to that. Don't you see how important this is?"

"I'm . . ." Andy began, searching his mind for a way to put it.

Race finished the thought for him. "Afraid. Of course you're afraid. Any damn fool would be, seeing Bub. We've been taught to fear him since we were born. But if I can paraphrase Samuel Butler, we don't know the Devil's side of the story, because God wrote all the books. Just think about what we can learn here."

"You're military," Andy accused. "I'm sure the weapons implications of controlling the Prince of Darkness aren't lost on you."

Race lost his friendly demeanor, his eyes narrowing.

"We have an opportunity here, Mr. Dennison. An opportunity that we haven't had since Christ walked the earth. In that room is a legendary creature, and the things that he could teach us about the world, the universe, and creation itself staggers the imagination. You've been chosen to help us, to work with our team in getting some answers. Many would kill for the chance."

Andy folded his arms. "You expect me to believe not only that the devil is harmless and just wants to have a chat, but that the biggest government conspiracy in the history of the world has only good intentions?"

Race's face remained impassive for a few seconds longer, and then he broke out laughing.

"Damn, that does sound hard to swallow, don't it?"

Andy couldn't help but warm a bit at the man's attitude. "General Murdoch . . ."

"Race. Call me Race. And I understand. I've been part of the Project so long the whole thing is the norm to me. You need to eat, rest, think about things. We'll grab some food and I'll show you your room."

"And if I want to leave?"

"This isn't a prison, son. I'm sure you weren't the only guy on the President's list. You're free to go whenever you please, so long as you never mention this to anyone."

Andy took a deep, calming breath and the effects of the adrenaline in his system began to wear off. Race opened the gate and they began their trek back down the hallway.

"The world really is going to hell, isn't it?" Andy said.

Race grinned. "Sure is. And we've got a front row seat."

CHAPTER 2

Breakfast was light but nourishing, consisting of banana muffins, sausage, and coffee. The coffee was the only thing fresh. The food, like all food in the compound, was frozen and then microwaved. Race told Andy that refrigeration had been possible since the compound was created, but the small group of people who lived here didn't warrant the constant trips to refresh supplies. Instead, two huge freezers were stocked several times a year with everything from cheese and bread to Twinkies and Snickers. Milk, an item that didn't freeze well, was available vacuum-packed. "How many people are here right now?" Andy asked, stirring more sugar into his coffee.

They sat on orange chairs at a Formica table with a sunflower pattern. Green 2—or the Mess Hall as Race called it—doubled as both a dining area and a kitchen. The decor, save for the microwaves, was pure 1950s cafeteria.

"Eight, including you. The holies, the priest and the rabbi, leave for brief periods every so often. Everyone else is here for the long haul. Believe it or not, except for the isolation and the fact that you don't see the great outdoors, this is almost like a resort. We've got a sauna, a four lane swimming pool, a full library, even a racquetball court."

"Who foots the bill for all of this if only the President knows about it?"

"Social Security. Now you know why the benefits are so low."

Andy used his fist to stifle a yawn. The food was settling well and he suddenly realized how tired he was.

"I'll show you to your room," Race said. "If you haven't had a chance yet, take the time to make a list of things you need from your apartment; clothes, books, whatever. I know you've got some things already en route, toiletries and such, but anything else you might need, just holler. That goes for things you might need for research too. We have a blank check here, no questions asked. Back in the sixties, as a joke, two guys asked for a Zamboni. Came the next day. Sure pissed off President Johnson. That man could curse like no one I've ever met."

"I'm still not convinced I'm staying."

"That's fine, but it's a funny thing about Bub. We've had people scream, faint dead away, become downright hysterical the first time they see him. But we've never had one leave without finishing their job. Curiosity is a powerful motivator."

It also killed the cat, Andy thought.

They left the Mess Hall and headed down the Blue Arm via the Octopus. As they walked, the door to Blue 5 opened and a woman came out into the hallway. She was petite, and the lab coat she wore was too big for her even though the sleeves had been rolled up. Her hair was blue-black and cut into a bob, perfectly framing a triangular Asian face.

Andy was immediately entranced. It had been a long time since he'd been in the presence of a beautiful woman. The last was his ex-girlfriend, Susan. Pre-Susan, he'd dated a lot. His looks were okay, but the ability to speak in dozens of languages was something women really liked. Post-Susan, he'd been a desert island. She'd taken more than just his heart. She'd taken his confidence as well.

"Dr. Jones, this is Andy Dennison, the translator. Andy, this is Dr. Sunshine Jones, our resident veterinarian."

"Hi," Andy said, smiling big. "You know, when I was a kid I had a retriever named Sunshine. I loved that dog."

Dr. Jones stared at him, her face made of marble.

"Not that I'm comparing you to a dog," Andy said quickly. "But it's a small world, both you and my dog having the same, uh, name." She didn't respond. Andy's smile deflated.

Race, who watched the exchange with barely concealed amusement, cut in to give Andy a hand.

"Mr. Dennison was called in at three this morning. He just met Bub an hour ago. You could say he had the typical reaction."

"Hey, I'm from Chicago," Andy said, trying to recover. "I'm not bothered by too much."

"Is that so?" Dr. Jones said. Her voice lacked the faintest trace of good nature. "Bub's next feeding is at noon. Maybe you'd like to lend a hand?"

"Sure."

Dr. Jones nodded, then walked down the Blue Arm to the Octopus. Andy waited until she'd gone through the door before commenting.

"Very intense lady."

"She's been here a week, since Bub woke up, and I haven't seen her smile once. Does a helluva job though. She's the one who figured out Bub's, uh, nutritional requirements."

"Which are?"

"Remember those sheep you smelled?"

Andy frowned, the banana muffins doing a flip in his stomach.

"Well," Race said. "Here's your room."

Race opened the door to Blue 6. Andy gave it a quick glance over. It was set up like a hotel suite: bed, desk, TV, dresser, washroom. The only thing missing was a view.

"Our water heater is on the fritz, so all we got is lukewarm for the time being. That phone on the nightstand is in-house only. All the rooms in Samhain got 'em. Hit the pound sign and then the number of the Arm followed by the room number. Blue Arm is number one, Yellow Arm number two—there's a list next to the phone. I'm in Blue 1, so just hit #11 to get me. Or hit *100 and go live over the house speakers."

Andy yawned, knowing he wouldn't remember any of that.

"The only outside line is in the control room," Race continued, "and for obvious reasons that's restricted. If you need to get a message to the rest of the world, you have to go through me."

Andy looked at the bed and felt his will drain away.

"Do I get a wake up call?"

"I believe you've already got one in the form of Dr. Jones. I know a thing or two about being macho, but I'm not sure you should witness a feeding just yet, even to impress the cute doctor."

"It's that bad?"

"I've seen action in two wars, son, and it's that bad."

Andy took Race's outstretched hand and mumbled a thank you, though he wasn't really sure what he was thankful for. He was three items into his list of necessities when he fell asleep.

A buzzing woke him up. Andy wasn't sure where he was, and when he remembered, he couldn't figure out what the noise meant. It turned out to be his phone, humming like an angry bee.

He lifted the receiver.

"Mr. Dennison? This is Dr. Jones."

Andy blinked and said good morning. The clock on the dresser said 12:07, so it was technically afternoon, but that didn't enter into his sleep-addled head.

"Can you meet me at Orange 12, say in fifteen minutes?"

"Sure. Orange 12."

The doctor hung up. Andy rubbed his eyes and extended the motion into scratching his chin. Stubble. He sat up in bed. Thought about the demon. Felt his heart begin to race.

Pretend it's just another translation job, he told himself.

A suitcase that he recognized as his own was sitting

next to the bathroom door. When he calmed down, he opened the case to find clothing and sundries, packed neater than he'd ever been able to. His electric razor was in a zippered pocket, and he took that and his toothbrush kit into the bathroom with him.

After a shave and a brush he hopped into and out of a tepid shower, using soap in his hair because he hadn't bothered to look for shampoo. Five minutes later he was dressed in some khakis and a light blue denim shirt. After a brief indecision he left two buttons open at the neck rather than one, and was then out the door and headed for the Orange Arm.

When he reached the center of the compound—the Octopus as Race had called it—he found two men sitting at the center table. Both were at least thirty years his senior. The one on the left wore round Santa Claus glasses on an equally round face. He had a balding head and a gray goatee, and his large green sweater was tight on his rotund body. The other man was his comic opposite; long and gaunt, cheeks sunken rather than cherubic, scowl lines instead of smile lines. He looked uncomfortable in his jeans, whereas his companion looked at home in his.

Andy recalled Bert and Ernie from *Sesame Street*.

They were in an intense conversation when Andy entered, and his arrival didn't warrant an interruption.

"As usual," the chubby one said in a voice deep and full, "you're narrowing your concept of Christian hell to church teachings, with Dante, Milton, and Blake thrown in for good measure. But the concept of an Underworld goes back to Mesopotamia almost four thousand years ago, which predates both Christianity and Judaism."

The thin man sighed as if the world rested on his shoulders. "I'm aware of Mesopotamia, as I am of Egyptian, Zarathrustrian, Grecian and Roman beliefs in Hell." He had a thin, reedy voice that matched his appearance. "I'm also aware of the complexities of explaining the presence of evil in a divinely created universe. But it seems to make more sense to have an embodiment of evil in the form of Satan than a dualistic God who is both forgiving and wrathful."

"Fa!" the fat one said, raising up his hands and rolling his eyes. "Enough with Yeoweh's dark shadow. From the second century BC, my people have believed in a distinct malevolent deity, in this case Mastema, who was created by ha-shem to do His dirty work, namely, punishing sin. It can be read that Mastema, not Adonai, was the one behind the trials of Job. The same Mastema who tempted the prophets Moses and Jesus."

The thin one winced. "I hate it when you call Jesus a prophet."

"You must be the holies," Andy said. It was the first opportunity he'd had to get a word in.

"What makes more sense," the fat man turned to Andy. Andy guessed correctly that he was Rabbi Shotzen. "The devil as a fallen angel, or the devil as a purposeful creation of God to be an alternative to His light?"

"I'm an atheist," Andy said.

There was a moment of silence.

"How can you refuse your own eyes?" asked Father Thrist. "You saw Bub, correct?"

"Yeah."

"Well, he's unmitigated proof that God must exist. For there to be devils, there must be hell, and if there's hell, there's a heaven and a God."

Andy decided he didn't want to get drawn into this conversation.

"I saw a thing, that looked like what we call a devil. I can't draw any more conclusions than that."

"Another Thomas," Thrist said to Shotzen. "Here we have, in captivity, one of Satan's minions, and everyone who sees him doubts. Why not set him free? The world wouldn't tremble with fear, as predicted. Bub would probably go on the talk show circuit and then become a sponsor for soft drinks."

The agitated priest turned to Andy again and pointed a finger, a gesture he seemed comfortable making. "Satan's greatest feat is to convince us he doesn't exist. He doesn't want us to believe in him, and that makes it easier for him to spread his evil. Lucifer is the Master of Lies."

"I disagree, Father," Shotzen cut in. "God wants us to know the devil exists. It's his infernal existence that steers us towards the path of truth and light."

Andy headed for the Orange door, content to leave the philosophical demands of the situation in other hands. The discussion continued without him; in fact, Andy guessed they hadn't even noticed he'd left.

The Orange Arm looked newer than the rest of the facility, with brighter paint and shinier tile, but the smell was barnyard fresh. Andy wrinkled his nose.

Dr. Jones was waiting for him in front of Orange 12, holding a clipboard that commanded her attention. She didn't look up at Andy as he approached.

"I'm ready for lunch," Andy said. He tried on a small grin.

She walked into Orange 12 without replying. Andy followed. The room was large, almost the size of Bub's habitat. Several empty pens were off to the right, and to the left side was a fenced area where almost two dozen sheep milled about. For all his travels, Andy had never seen a sheep before, and was surprised at how big they were. They were waist high and fat, like a bunch of gray marshmallows on toothpick legs.

"Is that actual grass they're on?" Andy asked.

"Astroturf. My idea of turning this part of the complex into a biosphere was rejected as too complicated. The turf wears well and is easy to clean."

"It looks like they're eating parts of it."

"Yeah, I told them that would happen. Come on."

Dr. Jones went to a set of lockers near the pens and removed a leather harness that resembled the reins for a horse. The reins were handed to Andy, and the doctor reached back into the locker and took out a half dozen boxes of Cap'n Crunch cereal. She walked up to the fence and rang a large cowbell hanging from a pole. All of the animals turned to look.

"They eat hay, but they love breakfast cereal. To get them to approach I have to bribe them. The problem is they're skittish. Every time they come to get the treat, one of them is taken away."

Dr. Jones began opening boxes and pouring them into the trough inside the fence. The sheep watched for a minute before the first of them approached. He stuck his face in the crunchy treat and began snacking. Dr. Jones patted him on the head.

"You want the harness?" Andy asked.

"No, this is Wooly. He's the Judas sheep. He always comes first, and then the others follow. If we snagged him, they'd all be too afraid to come the next time."

Wooly grunted his agreement, sucking up the cereal

like a vacuum. Soon he was joined by two others, muscling their way in. Dr. Jones grabbed one of them by the scruff of the neck, gathering up wool in her fist. It appeared rough, but the animal didn't seem to notice and continued its binge.

When the cereal was gone, Dr. Jones deftly slipped the harness over the sheep's head, tightening the straps with her free hand. She held the reins in her armpit and opened the last box of cereal, luring her captured animal over to the gate. Several of the other sheep followed, and Wooly snorted his disapproval at being left out.

"Shoo the others away while I open the gate," Dr. Jones told Andy.

Andy, feeling quite the dork, flapped his hands around and made hissing noises. The sheep just stared at him, and out of the corner of his eye he thought he saw the stoic Dr. Jones smirk.

"Go on sheep! Go! Move it! Go on!"

The herd slowly backed off, and Dr. Jones opened the gate and led her captive to one of the pens. Once it was safely locked in she went to fetch her clipboard.

Andy gave the sheep a pat on the head and stared into its alien eyes with their elongated pupils. Bub's eyes. He shuddered, realizing he didn't want to see the demon again so soon.

With a tape measure Dr. Jones checked the sheep's length and its height at the shoulder. She noted the measurements and then pressed some buttons on a digital display next to the pen. It registered the sheep's weight. She jotted this down as well.

"So, do people call you Sunny?"

"Not if they want me to reply."

Ouch, Andy thought. *How can someone so cute be so cold?*

"I thought all vets were supposed to be cheerful. Something to do with their love of animals."

She gave him a blank stare, and then began to examine the sheep's teeth.

"What do you go by, then?"

"Sun. People call me Sun."

"Sun. It's unique."

"My mother was Vietnamese. She fell in love with an American soldier, who brought her to this country before Saigon fell. Sunshine was one of the first English words she learned. She didn't know any better."

"Oh, I think she did. It matches your cheerful disposition."

Sun was now looking into the sheep's eyes, holding their lids open. The sheep protested the inspection by twisting away.

"Wait a second," Andy said, snapping his fingers. "You're Vietnamese."

"Don't say it," Sun warned.

But Andy, a grin stretched across his face, couldn't resist. "You're a Vietnam vet."

Sun's face became even harder, something Andy hadn't thought possible.

"Never heard that one before. Open the pen there."

Andy lifted the latch on the gate and Sun led the sheep out of the pen and over to the entrance door.

"I've visited Vietnam twice," Andy said. "Beautiful place. All of those war movies make it look like hell, but it's actually very tranquil, don't you think?"

"I wouldn't know. I've never been there. I'm an American."

Andy decided to shut up.

They led the sheep through the hallway and into the Octopus, where the rabbi and the priest were still arguing.

"Here comes another one, wretched thing," Rabbi Shotzen pointed to the sheep with his chin.

Father Thrist frowned. "I don't understand why you can't kill the sheep humanely first." He crossed his arms, obviously uncomfortable.

"Bub only takes 'em live, guys," Sun answered. "You know that."

The Rabbi said, "What about some kind of painkiller? Morphine, perhaps?"

"We don't know how that would affect Bub's unique anatomy."

"How about a cigarette at least? A last meal?"

"He had Cap'n Crunch," Andy offered.

"You gentlemen are more than welcome to perform the last rites, if you wish," Sun said.

Again, Andy caught the faintest hint of a smirk.

"Sacrilege," the Rabbi said. But he approached the sheep and held its head, speaking a few words of Hebrew.

"Perhaps Bub can be trained in the ways of shohet," Andy said. "Then he can eat according to shehita."

If Shotzen was impressed by Andy's knowledge of his people's tongue, he didn't show it. Instead the chubby holy man shook his head in disagreement.

"Bub won't eat kosher meat. He's trefah, a blood drinker."

The rabbi went back to his seat. Sun walked the sheep to the Red door.

Father Thrist refused to look.

"Rabbi Shotzen says that prayer every time we feed

Bub a sheep," Sun told Andy when they entered the Red Arm.

"It wasn't a prayer. The rabbi simply apologized to the sheep, because it wasn't going to be killed by a proper butcher, according to the Jewish laws of slaughtering animals humanely."

Sun punched in the code for the first gate, and Andy made sure he noted the five-digit number. The titanium bars swung open, but the sheep didn't want to budge.

"She smells him," Sun said. She took a black swatch of cloth from her coat pocket and slipped it over the animal's eyes. "They're calmer when they can't see."

With some firm tugging and a sniff of cereal, the sheep moved forward.

"You're a vet, you're supposed to take care of animals. Doesn't this bother you, marching one off to death?"

Sun sighed. "Have you ever eaten a hamburger?"

"Sure, but . . ."

"Bub's a carnivore, like a lion, like a shark, like you and me. As much as everyone around here is shocked by Bub's eating habits, if they ever visited a slaughterhouse they'd be a thousand times more repulsed."

"But you're a vet."

"I'm a vet who eats hamburgers. I also spent six months in Africa studying lions."

Andy said hello in four African tribal languages.

She wasn't impressed.

They came to the second door, and Andy punched in the numbers on the panel. Nothing happened.

"Two different codes," Sun said. "You can't have a secret government compound without security overkill."

The sheep tried to bolt at the sound of the heavy door clanging open, but Sun had a tight grip on the reins.

Andy stopped at Red 14 and grasped the door handle but he didn't turn it right away. The moment stretched.

"You don't have to go in," Sun said. "I just needed you to help in Orange 12."

She was giving him a graceful way out, but he knew her opinion of him would drop even further if he took it.

Andy turned the knob and entered.

The smell hit him again, heady and musky, almost making Andy gag. This time the room wasn't empty. Standing among the medical equipment was a man in a lab coat. He was tall and intense looking, with a thin line for a mouth and wide expressive eyes. His hair was light gray, short and curly. Andy put him at about forty, but he could have gone eight years either way.

"Oh good, feeding time," the man said.

"Dr. Frank Belgium, this is Andy Dennison," Sun said. "He's the translator."

"Good good good, we're in need of one. Attack the mystery from all angles, the more the better. Yes yes yes."

"Frank's a molecular biologist." Sun said it as if that was explanation for Dr. Belgium's weird speech patterns and birdlike movements. "How's the sequencing going, Frank?"

"Slow slow slow. Our boy—yes, he is a boy, even though there isn't any evidence of external genitalia—his bladder empties through the anus, like a bird. He has 88 pairs of chromosomes. We're looking at over 100,000 different genes, about quadruple what humans have. Billions of codons. Even the Cray is having a hard time isolating sequences. Nothing yet, but a link will show up, I'm sure it will."

"All life on earth, from flatworms to elephants, share some DNA sequences," Sun explained. "Dr. Belgium believes Bub also shares several of these chains."

Dr. Belgium nodded several times. "Bub's got the same four bases as all life, the same 20 amino acids. Even taking into account his . . . *different* anatomical layout, I believe he's terrestrial, that is, he has earthly relatives somewhere. We're trying matches with goats, rams, bats, gorillas, humans, crocodiles, pigs, everything that he looks like he may be a part of, to fit him into the animal kingdom . . . but now it's feeding time, so let's see if we can witness another miracle, shall we?"

Sun led the sheep past Andy and over to Bub's habitat. Andy, who'd been avoiding looking in that direction, forced himself to watch.

At first, Bub wasn't visible. The dwelling was filled with a running stream and trees and bushes and grass, as deep as a basketball court and about thirty feet high. The foliage was so dense in parts that even a creature Bub's size could apparently hide in it.

"All fake," Dr. Belgium said. "Fake brush, fake rocks, fake stream. It's supposed to resemble the area where he was found, in Panama. I don't think he's fooled."

"Where is he?" Andy asked, cautiously approaching the Plexiglas shield. He squinted at the trees, trying to make out anything red.

Bub dropped from directly above, the ground shaking as he landed just three feet in front of Andy.

Andy yelled and jumped backwards, falling onto his ass.

Sun laughed. "Did you forget he could fly?"

Andy didn't notice Sun's amusement. Bub was crouching before him, his black wings billowing out behind him like a rubber parachute.

Andy's mouth went dry. The demon was the most amazing and horrifying thing he'd ever seen.

Hoofs big as washtubs.

Massively muscled black legs, with knees that bent backwards like the hindquarters of a goat.

Claws the size of manhole covers, ending in talons that looked capable of disemboweling an elephant.

Bub approached the Plexiglas and cocked his head to the side, as if contemplating the new arrival. It was a bear's head, with black ram horns, and rows of jagged triangular teeth.

Shark's teeth.

His snout was flat and piggish, and he snorted, fogging up the glass. His elliptical eyes—black bifurcated pupils set into corneas the color of bloody urine—locked on Andy with an intensity that only intelligent beings could manage.

He was so close, Andy could count the coarse red hairs on the demon's broad chest. The animal smell swirled up the linguist's nostrils, mixed with odors of offal and fecal matter.

Bub raised a claw and placed it on the Plexiglas.

"Hach wi' hew," Bub said.

Andy yelled again, crab-walking backwards and bumping into the sheep.

The sheep bleated in alarm.

Bub, as if commanded, backed away from the window. His giant, rubbery wings folded over once, twice, and then tucked neatly away behind his massive back. He walked over to a large tree and squatted there, waiting.

Sun led the sheep past the Plexiglas and to a doorway on the other side of the room. They entered, and a minute later a small hatch opened inside the habitat, off to Bub's left.

Andy mentally screamed at Sun, *"Don't open that door!"* even though the opening was far too narrow for Bub to fit through.

Bub watched as the sheep walked into his domain. The door closed behind it.

The sheep shook off its blindfold and looked around its new environment.

Upon seeing Bub it let forth a very human-sounding scream.

In an instant, less than an instant, Bub had sprung from his spot by the tree and sailed through the air almost twenty feet, his wings fully outstretched. He snatched up the sheep in his claws, an obscene imitation of a bat grabbing a moth.

Andy turned away, expecting to hear chomping and bleating. When none came, he ventured another look.

Bub was back by the tree, sitting on his haunches. The sheep was cradled in his enormous hands, as a child might hold a gerbil. But it was unharmed. In fact, Bub was stroking it along its back, and making soft sounds.

Sheep sounds.

"He's talking to the sheep," Dr. Belgium said. "He's going to do it. Here comes the miracle."

Andy watched as the sheep ceased in its struggle.

Bub continued to pet the animal, his hideous face taking on a solemn cast. There was silence in the room. Andy realized he'd been holding his breath.

The movement was sudden. One moment Bub was rubbing the sheep's head, the next moment he twisted it backwards like a jar top.

There was a sickening crunch, the sound of wet kindling snapping. The sheep's head lolled off to the side at a crazy angle, rubbery and twitching. Andy felt an adrenaline surge and had to fight not to run away.

"Now here it comes," Dr. Belgium said, his voice a whisper.

Bub held the sheep close to his chest and closed his elliptical eyes. A minute of absolute stillness passed.

Then one of the sheep's legs jerked.

"What is that?" Andy asked. "A reflex?"

"No," Sun answered. "It's not a reflex."

The leg jerked again. And again. Bub set down the sheep, which shook itself and then got to its feet.

"Jesus," Andy gasped.

The sheep took two steps and blinked. What made the whole resurrection even more unsettling was the fact that the sheep's head hung limply between its front legs, turned completely around so it looked at them upside down.

Andy's fear changed to awe. "But it's dead. Isn't it dead?"

"We're not sure," Sun said. "The lungs weren't moving a minute ago, but now they are."

"But he broke its neck. Even if it was alive, could it move with a broken neck?"

The sheep attempted to nibble at some grass with his head backwards.

"I guess it can," Sun said.

"Amazing," Dr. Belgium said. "Amazing amazing amazing."

"Shouldn't you get the sheep?" Andy asked. "Run some tests?"

"Go right ahead," Sun said. "The door's over there."

"Probably not a good idea to go in there before Bub's eaten." Dr. Belgium said.

Andy said. "Can't you tranquilize him or something? Race said he went into the habitat before."

"Twice, against my insistence, but only to get some stool samples and to fix a clog in the artificial stream. Both times Bub ignored him. Even Race isn't insane enough to go in there and take his food away. And I'm not going to tranquilize Bub until we know more about his physiology. We don't know what tranquilizers would do to him."

Bub barked a sound, similar to a cough. The sheep trotted around in a circle, head swinging from side to side, trying to bleat with a broken neck.

Bub coughed again.

Or was it a laugh?

The sheep swung its head around at Bub and screamed. Bub reached out and grabbed the sheep. The grab was rough, all pretense of tenderness gone. Holding a hind leg in each claw, he ripped the sheep in half and began to feast on the innards.

Andy's stomach climbed up his throat and threatened to jump out. He put a hand over his mouth and turned away, the munching and gobbling sounds filling the large room.

"From amazing to horrible," Dr. Belgium said, returning to his computer station.

"He eats everything," Sun said, putting the reins in her coat pocket. "The skull, bones, hide, even intestines. Doesn't waste a crumb. The perfect carnivore."

Andy threw up, seeing the banana muffins for the second time that day. He apologized and fled the room, his brain scrambling to remember the code number for the gate. He managed, but got stuck when he reached the second one.

This was insane. This whole project was insane. Andy felt no curiosity at all—only terror, revulsion, and anger at being suckered into this mess. He gave the bars a shake and a swift kick, swearing in several different languages.

Sun came up behind him and punched in the correct code.

"Thanks," Andy mumbled.

He took off down the hall, barely noticing the deep frown of concern on Sun's face.